OWL DREAMS

OWL DREAMS

JOHN T. BIGGS

an imprint of
Roan & Weatherford Publishing Associates, LLC
Bentonville, Arkansas • Heber City, Utah
www.roanweatherford.com

Library of Congress Cataloging-in-Publication Data
Names: John T. Biggs, author
Title: Owl Dreams/John T. Biggs
Description: First Edition | Bentonville: Rogue River, 2026
Identifiers: LCCN: 2026941661 | ISBN: 979-8-89299-188-9 (trade paperback) |
ISBN: 979-8-89299-189-6 (eBook)
Subjects: FICTION / Magical Realism | FICTION / Psychological | FICTION / Southern
LC record available at: https://lccn.loc.gov/2026941661

Rogue River trade paperback edition July 2026

Editing by George "Clay" Mitchell & Don Money
Cover Design by Casey W. Cowan
Interior Design by John Bredesen

*To my wife, Margaret Anderson Biggs for being a source of stability
in my otherwise chaotic life.*

To William Bernhardt for coaching and workshopping this book.

*To Regina Williams, for publishing my short fiction
when no one else was interested.*

To Bill and Pam Wetterman for their critiques and evaluations.

*To Dusty Richardson, the late great writer of Western Fiction,
for his encouragement.*

Acknowledgments

I LEARNED A lot about the art of the narrative from listening to Choctaw storyteller Tim Tingle and reading his Oklahoma Book Award winner, Walking the Choctaw Road. The title of this book came from one of the anecdotes he passed on at the first Red Dirt Book Festival I attended.

1

SARAH REACHED INTO her purse and retrieved the sticky note her mother had taped to the refrigerator. Sticky notes and tape, an early sign Mom was off her meds.

Meet me at the Dog House Drive-In at 12:30 p.m. I have a big surprise. It was signed, *Your loving HALF-SISTER, Marie Ferraro,* followed by three smiley faces.

Sarah knew, when Mom became her big sister, the surprise would be a man, and that would be hardly any surprise at all. She stood in the parking lot, getting the lay of the land. Always good to have an escape route planned when Mom was in half-sister mode.

The sound of Italian shoes on macadam closed in behind her. *Marie* had arrived.

"There's a problem, Sarah."

Marie took her daughter's arm and turned her to the left. Two clean-cut young men with exceptionally good posture stood in the parking lot. They wore inexpensive-looking sport coats that bulged over one hip and matching Foster Grant sunglasses. Unless this was the new look for Mormon missionaries, they were FBI.

"I wanted you to meet Archie," Marie said. "You're going to love him."

"Your new boyfriend?" Sarah looked at her watch and tried to figure out if she still had time to get to class.

"We should have gone to a sushi place," Marie said. "Federal agents hate sushi."

"I'm missing a presentation on Pueblo artifacts for this," Sarah said. "Couldn't I just watch the video on the next segment of *Cops*?"

"It'll be over in a minute, Sarah, and anyway, anthropology is a waste of time."

Marie had been conducting her own Study of Man since puberty. She didn't have everything worked out yet, but she was getting better. An illegitimate daughter at age fourteen hadn't slowed her down at all. The walk, the talk, the sultry look, all the moves that made the wheels of history turn for thousands of years still worked as well as ever for Sarah's mother and sometimes-half-sister.

"I promise you, Sarah, you can learn everything you need to know from Nicholas Sparks novels and Lifetime TV." She strolled toward the FBI agents like a Victoria's Secret model walking down the runway.

"Excuse me, gentlemen." She crowded into the agents' personal space—way in—touched one of them on the hand and bumped the other with her hip. Both contacts lasted longer than necessary.

"I was wondering…." She kept her hip against one man while speaking to the other—sexually ambidextrous. How long did it take to perfect a skill like that?

"I was just wondering…." The tip of Marie's tongue played over her lips, which somehow made the front of the agents' pants stand out more than their pistol bulges. It didn't matter what Marie was just wondering because these men were ready to listen. She held both of one agent's hands and bound the other one securely with the pressure of her hip. They didn't stand a chance. Harry Houdini in his prime couldn't break free from Marie Ferraro's estrogen grip.

Sarah had watched her mother demonstrate sexual jujitsu a thousand times. Use an opponent's weight against him. Pin him to the floor with the power of his own erection. So easy for a woman like Marie, who knew everything there was to know about the weakness of the stronger sex.

"I was just wondering if you and your partner would care to join us for lunch—you know, you look just like Cary Grant in *North by Northwest*." She said this somehow to both agents at once. Now she had each of them by one hand, leading them toward Sarah, who was shaking her head no and thinking about the lecture she was missing.

The agents had probably never seen *North by Northwest*, but they were being treated to a colorized description of the major plot points on the parking lot of the Dog House Drive-In while Marie Ferraro's boyfriend, Archie, escaped.

Sarah looked around, trying to figure out which lawbreaker belonged to her mom. There were lots of possibilities. Guys with horror-show scars and arcane tattoos that anthropologists would study in a thousand years when they were safer to approach. Either bad guys all liked hot dogs, or they were getting into practice for when they ordered their last meals before they were humanely executed with intravenous injections.

That one, coming out of the restaurant. Apparently, you could eat inside the Dog House Drive-In even though there were bars on every window. The place looked like a jail so its customers would feel at home. Sarah locked eyes with the tall, lean, possibly Hispanic man wearing distressed jeans, sneakers, and a Hawaiian shirt. Her suspect slipped his hand into the waistband of his pants the way a professional baseball player adjusts his penis, and before she could say, "Nine-one-one, what's your emergency?" he pulled a pistol from his belt and aimed it at the FBI agents.

Marie pushed the agents in front of her and lay down on the parking lot, gracefully, like people used to do in Hollywood's golden age. Sarah dropped to the macadam—less like a movie star, more like a marionette whose strings were cut.

Mother and daughter rolled to safety, more or less, while the cops and the gunman fired bullets in every direction and covered the macadam with hot brass, like a metal hailstorm. Nobody hit, no glass broken, no bullet holes anywhere to be seen. Thank God for the wide-open spaces of Albuquerque.

It ended when the gunman ran out of bullets and the FBI agents didn't. One of them said, "On the ground, asshole," and the other repeated the statement with a little more volume to make up for coming in late.

The gunman put his pistol on a faded yellow line beside a handicapped parking space and nudged it in position so that neither the barrel nor the grip touched unpainted asphalt. Then, he pushed loose gravel aside, creating a relatively clean space a little larger than the shadow he cast on the macadam, and lay face down with his arms extended.

"I'll bet he keeps his cell nice," Marie said.

One of the agents read the gunman his rights while the other pushed his face onto the parking lot and cuffed his hands behind him. "And if you can't afford an attorney, one will be appointed to defend you." The agent reading the little laminated card did look a little like Cary Grant, but he had a southern accent and a stutter when he asked if the shooter wanted to give up his rights.

"Looks like he's already given up everything else," Marie told Sarah.

"Is that Archie, Mom?"

"Heavens no, Sarah, this is New Mexico."

"What's that mean?"

"Lots of bronze-skinned people around with guns and warrants. Those agents just arrested the wrong one." Marie pointed to a quiet disturbance at the most distant corner of the parking lot. A man sat on the asphalt with his hands in the air while his car backed onto Central Avenue.

"Archie's borrowing a Toyota Prius for a while," Marie said. "Come on, I'll drive you back to school."

2

I T HAD ONLY been a day since Sarah had just missed being collateral damage in a parking lot gunfight. But growing up with Marie had made her accustomed to drama, so she didn't look through the peephole before she opened her apartment door.

A large dangerous man stood in front of her. He smiled, but wolves do that, too, before they bite you. He took a step forward and extended his right hand. There wasn't a gun in it—that was a plus—but a man like this wouldn't need a gun.

When she didn't shake his hand, the man raised it, the way Indians always seemed to do in old-time Western movies, but he said, "Hello," instead of "How."

Sarah shook her head the way boxers do when they've been hit too hard to think clearly. She tried for a standard greeting, like "How are you," "Pleased to meet you," or just "Hi," but the words came out all at once and sounded like a frog doing an imitation of a horse.

The man's smile grew wider. Not exactly friendly, not exactly safe, but Sarah had to admit he was handsome in a prison-pen pal-boyfriend sort of way.

"Native American." Sarah knew that was the wrong thing to say, especially for an honors anthropology student at the University of New Mexico, but it was too late to take it back, so she extended her hand and hoped modern indigenous people didn't have some kind of complicated secret handshake she wouldn't learn about until graduate school.

His hand swallowed hers completely. His touch was firm and callused but so gentle that her pulse rate approached normal—until she got a close look at the prison ink on his arms. This man wasn't like the Navajo and Pueblo she saw on the streets of Albuquerque every day. He wasn't like the old-time indigenous people she studied in anthropology classes. He was the kind of Native American you saw through bulletproof glass and iron bars—the kind who made negative stereotypes possible. She took advantage of the calm before the storm to get a good look at his face, in case she had to describe him to a police artist later on.

High heels clicked across the hardwood floor behind her. Was her mother coming to her rescue? Unlikely.

"Sarah. I see you've already met Archie. What's the matter? Cat got your tongue?" The dangerous-looking man crossed his arms, perfectly framing the *"Free Leonard Peltier"* banner on his T-shirt.

He said, "No problem. I have that effect on women… men, too, for that matter. My name is Archie Chatto."

Sarah felt herself relax. "You mean the boyfriend from the Dog House Drive-In."

Archie said, "Your big sister here has told me all about you. Haven't you, Marie?

"Why, yes." Mom flashed her an apologetic look and filled in the blanks in their made-up family history. "Sarah and I had the same mother but different fathers. That's why she has such an odd last name."

"Bible," Sarah said. "It *is* a weird name, and there's an even weirder story behind it. Maybe Marie will tell you all about it someday. Too bad I couldn't have a regular old Italian name like Ferraro." She looked at Mom to make sure she had it right. Last names were like boyfriends for Marie. When one got inconvenient, she just found another.

"There are lots of things Archie will find out in time." Marie paused for effect. "If I decide to tell him." Her smile was as innocent as bait in a mousetrap. She talked while Archie and Sarah listened. That was good because it gave Sarah an opportunity to learn her role in her mother's latest drama.

It was good for Archie because it gave him a chance to be in close proximity to Marie, a place almost every heterosexual man in the world wanted to be.

Sarah never understood why men reacted to her mother the way they did. She knew there were biochemical explanations that had to do with things like dopamine and oxytocin, but Marie had a simpler explanation.

Men are stupid. She explained it years ago in the five-minute birds-and-bees talk most parents skillfully avoid. According to Marie, men are simpletons who want to be kings. Weak ones think they're strong. Short ones pretend to be tall. Ugly ones preen in front of mirrors for hours every day. She blamed it on testosterone, the hormone that makes them fight, lose their hair, and fall in love with women who drive them like rental cars.

Biology was Sarah's weakest subject. She hoped it stayed that way.

Marie kissed her new boyfriend on the cheek just below a scar that looked like someone's initials. "Archie's a full-blooded Apache. You know what *that* means."

Sarah knew all about the migration of Athabaskan tribes across the Bering Strait and through the Rocky Mountains, but that probably wasn't what Marie had in mind.

3

"**F**EDERAL AGENTS CAME to the college, Mom." Sarah struggled to maintain a civil tone of voice. "You could have told me a little more about him. It's been two days since he was here."

Marie struck a very convincing disappointed mother pose.

"He's trouble, Mom. More trouble than your boyfriends usually are." That was Sarah's best argument, and she knew it was useless. Persuading Marie of anything had always been impossible unless she read it in a romance novel or saw it on Lifetime TV.

"Time for another lesson in practical anthropology," Marie said. "Everyone with a Y chromosome comes with a certain amount of baggage."

Sarah had heard her mother's treatise on men before. They sold drugs the way women sold Mary Kay. Robbing a convenience store could be thought of as a male shopping alternative. Prison was a masculine version of finishing school. And warrants came standard with every pair of testicles.

"Testicles." Marie said that word more than most women. "Testicles are where all the baggage is packed. That's just how things are." The fact that her boyfriend had killed a federal agent did not bother her at all.

"Men are like cats, not understandable in any proper sense of the word. They aren't for us to judge."

That was one point upon which Sarah and her mother could agree. People in black robes would do that as soon as Archie was in custody.

"He's a *killer,* Mother." Not Mom's first killer. Probably not her last, but most of them didn't capture the interest of federal law enforcement like this one.

"Archie's an Apache," Marie said. "Didn't those anthropology classes teach you anything?"

"The FBI interviewed my department chairman. They actually got to meet him before I did."

"College is supposed to make you more open-minded."

"Apparently, they think I might be hiding him." Agents hadn't come to their apartment yet, but there was no doubt they were watching.

"You'll learn more from Archie than you will from books and men with letters after their names," Marie said. "He's a real live Apache warrior. Think of him as a modern version Geronimo. That's how he thinks of himself."

"Geronimo." Sarah didn't know a lot about the old renegade warrior, but she knew enough.

"Geronimo's first family was killed," she told Marie. "He was shot and stabbed numerous times. He and his followers nearly starved while government troops chased him all over Mexico and Arizona. He surrendered more than once. The last time finally took."

That paused the argument long enough for Marie to mentally reconfigure the conquest of the American west.

"At Skeleton Canyon, Arizona," Sarah said. "In case you want to look it up. Geronimo surrendered to General Nelson Miles. He spent the rest of his life in custody."

"Archie's clever," Marie said. "He'll stay right here in Albuquerque. He won't go anywhere near Arizona." It had taken her five seconds flat to work things out to her satisfaction. In the cinema of Marie's mind, her boyfriend had become a Native American insurgent in the most recent sequel of the Apache wars. It was the Indians' turn to win.

"Anyway…." Mom shifted gears smoothly and moved on with her plans. "Don't you think he looks just like Cary Grant in *North by Northwest*?" All of her boyfriends gradually took on the features of the Roger O. Thornhill character in the Alfred Hitchcock classic.

"And he's just as tricky too. The bad guys will never catch him." During her manic phase Marie lived by a simple code. Keep negative thoughts out of your mind. Sit back and enjoy the ride. The scenery is splendid.

"I've always wanted to get married at Mount Rushmore." Marie had plenty of experience planning weddings. This time there would be no Justice of the Peace in a county courthouse. She would marry her renegade Apache standing before the benevolent stone heads of dead American presidents. No formal ceremony because of the groom's criminal status, but symbolism was the most important thing.

ARCHIE COULD HAVE stayed free longer if Marie knew how to cook, but she'd dropped out of high school to become an almost-never-stays-at-home mother and hadn't gotten around to Home Economics.

She had a hankering for chile rellenos, and Archie couldn't say no.

"Any Old Town restaurant should be safe enough," Marie reasoned. "The prices are too high for government expense accounts."

Things looked good in Padilla's Mexican Kitchen. The lunch crowd was heavy, and the margaritas were murky with tequila.

"Men in suits," Archie told Marie as the hostess took them to their table. "Lots of men in suits."

Marie told him not to worry. "There's a Kirby vacuum cleaner sales convention in town. Those guys wear suits almost as much as federal agents."

"Feds take it really serious when you kill them." Archie sat with his back to the wall and asked the hostess if they had buffalo on the menu. "Always wanted to die with the taste of buffalo in my mouth."

Marie laughed and kissed him on the cheek, but she noticed the two men at the next table. The only two men in the restaurant who were looking at Archie instead of her.

"Probably gay vacuum cleaner salesmen." Just to be sure, Marie gave them her most seductive smile. Their eyes turned toward her like two pairs of compass needles redirected by a shift in the earth's magnetic field, but their hands slid underneath the bottom buttons of their Brooks Brothers jackets.

"Oops." That was Archie's cue to surrender.

He stood and announced at the top of his voice, "I'll go without a fight." He tried to nudge Marie away, but she wouldn't leave.

"I want to make a statement first." He showed them his hands, like a cruise ship magician getting ready to amaze the crowd.

The federal agents looked nervous. There were too many patrons in the restaurant for a gunfight. Marie positioned herself in front of Archie so they couldn't get off a clean shot, and there were probably security cameras around ready to capture footage for the evening news. If things went wrong—and she couldn't imagine they would—her final moments would be captured on the evening news. She tried to think of some dramatic last words that would sound good in a Lifetime TV movie.

One of the agents said, "Go for it, Chatto," while the other finished his last bite of his enmolada and fished his Miranda rights card out of his pocket.

Archie kissed Marie on the lips long enough to make the agents nervous. Then he recited the same surrender speech he always made when it was time to spend a little time in prison. It was a good one. Geronimo used it first over a hundred years earlier.

"I was warmed by the sun, rocked by the winds, and sheltered by the trees as other Indian babes," he said. "I was living peaceably when people began to speak bad of me. Now I can eat well, sleep well, and be glad. I can go everywhere with a good feeling." Archie finished it appropriately—with a war cry.

The customers gave him a rousing round of applause and then got back to their midday meals. Marie sobbed quietly as the agents led her boyfriend away. She walked a fine dramatic line, demonstrating a suitable amount of anguish without stealing the show. She checked her reflection in the chrome napkin dispenser on her table. Her mascara was adequately streaked. She left a twenty-dollar bill on the table even though neither she nor Archie had been served.

"ARCHIE'S THE LOVE of my life." Marie raised her right hand and crossed her fingers.

"Crossing your fingers means you are lying," Sarah said.

"Whatever." Marie uncrossed them and repeated herself. "This time's for real. The other times were just for practice."

Ordinarily, Marie's romances ended as soon as her lovers were Mirandized, but she couldn't seem to stop crying over Archie Chatto. He had won her heart. He would take it with him to the federal prison in El Reno, Oklahoma where he'd be held awaiting trial. Marie swore she'd join him there.

"He gave up his freedom for me. It's the least I can do."

Sarah didn't mention the federal agent he had killed or the warrants for other lesser crimes or all the times Archie Chatto had spent behind bars when Marie wasn't in the picture. She hid Mom's car, had her SSI check deposited in a different bank account, and waited for her passion to focus somewhere else. It had been four years since she and Mom left Oklahoma and came to Albuquerque. That move had followed another of Marie's disastrous love affairs. Sarah had no intention of ever going back. She was now the legally responsible adult in the family, the grownup who could sign documents and write checks. What could her mother do except pout and whine and go missing days at a time?

That is what she did, of course. A few days passed, and Sarah didn't see or hear from Marie. Nothing unusual about that, but then a few days more and then a week, and Sarah started to worry but only a little.

Marie would assemble a new collection of devoted friends, the way she always did. A number of potential lovers would be drawn under her spell, and when that group reached the critical mass, she'd pair up with the least suitable candidate. Marie's new paramour would use all his resources to satisfy her every whim until he was financially exhausted, arrested on an outstanding warrant, or finally realized she was crazy. Then Marie Ferraro would become Mom again. That cycle would repeat itself until Marie's mood reached the peak of optimism and began its relentless slide into the black pit of depression.

Sarah considered how much easier life would be if her mother looked more like a crazy person, if she had a tremor in her voice, stepped over cracks compulsively, or wore her hair in a Bedlam style. It was hard to recognize just how crazy Marie was until you got to know her. She seemed clever and exotic at first, especially to men.

She attracted male admirers the way a Venus flytrap collects insects, with a combination of pheromones and sugar-rich nectar. Once they were firmly tangled in her embrace, she would soak up their emotional nutrients and cast their empty husks aside without the slightest bit of malice.

She relished the taste of her victims during the manic phase of her illness and regretted their plight during her depressions, but her hunger never lost its edge.

Marie swore Archie would be different, but from Sarah's perspective, things looked pretty familiar. Another boyfriend had been hauled away in the back of a police cruiser, and her mother was out and about, undoubtedly luring a vulnerable male to his doom.

4

SARAH DIDN'T HAVE to wait long outside her department chairman's office. She was prepared to plead for a verbal reprimand or a single, easily-overlooked line in the nebulous permanent record educational administrators value so highly. She might be able to produce a tear or two if it came to that. She sorted through all the bad things that had ever happened to her, looking for the proper motivation. The list was endless.

She began formulating an apology as soon as the secretary closed the door behind her, but Professor Lindsay cut her off.

"Finally, I have a student who takes an active interest in the struggles of indigenous Americans."

Who could have guessed that Archie Chatto was the descendant of one of the Indian scouts who had helped the U.S. Army bring an end to the Apache wars?

"Betrayed, every last one of them," Professor Lindsay said. "Cashiered out of the cavalry and shipped off to Florida on a cattle train. And now the U.S. government is persecuting the great-great-grandchildren of those brave warriors."

Sarah wasn't sure about the number of greats in Professor Lindsay's calculation, and she was even less certain of Archie Chatto's lineage, but she didn't argue. The department chairman wasn't upset in the least over his exchanges with the FBI. In fact, he was delighted. He enumerated constitutional amendments too fast for Sarah to keep track as he rose to his feet and shook her hand. He escorted her to an ugly institutional vinyl couch on the wall of his windowless office and took a seat beside her.

"Archie will overcome the outrageous charges the government has brought against him," Dr. Lindsay told her. "With my help, and yours, and the assistance of your wonderful mother."

Sarah expelled the breath she had been holding long enough to make her dizzy. "You know my mother?" Now she could see the signs—the way Professor Lindsay's voice trembled with barely controlled emotion, the way his eyes danced around the room when his mind settled on Marie. "She's told me everything. I was dubious at first, but your mother is very persuasive." Was no man immune to Marie Ferraro's charms?

Professor Lindsay invested several long seconds looking Sarah over. His manner was intrusive, but at least it wasn't lecherous. He examined Sarah the way a coin collector would evaluate a potential purchase.

"The resemblance is only... well, slight. Between you and your mother, I mean."

Sarah knew exactly what he meant. Marie had a mysterious quality that a physical anthropologist couldn't measure with a Boley gauge or weigh with a scale, and that quality had transformed Professor Lindsay's brain into scented KY Jelly. There were many things she could have said to her department chairman at that moment, but she knew from past experience that her warnings would go unheeded.

Marie had turned her bipolar condition into an asset. When she was manic, she made men feel good, and when she was depressed, she made them feel responsible. Eventually she always did something crazy enough to turn her lovers' infatuation into panic. Dr. Lindsay had not reached that stage.

"Your mother needs you in Oklahoma. We can arrange for a leave of absence while you go to her."

"Mom's in Oklahoma?"

"My daughter, Victoria, has a guest house you can stay in," Professor Lindsay said. "She is solidly behind the struggle for Native American sovereignty."

The fact that Archie Chatto was on trial for murder didn't figure into the department chairman's equation. Archie was an Apache, after all, a member of an endangered species. Like the American timber wolf, Archie would be forgiven the social peccadilloes that attend living off the land.

MARIE CALLED FROM Oklahoma a few days later with a plea for help. Grady County sheriff's deputies were holding her on a charge of grand theft auto.

"I never intended to keep the car. I just needed transportation." Marie didn't expect much understanding from the legal system. There were all those outstanding Oklahoma warrants and her well-established status as a mental patient. *"They'll put me in a mental hospital—probably Flanders. I can't go there again, Sarah. They might never let me out."*

Sarah knew that wasn't true. Her mother had been involuntarily committed to mental hospitals many times. They always let her out. But it wasn't only men that Marie Ferraro could manipulate. She could work spells on her daughter too. All she had to do was use the magic words, and Sarah couldn't refuse.

"Please, Sarah. Please come and help me. I need you."

5

WHEN THE WIND blew, she talked to Robert Collins, and in Oklahoma, the wind blew all the time. She brought him words of wisdom, told him jokes, whispered secrets he didn't want to know. The wind was a tireless talker, and Robert listened carefully to everything she had to say. No wonder he was crazy.

"She has no voice of her own." He'd told this story now to fifty-six Medicaid psychiatrists before his current one. Their faces and professional degrees were interchangeable—no point in learning names. They all answered to Doctor.

"She gathers cast-off words and phrases. Puts them into brand new sentences."

This doctor mouthed the word, *"She?"* He raised his eyebrows, making it into an unasked question, but he didn't ask it out loud. He wanted Robert to do most of the talking.

"She." Robert shrugged. Didn't everybody agree on the gender of the wind? Nothing Freudian about it.

"Please go on," the doctor said.

Robert couldn't blame him for the low-energy style. Psychiatrists earned less than plumbers, and their profession was uniquely unpleasant.

"What does she tell you?" The doctor lifted his Mont Blanc pen and made a series of quick, arcane entries in Robert's chart.

Robert didn't judge him for keeping is comments brief. There were far too many schizophrenics in Oklahoma City. Inconvenient citizens, as unfathomable as stray cats but not as dangerous—usually.

The group home where Robert lived was infinitely superior to Flanders Mental Hospital. He could stay there as long as someone with a medical degree said was sane enough.

"She tells me I'm no danger to myself or others." Robert pointed to the note pad, but the doctor didn't write that down. This time-honored Jedi mind trick didn't work this time.

The psychiatrists checked him out in these weekly sessions, made sure he hadn't crossed that institutionalizable threshold once again. Talking to the wind took him right up to the welcome mat.

"Really, Robert? What else does the wind tell you?"

He could give the doctor an example. Perhaps a snippet from a political speech the wind had brought him earlier this morning. A few phrases that blew in from the southeastern corner of the state complete with a Little Dixie accent. He could imitate the tone and cadence perfectly, but he really wasn't sure about the content. It was politics after all, not much different than schizophrenia. So, he shrugged instead. There would be plenty to say when he got back on the streets. The wind was a good listener, better than the nameless parade of shrinks who questioned his version of reality.

The doctor looked nervous. He pretended to scratch his shoulder with his left hand so he could check his watch. Digital. Precise. Made in China.

Robert told him, "We can cut the session short. I don't mind." The voices hadn't told him to do anything dangerous or illegal, but the psychiatrist needed another thirteen minutes to satisfy his Medicaid requirement. Big Brother might be watching.

"Please go on." The doctor's eyes moved to a travel poster on the wall of the cramped little room—somewhere in the Caribbean. Robert started to ask if that's where he went to medical school but thought better of it.

"Well, doctor." Shrinks always recognized stalling tactics. As long as the fifty-minute hour was filled to the brim, they didn't usually care, but this one tapped his hundred-dollar ballpoint pen on his front teeth and looked at his watch again.

Ten minutes left, enough time for the Cliff Notes version of Robert's life story—suitable for a quarterly assessment. He could make a show of clarity in this stuffy little room the voices couldn't penetrate. An open window would have blown the illusion of sanity away.

"The wind tells me my parents were archeologists." Lovers, sifting through the remains of a lost civilization, but Robert didn't say anything about that.

"I was conceived on site." He didn't explain how an ancient shaman's spirit took advantage of the situation. Delusions with too much texture looked like serious psychopathology.

The doctor checked his watch again. He flipped through Robert's record checking today's responses against previous sessions.

Damn.

"You believe an ancient indigenous spirit lives inside your body?"

When all else fails, try the truth. "Sometimes, I do."

There were weeks, even months when the whole idea seemed preposterous, especially when he took his medications. During periods of clarity, Robert knew he was an orphan who had been in foster care from the age of three. His archaeologist parents were no more than a mental program malfunction, but they were at least as real as the science of psychiatry.

"Mostly, I don't."

The doctor didn't speak, but his body language shouted accolades. With a flourish of his Mont Blanc, he made a note in Robert's chart. His lips moved as he wrote, *Touching base with reality.* He drew a five-pointed star beside the entry.

The pentagram. An appropriate sign to designate the loss of a man's soul. It didn't matter to the doctor that Robert Collins's life was interesting when the spirit of an ancient shaman lived inside him.

"Tell me, Robert. What does the wind think the future has in store for you."

"Partly cloudy skies tomorrow with only a small chance for rain. That's a good thing because the house I live in has a leaky roof." No need to tell the doctor something big and dangerous is coming soon. Robert might be crazy, but he wasn't stupid. He knew from past experience how terribly wrong things could go in the final minutes of a session.

"You should keep your umbrella close at hand just the same. Even the wind can't predict the weather in Oklahoma."

The psychiatrist tapped the crystal of his wristwatch as if that would hurry the session along. He held his watch so that Robert could participate in the countdown. 58, 57, 56…. All conditions were go.

NO ONE PROTESTED when DHS bought rundown houses on the northeast side of town and converted them to group homes for the mentally challenged. The neighborhood where Robert lived didn't quite rise to the status of a ghetto, but the streets were ruled by teenage gangsters with an unlimited capacity for violence. The youthful offenders committed armed robberies, sold drugs, and shot each other with impunity, but they treated the residential clients of the group homes with reverence.

Robert walked the streets of the most dangerous quadrant of Oklahoma City in complete safety because he was crazy. Like the Cheyenne and Sioux of the Great Plains, the Crips and Bloods around N.E. 36th Street cherished and protected the insane.

The wind was in a playful mood, nudging him this way and that, pelting him gently with dandelion seed and bits of cast-off paper. She chased herself into a whirlwind and embraced him in the center. The wind's happiness was contagious, and Robert soon found himself singing a song he heard many years ago but only just remembered.

The tune was wrong. Lyrics fit poorly into stanzas. The rhyme and meter missed the mark, but in Robert Collins's mind, the effect was serious perfection.

A young black couple crossed the street to avoid contact with the crazy white man who sang to an invisible audience. Robert watched them evaluate the area for potential cover. He smiled and waved, but that didn't seem to put them at ease.

They paused in front of the Wise Owl Child Development Center, even took a few steps toward the door. Robert kept on walking, careful not to stare—proof he wasn't a threat to himself or others. He sang louder as he drifted away from the young couple, away from the child development center like a flying insect moving at the wind's discretion. No one would interfere with him in this part of town, and no one would complain to the authorities.

When the song lyrics finally ran their course, he found the wind had stopped him within the boundaries of Riverside Gardens Cemetery. A glossy black hearse turned into the entrance and led a string of cars between two square stone pillars that served as pedestals for a pair of weeping angels.

Riverside Gardens Cemetery was one of the oldest graveyards in the region, established well before statehood. Robert visited often. The burial park was one of the few peaceful well-kept expanses of green within walking distance of his group home. Rich and poor were buried together here. Blacks, whites, and Native Americans lay in peaceful coexistence under carefully maintained lawns. The status of the dead was differentiated only by their headstones. Dust-bowl-paupers slept under degraded blocks of limestone with barely legible names and dates. Granite monuments and marble statuary adorned the graves of oil millionaires and industrialists.

The only segregated part of the necropolis was the oldest eighth acre in its exact center. The dead in this section of the graveyard were fenced in by a sandstone wall built when Oklahoma City was still an unnamed section of Oklahoma Territory. A bronze plaque beside the only entrance identified the place as the Indian Baptist Cemetery.

Robert never went inside the sandstone wall. The place was spooky, too spooky even for a white man whose body is inhabited by the spirit of a dead shaman.

The rest of Riverside Gardens was carefully manicured, but Indian Baptist Cemetery was overgrown with thistles and moonflowers. Cottonwood trees grew as haphazardly as Robert's thoughts. Fallen limbs provided nourishment for yellow puffballs as big as Christmas ornaments.

Tipped slate tombstones barely held their own against the deadwood and the weeds. They sported epitaphs written in the graceful looping Cherokee alphabet. Failed wooden crosses without lettering or numbers marked the final resting places of Creek and Seminole freedmen.

Three redbrick Choctaw bone-houses dominated the little graveyard. The names—Tingle, Byars, and Maytubby—were spelled out in green colored tiles over their doorways. Only the Maytubby building was in good repair. Its roof was straight, its entryway swept clean. A life-size figure of a white owl decorated the rusty metal door. Simple shapes of plane geometry arranged by a clever anonymous artist to resemble a nocturnal bird of prey.

"Post-modern abstract representation," the wind told Robert. He had no idea what she meant.

He turned away from the Indian Baptist Cemetery and watched a newly arrived funeral procession follow a winding gravel road toward a yellow canopy at Riverside Gardens's northern border.

"A graveside service," the wind told him. She would sweep through the open walls of the pavilion and collect solemn words. She would mix them into phrases from playgrounds, political rallies, battlefields, and prison yards. She would use the borrowed words to fill Robert's ears with things no one else could know. The wind spoke in a thousand voices, each one fully charged with its own emotion. She was impossible to ignore.

A black SUV turned away from the procession and headed toward the Indian Baptist Cemetery.

"Watch what he does!" The wind borrowed the voice of a scorned wife who had used that phrase to instruct a private detective. The words were as sharp and angry as a switchblade.

"Don't get too close!" A mother's words this time, warning her child away from a space heater.

A man rolled out of the passenger door of the SUV as it stopped at the entrance to the Indian Baptist Cemetery. A Native American man.

He struggled to his feet. His head bobbed in a perfect imitation of a chicken evaluating the final hundred yards leading to a rendering plant. Methamphetamine users moved their heads like that, but this man was no addict. He was clean-shaven and well-dressed with glossy black shoes, well-tailored pants, and a blue blazer. A name tag pinned to the pocket of the blazer identified him as *J. Mankiller, Casino Manager.*

The driver stepped out of the SUV. His skin was bronze, like his passenger's, but his features gave no clue of his race or nationality. He made a wide circle around the vehicle and closed in on the disoriented passenger with the slow deliberate motion of a wolf cornering a rabbit.

The wolf waited for an opening as if he had done this kind of thing many times before.

"You killed my wife." The passenger barely spoke above a whisper, but the wind picked up his words and carried them to Robert.

"You took my daughter."

The wolf did not answer. He had his quarry trapped between himself and the SUV.

The passenger reached into the inside pocket of his blue blazer. The wolf stepped back in case his rabbit might have a weapon, but it was only a piece of paper.

"I know where she is."

The wolf snatched at the paper, but he only tore away a corner.

"I know where she is."

The wolf extended a closed fist in the passenger's direction. He turned his hand over and opened it so the rabbit could see the mound of yellow powder resting on his palm.

Robert watched the driver blow the yellow powder into the passenger's face. The man fell backward against the SUV, slid down the door, and sat on the ground. The driver reached for the paper in the passenger's hand, but the wind snatched it away before his fingers closed around it.

The paper blew left and right, as unpredictable as a dragonfly. It followed a jagged meandering route, until it dropped like a heavy stone at Robert's feet. He picked it up.

"Run!" The wind shouted the order to Robert in a voice borrowed from a football coach. He waited long enough to see the wolf stuff his victim back into the SUV.

"Run, run, run, as fast as you can!" It was the voice of an enthusiastic grandmother telling the story of the gingerbread man to a three-year-old who was hearing it for the first time.

Robert knew he couldn't outrun the wolf's SUV, but the man couldn't drive among the gravestones, and he couldn't chase him down in front of witnesses. So he sprinted toward the graveside service. After a dozen steps, he heard footfalls on the gravel road behind him—fast, efficient footfalls that would close the distance between them in minutes. But in seconds Robert reached the safety of the funeral canopy.

Bad news. It was an African-American funeral. He couldn't blend seamlessly with the mourners, and they would not interrupt their service to defend a crazy white man in a fight that did not concern them.

Robert continued running but looked over his shoulder to check the progress of his pursuer. A strategic mistake. The wolf had dropped back, and Robert might have been able to escape over the cemetery fence, but he tripped on a wrinkle in the artificial turf under the canopy and went sprawling over a group of mourners. The wind collected a wide assortment of expletives as a result of his blunder, but he lost the opportunity for a clean getaway.

He scrambled to his feet, ran to the open coffin.

"Jesus, take this man to your bosom," he sang out in his loudest most sincere gospel music voice. The wind provided Robert with the kind of religious vocabulary spoken at tent revivals and river baptisms.

"This sinner has been washed in the blood of the lamb." Robert did crazy things all the time. He usually didn't realize it, so he usually didn't feel embarrassed. This time he did. He bent over the corpse and kissed both of the dead man's cold, heavily rouged cheeks while he stuffed the paper he was carrying into the pocket of the dearly departed's burying shirt. Then he turned around to take stock of his circumstances.

The wolf was nowhere to be seen. He'd been discouraged by Robert's antics. Now the crowd of mourners posed a more immediate threat.

He ran around the coffin and away from the crowd, worrying too much about the impression he left behind and not enough about the obstacles in front of him. He traveled only a few yards when he stumbled over a headstone and rolled into an open grave.

Robert's head made a sound like an under-inflated basketball as it thumped against the edge of the concrete vault. He rolled onto his back and looked at the perfectly rectangular patch of sky at the top of the grave.

"You all right?" The speaker was a large black man dressed in well-worn working clothes. He wore a broad-brimmed green gardener's hat that kept his face hidden in a shadow. He walked around the edge of the grave in a stride that was simultaneously rough and graceful.

Robert tried to answer, but the words stuck in his throat. The surface of the world was very far away, so much farther than the six feet mandated by tradition.

"You all right?" The margins of the grave framed the man like a surrealistic portrait. Reflected sunlight found its way under the brim of his hat and revealed a face distorted by concern. A hummingbird hovered over the man's right shoulder, and there was something else. His proportions were wrong, squat and thick, like an image in a fun house mirror.

As other people gathered beside the man, Robert could see that he was large but also relatively short, not even as tall as some of the female mourners.

That seemed impossible, but after a few seconds of careful observation, Robert solved the problem. The big man had no legs below his knees.

"Who are you?" Robert asked him.

"They call me Big Shorty."

But the wind told Robert his real name, "Baron Saturday," accented with delicate Acadian French vowels she'd carried from the bayous of Louisiana.

"Baron Saturday." Robert repeated the name with the same precise Creole intonations.

A fellow halfway house client had told him all about the Voodoo Loa of the dead. Baron Saturday was supposed to wear a white top hat and a black tuxedo, not overalls and a gardener's hat.

Robert meant to ask the big, short man about that, but before he could, the rectangle of light at the top of the grave receded to a small bright point and then disappeared altogether. The last thing he heard before his world slipped away was discordant music—Bartok or tinnitus or maybe just the wind. He knew he wasn't dying. His head hurt far too much.

6

"THANK GOD I'M nothing like Marie," Sarah mumbled under her breath as she entered the common area of Flanders Mental Hospital.

The great room was large and well illuminated by skylights and windows with a northern exposure. Architecturally interesting nooks and crannies gave the illusion of privacy without obscuring the vision of staff nurses. Gaming tables and benches made of cast concrete offered the opportunity for cards, chess, and checkers but couldn't be converted to battering rams and blunt instruments. Identical overstuffed couches, bolted to the floor around the perimeter, created semi-private micro-environments.

Three televisions mounted at strategic locations allowed patients the viewing choices of sports, drama, or music video. Cable news and religious channels had been blocked. Prozac couldn't overcome the stimulatory effects of current events and Jesus.

Over the years, Sarah had visited her mother in places like this many times, often enough to know that in spite of initial impressions, there was nothing common about the common area of a mental hospital. Even the most cunning interior design could not hide the simple truth about Flanders for more than a few seconds. The place was a crazy house.

Clients were permitted to use the commons only if their disorders were manageable. Sarah was impressed with euphemisms used by the mental health establishment. The clients of Flanders were patients, forcibly confined and given unwanted medications to alter mental states they didn't want to change. A disorder was considered manageable if its decibel level didn't consistently exceed hospital background noise. That could be pretty loud.

The collection of behaviors in the common area was both predictable and bizarre. Some clients engaged invisible companions in animated conversations. Others rocked obsessively, sang tuneless songs in private languages, paced the room like participants in a zombie parade, or wavered between uncontrollable tremors and catatonia.

"We're being watched," Marie Ferarro told her daughter.

Sarah knew her mother's suspicions weren't a symptom of her disease. The staff in the common area was discretely absent but could appear as suddenly and mysteriously as a magician's illusion if a client disrupted the questionable serenity of the room.

"They have hidden cameras all over the place," Marie said. "And microphones and spies."

Sarah didn't believe professional spies were imbedded in the client population, but there were snitches aplenty. The difference would be lost on Marie in her current mental state. The doctors had settled on Thorazine as the most appropriate means of managing her manic behavior. The drug gave her complexion a permanent blush. It dried up her saliva, made her hands tremble, and transformed her confidence into confusion. Sarah hoped to persuade someone in authority to reduce the dosage, but doctors were scarce in mental hospitals, and they avoided the relatives of clients the way celebrities avoided paparazzi.

Marie lowered her voice to a slurred whisper. "Archie's reaching out to me." The tip of her tongue explored the vermillion border of her lips as if it had an alien purpose of its own. Marie covered her eyes with her hands but peered through the spaces between her fingers. Her breathing was deep and noisy. Sarah watched the second hand of her Timex while she counted respirations.

Twenty times a minute—was that hyperventilation?

"Yesterday, I held a cup of coffee in my hands." Marie's whisper was barely audible but carried as much emotion as a scream.

"Archie's vibrations buzzed my fingers like a captured hornet." According to Marie, he spoke into his own cup of coffee in a prison cafeteria fifty miles away, broadcasting expressions of love on the emotional wavelengths of the cosmos. Marie thought Nicholas Sparks should incorporate the concept in his next novel. She planned to send him the idea eventually but would use a traditional means of communication like the postal service or email.

"Fifty miles is no distance at all for a man like him." Marie swore the persistence and intensity of the vibrations were as reliable as his signature. Archie's love for her shook the walls, the windows, even the floor of Flanders Mental Hospital.

"It's like *Message in a Bottle*." Marie drew a deep breath between each word. "But the bottle cap is stuck so tight, I can't get it open." She gripped an invisible bottle in her left hand and struggled to unscrew its imaginary cap with her right. The act transformed her simile into a full-blown hallucination. Marie's emotions and her invisible bottle were at the breaking point.

Sarah looked around the room for help, but Marie's current mental state would be acceptable to the Flanders Angels of Mercy. She was quiet. She was not a physical threat to herself or to anyone else. The only pain she suffered was mental, and in a hospital like Flanders, internal turmoil was a matter of course.

Marie's breathing increased in frequency. Way too fast for simple anxiety. Her fingers curled into spastic claws. Sarah knew that was brought on by too much oxygen too fast. The spasms would intensify and spread into the large muscles of Marie's arms and legs.

"Slow down, Mom." Sarah knew from past experience she couldn't talk Marie down, but she didn't know what else to do. "Breathe slower. You'll make the spasms worse."

Marie began a series of rhythmic silent screams as noiseless and as relentless as a shark attack. Sarah would have run for help if she could have done so without leaving her mother's side. She was afraid to call out, afraid overzealous staff members might interpret her vocalizations as a threat to peace and stability. Even for Marie, she would not risk being mistaken for a disruptive Flanders client. Psych nurses were quick on the draw with hypodermic syringes, and they weren't particular whose butt was loaded full of sedatives.

A series of pokes with a stiff index finger ended Sarah's period of indecision.

"Not good." The finger's owner was a tall, balding, male client as thin and fragile as an Auschwitz survivor. He continued poking Sarah well after he had her full attention.

"Seen this before." He counted ten pokes, then withdrew his hand, blew on it, and licked his fingertips. "Sweet." He trained his gaze on a spot two inches above Sarah's head. "Not good at all. Ben will get Doctor Collins." The man's walk reminded Sarah of Charlie Chaplin. A lot of people walked like that at Flanders.

After several minutes, Ben returned, accompanied by a handsome young man with lustrous black hair and deep blue eyes. He introduced himself as Robert.

It was rare to find a doctor who didn't use his title to put distance between himself and lesser humans. A doctor whose humanity hadn't been erased by higher education—amazing.

Even more amazing, he was an absolutely charming man. A first for Sarah. Her attitude toward members of the opposite sex had been tainted by Marie's romantic escapades. Sarah usually found men about as desirable as exotic venomous reptiles, but she might make an exception for Dr. Robert Collins. He seated himself beside Marie. Her silent frantic screaming had intensified, but he brought it to a sudden stop by taking her hand. A man's touch always got Marie's attention. She smiled at Dr. Collins through her Thorazine haze.

"Tell me what you need," he said. "We'll look for it together."

Marie's breathing approached a normal rate. "Archie's calling me. But I can't hear him inside this place."

"I understand." Sarah didn't doubt the truth of that statement. Apparently, neither did Marie. "Work with me. We can bring him closer."

Sarah had never seen a doctor do what Robert did. It was something like hypnosis and something like meditation and something like two crazy people talking to each other. Robert Collins had perfect rapport with Marie Ferraro. Sarah watched as he guided her mother through several seemingly pointless mental exercises to an incomprehensible conclusion that Marie understood completely. As Sarah's mother sorted through her thoughts and emotions, her facial expressions changed as clearly and concisely as a lesson in method acting.

"I'll hear him better when I'm outside," she said. "Until then, feeling his vibrations will be good enough."

Robert nodded in agreement. He gave Marie's hand a gentle squeeze, ending the session as it began.

"Screwing someone's head on straight requires some delicacy," he told Sarah. "The threads are easily stripped."

Collins was quite a man, good looking but not arrogant, smart but not superior, a doctor of the mind who preferred happiness over sanity. He could definitely change Sarah's attitude about the effectiveness of psychotherapy. Maybe about men in general.

There was no wedding band on his finger, but that didn't rule out a significant other. She wanted to ask him straight out. That's what her mother would do. Move boldly and make corrections as conditions demanded, like a juggler on a tightrope. Sarah wished for a moment she could be just a little more like Marie, but she was accustomed to stifling such impulses.

Maybe later, she thought. Maybe she could arrange to run into him outside of Flanders Hospital. A mental institution didn't seem the most appropriate environment for exploring relationship possibilities. Not even Nicholas Sparks could twist that idea into a believable story.

Sarah didn't think to ask Dr. Collins if he would take charge of her mother's therapy until she reached the security doors at the entrance of the hospital. Her thought processes had been put on hold by the strength of the doctor's personality, but she knew she should take immediate action before one of the other doctors did Marie irreparable harm. If something developed between Sarah and Robert while Marie was being treated, so much the better.

She made her way to hospital administration and eventually found a secretary who seemed sympathetic to her cause.

"It's nice when one of our psychiatrists gains the confidence of a family member." The secretary ran her fingers over her computer keyboard, brought up the appropriate screen, and asked for the doctor's name.

"Robert Collins." Sarah watched the cooperative smile slide off the helpful woman's face.

"Did he say he was a doctor?"

Sarah mentally reviewed her encounter with Collins. She was surprised at the detail.

"I guess not." She was ashamed to admit feeling a little disappointed at Robert's loss of professional status.

"Is he an intern, a psychiatric nurse, an orderly?" Surely a man with Robert's expertise wasn't a mere visitor.

"He's a client," the secretary said. "Brought in by the police after he disrupted a funeral. They say he talks with the wind."

Perfect, Sarah thought. *Maybe I* am *my mother's daughter after all.*

7

A S HASHILLI MAYTUBBY drove his black Chevy Tahoe along the Kilpatrick Turnpike, he composed a prayer-song to the enemies of his ancestors. He wasn't good at music, but he did well with words, so he borrowed tunes from Paul McCartney and sang lyrics about white men's treachery and Choctaw magic.

Grandfather would approve. The old man had been a Beatles fan in his youth. He'd been a lot more generous with his records than his magic. He liked the Rolling Stones and the Dave Clark Five, all the British groups, because they were descendants of white people who hadn't come to America to steal tribal land. He was grateful to Europeans who stayed where they belonged.

On more than one occasion, Grandfather told Hashilli, "Not all whites are bad, just the ones on this side of the Atlantic." He'd been so narrow-minded.

Grandfather couldn't admit that white people brought the seeds of modern magic to the New World when they came. Without things like telephones, computers, and copy machines, witches like Hashilli would be lost. He appreciated motor vehicles most of all.

His SUV carried him quickly from one destination to another. He could look into his victims' eyes at the moment of deception, steal little pieces of their souls along with their money, and then move on. The essence of witchcraft.

He briefly considered calling Victoria Tiger to tell her he'd been delayed but decided against it. Victoria wouldn't complain. She was too consumed with white guilt to judge Hashilli harshly.

Indian time was something Victoria had learned about from her father. It was an integral part of the culture she'd been looking for, ever since she'd married Albert Tiger. Her husband's obsessive punctuality was a source of bitter disappointment. Five minutes early for every appointment, as measured by his Rolex watch.

Albert was an ambitious casino manager, with an appalling lack of Indian ways. He was a modern man living in the modern world and hardly gave a thought to things like Indian Removal and genocide. Victoria was an old-fashioned girl whose morality came from sometime in the 1960s. She was desperate to apologize for the cultural atrocities of her ancestors. That difference in worldview made them vulnerable to Hashilli's style of sorcery.

The Tiger estate was in a wooded area west of Oklahoma City. It was close enough to the casino to be handy for Albert but secluded enough to allow for the privacy both he and Victoria valued.

"A good place to raise a son," Victoria told Hashilli the first time she invited him onto the property. Baby Andrew was the first boy-child of his generation. Hope of immortality for the Tiger line.

Hashilli didn't remind Victoria that traditional Muskogee heredity is matrilineal. Bloodlines are insignificant in matters of the heart. Hashilli Maytubby understood the value of an only child, and in the fullness of time, Victoria and Albert Tiger would understand it too.

Within a week, Andrew Tiger would be a possession of Hashilli's. The baby boy would fetch a hefty ransom. The magic of electronic funds transfer would make Tiger money disappear into a bank account on Grand Cayman Island. It would jump across oceans and continents to Bermuda, Wales, Israel, and Switzerland. This kind of magic was much more profitable than changing into an owl to frighten superstitious Indians.

Victoria and Albert would never see their son again, regardless of the price they paid. If things went as Hashilli hoped, baby Andrew would be absorbed into the Maytubby line. If not, he'd be auctioned to the highest bidder. There was an ever-increasing number of would be parents who had money but lacked reproductive wherewithal.

Hashilli drove through the open gate. What good are gates when the owners leave them open? Not that the Tigers's gate would hinder him in the slightest. On his last visit, he had watched Victoria enter the code. She recited the numbers out loud as she keyed them in. Victoria Tiger trusted Hashilli. And why wouldn't she? He was a respected antiquities consultant for the Oklahoma Western Heritage Museum. She knew this because Hashilli told her so. White women married to Native men were such easy marks.

A small copse of red cedar trees made the house invisible from the road—the perfect place to stage a kidnapping. Hashilli had cautioned Victoria that discretion was of utmost importance. It was best if no one, not even her husband, knew of their plans while they were in the formative stages.

Hashilli, the respected antiquities dealer, had discovered something while authenticating museum documents, something that would make important people nervous. Especially casino owners who wanted to stay in the good graces of federal agencies.

Hashilli knew how to set the hook. He fabricated a discovery based on Victoria's vanity and total confidence in government treachery. Promises had been made to Albert's great-great-grandfather by President Andrew Jackson. Hashilli found a letter. It was all hush-hush.

"The document might not be enforceable, but it is an important piece of Albert's family history."

That was all it took. Victoria had given her husband a son, and now she would give him part of his heritage. Enforceability be damned.

As Hashilli pulled into the circular drive and parked under the porte cochere at the front of the Tigers's home, he saw a low-end, late model Subaru Outback parked beside the guesthouse. The Tigers had company. Trouble he didn't need.

The moment he was inside the house, he reminded Victoria how easily the Jackson document could upset the political apple cart.

"Maybe we should wait until your visitor is gone before proceeding."

"Sarah's got other things on her mind." Victoria repeated the story her father had told her when he arranged for Sarah to stay in the guesthouse.

Hashilli had thoroughly researched Victoria's background. He knew all about Dr. Carson Lindsay, but he pretended to be surprised.

"She's Dad's favorite student." Victoria added embellishments she learned from Sarah since her arrival.

"A visiting anthropologist with a crazy mother." Hashilli could handle Sarah Bible if it came to that, but he didn't like loose ends. "Does she know about the Jackson document?"

Victoria retrieved a rescue inhaler from her purse and took two good blasts. "Don't worry. I might have mentioned the letter, but Sarah wasn't curious, and I didn't tell her anything about our arrangement." Her breathing became more regular as the medication did its work.

"How's the asthma?" Hashilli didn't need another medical emergency when the time came to snatch Andrew Tiger. His last victim stopped breathing when he blew the *spirit powder* into her face. The coroner called it respiratory arrest. The woman's husband called it murder.

The dead tell no tales, but they don't pay ransom either. It wasn't a total loss. Gay couples pay good money for healthy babies with no strings attached. So do middle-aged Caucasian women who waited too long to have children.

"Pollen allergies," Victoria said.

That bit of information didn't reassure Hashilli in the least. If this woman died, he wouldn't even try for a ransom. If the child proved a suitable heir, he would keep him, otherwise he'd settle for a quick, clean sell.

"My source needs two thousand dollars." The price was the clincher. Neither expensive nor cheap, high enough to reflect the document's authenticity but not so high it would shake the buyer's confidence.

Hashilli promised he would front the money. That raised Victoria Tiger's trust to the next level.

"Reimburse me when I bring the document, and don't say anything to your visitor." He flashed a smile copied from a presidential candidate, sincere but unenthusiastic. It was the perfect facial expression to convey the willingness but not necessarily the commitment to proceed.

He invested the remainder of his visit milking Victoria for every bit of information she had about her guest. He had to be certain no intruders would be present when he abducted the Tigers's child.

8

SARAH HOPED A few drops of blood wouldn't spoil Victoria Tiger's Native American dessert. Ginsu knives were every bit as sharp as advertised, and slicing pumpkins called for a high level of food-prep dexterity.

"Thanks so much for helping." Victoria walked around her scrupulously clean, commercial grade kitchen, explaining the nuances of "Pumpkin Corn" dessert while trying every trick she knew to make baby Andrew happy.

"Andy won't let me cook. He screams when I put him down."

Sarah wondered how much more volume the little boy could muster if his feet touched the floor.

Shut up, you little bastard. So many unworthy thoughts. She wanted none of them. Sarah selected an ear of blue corn from the colander in the kitchen sink and did her best to ignore the audio portion of motherhood.

"Careful not to slice into the cob." Victoria tried to tickle Andrew into submission, but the baby wouldn't be distracted. She used one hand to set the temperature on her oven, and Andy took it to the next level.

How much snot could that little nose produce? Andrew had no interest in having it removed. He screamed louder when Victoria wiped his face with a wet paper towel, louder still when she ran through her repertoire of funny faces, and loudest of all when she lifted his tiny shirt and blew on his belly.

Sarah wondered exactly what aspects of motherhood Victoria found enjoyable. Birthing a child was bad enough. After that came sleepless nights, dirty diapers, childhood illnesses, temper tantrums, peer conflicts, teacher parent conferences, bad attitudes, broken hearts, driver's license, college entrance exams, tuition bills, bad marriages, divorces. Then grandchildren started the process all over again.

She raked the severed corn kernels with just a few of her own epithelial cells into a pie pan and put it into the oven to bake.

Why didn't she see the attraction that was so obvious to every other woman in the world? Sarah had zero understanding of the most basic building block of human culture. Marie hadn't gotten it either. Maybe there was a defective family unit gene passed down from mother to daughter. Sarah wanted Victoria to explain the nesting instinct in terms a non-believer could understand. She almost worked up the courage to ask the question.

Instead, she asked, "Is this a traditional Creek dish?"

Victoria made a show of checking on the blue corn. She propped Andrew on a hip, slipped an oven mitt over one hand, using her teeth for leverage, and carried the slightly parched corn over to the stovetop.

"It's kind of embarrassing." Victoria's voice was barely loud enough to be heard over Andrew's caterwauling.

"The Creek in Albert's family are totally integrated into white society."

Andrew took a break from crying for a moment. It lasted until Victoria made a madhouse happy-face.

"They've kept nothing of their culture." Victoria looked as though she might be about to give Andrew a lesson in tear production. "They have forgotten everything."

"Thank God for people like Hashilli." Victoria choked on the name.

"Who?"

"You're doing that all wrong." Victoria pushed Baby Andrew into Sarah's marginally willing arms. She adjusted the heat under the pumpkin slices and sprinkled blue corn kernels into the orange mush.

"Now for the whole-wheat flour and honey." She stopped suddenly in the middle of her project and stared at Sarah. "Well, will you look at that?"

But Sarah had turned her all her attention to Baby Andrew. The little boy looked into her eyes as though they were the most fascinating things he had ever seen. A smile spread over his face in jerky increments like time-lapse photography of a blooming flower. Andrew touched Sarah's nose with a tiny hand and disarmed her with baby noises that made her want to cover him with kisses.

"I think I get it now." Sarah meant to keep the thought internal, but Andrew had weakened her defenses with baby magic.

"What?" Victoria held her hands out to take the baby, but Sarah wasn't ready to relinquish possession.

"I think your pumpkin corn dessert is burning."

Andrew grasped a few strands of Sarah's hair. It only hurt a little.

She studied his face. No features he could call his own. The baby's eyes were seriously blue. She hoped they'd stay that way. She'd seen eyes like that only once before.

Robert Collins. Damn! What made me think of him?

9

A RED DOT in the center of his forehead and a little unortho-
dox brushing of his hair transformed Hashilli Maytubby into
the famous Doctor Moon, renowned psychiatrist from the
mysterious Asian continent.

So easy to fool the educated class. The intelligentsia kept their minds
wide open—no need to pick the locks or crawl in through an upstairs
window. An enigmatic smile and an exotic birthplace inspired confidence. The suggestion of bigotry closed avenues of inquiry.

Dr. Moon's accent was American television English. He added texture by occasionally mixing up his V's and W's, but people were careful
not to notice. The famous doctor's body language made it clear he was
a sensitive man.

He was a genius healer from the transcendental world of Buddha
and Mahatma Gandhi. He entertained no questions about his history.
He had no publications of note or research fellowships at prestigious institutions, but everyone remembered hearing his unusual name. They all
knew the reputation of the famous Doctor Moon. Details and context
be damned.

He moved through Flanders Mental Hospital like a phantom, unhampered by duties or obligations. He had no patients of record. He wrote no orders. He attended group sessions when it pleased him, and it seldom did. Dr. Moon was a psychiatric consultant, which is to say, the state of Oklahoma paid him a substantial monthly retainer to do whatever took his fancy.

No one would object when he followed Marie Ferraro onto the hospital grounds where trustee-patients had minimal supervision. He carried a clipboard and pretended to take notes on her behavior.

He was not the only psychiatrist to take an interest in the remarkable bipolar patient. Her miraculous improvement was the subject of much debate among the psychiatric residents. Marie's mood hit bottom and rebounded like a Superball. The nurses confided in Dr. Moon that her improvement began when she met the young schizophrenic, Robert Collins. Dr. Moon didn't believe that was a coincidence.

The mother of the woman living in Victoria Tiger's guesthouse was friends with the man who had stolen evidence from Hashilli. At the Maytubby bone-house. In full view of the ancestors. Power was at work here, the kind of power Grandfather never taught him to control.

Most psychiatrists wanted to vanquish, or at least manage mental illness, but not the famous Dr. Moon. He recognized wisdom in the ravings of lunatics. Blunting those ravings with electroconvulsive therapy and drugs squandered a valuable resource.

What did Marie Ferraro and Robert Collins talk about when they were together? Were they mustering the forces of creation against him? Did they speak with Maytubby ghosts? Had they somehow made contact with Grandfather?

Dr. Moon followed Marie from a discrete distance. He milled about the grounds, feigning interest in the group dynamics of the outdoor client population. He followed her for most of the afternoon and well into the early evening. She was a charming woman, who devoted more attention to her appearance than the average mental patient.

Marie had the grace of a ballet dancer—her posture comfortably erect, her stride smooth and elegant. The wind brushed her hair in ways that would be envied by stylists in the finest New York salons.

Not beautiful. Not like an actress or a runway model, but Marie Ferraro was pretty. That word had not invaded Hashilli's mind for a very long time.

Needs wait in ambush. He hadn't wanted a woman since his teenage years. Even then, he'd not desired a particular female, just the generic female category. Just parts of women really. Curves and scents, sensual motions, and beguiling smiles. Lust had no need for names and faces.

It was good to know his body could still respond.

Marie Ferraro seated herself on a cement bench beside a koi pond donated to Flanders by a dentist with a crazy wife and a guilty conscience. She turned toward Hashilli. She smiled. She greeted him with a finger wave as delicate as a butterfly.

His clandestine intelligence-gathering mission was not clandestine after all. He suspected this woman always knew when a man's appreciative eyes fell on her. A kind of power he had not encountered until now.

A tiny sparrow hopped out of the underbrush and made its cautious way to Marie. Too late in the season for a fledgling, but the little bird could not fly. The woman extended her hand to the bird, and it hopped onto her index finger.

Grandfather coaxed birds into his hand the very same way, but the old man had never shared the trick.

Did the sparrow believe that this woman would somehow offer protection? Would she?

Marie turned her attention to Hashilli once again and accelerated his heart rate with a fragile smile.

Available.

For a brief moment, he envied the bird perched on Marie Ferraro's finger. He wanted to hop between her hands, preen himself a scant two feet from her face, and inhale air that had been inside her.

Marie held the sparrow over her head, examining the bird in the waning sunlight. Hashilli could see now why the sparrow couldn't fly. He could see why it sought the protection of another species. The little sparrow had no tail.

Probably lost those feathers to predator. Stray cats passed through the perimeter fence at will.

Marie whistled a poor imitation of a birdcall. She held the sparrow high over her head, offering it the opportunity to fly away. She had not seen the creature's fatal disability, and anyway, her birdcall was unconvincing. Too full of wind for a songbird, too sweet for a bird of prey.

A shadow traced circles around the bench where Marie sat. Each circle was smaller than the last. Hashilli recognized the shadow. He'd watched for such a shadow his whole life. He wondered how the woman could be unaware of the manifestation of power at her feet.

She favored Hashilli with another smile just as a great horned owl dove from the sky and snatched the sparrow from her hand. When she turned to see what had displaced so much air, the little bird was gone.

"Her wings made quite a racket," Marie called out to Hashilli.

Could she be so blind to power? He walked over and took the hand that offered up the sacrifice. "Before long the sun will set. Time to go inside."

Her hand was warm and supple. An exchange of energy passed between them, like static electricity in slow motion. Marie followed him as if he were leading her onto a dance floor. He suppressed the impulse to put an arm around her shoulders.

"My name is Doctor Moon," Hashilli told her. "Perhaps you've heard of me."

"Perhaps I have."

"I've been studying your case. You are a very special client."

"How nice of you to say."

Hashilli wondered if he and Marie shared a common destiny. "I want to see you privately. As a private client, I mean."

The words sounded clumsy and coarse, even as he said them. He hoped she wouldn't consider him boorish. He could take her as a private client even if she objected, if it came to that, but Hashilli wanted Marie to come to him willingly.

She looked young, but she had a daughter in college. Could she still bear children? Could the spirits have another reason for pointing her out? Was this Grandfather's handiwork?

10

ON SARAH'S LAST visit, Marie's hair had been tangled, her buttons were misaligned, and her shoes were on the wrong feet. Now her medication schedule was down, her lips were the color of Galia 03 Rosy Nude lip gloss, and her eyes were outlined with Urban Decay 24/7 glide-on eye pencil.

Sarah didn't bother to ask where her mother got the improved outlook on life and the cosmetics. It was obvious. Marie had found a male admirer with a credit card. Inside a mental hospital. How did she do it?

"I feel Archie's vibrations, everywhere. Robert taught me how."

Just perfect, Sarah thought. A bipolar patient taught by a schizophrenic to fine-tune telepathic broadcasts from a sociopath. The lunatics were definitely running the asylum.

"I know how this looks, Sarah. You've seen my mood swing before, but this time it's different."

"It's always different. Otherwise psychosis would be boring."

"This time love is real. Not just a delusion. Doctor Moon could tell you. He planned to be here for your visit. Something important must have come up."

"Did Doctor Moon graduate from a medical school, or did a mental patient confer his degree, like Doctor Collins?"

"He brings me cosmetics. Smuggles them in a plain brown wrapper. Don't you think that's cute?"

"Now you have the shrink you've always wanted. Generous, flexible, putty in your hands."

Marie checked her face in her brand-new compact mirror. "He's quite famous. Everybody says so, but no one seems to know specifics."

"Perfect casting for a mental hospital. A doctor who is both famous *and* mysterious. Does Doctor Moon approve of your fixation on Archie Chatto?"

"Doesn't disapprove—at least I don't think so." Marie motioned to someone across the room.

Sarah knew, without looking, that someone would be Robert Collins.

Be polite but distant. He couldn't help being a schizophrenic, and he seemed to be good for Marie.

Robert shook Sarah's hand. He kissed her mother on the cheek. His greeting was warm and appropriately noninvasive. The man did not have the look of a mental patient. He didn't talk like one either.

There was symmetry about Robert Collins's face, appropriate for a television personality but totally out of place on a crazy man. His eyes beamed with intelligence, as untainted with guile and as blue as Andrew Tiger's.

Bluer than the evening sky.

Bluer than the Atlantic Ocean.

Bluer than the bluest crayon that Crayola ever made.

She forced herself to stop thinking of Robert Collins's eyes in comparatives and superlatives, especially those involving pigmented petroleum products. What would she do next? Write his name in the margins of her classroom notes?

"I'm so happy to see you again," Robert said to Sarah, and she was somewhat surprised and slightly disappointed to find she was also happy to see him.

He walked Sarah and Marie to one of the couches lining the perimeter of the commons and took a seat between them.

"I have something important to show you." He opened a copy of the *Daily Oklahoman* and spread it over his lap. He read the headline of the featured article out loud. "Casino Manager commits suicide."

There were accompanying photographs and a detailed description of the travails Jimmy Mankiller had endured prior to ending his own life.

"Like Wilma Mankiller." Sarah wondered if the victim was related to the much-admired former chief of the Cherokee Nation.

"His wife died of a mysterious allergic reaction last month," Robert said. "His daughter is missing. They say he was skimming profits from the casino and wiring them to temporary offshore accounts."

"Did you know him?" Sarah lifted the paper from Robert's lap and studied the pictures. She wasn't really interested. There were stories of suicides, murders, and accidental deaths in the paper every day, but she didn't want to appear callous if Robert had a personal stake in this one.

"I only saw him once. The day they brought me to Flanders. Apparently, the day before Mister Mankiller died." He gave Sarah and Marie a brief rundown of his encounter in the cemetery. He pointed to the largest, clearest photograph of Jimmy Mankiller. He traced the shape of the dead man's face with the tip of his little finger.

"This is the man I saw subdued in Riverside Gardens Cemetery."

Robert folded the newspaper so the picture was centered on the page. He handed it to Sarah. "There is something else I have to tell you. Something you may find difficult to believe."

From the look on Marie's face, Sarah could see she totally bought into Robert Collins's story. So far, it was not totally unbelievable. Casino managers who were skimming tended to have impressive runs of bad luck. Their family members went missing and died mysteriously. People who stole from casinos often fell down flights of stairs. They ran into doors. They committed suicide in record numbers. Notorious thugs ran gambling houses. Incorporating didn't make them law-abiding citizens.

"Go ahead," Sarah said, hoping very much that Robert Collins wouldn't venture too far into outlandish territory. "I'm listening."

"The man who subdued Jimmy Mankiller in Riverside Gardens Cemetery was Doctor Moon."

Marie inhaled so fast she choked on her own saliva. It took several seconds of back slapping and gasping before she breathed easily again.

"Impossible. Delusions come and go. Take it from one who knows." She shifted into her *poor dear* tone of voice and promised him Dr. Moon was a bona fide doctor of psychiatry, not some imposter who sneaked into a mental hospital on some secret criminal agenda.

"Everyone at Flanders knows him. He's famous."

Sarah was forced to weigh the judgment of two crazy people. Her mother had the edge.

"The man in the cemetery looked different, but he was Doctor Moon. I know it." The steadiness of Collins's voice, his posture, his unwavering eye contact were all unambiguous signs of a man who believed what he was saying.

"How can you be certain?"

"There was an open window in my room," he said, as if that explained everything. "I can barely hear the wind when I'm on my medications, but she was loud and clear when she told me about the famous Doctor Moon."

The arm of the couch set limits to the distance Sarah was able to edge away from him.

"I know it sounds crazy, but I can prove at least part of my story."

Marie was no longer listening. She opened Robert's newspaper to the comics section and asked, "Whatever happened to Little Orphan Annie, anyway? And Dick Tracy? He was my favorite."

Robert directed his full attention to Sarah. "Jimmy Mankiller had something written on a paper. He discarded it before Doctor Moon knocked him out with his yellow powder."

Crazier and crazier.

"Jimmy dropped like a rock, but the wind brought the evidence to me."

Sarah knew she should call for a staff member, or at least beat a hasty retreat to the exit, but she sat still and listened.

"I hid the paper where he couldn't get it," Robert said. "Before they took me away."

Sarah cleared her throat several times, but her voice still felt raspy when she asked, "Where did you hide the paper?"

"In the shirt pocket of a dead man. Just before he was buried. I don't remember the man's name, but I'm certain I can find the grave. That paper will prove everything."

Sarah looked at her watch. "Got to go. Late for… an appointment." She waved to her mother as she headed for the door. "Sorry, Mom. Have to cut the visit short. See you again real soon."

She promised herself she would talk to someone on the staff before she came back. She wanted Robert Collins to be kept far away from her mother.

11

HASHILLI UNDERSTOOD THIS much about teenage boys—they like pizza, beer, and naked girls. Oklahoma City boasted many establishments where all three legs of the motivational stool could be obtained. Yellow Pages ad executives called them Gentlemen's Clubs.

First came the false IDs.

"Dude, how did you get our pictures?" The tall boy did all the talking. His two buddies fondled their fake drivers' licenses and waited for orders.

Hashilli showed his new recruits a six-pointed gold star with official-looking letters engraved across the middle. He flashed his fake government agency ID. He loaded the boys into his black SUV and drove them to a windowless cement block building with the name *Nasty Boyz* painted in man-size red letters on all four sides. His passengers were too busy being manly to ask about the three shovels in the rear storage area. Hashilli had known it would be this way. Gentlemen are discreet.

"Your first assignment," Hashilli told the tall one. "Infiltrate a strip bar and pass yourselves off as ordinary patrons." Drinking beer and watching naked girls dance around poles. It was an onerous responsibility for three teenage boys. Hashilli imagined debauchery morphing into patriotism in their minds. God, country, beer, girls. Their window of opportunity was wide open.

"But how did you get our names, dude?" The tall one was persistent but not intelligent. Teenage boys hang out in malls. They broadcast their names like candidates for the local school board. They put their most personal information all over the Internet and then wonder why they have no secrets.

Instead of answering, Hashilli picked at an imaginary piece of lint on his cheap, black blazer. The jacket looked like it might have been purchased at a cops' plain-clothes uniform store. Its thin fabric kept his body at a marginally uncomfortable temperature.

Grandfather could change into an owl or a coyote. Hashilli's style was more contemporary. He shifted his position so the boys could see the 9mm pistol suspended under his left arm—just to remind them who he was.

He gave them each a hundred dollars in ones and fives for lap dances and beer.

"Your mission, if you choose to accept it." Was there ever any doubt?

Hashilli pressed a twenty-dollar bill into the bouncer's hand. That was all it took to keep the mean-looking cowboy with no front teeth from inspecting the fake IDs too closely. The bouncer's two missing fingers didn't compromise his ability to accept a bribe.

"Watch out for my boys," Hashilli told him. "You'll get twenty more if they leave without bruises."

One of the bouncer's eyes winked at Hashilli. The other found the ordinance lump at his left shoulder.

"Happy to cooperate with law enforcement," the bouncer said.

Hashilli retired to a booth in the corner and practiced being invisible. Grandfather perfected the art, but Hashilli didn't have it yet. At his best, he was almost completely invisible to women, but men could still see him a little, and the meanest men could see him best of all. *Nasty Boyz* was a good place to have a badge and a gun. Playing the role of an incompetent undercover cop was the simplest kind of magic, and it kept the magician safe.

The crowd around the bar looked like the waiting room at a free clinic. A hundred dollars was enough to get a teenage boy infected with a dozen STDs. Hashilli wondered how long it took for the first symptoms of herpes to emerge. Syphilis, gonorrhea, hepatitis, AIDS—so many possibilities. Bacteria with antibiotic resistance, viruses with edges sharp enough to slice through latex, and teenage boys who never learned to say, "No thank you."

Hashilli felt a pang of conscience as he watched his boys resonate with the frenzy of the drunken crowd.

The dancers spun around brass poles and distorted their backs into shapes the patrons had only seen in wet dreams. The evening was young, and so were the girls, some of them anyway. They wore needle tracks, six-inch pumps, and dollar bills stuffed into G-strings that wouldn't interfere with gynecological examinations. One at a time, the boys went into a curtained section of the bar for private dances.

Hashilli didn't get it. Grandfather hadn't gotten it either. Urine, feces, and reproduction were close neighbors in the small region of a woman that most men found so enchanting. Blood and deteriorated endometrial tissue leaked out of the reproductive orifice on a schedule almost as reliable as Old Faithful's. There were vaginal secretions with the consistency of phlegm, and odors that spawned a thriving industry of feminine hygiene products. Yeast grew inside of women and bacteria and worst of all, human seedlings that looked like chicken embryos you wouldn't want to eat for breakfast. But vaginas still attracted ordinary men more than free admission to a monster truck rally.

Hashilli had to admit some of the girls had nice breasts. And their buttocks reminded him of things he hadn't thought about for a while, but he didn't have long to ponder the feminine mystique. A drunken cowboy in the private dancing area wanted his money back.

"Twenty dollars and I can't even touch her titties."

It was the most articulate statement Hashilli had heard in *Nasty Boyz* all evening.

The bouncer charged across the room, knocking several patrons to the floor. He pulled the curtains of the private area aside and broke the cowboy's nose with a well-placed right jab. He took a step back and waited for the aggrieved patron to refine his complaint. The argument was over. Diplomacy won out. The blood spatters on the dancer only made her more desirable.

Hashilli thought the world would be a safer place if the bouncer were in charge.

Time to collect his boys. They were properly fueled on testosterone and alcohol. The proper frame of mind to rob a grave.

RIVERSIDE GARDENS CEMETERY was a scary place at night. The moonlight reflected off the polished granite tombstones and cast distorted shadows that followed the three teenage boys as they searched out the grave they had come to desecrate.

The tall one led the way. He'd driven them to the edge of the cemetery, then parked his car and ventured into the land of the dead, as if robbing graves was something he did every night.

"Wish I had a cigarette." He pretended the tremor in his voice was the result of an unsatisfied nicotine addiction. His two companions didn't notice. They were too busy listening to the sounds of their own breathing and wishing they had not taken money from the mysterious federal cop.

"There is a paper in the dead man's pocket," he had told them. "Bring it to me, and I'll give you each another hundred." He provided shovels and a map. The map was hard to read in moonlight, and carrying shovels through a graveyard was just plain creepy.

When the tall boy came to a sudden stop, the other two members of his team bumped him. The last boy in the line dropped his shovel. It fell against a gravestone and rang out like a dinner bell. They stage whispered the word "shit," more or less simultaneously, then dissolved into a nervous laughing fit that sounded like a monkey house at feeding time.

The leader checked the name on his map against the inscription on the stone.

"Roosevelt Washington? What the hell kind of name is that for a dead man?"

His companions encouraged him with grunts of approval. They moved to the perimeter of the grave and imagined the dead man listening to their footsteps from within his coffin.

"What if it's some kind of trick?" one of them asked the tall one.

"You mean like there is a vampire down there waiting to suck our blood? Or a zombie that wants to eat our brains?"

That was it exactly. The tall one listened while his companions journeyed down the verbal trail of supernatural speculation.

"Or a ghost."

"Or a demon."

"Or a doorway to another universe."

"Or something more ordinary, like an atom bomb or some kind of bioweapon." So many possibilities, and none of them good.

"Just a dead man," the tall one said, as if that weren't bad enough. "A dead man named Roosevelt Washington with a paper in his pocket." The leader had never seen a dead man and suspected his companions hadn't either. He backed a little farther from the grave, waiting for someone else to call the whole thing off. Who would be the coward? Who would be responsible for telling the federal agent they had failed America? The Fed promised he would find them later on, "to settle accounts." And he would. The leader didn't doubt it for a minute.

"Half now and half when the job is finished," the stranger had said when he gave them their retainer. He'd snapped each hundred-dollar bill like a shoeshine rag. He creased the money down the middle and stuck them in the waistbands of their jeans, like they were dancers in a gay strip club.

The boys jumped at a rustling sound that came from behind Roosevelt Washington's headstone. The tall one wanted to believe it was an animal or a figment of their collective imaginations. He'd heard of mass hallucinations. Was a group of three a large enough mass to generate an apparition like the one materializing out of the darkness?

A black man with a neck and shoulders like a professional wrestler's lumbered toward them. He looked as solid and as heavy as a commercial grade refrigerator, so heavy the earth would barely hold him. He seemed to be wading knee deep through the topsoil of the cemetery until he stood on Roosevelt Washington's grave. That's when the boys saw the black man's legs were missing below the knees.

When teenage boys scream, they sound like little girls, and when they run in panic, they stumble and fall a lot. Fear of the mysterious federal agent no longer figured into their plans. They abandoned the stranger's shovels and escaped from the ghost of Roosevelt Washington as fast as they were able.

The tall one wore a crucifix around his neck, and he clutched it in his right hand, improving his confidence in Jesus but significantly compromising his balance. Would this creature be repelled by the power of the cross? He knew from watching old-time horror movies that monsters followed a rigid set of rules. He could remember none of those rules at that moment.

The boys sprinted through the cemetery gate without a backward glance to see if the ghost of Roosevelt Washington followed them. Their feet pattered over the city street like a poorly synchronized tap dance, and the air passing through their open mouths sounded like old men laughing.

Back within the confines of Riverside Gardens Cemetery, Big Shorty collected the would-be grave robbers' shovels from the carefully manicured lawn.

Never been used. Vandals usually took their tools with them when they ran away.

This was not the first time he encountered nighttime intruders in his cemetery, and he supposed it wouldn't be the last. Shorty didn't understand their motivations, and he supposed he never would. The boys—it was always boys—never stuck around to answer questions, and they ran way too fast for him to catch.

A double amputee had to face up to his limitations. Big Shorty didn't make friends easily among the living, but the dead slept in peace while he was around, and that was all that really mattered.

The new shovels would find honest work in his hands.

12

THIS WAS THE first time the security gate had been closed since Sarah moved into the Tiger's guesthouse. She retrieved a calculator from her shoulder bag and did some quick computations. Seventy-two possibilities for the Tiger's four-digit security gate code. Or was it 362,880. Or another number too large for the digital display? A calculator was useless to a social scientist.

"Math is hard." She remembered the quote from *Co-ed Barbie*, the greatest philosopher who never lived in the twentieth century, but the four simple numbers eluded her.

Sarah relaxed and waited for the number to take shape in her mind. A date. Something everyone would know and no one would think of. Then it came to her, the year Oklahoma became a state. So simple she hadn't bothered to write it down. Sometime after the Dakotas but before Arizona. A date that will live in infamy—no, that was Pearl Harbor, during the administration of another Roosevelt.

She started at 1904 and worked her way up. Three entries later, the gate opened—1907, my how time flies.

A black SUV with a Choctaw Nation license tag was parked at the Tiger house. Victoria's antiquities dealer.

If Sarah remembered correctly, the man with the unusual name had a letter from Andrew Jackson to one of Albert's ancestors making a number of promises he hadn't kept. Sarah had never come across a reference to any such letter in her studies, but it was certainly possible. Jackson made a lot of guarantees before he banished the civilized tribes to Indian Territory and as far as she was aware, he hadn't kept any of them.

Victoria promised to have her father authenticate the document before any money changed hands, but Sarah doubted she would follow through. A few thousand dollars was no problem for the Tigers. The Crazy Snake Casino floated on a virtual river of money, and the tribe was generous with management.

Times had changed now that Oklahoma tribes had discovered the lucrative gaming industry. They were in the process of reacquiring their stolen land a few acres at a time, buying it with dollars won from white people in games of chance. Suddenly, there were a lot of wealthy Native Americans in Oklahoma.

In the past, everything of value was stolen from the tribes. Sarah hoped history wouldn't repeat itself. She hoped this Native American antiquities dealer was the real thing.

Hashilli sounded like an authentic Native American name. Maybe she'd Google it. Most Oklahoma tribal members didn't use indigenous given names, not even the artists and the storytellers.

None of my business, Sarah decided, but she found herself looking out the guesthouse kitchen window, spying on Victoria Tiger instead of working on her research paper. Should she phone Professor Lindsay, tell him what his daughter was up to? Would he appreciate her intrusion into Victoria's private affairs?

Leave it alone. Unless something happens, just leave it alone.

But then something did happen. A man with bronze skin and a conservative gray business suit emerged from the Tiger home carrying Victoria's baby boy. A first-time mother didn't grant this privilege to just anyone. She must really trust this antiquities dealer.

Hashilli had the body type and facial features Sarah had come to associate with the so-called civilized tribes, a mixture of every race that inhabited the new world painted on a Native American canvas. Neither remarkably tall nor remarkably short. Slightly barrel chested with narrow hips. A full head of black hair with a texture that would vary with seasonal humidity. Sarah catalogued his attributes as if she were preparing a description for the police.

Victoria is a gown up. She makes her own decisions. I shouldn't be suspicious. Those were three good reasons to walk away from the window and quit spying on her host. She took a step backward but kept her eyes fixed on the antiquities dealer the way she'd watch a stage magician—to see if she could figure out his tricks.

Hashilli left the front door open, but Victoria didn't follow. He fastened baby Andrew into a child seat in the back of his SUV. Quick and efficient. No missteps. Undaunted by the belts and fasteners that puzzled most men.

His eyes met Sarah's as he returned to the SUV after shutting the front door to the Tiger's home. He gave her a perfunctory wave. Nothing wrong here.

So where's Victoria? The social constraints holding Sarah back stretched to their elastic limit and popped like a rubber band. She bolted from the window, pulled her front door open, and sprinted toward the black SUV.

Hashilli paid her no attention. He seated himself behind the steering wheel of the large black vehicle. He started the engine. He backed the SUV toward the gate.

So I can't see his license plate, Sarah realized. A Choctaw tribal plate. She'd seen it earlier—was the number 1907? No, damn it, that was the gate code.

She ran after the SUV, cursing Hashilli, cursing herself for her inaction. The vehicle pulled away, leaving Sarah in the dust. Hashilli gave her another wave, like a soldier waves to his girlfriend when he goes off war.

Cry all you want, little girl. History won't slow down for tears.

Tears of desperation. Tears of failure. They were a waste of good saltwater. They blurred the vision, and Sarah needed to see clearly. She hadn't meant to chase the SUV so far. It was a long run back to the house to check on Victoria. Maybe everything was all right. Maybe she had made a fool of herself chasing after an innocent man.

But she knew that wasn't the case. The front door stood open, exactly as Hashilli left it. Sarah left it that way too as she charged inside. She'd apologize for the intrusion later, if apologies were necessary.

"Victoria!" Sarah scanned her surroundings as she moved into the home's interior.

Everything in place, as it always was in the Tiger home.

"If you can hear me, please answer!" Hysteria cracked her voice. The pervading silence was proof that something dreadful had happened. Victoria's adoption of indigenous ways had not yet extended to eliminating the background noise of television and radio.

Sarah almost tripped over Victoria as she hurried through the formal living room. Sprawled in the middle of the floor on a Navajo rug fine enough to be a museum piece. Like an aesthetic death scene, like the cover illustration on a Robert B. Parker novel? The disjointed thought didn't slow Sarah down. She rolled Victoria onto her back, checked for a pulse in her neck, listened for breath sounds. They were loud and raspy but regular.

"Has pulse. Is breathing," she said aloud because that is what she had learned to do in the Red Cross CPR course she had taken earlier that year. She used the Tigers's landline to call 911. The operator told her that an ambulance had already been dispatched.

Impossible. Sarah was the first one on the scene. Unless Hashilli… the 911 operator didn't want to hear Sarah's theories.

She walked around Victoria. Searching for clues, like Nancy Drew. A note lay beside Victoria. It read, *I'm feeling faint. Left Andrew with a dear friend in case something happens.*

The hand was shaky but feminine. Why would Victoria write a note instead of calling a doctor? Why would a dear friend take the baby and not stay with the mother? Maybe Sarah had been watching too many *Law and Order* reruns.

A vacuum cleaner sat in a corner by the fireplace—not unusual. Victoria Tiger was a clean-freak, but a thin patina of yellow dust coated the glass-topped coffee table beside the unconscious woman. Like pollen dropped by a floral display.

Not in the Tigers's house. Not with Victoria's asthma. The sound of sirens brought one thought. If this Hashilli was a dear friend, then I'm Hillary Clinton.

"HOW COULD THIS happen?" Albert charged into the emergency waiting area where Sarah had been sitting for the last three hours. He stood well within the borders of her comfort zone and glared at her. The families and friends of other patients turned their attention Albert's way, but no one interfered.

Sarah told him exactly what had happened. When that didn't satisfy him, she told him two more times.

After each account, Albert told her, "That doesn't make sense!" He raised his voice a few decibels with each repetition. "Victoria wouldn't do that. She'd never hand Andrew to a stranger."

Sarah didn't disagree. She recited the facts she knew one more time. Hashilli was an antiquities dealer, selling something Victoria wanted to buy. "A letter from President Jackson to one of your ancestors. She wanted to surprise you."

"Well, I'm surprised!" Albert shook his head. Victoria's respiratory distress was under control. The EMT's quick response made all the difference, but that was one of the things that made no sense.

"Who called the ambulance, Sarah? If you know something, tell me now."

Sarah sat up a little straighter in the waiting room chair. Pleading innocence irritated her. She was just about to say something she'd probably regret when Albert's cell phone rang. He showed her his caller ID. Victoria.

The Kidnapper.

Albert's skill at verbal confrontation was notorious at the casino. The one and only time Sarah had ever been there, he'd vanquished a disgruntled employee in seconds. But now, he sputtered one-word answers into the phone, then turned it off. The creases around his eyes deepened and then vanished as if chased away by a Botox injection.

"I understand what happened now." The angry energy seeped out of Albert's voice like water through a sluggish drain. His words were slow and sticky.

"I shouldn't have spoken to you so sharply. There's no problem."

"Was that Hashilli?" Sarah asked.

"Funny name," Albert said. "*Changing Moon.* One of the few Choctaw tribal words I know."

"Changing moon." That phrase nagged at Sarah's memory. Something she heard only a short while ago.

"I could be wrong. Long time since I studied native languages." If Albert had been puffed up before, now he was deflated.

"I don't think you are wrong." Sarah recalled her last encounter with Robert Collins. He'd shown her the newspaper article about Jimmy Mankiller, the casino manager who'd been skimming, the man whose wife died mysteriously, the man whose child disappeared. Robert saw the driver of a black SUV subdue the hapless casino manager with yellow knockout powder.

She thought of the dust on Victoria Tiger's coffee table. She thought of the man Robert had accused murdering Jimmy Mankiller. The famous Dr. Moon.

"Never met an Oklahoma Indian with a name like Hashilli." Albert wasn't interested in talking about his missing son any longer, and Sarah knew why.

The kidnapper had taken charge. Hashilli was telling Albert Tiger what to do, and Albert wouldn't argue. Not if he wanted to see Andrew again—alive.

Sarah had to talk to Robert Collins about this doctor/antiquities dealer who abducted Andrew Tiger. Native Americans had a long history of respecting the delusions of the insane. Maybe they were onto something.

13

HASHILLI PARKED HIS SUV beside the Indian Baptist Cemetery. The sun was still too high to test the child. Ten more minutes. Fifteen at the most. The motion of the SUV had rocked Andrew to sleep, but now he was waking up. He'd want his mother soon. Hashilli knew the pattern. First the little boy would pull at his child seat restraints, then he'd cry like a guest on *Oprah Winfrey*, only louder and longer. God, how Hashilli hated babies. Roly-poly, chubby cheeked, little shit machines. Eyes full of tears and heads full of mush.

Andrew smiled at him like a stroke victim. A cloudy stream of drool dripped from the baby's chin. Admittedly cute. That's why their mothers didn't kill them—usually.

These days, babies were in short supply for women who'd put off getting stretch marks until too many ripe plums had fallen. Andrew would fetch a handsome price if he didn't satisfy the Maytubby ancestors. White enough to command top dollar in the grey adoption market where lawyers peddled infants the way used car salesmen moved low-mileage one-owner luxury sedans.

The baby gurgled a persuasive string of nonsense syllables, charming little manipulator. This child came equipped with the perfect skill set for a twenty-first century witch. Hashilli had high hopes.

"Maybe you'll be the next great Choctaw sorcerer." No butchered syntax or infantile speech impediments were necessary to hold the little one's attention. With babies it's all about cadence and melody.

Andrew's head wobbled in agreement. He spewed a fine mist of saliva and seemed to be completely satisfied with his accomplishment. Hashilli liked Andrew just a little.

Had Grandfather liked Hashilli just a little?

"The old man brought me here," he told Andrew. "Almost forty years ago." Things were simpler in those days. No kidnapping necessary.

"Bought me from a homeless Seminole woman."

Andrew's face twisted into its tear-shedding configuration but relaxed when Hashilli favored him with a conspiratorial wink.

"Paid her twenty dollars and a two-for-one coupon good at any MacDonald's." Hashilli didn't know if this was true or just another one of Grandfather's stories. The old man told so many.

"When he sat me in the doorway of the bone-house, the afternoon sun cast my shadow in the shape of an owl." Witches didn't reproduce like lawyers and dentists. The forces of creation chose them the same way a hunter picked the best hound from a litter. Witches were marked in ways invisible to the living but obvious to the dead. This mixed race Creek baby could be the one.

As the sun moved into the proper position for the test, Andrew squirmed in his baby seat. Hashilli took it as a sign of readiness, but the baby might be simply redistributing the bowel movement that already stained both legs of his jumper.

"Sorry little one, witches don't change diapers."

HASHILLI STAYED AT the cemetery longer than he should have, long after Andrew failed the test. Like all of the stolen children before him, the Tigers's baby did not cast a witch's shadow.

"But you will fetch a handsome price," Hashilli told Andrew. "You will break the heart of your old family while you make your new one happy." Balance was the core of power. Kidnappers generally murdered the children they stole, but Hashilli never did. He was wicked, not cruel. There was no quicker way to squander power than taking innocent lives.

The Tiger baby would go to The Wise Owl Center, one of Hashilli's most altruistic concerns. Good could be as profitable as evil if a clever witch used other people's money to pay the bills.

Hashilli shared Grandfather's best advice with baby Andrew. "Be many things to many people. Friends and enemies stumble over each other, and your trail is lost." The child squirmed as Hashilli fastened him into his baby seat.

"Be calm, little one. You can still be a man of power, even if you're not a Choctaw witch. Magic is all about money these days." Hashilli had so few opportunities to talk about his work.

He told Andrew about the secret of zeros. "The difference between a one-dollar bill and a ten and a hundred is how many little circles follow the number one." Zeros were as imaginary as Santa Claus but a lot more convincing. Especially in the digital era, where wealth consisted of electrons wrangled into the proper files.

Andrew gurgled. His crusty diaper seemed forgotten for the moment. Perhaps this baby was too pretty to be a witch, his features too regular, his personality too appealing. A witch wears his persona the way a snake wears his skin. He could shed it and grow another when the time was right. Rich man. Poor man. Beggar man. Thief. Doctor. Lawyer. Indian Chief. When the modern shapeshifter plies his trade, the soft money from government grants and the hard money from annual budgets collects around him like iron filings around a magnet.

"You're pretty enough for politics," he told Andrew. The baby responded with a distress cry that would have brought gorillas running from the jungle if they had been in the Congo.

What other African entities might that cry have summoned? Hashilli drove slowly toward the only passageway between Riverside Gardens

Cemetery and the land of the living. He scanned the monuments for signs of the giant black man with stumps for legs.

Baron Saturday.

Robert Collins called him by name from the bottom of a grave. The insane see power with crystal clarity.

Andrew pulled off a baby shoe and threw it against the back of Hashilli's seat. Precursor to a tantrum.

Indian mothers strapped their babies into cradleboards and propped them in the corner of a lodge. Didn't they? Times were different now. So were children. Babies needed interaction. They needed entertainment. Or else they raised hell.

Hashilli was up to the task.

"Archiving documents," he told Andrew. "That was my real breakthrough business back in the day."

He stretched his vowels to their elastic limit and added a simple melody. He followed up with a song devoted to backing up computer files and a poem with a payroll management theme. Economic rap music at its infant-pleasing best, without one derogatory reference to women.

The baby smiled at Hashilli's image in the rearview mirror. "Innocence—the perfect disguise." Too bad the Maytubby ghosts rejected him. Important ghosts, but not Grandfather. The old man's bones lay in the mud at the bottom of Lake Texoma, his outer shadow lost beyond all hope of redemption. Hashilli smiled at the memory.

NO ONE GREETED Hashilli when he entered the intake section of the single open-concept room of the Wise Owl Center. The clerical staff looked up from their Sudoku and crossword puzzles long enough to evaluate the threat to their employment. None at all. In the Wise Owl Center, Hashilli was Mr. Luna, a well-respected social worker from the Department of Human Services. He brought babies to the center all the time. The infant in his arms was just one more. Mr. Luna smiled and waved.

"Don't mean to interrupt your work," he said without a trace of cynicism.

Desks were scattered around the perimeter of the large room. The nursery occupied the center, segregated by a waist high wall. A Plexiglas extension had been added to baffle sound without obstructing vision. It reminded Mr. Luna of the cough shield over the buffet line at the Golden Corral. There were four entrances to the nursery area. He took the closest one.

A nurse practitioner frowned at the unhygienic condition of her newest client. She gave Mr. Luna a look almost as nasty as the new baby's bottom. "Your babies are always soiled and cranky."

She was African American. Mr. Luna was a big believer in diversity. It was the modern equivalent of protective coloration.

He watched the nurse apply a little warm water. She swabbed the baby's bottom with sanitary wipes while she half-hummed half-sang a generic lullaby.

"Get DHS to buy you wipes and diapers, Mister Luna. This baby's butt looks like raw hamburger."

"I'll look into it." He never used the nurse's name. His way of keeping distance between the Wise Owl Center staff and himself. A modern shapeshifting witch couldn't become entangled in personal relationships. But Hashilli knew her name, all right. He knew quite a lot about Nurse Practitioner Jemima Coinpenny.

Her family brought their Haitian religion and a little of their language with them when they moved from Louisiana to the all-black town of Boley, Oklahoma. Her Creole nickname, Ti'Mama, and the string of Mercury dimes she wore around her left ankle were proof she still respected the Voodoo Loa, even though she'd checked the Catholic box on her employment application. Hashilli used her as a barometer of local Voodoo activity. In just a few centuries, African sorcerers had displaced Indian mystics in Mexico, the Caribbean, and in Hispanic sections of North America. Eventually they'd move into Oklahoma, but as long as this nurse's friends and associates were mostly Muslims and Baptists, Hashilli felt relatively safe. When that changed, it would be time for his Mr. Luna persona to take cover.

Ti'Mama pronounced the little boy healthy and well nourished. Not the case for many of the babies Mr. Luna brought to the Wise Owl Center. She placed a bracelet around his ankle. It identified him as baby *MT186.*

"I have a priority family," Mr. Luna told the nurse. "I don't expect this one to be here very long. A few days at the most."

"It'll take longer than that to treat his diaper rash." She tickled the baby's cheek, eliciting a smile.

"Teenage mother," Mr. Luna said. "Tried her best to keep him but couldn't manage." That would satisfy Ti'Mama Coinpenny's curiosity. Babies at the center always had sketchy histories. If the nurse learned too much about them, the truth might break her heart.

The Wise Owl Center was already decades old when Hashilli first infiltrated it. The state of Oklahoma started funding the center when the declining birthrate among the middle class made orphanages obsolete. Taking over the operation required only three identities, and two of them were invisible. Easy work for a competent shapeshifter.

No one at the center had ever seen the director or the lawyer who handled the lucrative private adoptions. Mr. Luna was the go between, and no one suspected he was all three people. Selective blindness was the key to the operation's success.

Mr. Luna left day-to-day management in the hands of the slightly dishonest staff. He permitted them to convert a small percentage of the center's resources to their personal use. Not much—padded expense accounts, state subsidized automobiles, occasional cash bonuses for meetings never attended.

As long as things ran smoothly, as long as the absentee director didn't take an active interest, the minor thievery could continue. It was a management style that worked. The clandestine self-directed monetary redistribution program made the staff feel guilty, and guilty people were easy to manipulate.

That's how modern witches do it. No spectacle of smoke and mirrors is necessary to bend people to your will, just careful planning and a willingness to accept the fact that people are no damn good.

The Mr. Luna persona gradually evaporated as Hashilli exited the front door of the Wise Owl Child Development Center. Being Mr. Luna always left him with a good feeling. When Hashilli assumed the social worker identity, he almost forgot he was a murderer, a kidnapper, and an extortionist—almost but not quite.

A shape-shifter kept a locked compartment in his soul where his original identity remained intact. At the same moment he was a respected social worker, he was also a wanted man whose fingerprints were on file with the police. Youthful indiscretions.

Hashilli borrowed fingerprints for each of his personas. There were plenty of swirls and deltas to go around, thanks to his record archiving business. He had access to forensic identifiers that would be an insurmountable obstacle for any police investigation. Too bad he couldn't change the patterns on his fingertips.

His reckless youth had led to many brushes with law enforcement. If he should be arrested, he would be quickly identified.

If only he could turn into an owl or a coyote, like Grandfather. He mulled over the lost simplicity of the early twentieth century. When his mind settled back in the present, he saw Baron Saturday lurching down the sidewalk on his leg stumps.

"What are you doing here?" Hashilli hadn't meant to speak, but the words were out now, and he couldn't take them back.

The black man held two paper bags. He looked at one and then the other.

"Been to Homeland. Man has to eat." No trace of Creole accent colored his language. No black urban or rural influence either. The absence of history in a human voice marked the speaker as a creature of power. Hashilli hadn't thought the Voodoo spirit could follow him out of the cemetery, but here he was.

"Baron Saturday!" The words popped out like an unanticipated gas bubble. Calling a malevolent spirit by name could give him a handhold to pull himself inside your soul.

Deep horizontal wrinkles formed across the black man's brow, as evenly spaced and parallel as the lines on a stenographer's note pad.

"Big Shorty." The black man said the words slowly and clearly, like a speech therapist instructing a backward child. "Not Baron anything. People call me Big Shorty."

Hashilli's eyes froze on the leather pads covering the walking surfaces of Big Shorty's stumps. "I've seen you at the cemetery. I didn't know you could leave."

Big Shorty lumbered forward. He stood as tall as Hashilli's shoulders. His head was approximately the diameter of Hashilli's waist. The black man pulled his lips back over his teeth in what might have been a smile if it looked less predatory. The gold in his bicuspids glinted in the sun.

"I'm the caretaker at Riverside Gardens, not a prisoner. I can leave anytime I want."

Big Shorty walked past Hashilli. His stride was rough but with a trained athletic quality, like a hurdle jumper on a practice lap. "Maybe I'll stop by and say hello next time you go to that old Indian boneyard."

Hashilli followed Baron Saturday with his eyes until the African blended with the horizon—a long walk for a man without legs. Did the Loa of the Dead really shop at Homeland?

14

SARAH FOUND ROBERT Collins milling around the Flanders common area. The morning nursing shift chased the at-liberty clients out of their rooms by 9:00 a.m. Unless they had outside privileges or therapy sessions, there was no other place to go.

"Come with me." A yellow legal pad and an arrogant facial expression gave Sarah untouchable status within the mental institution. People who take notes are to be avoided at all costs. She could be an attorney or a community organizer or a relative looking to cause trouble. No one—not the clients nor the orderlies nor the doctors nor the nurses—wanted their names written down on her yellow legal pad.

Sarah led Robert to a bench on the periphery of the Commons and chased the occupants away with a series of meaningless questions. *Who was Britney Spears's first husband? What is the capitol of South Dakota? Where were you on September 11, 2001?* She printed the month, day and year in large Catholic School block letters across the top of the page and underlined it twice. By the time she finished, the clients had moved on.

"Paranoids are easy." She pointed at the precise spot where Robert was to sit. He responded like an obedient dog, but Sarah wasn't quite ready to reward him with a treat. "Tell me again about your encounter with Doctor Moon in the cemetery." She listened carefully while Robert repeated the story. He paused and stumbled over words. He struggled with the time line. But the elements didn't change. Robert had hidden a paper in a dead man's pocket—evidence Dr. Moon was a kidnapper.

Sarah made him repeat the story two more times. No evolution or elaboration of the facts. Some of Robert's story might be delusion or hallucination, but the essential parts were grounded in reality.

"I'm going to break you out of here, but first we need a plan." Sarah had two pens, red for problems, black for solutions. She learned this strategy from a CPA her mother had once taken as a lover. "A criminal without a plan is an inmate in training." Robert was already an inmate of sorts, but it didn't pay to dwell on that. "What can we try, and what could go wrong? Tell me anything you can think of."

"Well...." The worry lines on his forehead looked like a study in contour plowing.

"Hey, we're brainstorming here," Sarah told him. "Seriously. There are no stupid suggestions."

"I guess we could run for it. But then we might get caught."

"Okay, right." He wasn't going to be much help.

"Harry Potter used a cloak of invisibility," Robert said. "I don't suppose you have one of those."

"Robert, please...."

"Or a shrink ray, like in *Fantastic Voyage*."

"Okay, so there is such a thing as a stupid suggestion."

"I usually get my best ideas from the wind," Robert said. "And the wind doesn't blow much inside Flanders."

"I guess that explains it." If things went dreadfully wrong, Sarah supposed there might be dissertation possibilities for an anthropology student in a women's prison. "Just sit quietly and let me work on the plan."

Robert made a zipper sign across his lips and affected a blank stare. It looked like he'd been practicing. Sarah waved a hand in front of his face. No response. Just like the Royal Guards at Buckingham palace. Good-looking ornaments without apparent function.

For as long as Sarah could remember, she'd watched Marie's boyfriends engage in all manner of criminal activities. Bad guys like to act on ideas while they are fresh and new, before they blur into incomprehensible smudges like prison tattoos. That's why they steal cars with sleeping children in the back seats, televisions they can't carry, jewelry they can't sell, and drugs they can't identify.

Not one of them had ever stolen a schizophrenic? Was that even a crime? If so, was it a felony or a misdemeanor? She might run a few words through Google later on and see what the Internet had to say.

Run away, but they might catch us, Sarah wrote in red. Maybe it wasn't such a stupid idea. *Walk, don't run,* she wrote in black. Robert didn't look all that crazy. He could be a visitor or a staff member or even a resident. She'd mistaken him for a doctor when they first met. Sarah could walk Robert out of Flanders if she could think of some place within the institution where people wouldn't know him.

Some place with exits. Sarah had become well acquainted with the institution's security system over the years, thanks to her mother's frequent involuntary admissions.

There was just one locked-down area, reserved for clients with a recent history of violence. Fortunately for Sarah, Robert Collins did not fall into that category.

The internal security force consisted mostly of burly orderlies and male nurses who could immobilize disruptive clients long enough to inject them with pharmaceuticals designed to quench their inner fires.

Unarmed Rent-a Cops restricted access to the institution by walking visitors through a metal detector and going through purses. They kept a naughty-list and checked it twice just like Santa.

The most important thing about psychiatric patients is that no one except for hospital administration wants them out. A client might stumble onto a clever escape plan, like walking through the front door when no one was looking, but friends and family members usually wouldn't help. Breaking Robert Collins out of Flanders should be as easy as stealing garbage from a city dump.

"I can pick locks if it comes to that," Sarah told Robert. "Marie's old boyfriends taught me how to forge IDs, disable alarms, and hotwire cars."

He looked at her but kept his vow of silence.

Sarah hoped the emotion in Robert's eyes was admiration, but it looked a lot like love. "There are lots of ways to get you out of here. The best plans are usually the simplest."

At-liberty clients moved freely within unrestricted areas of the hospital. They could read, play games, or watch television in the common area. There was a makeshift movie theater, complete with automated popcorn and soft drink concessions. There was a cafeteria where clients could enjoy institutionally prepared meals with visitors, alongside doctors and other staff members.

Cafeteria. Sarah wrote that word in black. Thanks to her mother, she had eaten many meals in similar facilities. The cafeteria was a gaping hole in the flimsy fabric of the hospital's security net. Food service workers entered and exited the kitchen through a back door that opened onto a small employee parking lot.

Cafeteria workers didn't interact with clients or professional staff. Sarah had overheard one food service employee advise another, "Don't look them in the eye. It turns them wild." She was never certain exactly who might be provoked to violence by an incautious brush with minimum wage eyes, but neither were the workers. Their gazes moved from the unsightly tubs of overcooked meat and vegetables to the abstract pointillist patterns of the terrazzo floor. They might be able to identify doctors, staff, or patients by the styles of their shoes but never by their faces.

The only glitch in Sarah's plan was that it might succeed, and then she would have a schizophrenic on her hands. So far Robert had been reasonable and well mannered. But stability was not a hallmark of mental illness, and God only knew how he'd behave after she broke him out.

Would he wander off to attend conventions of aliens and talking buildings? Would he become her permanent inconvenient sidekick, filling in when her mother lapsed into periods of relative sanity? How would she get rid of him, once he'd helped her find the evidence she needed to rescue Baby Andrew?

Sarah resisted the impulse to write that problem on her legal pad in bright red letters. Maybe she wouldn't want to get rid of him. Sarah's experience with men was limited to say the least, but aside from a few major-league quirks, Robert was better than most. If she set aside the fact that he talked with the wind, he was perhaps the most down to earth man she had ever met. Was this how her mother started out?

She put her doubts aside for the moment. She wasn't taking Robert as a lover, even though she wasn't totally repelled by the idea. She was enlisting his help in recovering Andrew Tiger. She was acting purely out of altruism.

Altruism! The word had a nice ring to it, so much better than delusion or rationalization. Sarah didn't like to spend too much time considering what she was about to do. It reminded her too much of her crazy mother's past adventures.

MARIE FERRARO SCOWLED at Robert and Sarah from the far side of the commons. The famous Dr. Moon had told her all about Robert Collins. She'd warned her daughter, but Sarah wasn't listening.

Robert smiled at Marie and waved. The boy was charming, just the kind of man who routinely swept her off her feet when she was Sarah's age. A good-looking man with an easy smile and a way with words as dangerous as a rattlesnake—more dangerous. Men seldom give a warning before they strike.

But you survive the poison. Marie knew that from hard experience. When it came to men, Marie knew everything there was to know. Even the worst of them had shining moments, and it's easy to be taken in when their motives seem so pure. Like when Robert taught her how to be close to her true love, even though Archie was locked in prison fifty miles away.

You have your ways, Robert Collins. I'll give you that. Thanks to him, Marie could sense the bits of Archie floating in the world around her like miniature swarms of invisible insects. When conditions were right, Marie felt her lover's presence as clearly and completely as if he were standing right beside her.

When Archie breathed, he released his bittersweet Apache essence into the wind. Wild Indian molecules tantalized the olfactory centers of Marie's brain. They mixed with her saliva and left a taste that reminded her of champagne. When she walked outside, the wind carried Archie's voice to her. Proper nouns and adjectives, never a complete thought. Just enough to let Marie know her name was on his lips.

Thank you for that, Robert Collins. She would have been taken in completely if not for the famous Dr. Moon.

"The boy is not all bad," the doctor told her. "But the bad outweighs the good. It's his nature to be devious."

The young man's helping hand would finally close on her soul in a relentless grip of death if she let it happen. Sarah and Robert huddled together on a couch as far away from the televisions as they could get. Planning something and Marie couldn't stop it. All she could do was stand apart and scream at them with her body language. No use. Men never listened to Marie unless they were in love, and Sarah never listened at all.

"I WON'T LET you down," Robert promised Sarah. "I'm desperate to get out of here. The medications make my mouth dry, and the wind doesn't talk to me."

She tried her best to ignore his motives for wanting to escape. She needed something tangible to take to the police, something that would convince them Andrew Tiger had been kidnapped, in spite of denials by the boy's parents.

"Do what I say, and don't start acting crazy," Sarah said.

Robert wanted to take Marie along. "We need to get her away from Doctor Moon."

"How many inmates do you think I can break out of this asylum?"

"Clients," Robert said. "They call us clients."

LUNCH AT FLANDERS Mental Hospital blended seamlessly with breakfast and dinner to accommodate rotating staff schedules and clients whose internal clocks had been reset. It passed for enlightened therapy. Snacks kept mental patients on the straight and narrow better than Prozac. They were cheaper, too, bought with good behavior commissary credits, redeemable Monday through Saturday from nine to five and noon to six on Sunday.

Psychiatrists called the policy "passive socialization." It turned the cafeteria into a demilitarized zone, where everyone ignored aberrant behaviors and unprofessional activities unless they got too loud or too disgusting. No one paid the slightest attention when Sarah led Robert into the facility with two white clinic coats tucked under her arm.

"Borrowed from a laundry hamper," she told him. The jackets smelled like Gillette Sports Stick and isopropyl alcohol.

"With any luck, no one will notice you're gone until the evening count." She made Robert sit at a table while she purchased them club sandwiches and coffee. Sarah hoped the food and the caffeine would reduce the effects of his medications and allow him to walk more like a fatigued psychiatric resident and less like an actor in the latest *Living Dead* movie.

Robert ate with gusto. His eyes were sharp. His speech was crisp. "I ditched my morning meds. Pouched them like a hamster." He inflated his cheeks to demonstrate the technique.

"Stop it." Her right hand squeezed the air out of Robert's mouth along with a stray piece of lettuce.

"I hope your coordination is as good as your appetite."

"I'm hardly crazy at all right now."

He seemed to be in a zone of sanity therapists could never consistently produce with medications. Somewhere between being doped into oblivion and talking to the wind. Sarah could see that Robert's sense of taste was fully functional. He obviously relished the whole wheat bread and the turkey bacon in his sandwich. His other senses were awakening too. When she stood and pushed her hands through the arms of her clinic jacket, Robert checked her out.

So damned obvious. But it felt good to be appreciated, even by a mental patient.

"Keep your mind on business."

Her comment elicited a blush. Robert had his winning ways. No guile, no undercurrent of violence. Totally different from Marie's boyfriends. Except for the poorly-concealed sexual agenda. Every man had that.

"It's time," she said. "Walk beside me. Let me do the talking."

Before Robert could object, Sarah grabbed his hand and pulled him toward the entrance to the kitchen.

"You won't need this." She threw his clinic jacket over her shoulder like a warrior's banner. Robert demonstrated no signs of that irritating masculine desire to be in charge. Not manly, perhaps, but nice.

"We'll get to the bottom of this." Sarah adopted the tone of a reasonable but angry mother who had decided to administer a spanking but hadn't quite settled on a target.

The cafeteria workers busied themselves with bussing dishes or inspecting the walk-in freezer. Heads turned away as Sarah as walked briskly through the kitchen with Robert in tow. Pots and pans stopped rattling. Institutional silverware stopped clinking. The only sounds in the kitchen were Sarah's threatening utterances and the hostile clatter of her shoes punishing the terrazzo floor.

"Not so fast!" A burly man with a café au lait complexion and three days' worth of facial stubble stepped into Sarah's path. His hair net wasn't up to its job and neither was the laundry that cleaned his knee length lab coat. Across his ample left man-breast, the word "Supervisor" was embroidered in faded black thread, just over a beet stain that almost obscured his name.

"Tommy." Sarah hadn't meant to say the name out loud. She gave Robert's hand a jerk, and he came to rest at her side.

"You docs don't belong here," Tommy said. "Back here it's just me and my people." The supervisor smiled. Something green had lodged between his front teeth.

Sarah worked hard at ignoring it. Robert didn't.

"I think it's spinach," he said. "But it might be a very old piece of lettuce."

That was just one of many things Tommy didn't understand. He pointed toward the dining room. "Get out!"

Tommy was a man of few words, but Sarah had a few of her own. "Supervisor Tommy, just the man we're looking for." Too bad she'd left her yellow legal pad in the common area.

"Say what?" Tommy pinched his nose, then wiped his fingers on his lab coat.

"I'm Doctor Sarah Jessica Parker, and this is my assistant, Doctor Robert McNamara. We're food inspectors, Tommy. Can you guess why we're here?"

"I ain't did nothing wrong." Tommy smoothed his lab coat with his questionably clean hands, then tucked stray locks of hair under his net. "I know my rights." He recited two of them. "I don't have to say nothing. I want my union rep."

Sarah released her hold on Robert. She held her open hand three inches in front of Tommy's face, like a traffic cop in a very bad mood. Tommy stepped back. Red blotches appeared on his neck and face. His pupils contracted. His jaw muscles tightened. Marie's boyfriends usually looked this way just before holding up a drugstore. Sarah said, "Cool it, Tommy. No biggie, just a standard complaint." His blotches faded slightly.

"About the beef tips." There were always beef tips, weren't there? Sarah pointed to the serving area without looking. "Robert, bring the tub of beef tips over here. Use oven mitts, in case they're hot."

"Who complained about the tips? Everybody loves the tips. Just like the ones at the Golden Corral." His blotches went back to their previous shade of red.

By this time, Robert had lifted the heavy serving tub out of its well. "Not hot at all. Barely room temperature."

"That's how the crazy people like 'em." Tommy took a step toward Sarah. His jaw muscles clenched with the rhythm of a beating heart. "The shrinks like 'em that way too. Even the colored nurses."

"Stop!" Sarah raised her hand again, in what felt like a modified Nazi salute. "It's not the tips. It's what is in the tips."

Robert came to an unsteady stop beside Sarah, his eyes fixed on the heavy serving tub, careful not to spill the gravy. Sarah stepped on his closest foot and gave him the slightest shove—just enough to send Robert and the tub falling in the supervisor's direction.

"Damn!" Tommy wasn't so proud of his beef tips now that he had a closer look.

He'd need a new lab coat. At least some good would come of this.

"Damn!" Tommy muttered something about workman's compensation and official complaints, notarized and signed with a sterling silver ballpoint pen in a lawyer's office. "As soon as I get cleaned off, there'll be hell to pay."

But by that time, Dr. Sarah Jessica Parker and Dr. Robert McNamara were in the parking lot, on their way to Sarah's car.

15

THE WIND MET Robert as soon as he stepped out of the hospital. He was glad she wasn't jealous of his new companion. "This is Sarah. I think she might be my girlfriend." He whispered in tones only the wind could hear. Sarah didn't know about their relationship yet.

"But she will," the wind assured him in a voice borrowed from a female country and western singer. "You know she will."

Sarah picked up her pace so the two of them were almost running. "So far, so good. Just don't go crazy on me, at least not yet."

When they reached her car, Robert asked if they could ride with the windows open.

"Why not?"

His old friend's fingers felt good running through his hair. She celebrated Robert Collins's freedom by blowing metric tons of wastepaper along the streets like confetti.

Sarah said, "Your friend's a litterbug."

No response from Robert. He was busy reading a section of *The National Enquirer* that had just blown into the passenger window.

"Did you know *Fox News* is run by aliens?" He dangled the yellowed newspaper fragment near the steering wheel until Sarah final-ly looked. He watched her lips move while she read one headline, then another.

"Thank you, Robert. I'd never have guessed Kim Kardashian was born with a penis." She turned her attention back to the road while she fumbled for the control that raised the passenger side window.

"The wind brings me all the latest news, fresh from the grocery store dumpsters." Robert hadn't expect Sarah to take the news about Kim Kardashian so hard. He turned the dash-vents toward his face and re-solved to be satisfied with that at least until they reached the cemetery.

But the moment they left the relatively windless environment of her automobile, the wind was back, and Robert picked up where he'd left off.

"The wind thinks you are pretty."

"Flattery will get the wind nowhere."

"The wind likes you a lot."

Sarah locked her Subaru Outback with the factory-issue remote con-trol attached to her keychain. She pointed the device at Robert and fiddled with its buttons.

"Damn!" She returned it to her shoulder bag. "I guess there's no way to turn you off."

Robert thought she might be joking. Whether she was or not, he was grateful for the attention. He stood in front of her as passive as the sculp-tured monuments scattered about Riverside Gardens Cemetery, waiting for the opportunity to please or impress.

"Robert...."

His name sounded important when she said it, even though he was pretty sure the look on her face was anxiety rather than affection.

"Are you okay, Robert?"

She put her hands on his shoulders and gave him a shake. "Hey, pretend you're not crazy, just until we find the right grave to rob."

He cupped his hand over his ear and listened to the wind sing-ing Anita Carter's version of Ring of Fire. "The wind is singing you a song." He bobbed his head in time to the music waiting for her to pick up the tune.

She didn't. Sarah gripped him by his earlobes and turned his face toward her. "We have several hours before the sun sets. We need to locate that grave so we can find it again in the dark"

"The wind says we should start at the old Indian Baptist Cemetery." Almost sane, he thought, but still no cigar.

"That's where I started running from Doctor Moon," Robert said. "The wind thinks we should retrace my steps."

Sometimes the wind was very logical.

SARAH HAD READ about Choctaw bone-houses, but the ones within the walls of the Indian Baptist Cemetery were the first she had ever seen.

"They look like mausoleums." She recognized the blending of indigenous and Christian customs. She wondered if Dr. Lindsay knew about these bone-houses. Aside from her academic interest in the Indian Baptist Cemetery, Sarah felt something else that had no place inside the mind of an anthropologist. She felt like the place might be haunted.

"Spirit garden," Robert said. His voice had almost none of the dreamy quality that dominated it only minutes before. Sarah looked at the leaves on the cottonwood trees inside the sandstone walls of the Indian Baptist Cemetery. No sign of the wind.

"This is a very creepy place." She stepped away from the wall and turned in a full circle to see if anyone was watching. Impossible to know for sure. Unwelcome observers could hide behind monuments or inside the old bone houses.

She didn't like this place, but someone did. Someone especially liked the mausoleum with the word Maytubby spelled out in green tiles over the door.

That building was in good repair, and the pathway to the Maytubby bone-house was clear of the tangle of deadwood and clusters of flowering weeds that covered everything else. Sarah had seen pictures of weeds like these in an ethnobotany course just a year ago, but none of that material stuck with her past the final exam.

"Moonflowers," Robert said. "Jimson weed."

Sarah recognized the two common names for Datura, the plant used by holy men on vision quests. Could Robert read her mind?

The wind didn't stir, and the ghosts—if there were any within the sandstone walls—were quiet.

Sarah tried to identify the distinctive yellow puffballs growing on the rotten cottonwood branches strewn about the graveyard. Ceremonial mushrooms. Hallucinogenic. She was sure of that much.

She pointed out the freshly painted white owl on the iron door of the Maytubby bone-house. "Could the artist be the famous Doctor Moon?"

The sound of footsteps on the gravel road behind them didn't leave Sarah much time for speculation. There was little doubt in her mind who she would see when she finally turned and acknowledged the approaching threat. She turned slowly, as if meeting a killer in a cemetery was something she did all the time.

"Mister Hashilli, I presume." Did he recoil a little, when Sarah called him by that name?

The psychiatrist-antique dealer-kidnapper aimed a boxy black pistol at a point midway between her and Robert.

"Sarah Bible." His words vibrated with a greedy enthusiasm. "So good to see you and your crazy boyfriend."

"He's not my—" Sarah cut her denial short. Her next words might be her last. She shouldn't waste them correcting the misperceptions of her killer.

"So convenient. It saves me so much time and trouble." He motioned with the gun for them to walk through the entrance into the Indian Baptist Cemetery.

The temperature dropped as they crossed the threshold. No bird or insect noises. Sunlight dimmed. Each step took them deeper into the land of the dead. If Sarah died inside this graveyard, would her spirit would be trapped here forever? Maybe she could run for it, vault the wall, keep the bone-houses between herself and Hashilli's pistol, then follow a twisted path to freedom using monuments for cover. She might have tried, for better or for worse, if there was at least a small chance

Robert Collins would follow. But the wind was blowing once again. Robert was oblivious to danger, content to leave his fate in the hands of an imaginary supernatural entity who read trashy periodicals snatched from dumpsters.

People's lives were supposed to run through their minds like a documentary movie when they faced death. At least that's what Sarah had been told. Her mind ran a newspaper headline instead. *KRIS JENNER REVEALS, KIM KARDASHIAN WAS BORN WITH A PENIS.*

Please don't let me die with that thought on my mind.

"So much to do," Hashilli said. "So little time, and so many people want to interfere." He marched them to the front of the Maytubby bone-house and tapped on the door with the barrel of his pistol. "Metal door. Keeps out grave robbers and salesmen."

He tapped the door again. "Avon calling." Hashilli fished a key ring from his pocket and sorted through it with one hand while he held the pistol in the other.

"Skeleton key. Perfect for a bone-house." The tumblers inside the lock fell into place with a snap. The door squeaked and sagged on its hinges as Hashilli pulled it open. He ordered Robert and Sarah into the musty dark interior, slipped the pistol into his belt, and used both hands to shove the door closed.

"My ancestors will keep you entertained," Hashilli said. "They don't get many visitors."

Sarah and Robert stood quietly listening to their captor's footsteps recede while their eyes adjusted to the darkness. Dim reflected sunlight filtered in through rectangular ventilation slits that circumscribed the building at the junction of the walls and roof.

"Out of one prison and into another." Robert ran his fingers over the oxidized brick walls around the metal door. He inspected several bricks and rapped his knuckles on each of them four times. If there was logic to the pattern, Sarah could not see it.

He cupped his hands as if he was trying to amplify a faint sound. "Baffled." He considered the word for a few seconds. "The wind can't help me here."

"It'll be pitch black when the sun sets." Sarah showed Robert her shoulder bag. "Hashilli must have important things on his mind or he'd have taken it." She reached inside, retrieved a small LCD flashlight and handed it to Robert. "No knives or guns, but I have a cell phone." She walked the perimeter of their little prison. She waved the phone around like a fairy's wand. She held it as high as her arm would extend and as close to the ventilation slits as she could reach, but she had no bars.

"A dead zone. No pun intended."

Robert had no interest in the telephone, but the flashlight was another matter. He shined the intense blue-white beam onto a series of yard-long rectangular boxes that lined the wall opposite the door.

"Bone boxes," Sarah told him even though he hadn't asked. "And if we're lucky, maybe a means of escape."

The older bone boxes had been lacquered, but the more recent ones were painted various shades of green. A shower of paint flakes fell as Sarah lifted the uppermost box and set it in the center of the sandstone floor. She removed the lid without difficulty, blew off a cloud of dust, and held it in front of her chest like a panhandler's sign. Robert's light illuminated a name spelled out in crudely carved letters.

"Timothy." He directed the beam of light over the skeletal remains of the Maytubby ancestor.

"Let's see what toys Timothy's ghost finds amusing." Sarah reached into the box and removed a hand full of ribs, a femur, an ulna, and several vertebrae.

Robert took two steps back, but he kept his light trained on the box's interior.

"No grave goods," Sarah told him. "Maybe this Maytubby didn't have any hobbies." She returned Timothy's bones to their container and shoved it aside.

Even in the dim light she could see Robert's jaw muscles were clenching to the point of spasm. How close was he to the breaking point? What would a panicked schizophrenic do? Her only frame of reference was a one-hundred level psych course at UNM and a few movies she wished she hadn't seen. *Psycho, The Silence of the Lambs, The Collector.* She was ashamed of having seen *The Hills Have Eyes*, parts I and II, but maybe she should have paid closer attention.

"Bring me another box." She'd involve him more in the escape attempt. Take his mind off their desperate situation. "Be careful not to drop the light."

Robert looked the bone boxes over as if he were selecting a complicated reference volume from a library bookshelf.

"Loved ones leave things with their dead," Sarah told him. "Things they treasured in life. If you don't believe me, ask the wind."

Robert cocked his head at an odd angle, like a dog listening to a curious sound beyond the range of human hearing. When a gust of wind blew leaves against the outside of the bone-house, the tension evaporated from his face. His shoulders relaxed. His knees bent slightly. He lifted another box off the stack and set it in front of Sarah. The name on this one was Helema.

Over the next hour, the two captives went through painted boxes with relatively conventional names, like Tom, John, Lizbeth, Amantha, Randolph, and Suzan. They also opened older lacquered boxes with more exotic names like Talako, Masheli, Nakui, Hanan, and Sinti.

Grave goods had been placed in all the old boxes and in at least half the modern ones. Sarah found pouches of tobacco, packs of cigarettes, amulet bags, a jar of pickles, a fishing pole with an assortment of lures, and a collection of hand carved wooden animals stored in a felt bag along with a folding knife.

"Sinti was a woodcarver." Sarah opened the knife and evaluated its blade. "Not much good as a weapon." She handed it to Robert and told him to work on the doorframe. The hinges were imbedded between a double layer of brick. If they could uncover those, it would be a simple matter to escape.

THE INN & OUT Motel was located halfway between the State Capitol building and the Oklahoma City Zoo. Not one of Hashilli's profitable enterprises but a handy place to commit murder.

His Seminole persona, Mr. Niilhaasi, bought the Inn & Out with money diverted from the Bureau of Indian Affairs. A place where state legislators could meet with troubled youth. Funding dried up long ago, but the meetings were going strong. Fifty dollars for a *half and half*. More kinky interchanges were negotiable. Rooms charged separately— no checks or credit cards thank you.

Hashilli shape-shifted into Mr. Niilhaasi as he pulled his SUV into the motel parking lot. A diminutive Vietnamese woman greeted him as soon as he opened the door.

"Bi'ch Pham," he said. "Always a pleasure."

"Mister Niilhaasi." She offered her hand. He took it but pulled away quickly after a light squeeze.

"I have cold fingers. Means my heart is warm." She waved her French manicured hand in front of him. "Like my new rings?"

His eyes dropped to the shadow of Bi'ch Pham's hand on the macadam of the parking lot. It twisted like a deadly Asian snake.

"Four rings. All jade. Like my name. You remember?" She'd told Mr. Niilhaasi the meaning of her name the day he hired her. "Pronounced Bik, not bitch. Means jade. Very pretty name."

When she moved her hand closer, Mr. Niilhaasi stepped back. If she touched him again, he'd freeze solid. Bi'ch Pham had killed men with that hand. She hid single-edged razor blades in her hair, shuriken throwing stars in her bra, and derringers in places he didn't want to think about.

"Very nice, Ms. Pham." Looking at the rings was better than looking into her eyes.

"You got Chickasaw tags, Mister Niilhaasi." She recited the number.

He should have changed them when he left the cemetery. Bi'ch Pham noticed everything.

"I need a room for at least an hour. Two hours would be better."

She made a sound that Mr. Niilhaasi translated loosely as, "Tsk-tsk."

She pointed to the yellow crime scene tape across a nearby doorway. "Police closed number seven earlier today. Toilet stopped up in number four. You need toilet for your date, Mister Niihaasi?"

He stifled the urge to explain. "No toilet necessary." He walked into the motel office and wrote Sarah Bible's name into the register, exactly the way she wrote it when she signed in at Flanders.

More perfect than necessary. The police would never run the signature past a handwriting expert. Not after they found Sarah's body in room four, strangled by her schizophrenic lover who she broke out of a mental hospital earlier the same day.

Bi'ch Pham turned her back while Mr. Niilhaasi opened the motel safe and removed a baggie of his spirit powder. She pretended not to notice the yellow powder in the safe, stored right beside her vials of crack and bindles of heroine.

Mr. Niilhaasi didn't have to pay his motel manager. She lived off drug sales, cash room rentals, and…. "Ms. Pham, do you have any video cameras working in room four?"

"Why, Mister Niilhaasi, you think I'd do something like that to you?"

He'd give the place a thorough check before he dragged his unconscious victims into the room.

SARAH HAD EXPECTED the mortar between the bricks to crumble free without much effort, but after two hours, Robert had only removed three bricks. No sign of the hinges, and the LCD flashlight was losing its intensity.

The wind whispered to Robert through the spaces where the bricks had been removed. She was free with advice, but none of it was useful.

"The wind says we'd better think of something fast. Doctor Moon will be back soon."

Sarah busied herself looking through more bone boxes. "Maybe you could ask her to save her breath until she has enough to blow the roof off of this place."

Her cynicism was wasted on Robert Collins. "No good—it's way too sturdy."

"Maybe if it were made of sticks or straw."

"Yes, that would make it easier." If he had heard the story of the three little pigs, it hadn't made much of an impression.

The blade of the folding knife broke just as the fourth brick was loose enough to tease out of its recess.

"Bad luck," said Robert. "I just uncovered the edge of the top hinge."

Perhaps Sarah could have found another folding knife if they had just a little longer. Perhaps Robert could have removed enough brick to loosen the hinges and dislodge the iron door. If things had worked out differently, Robert and Sarah might have escaped, retrieved the missing paper they sought, and taken that evidence to the police.

Hashilli knocked on the metal door and said, "Avon calling."

Sarah turned her flashlight off when his key rattled in the lock. The crescent moon over Hashilli's shoulder provided enough light to make his pistol look big and dangerous but not enough to illuminate the dark interior of the bone-house.

"Step where I can see you." He pointed to the spot where he wanted them to stand with his left hand. It was closed into a tight fist.

Nerves, Sarah wondered, or is he holding something?

Robert took two paces out of the deepest shadows and stood between Sarah and the muzzle of the gun.

"Where's the girl?" Hashilli scanned the darkness with a roll of his eyes, but he held his head and his weapon steady, giving no indication his attention was divided.

He tried to repeat his question, but a sudden gust of wind blew leaves and cottonwood seed around his head and into his face. Hashilli squinted his eyes and tightened his lips against the airborne particulates.

Sarah stepped from the shadows holding a Maytubby leg bone over her shoulder like an executioner's axe. She aimed for Hashilli's forearm, halfway between his elbow and his gun. She swung.

The bone moved two inches over Robert's head so fast its back draft disturbed his hair. A satisfying snap accompanied its impact. Hashilli cried out. He pulled his injured wrist against his body, but he didn't drop his pistol.

Sarah was left holding a brittle dagger shaped bone fragment.

Hashilli was injured and angry but not disabled or disarmed. He turned toward her, extended his left hand, and opened it revealing a clump of light-colored dust.

"A little powder for your face." He adjusted the position of his outstretched hand and estimated the distance to his target.

Sarah remembered the yellow dust on Victoria Tiger's coffee table.

She remembered Robert's account of Doctor Moon rendering his victim unconscious with a handful of yellow powder.

Hashilli filled his lungs with the thick musty air of the Maytubby bone-house.

Would holding her breath do Sarah any good? Should she close her eyes?

Robert stepped in front of her just as Hashilli blew the cloud of dust in her direction. The powder coated his face and hair. It reflected and intensified the dim light of the crescent moon.

Fairy dust.

Hashilli waited for something more to happen. Sarah could almost see his lips move as he counted seconds. One thousand one all the way to one thousand forty. Plenty of time for her to find one of the bricks Robert had dislodged from the bone-house wall.

"What...?" Hashilli sniffed the residue of powder remaining on the palm of his left hand.

Sarah stepped forward and clubbed him with her brick—not nearly hard enough. She might not get a second chance. Hashilli staggered backward and leveled his pistol at her.

Sarah threw her brick, a tenth of a second before he pulled the trigger. Her missile eclipsed the pistol's muzzle flash and absorbed the momentum of the slug. Ricocheting fragments stung Sarah's face, but they did not have the power to kill.

She stepped back into the shadows and went down on her hands and knees. There were three more bricks on the bone-house floor. She had to find one of them before Hashilli filled the air with bullets, but her eyes needed time to recover from the muzzle flash.

There. The sharp corner of a brick dug into her shin. It would cause a bruise if she lived long enough. She gripped brick with her right hand. She'd throw it harder this time, if he didn't kill her first.

The pitch was already in motion as she rose to her feet. Her eyes had partially adjusted to the darkness. Hashilli stood with his back to the door holding his pistol in a double-handed marksman's grip. He couldn't miss from this range.

A shadow moved beside Sarah. One of the Maytubby ghosts? No, it was Robert. Something shiny in his hand—her flashlight. Robert depressed the switch and covered Hashilli's eyes with a yellow circle of light. The batteries were low, but the flashlight did its trick. Hashilli's second shot went wild. Sarah's second brick did not.

It made a satisfying thud when it struck Hashilli's forehead. He made another satisfying thud when he collapsed onto the walk leading to the bone house door. Robert kept the flashlight trained on Hashilli's face.

Sarah asked him, "Do you think I throw like a girl?"

"A really mean girl," he said.

Hashilli lay motionless. Sarah nudged his body with her foot, a little harder than necessary.

"You bastard!" The words satisfied Sarah, even though Hashilli couldn't hear them. She poked the unconscious man with the toe of her shoe again. Some people might call the second nudge a kick.

"Damn bastard!" Sarah's vocabulary was sorely lacking in the expletive department, so she turned her attention to Robert.

"Why didn't Doctor Moon's magic powder knock you out?"

"I don't have a clue." Robert used his shirttail to wipe the yellow powder from his face. He collected a bit of the dust on his fingertips and brushed them with his tongue. "Moldy," he said, "with a bitter under taste."

Sarah guessed the powder was a combination of spores from the puffballs that grew in the Indian Baptist Cemetery, perhaps combined with pollen from moonflowers and a few other ingredients.

"I feel different," Robert said.

He looked different too—sharp eyes, erect posture. Not a sign of the confusion that dominated his persona ever since his antipsychotic meds had begun to wear off.

Sarah collected Hashilli's pistol. She found a set of keys and a billfold in his pockets. She put everything in her purse and told Robert it was time to finish what they had started.

She dragged Hashilli into the bone-house, making certain his pulse was strong and his airway open. "We'll turn him over to the police as soon as we collect the evidence you hid in the dead man's pocket."

"Shouldn't we just shoot him now?"

Sarah opened her shoulder bag and showed Robert the gun. "Think you can do it?"

His right hand moved toward the open purse and then veered away as if it had fallen under the influence of a powerful magnet.

"I guess not," he admitted.

"I'd be disappointed if you could." They settled for locking Hashilli inside his family crypt. Sarah knew from personal experience it made a very effective prison. But would it hold him until she and Robert did what they had to do?

16

SARAH SAID, "YOU'RE a hero."

But from the look on Robert's face, she knew he heard her say, "You're *my* hero." She knew it just a microsecond too late. Words like *hero* have the emotional impact of a meteor strike. She understood exactly what would happen next.

Robert would blush. He'd fidget as much as their fast walk through the dark cemetery would allow. He'd sputter a half-hearted denial. But after all that, he'd believe every word.

Men are simple creatures. They think of everything big important as a she—ships, cars, weapons, the sea. Even the biggest bad things have women's names. Does anyone believe Hurricane Bob could have wiped out New Orleans? The poor bastards live for female adulation, especially the young ones. They cosign loans, lie under oath, commit crimes. Most of them would die for a woman's postmortem praise. Sarah learned practically everything she knew about men at her mother's knee. They were dangerous creatures but deceptively easy to manipulate. She'd have to handle Robert with care. Stepping into Dr. Moon's magic dust had been an unambiguous act of heroism. But he wouldn't have done it for a man.

A complement here, a word of praise there, and he'd be hooked, a Sarah-junky, willing to do anything for a fix. Maybe he was already there. Lucky for him she was nothing like Marie.

Robert sang while they walked.

Out of tune, unrecognizable lyrics, but Sarah didn't object. Silence was the enemy. If Robert stopped singing, he'd fill the void with words he couldn't take back, and they didn't have far to go.

They found Hashilli's SUV about a hundred yards away from the Indian Baptist Cemetery.

"Downwind," Robert said. "If he parked upwind, I would have been warned."

Sarah opened her shoulder bag. She ran her right hand around its interior, shoving the contents into a chaotic jumble. After a minimal amount of swearing, she produced Hashilli's keys.

"Let's look inside."

No splotches of blood, bits of fiber, or spools of duct tape. The kidnapper had transformed the interior of the SUV into an evidence free zone. Even the child seat he used to transport stolen babies was gone.

Robert pointed out the brand-new shovel in the cargo space. Had Dr. Moon intended to do a little grave robbing of his own, or was he planning to convert a recently dug burial plot from single to triple occupancy?

"Like hiding a tree in a forest," Robert said.

Sarah didn't ask him to explain the thought process behind the statement. His style of logic seldom withstood the transition into language. She retrieved the shovel. She tested its weight and handed it off to her partner in crime. "Robbing graves is *man's work*. Ask the wind if you don't believe me."

"The wind stopped talking when Hashilli's powder hit my face. I don't hear anything. Not even a whisper."

"It'll wear off."

Robert stood quietly in the dim light of the crescent moon testing the sharpness of his shovel's edge, mulling over his limited knowledge of pharmaceuticals.

"Drugs never last forever." Sarah tried to sound more certain than she felt. Drugs didn't last forever, but sometimes their effects were permanent. Like vaccinations that altered the immune system and recreational drugs that remodeled the architecture of the brain. Ecstasy, methamphetamines—could Hashilli's powder be like one of those?

"Time to go," she said. "It's getting late, and we still have a grave to rob."

They made their way around monuments, mausoleums, and shrubbery until they reached a recently dug grave with a headstone that identified its occupant as Roosevelt Washington.

"This is it." Robert's voice had a rough unpleasant edge familiar to Sarah. She'd heard that quality in her own voice as a small child, every time her mother abandoned her to the care of strangers.

"It will all work out." She solidified her promise with a gentle hand on Robert's shoulder. "It always does if you keep your wits about you."

"As if I have any wits to keep," said Robert. "I haven't become sane, you know, just because I don't hear voices."

A recovering schizophrenic and no support group anywhere. Sarah wanted to tell him sanity was grossly overrated. She wanted to tell him character was more important, and intelligence, and empathy. An undergraduate anthropology student knew that much.

"For most of history, sane people believed in spirits, angels, demons, ghosts, and magic." Sarah directed Robert's attention to the graveyard with a sweeping gesture she had seen on a television game show. "Carefully landscaped city real estate, occupied by corpses, arranged in boxes so they'll face the east when they sit up to greet Gabriel's trumpet on judgment day."

Sarah Bible, graveside philosopher, quoted her favorite Paul Simon song. "Still Crazy After All These Years." The title said it all. She couldn't tell if her words made Robert feel better. Probably not, but at least he'd stopped complaining.

"Now dig." She pointed to the grave. "We haven't got all night."

Robert checked the place on his wrist where a watch would be if he owned a watch. "What's the hurry? Doctor Moon is safely locked away, and Roosevelt Washington's not going anywhere."

A sound like padded sledgehammers interrupted their conversation. The muffled-hammer noise thumped a line across the graveyard grass, moving in their direction with alarming speed.

A booming sports announcer's voice told them to stop what they were doing. The sound echoed off of granite tombstones making it difficult to choose an avenue of escape. An African-American man as massive as an offensive lineman, but not quite as tall as Sarah, lumbered out of the darkness. He was full of rage and rhetorical questions.

"Can't a black man be left in peace to molder in his own grave?"

Molder? Freaking out seemed Sarah's best option, but she hadn't decided what form that should take. Standing motionless was good for snakes and rogue grizzly bears. Maybe it would work for a graveyard apparition.

"How many people do I have to chase away from this man's final resting place? What did Mister Roosevelt Washington do in life that justifies this treatment?" The big man shook his head in disgust and was prepared to rail on for another several minutes about disrespecting the dead, but he stopped as soon as Robert called him Baron Saturday.

Roosevelt Washington's advocate fixed his gaze on Robert and lumbered a wide semicircle around the would-be grave robbers, forcing them to turn their faces into the light of the crescent moon. Sarah tried to keep her eyes on the man's face, but his stump pads were a powerful draw on her attention. His abbreviated limbs reduced the length of his stride, which made him appear to be running even though he moved no faster than a brisk walk. His pads drummed against the graveyard sod in a pattern that reminded Sarah of a beating heart.

"Two men have called me by that name." The volume of the big man's voice dropped several decibels, well out of the normal range for accusations.

"If I'm not mistaken, you were the first." He paused long enough to draw a breath and move two paces closer. "If I'm not mistaken, you spoke to me from the bottom of this very grave."

Robert looked from Baron Saturday to Sarah.

"I see him too. He's not the product of bad brain chemistry." She took a step backward as Baron Saturday moved forward. She would have taken another if she hadn't backed into Roosevelt Washington's tombstone.

"I'm real enough," said the legless apparition. "I'm no baron. No kind of heathen African God either." He turned his attention back to Robert. "My name's Big Shorty, but I already told you that."

A monster with a funny name. Simultaneously accurate and disrespectful, an unfortunate combination. Sarah doubted she could say this man's name and not append it with a nervous laugh.

How fast could Big Shorty run if it came to that? She wondered if Robert could keep up with her.

"Big Shorty, sir." Sarah said the three words quickly and then bit her lip to the point of bleeding. She composed herself for as long as it took to draw two breaths made uneven by suppressed laughter. "Big Shorty, sir, we mean no harm." She could have made that statement with more conviction if her companion wasn't holding a shovel.

"Twice in a week," Big Shorty said, "people have brought shovels to Roosevelt Washington's grave."

"What is it you people want? Is it those cast-off names his parents gave him? White folks haven't used those names for most of a hundred years. Can't take them back. Not from a dead man."

Robert held his hand up as if Big Shorty were a teacher who would look his way when it was time for him to speak.

"I put a paper in Mister Washington's shirt pocket," Robert said. "Sarah and I have come to get it back."

"Folks put letters into their loved ones' pockets all the time," Big Shorty said. "Reading material for the grave. A note for Saint Peter on judgment day. What family does is family business, but when a crazy white man puts a paper into a dead black man's pocket, I take it out."

Sarah wondered how often that policy needed to be enforced, but she didn't ask. The two men had reached a testosterone-fueled rapport, and she was now effectively excluded. A discussion between a recovering schizophrenic and a graveyard apparition was the very essence of *man talk*, and she was happy to be left out.

It didn't take Robert and Big Shorty very long to reach an understanding. Sarah understood why. They were both certifiably crazy. In a matter of a few minutes they were fast friends. Big Shorty promised to give Robert the paper he had hidden in Roosevelt Washington's pocket. The exchange would take place at Big Shorty's home, right there in the cemetery.

She could hardly wait.

17

"**D**ON'T GET MANY visitors," Big Shorty said as he escorted the would-be grave robbers to the caretaker's cottage behind the miniature Gothic-style chapel of Riverside Gardens Cemetery. Sarah understood the scarcity of guests. A giant black man with stumps for legs was likely to have a fairly empty social calendar, especially if he made his home in a graveyard.

The "cottage" was a prefabricated building assembled on site from metal and vinyl made in China. The exterior was faux stone with a green corrugated metal roof. Big Shorty had cultivated English ivy around the perimeter to blend the structure with the graveyard's ambience. From a distance, the effort met with reasonable success. In the light of the crescent moon, the manufactured building looked right at home. The cottage would lose some of its artificial charm with the morning sun. Even the most exuberant ivy could not hide its enamel gloss and factory edges.

"Holy ground." Big Shorty's voice was deep enough to sing base in a gospel choir but bore no trace of his ethnicity. He spoke with the clarity and precision of a professional narrator. "This cemetery is a border between the worlds of the living and the dead. The chapel keeps out the evil forces of both. That's why I came. That's why I stay."

The big man lumbered on his stumps faster than Sarah and Robert could walk. There were no exterior electric lights in the cemetery, but he had no trouble following the mulch pathways between the headstones.

"Put these soft trails in myself," Big Shorty said. "Easier on the legs than pavement."

Robert tried to ask Big Shorty a question, but as soon as Sarah heard the word amputation, she jabbed him in the ribs and covered with a series of loud, politically correct sneezes. The look she gave Robert penetrated the darkness like a roadside flare. She wasn't sure, but she thought Big Shorty chuckled.

Bless his heart. Sarah was only slightly ashamed of the patronizing cliché☒. Some people just didn't know when to be offended.

The cottage door popped open with a hollow metallic sound as soon as Big Shorty turned the latch. "Frame is warped. Ground shifts as the coffins collapse."

Big Shorty's explanation sounded right to Sarah. The man knew the territory. He was right at home in Riverside Gardens Cemetery.

"Been here since God was a teenager. Most folks would find it tiresome, but it suits me."

The inside of the cottage was spartan. Furnished with a laminated table, four folding chairs, and a couch. There was a kitchen sink, a gas cook top, and a miniature refrigerator that would have been at home in a college dorm room. As far as Sarah could see, there were no electrical forms of entertainment. No television, no sound system, not even a transistor radio.

Big Shorty hoisted himself onto the couch and gestured for his guests to find what comfort they could in the folding chairs. "Doesn't take much to entertain a man like me. When I get lonely, I go outside and listen to the dead."

Sarah couldn't tell if Shorty's smile was serious or humorous.

"Loud and clear at dawn and then again at dusk," Big Shorty said, "but you can hear them anytime if you listen close."

Sarah tried to think of some way to get Shorty back on the subject of the paper he removed from Roosevelt Washington's pocket. Crazy people don't respond to pressure. Adrenalin makes them crazier. Sarah had a lot of experience with the mentally ill.

"Did the voices tell you about the paper?" She worked with the care and precision of a spider-wrangler. Nudge the subject gently in the right direction. Whispers rather than shouts. Suggestions rather than demands. A slight tilt in the conversational terrain and Big Shorty would move where she wanted him to go. "You know. The one in Roosevelt Washington's pocket."

It would have worked, too, if Robert hadn't been so happy to find someone else who heard voices. "What do the dead say?"

Spider wrangler's rule number one—work with one arachnid at a time. Sarah tried to think of a way to re-direct the topic, but it was too late. Big Shorty was off and running.

"When ghosts come from the other world, they take the form of birds. Can't be bats or butterflies or mosquitoes. Those are something else entirely. Souls take the shape of birds when they visit. They sound like birds when they speak."

"How about parrots?" Robert asked. "Parrots are birds, and they can talk. So can parakeets and cockatoos."

"Now that is something to consider, but no bird like that has ever come to Riverside Gardens Cemetery."

They sat in silence listening to the souls who were perched in the ivy covering the caretaker's cottage. There were songs of whippoorwills and doves along with owl calls and warbling sounds of birds that Sarah couldn't identify.

After several minutes of listening to the boring conversations of the dead, she made a show of looking at her watch. She nudged Robert and commented on the lateness of the hour.

"About that paper in Roosevelt Washington's pocket…." Her plan only went that far. She looked at Robert, broadcasting as clearly as she could her desire for him to take the topic to the next level.

He reacted by moving his chair a few inches farther from Sarah as if a little more interpersonal space would solve her problem.

"I've been wondering." Robert tilted his head from side to side as though he were using gravity to align the words that would best suit the question he wanted to ask. "How did you lose your legs?"

Sarah's heart adjusted its rhythm to accommodate the gushing apologies she expected to be offering within the next few minutes.

Big Shorty looked at his stumps as if he just realized there was something missing.

"People hardly ever ask me that. All of them wonder, but they hardly ever ask." The gold cusps on his premolars glittered as his smile filled up the room. Somehow, he managed to be simultaneously terrifying and charming.

"My people come from the Cookson Hills, the heart of the Cherokee Nation."

Both Sarah and Robert were acquainted with the history of eastern Oklahoma. The region spawned and nourished more notorious criminals than they could count—Pretty Boy Floyd, Ma Barker, Machine Gun Kelly, and Wilber Underhill, just to name just a few.

Shorty pushed himself off his couch and lumbered to his gas cooktop. He lit a flame with a kitchen style match, filled a pot with water, and set it over the burner. Sarah wanted to tell him not to bother, but the big man went through the motions like they were part of a ritual, and she didn't interfere. He adjusted the flame and nudged the pot as if a half-inch this way or that made a difference. He didn't speak until he finished adjusting its position.

"The first Cherokee came to Indian Territory with black slaves, but they treated them like people instead of property." He sounded more sophisticated than Sarah expected, but it was hard to concentrate on his message while she watched him plod toward the couch. He stopped in front of Robert's chair as if he meant to have a men-only conversation. She usually complained about that kind of behavior, but it didn't seem like the time for confrontation.

"The tribe understood the value of family. They knew about responsibility, too, so when my great-great-grandpop moved his people to the hills, no slave hunters followed them with dogs."

Shorty held his arms out to his sides as if he were making an important point, but it didn't take Sarah long to decide he was struggling with his balance. She was about to rush to his assistance when the wobbling stopped. The old manipulator lowered his arms and smiled to let her know it was part of the spectacle he used to control people like her, who would always underestimate him. He turned his full attention back to Robert.

"The old man saw right from the start the Indians wouldn't fare any better in the territory than they had back east, and it didn't take long for history to prove him right. There was some shooting when the Civil War came—soldiers against soldiers, soldiers against the tribes, most everybody against the blacks—but that wasn't the worst of it. When the armies stopped fighting the white settlers came for the last few acres of Indian land. Some took it through marriage. Others marked out claims and wouldn't leave. Railroads took their share of territory real estate with grants, and the U.S. government used allotments to end what remained of tribal rule. When that was done, they made Oklahoma a state, with a legislature that loved its Jim Crow laws. I wasn't around for any of that, you understand."

He tipped back and forth, making progress toward his couch a few inches at a time. Shorty's version of pacing, Sarah guessed. He did that for a few moments and then flopped down where he'd been sitting with so much force the house shook.

"By the time I came along, the locals had forgotten about the black folks living in the hills. We stayed out of sight—hunted with bows and arrows, planted gardens in the undergrowth, cooked with smokeless fires. Grandpop taught us to speak so our voices were lost in the wind before they fell on prying ears." Big Shorty glanced at Sarah, as if he wanted to know if she had any questions, but turned to Robert before she had a chance to speak. A pair of crazy people bonding over a delusion.

"Grandpop was like a phantom. He could walk through the woods and not break a single twig. He could sit at the supper table and no one in the family would even look his way. It's no surprise we hardly noticed how old he'd grown. Grandpop had gotten so good at hiding, even Death couldn't find him."

Big Shorty winked at Sarah the moment he switched from telling his faintly believable family legend into a battle between spirits and mortals.

"I saw the Reaper lurking on game trails near our cabin. Glimpses mind you. Bits and pieces of his black robe caught in the underbrush, too, and there were animals he'd cut down with his scythe out of frustration. The more Death hunted Grandpop, the craftier the old man got. He dodged around the hills with so much stealth we'd think he was gone for good. But he'd reminded us he was still around with a kiss when we least expected it. Grandpop was family, and we kept on loving him, but after a while we began to wonder if the considerable troubles in Cookson Hills was Death's revenge for the old man who wouldn't die."

Big Shorty looked at the floor where his feet would have rested, if he had feet. He explained how his father gathered things Grandpop had touched and put them out for Death to catch his scent. Shorty's mother cut the old man's hair and scattered it around the forest. His brothers and sisters sang the old man's favorite songs.

"I didn't do any of those things. To this day I've never said his name out loud, and I suppose I never will. But I didn't try and stop them. I didn't warn the old man when I could have. And then one day it was too late."

He slumped on the couch for a few long moments before he retrieved a blue bandana from his pocket and dabbed at the corners of his eyes. Robert stood up from his folding chair and was about to move to Shorty's side, but Sarah stopped him with a wave of her arm.

"Miss." Big Shorty spoke to her but looked at Robert. He pointed to the boiling water on his cooktop. "There are teabags on the counter next to the cooktop. Would you throw four of them in the pot and turn the flame off?"

Woman's work. But how could she complain to a double amputee who had stopped them from robbing a grave. She'd done more menial things for crazier people.

Big Shorty picked his story up where he left off as soon as he heard the teabags splash into the water. "Death was mostly patient with his captured souls. He didn't mind when they changed into birds and fluttered off to visit places they had loved. Not Grandpop though. The Grim Reaper was afraid if he let the old man get beyond his reach, he'd never get him back. But holding Grandpop against his will was quite a trick, especially when he learned to turn himself into a bird."

Shorty stopped talking long enough to accept a mug of tea from Sarah. He stared into the golden-brown liquid while she walked a cup to Robert and took one for herself. She sat in her folding chair, watched steam rise in curlicues from her mug and disappear near the ceiling. She tried not to think about the unconscious man locked in the Maytubby bone-house.

Big Shorty sipped his tea. "I was collecting deadwood in the forest when Grandpop's spirit found me. It was fitting he took the shape of a hummingbird. The little creature had a white mark on his breast the shape of a lightning bolt that matched a scar on Grandpop's chest. He flitted here and there, silent except for the sound of his wings. The slightest movement in the trees sent him scurrying for cover. I could see he had no intention of returning to the land of dead. So I pulled my shirt pocket open wide, and Grandpa hummingbird flew inside."

Sarah's tea tasted like something that started in a discount box and then was stored past the expiration date. She winced a bit with her first swallow. Robert and Big Shorty drank theirs like it was ambrosia.

"You saved him?" Robert had totally suspended disbelief. Sarah wondered if the wind would help him sort through fact and fiction when he could talk to her again.

Big Shorty shook his head. "Back then I had two good legs. I could move faster than a roadrunner. I could jump high as a whitetail deer. I was young and strong and certain Death could never catch me, but, of course, I was wrong."

He rubbed his stump pads and shook his head in regret. He swallowed the rest of his tea in three gulps and then held the empty mug out for Sarah to take. She ignored him until it was clear he'd keep the mug front of her longer than she could pretend she didn't see it.

"Death's long black robe didn't slow him down a bit. He chopped my legs off with a swing of his scythe before I'd run a dozen steps. He put them into a burlap bag along with Grandpa hummingbird and flew off to wherever spirits go when they leave this world."

Shorty dabbed his eyes again and looked like he might break into a sobbing fit at any moment. Sarah couldn't tell if his emotions were authentic, but Robert looked like a true believer.

"I ran through the Cookson Hills when I had legs, tracking game and hunting plants that fill the belly. Now I lumber through a graveyard in search of Death."

"What will you do if you find him?" Robert asked.

"Wrestle him to the ground and demand he return my legs," Shorty said. "I've been punished long enough for sheltering Grandpop's soul."

Sarah looked into Big Shorty's eyes. She couldn't tell whether he believed his own story, but clearly Robert did. She'd been with so many crazy people in her life, delusions were starting to seem normal.

Big Shorty reached into his shirt pocket. For a moment she thought he was going to give her a look at Grandpa hummingbird, back for another visit from the land of the dead, but he withdrew a wrinkled piece of notepaper folded into a square.

"Had you for a moment didn't I?" Big Shorty grinned. He tossed the folded paper in Robert's direction. "That's the note you put into the dead man's pocket."

18

"NOT WHAT I expected." Robert silently read the note for the second time. "Not what I expected at all." He handed the paper to Sarah and slumped in his folding chair.

"It might be enough." Sarah held the note between her outstretched hands, turning it delicately to take advantage of the minimal illumination inside Big Shorty's living quarters. Most of the page was taken up by a drawing of an owl. A list of names formed two columns on the left-hand margin.

"Names of missing children, if I'm not mistaken," she said. "And this owl is identical to the one on the Maytubby bone-house door."

"Cherokee never cared too much for owls," Big Shorty said. "Not owl feathers or owl calls or even pictures of owls. None of the tribes from the old Indian Territory could abide night birds."

"Tribal superstition." Sarah folded the paper carefully and put it into a zippered compartment of her shoulder bag.

Easy words. Sarah knew next to nothing about the so-called Civilized Tribes. Not my fault, she told herself. The Five Tribes spend more time with politicians than anthropologists. She wouldn't let those excuses find their way to her lips.

"Death's emissary," Big Shorty said. "Odd to see something like that painted on a bone-house door."

"What now?" Sarah's mind had trouble finding traction.

"We need to check on Doctor Moon," Robert said, "and then decide what we should do."

Sarah could read the doubt in Robert's face. She could hear it in his voice. She understood his reasoning well enough. The cops would never take Robert Collins seriously. Not after they ran his record. They wouldn't even write his statement down unless it was corroborated by stable members of society. A legless cemetery caretaker and a visiting anthropology student with a crazy mother hardly filled the bill.

"The note will help." Sarah promised, even though she shared his misgivings. A simple drawing of an owl with a list of children's names didn't seem like much in the way of hard evidence, especially if the authorities learned it had been hidden in a dead man's pocket. "Victoria Tiger will testify, once Hashilli is in custody."

Big Shorty eased himself off his couch and lurched across the room as quietly as a galloping horse. The prefabricated metal building vibrated with every step, and the folding metal guest chairs shook in sympathy. If the late Helen Keller had been in the room, she would have interpreted Big Shorty's alarming stroll as an earthquake no less than seven on the Richter scale.

Sarah and Robert were out of their seats, preparing to take cover in a doorway or run into the questionable safety of the dark graveyard.

"Real show stopper," Shorty told his audience of two. "Always gets a standing ovation." He collected sealed beam flashlights from a shelf in the corner of his single room. "Owls have slippery ways. Let's find out if yours has flown the coop."

He led Sarah and Robert on a meandering pathway from the care-taker's cottage to the Indian Baptist Cemetery. "No lights and no con-versation till we get there."

Sarah understood that words and beams of light might alert Hashilli to their approach, but stealth was not something Big Shorty managed easily. The pads on his amputated limbs pounded a broken rhythm through the graveyard like a drug-addled drummer breaking in a new instrument. But it didn't sound like footsteps—not human footsteps anyway. If Hashilli were listening, he would know something was headed in his direction, but he wouldn't know what to expect until it arrived.

Robert tapped Sarah on the shoulder. He pointed to the empty space where Dr. Moon's SUV had been parked. Not a good sign.

The door to the Maytubby bone-house was still locked. Sarah retrieved Hashilli's pistol from her shoulder bag and handed it to Big Shorty. She didn't know whether he would pull the trigger if it came to that, but at least he looked dangerous.

It took her three tries to find the right key on Hashilli's key ring. Any opportunity for surprise was gone. If their prisoner was still locked inside the bone-house, he would be waiting for them, armed with bricks, skeletal remains, and grave goods. She pulled the door open as quickly as she could. Robert and Big Shorty flicked their sealed beams on and flooded the bone-house with enough light to blind their captive if he were still inside.

But he was not. The Maytubby crypt was empty, except for the remains of the ancestors, which Sarah noted had been returned to their boxes and filed, once again, like an orderly library of the dead.

Big Shorty pointed to an open space under the peak of the roof where the stars and the crescent moon shined through a pentagonal void in the wall.

"No mortar between the bricks at the top of the western wall," Big Shorty said. "So the ghosts can fly off to paradise."

"A supernatural escape route." That would have been useful information a few hours earlier. Sarah was embarrassed to find that her anthropology studies had left her somewhat less informed on this subject than the caretaker of a cemetery.

"Don't know much about the Choctaw," Big Shorty said, "but that's how they did it in the Indian Baptist Cemetery. People talk when they visit the dead. Keeps their minds away from their sorrows."

"What else have you heard people say?" Sarah asked. "What do you know about the Maytubbys? What do you know about Hashilli?"

"A grounds keeper tries not to intrude," he said, "but I've been watching that black SUV come and go for a long time." He stopped talking and listened to the night fliers rustling in the trees.

The screech of a something big followed by the sound of flapping wings made Sarah jump. She thought she saw the silhouette of an owl cross the moon, but she was so nervous, it might have been her imagination.

"Driver of that car is the only visitor who goes inside the sandstone wall," Shorty said. "Keeps the Maytubby place in good repair, but mostly he collects moonflowers and those yellow mushrooms."

He leaned over the sandstone wall and pointed out one of the big yellow puffballs growing close to the barrier. Sarah thought he might be about to pick it, but his fingers stopped a few inches away.

"We had these things back in the hills—ghost buttons. Grandpop said the smallest pinch can jar a man's soul right off the tracks."

"Or jar it back on track again." Robert's wistful tone aroused an unexpected pang of jealousy in Sarah. The wind was his old girlfriend who still came around but wouldn't speak to him. He desperately wanted her back.

Sarah almost asked him, "Is she prettier than me?"

But Big Shorty saved the day. "I've seen another painted owl like the one on the bone-house door." Big Shorty had shifted the conversation back on track before Sarah could embarrass herself. "A place not far from here. I've seen your missing man there too." He told them about his encounter with Hashilli outside of the Wise Owl Child Development Center.

Sarah had seen the place. She reached into her shoulder bag and found the wallet she had taken from Hashilli Maytubby. She flipped through it until she found his driver's license.

"How do you suppose the staff at the Wise Owl Center would react if we showed them Hashilli's photo ID?"

"They might know him by another name," Robert said.

"They might know Andrew Tiger by another name as well." Sarah might still be able to recover Victoria's little boy, even if Hashilli was beyond their reach. But first they needed a plan.

19

THE MEDICATION NURSE smelled of flowers, musk, and just enough pheromone to remind men how sweet life could be beyond the walls of Flanders Mental Hospital. Her tailored scrubs fit her well-proportioned body like a coat of latex paint. She moved with the sensual efficiency an exotic dancer—no wasted motion, completely aware of her male audience. Even women had to look. It was only natural she and Marie Ferraro would be friends. The nurse smiled as she loaded a daily dose of Zyprexa into a medication cup.

Marie was first to get her meds, full of energy because she was anxious to try out a slight of hand method for ditching her pills. A magician with a borderline personality disorder had taught her the trick. The most critical element of an illusion was picking an audience who wanted to be fooled.

"What's the difference between a psychiatrist and a used car salesman?" She told the nurse a new joke every day. Proof her depression was visiting relatives out of town.

"I give up, Marie."

"A used car salesman knows when he's lying." Jokes had to be short because the medication lists weren't.

The nurse chuckled as she moved on to her next patient. Flanders clients didn't stand in line for meds. Some of them wouldn't, but most of them couldn't because of the drugs.

Marie and the medication nurse acknowledged a truth the doctors wouldn't consider. Drugs don't cure psychosis. They make the psychotics feel too weird to act out.

In the good old days, shrinks used talk therapy. Not so much anymore. Old school psychotherapy had been incrementally discontinued until it consisted solely of collective discussions among patients. The groups were supervised by residents so recently out of school their credentials still had that new diploma smell.

Group sessions didn't do much good, but they were kind of fun. Marie was popular with the doctors and her fellow clients. Her *Vagina Monologues* were a welcome break from accounts of domestic abuse and self-recrimination. She reminded the depressed clients there were two sides to their psychosis. Hence the name bipolar.

She offered herself to the male clients as an object of obsession. As God intended. And she served as a vicarious example for the women.

There was an eager young female psychiatric resident who couldn't wait to hear another episode in Marie's exciting history. One of those intelligent women who did everything within her power to obscure her natural feminine charms. Every word was thought out in advance, every move choreographed to achieve maximum masculine effect, like a gay man pretending to be straight. The resident struggled to project professional confidence, but the character she portrayed lacked texture. Marie suggested the doctor watch medical soap operas. The pretty young psychiatrists and heart surgeons at General Hospital knew how to nurture the enthusiasm and good looks that had gotten them the roles in the first place.

The homework wasn't working. The resident's clothing didn't fit, and her makeup suggested a devotion to the Amish faith. She scratched herself in unbecoming places and didn't comb her hair. Marie knew crack whores with a better sense of style—at least in the early stages of their addiction. It was time to turn up the heat.

"Cosmetics are a woman's most valuable resource." Marie liked to warm the group up with a bit of background information that would prepare them for the main event, but this message was meant especially for the psychiatric resident.

"An attractive woman is a collage of color, scent, and form that creates sexual desire in a man and reminds him of his mother." Marie had practiced that statement in front of the mirror in the commons restroom. The group therapy space didn't have the echo effect that added gravitas to her words, but she made up for it with dramatic gestures. "It's a mental state that makes men anxious to please."

The doctor blushed. A sure sign she was absorbing the message. Marie would revisit important concepts in the future. But this was group, and now she had everyone's attention. It was time to delight her audience with story she had told to therapists and fellow patients so often she had the lines memorized. God she loved show business.

"I was thirteen years old when I met my first lover. He was wearing a ski mask and carrying a gun." She started the story at a different place each time and changed details here and there, but the theme remained the same.

"He came into Shamrock Bank in Coalgate where my parents were applying for a second mortgage." She pointed her finger like a pretend pistol and aimed it at one member of the group and then another.

"He spoke with so much emotion his voice broke when he said he didn't want to kill anyone but would." She told them how young the robber was, how full of life, as he lined the customers against a wall and warned the tellers about silent alarms and dye packs.

"I couldn't see his face, but I could tell the moment our eyes met there was more than money on his mind. From the moment he saw me, I was the driving force behind everything he did."

Marie showed group how the seduction was done. "Crude, because I was so young, but effective for the same reason." She demonstrated facial expressions. She showed her audience how she moved across the room, how she struck a sensual line as she raised her hands in symbolic surrender, how the rhythm of her breathing mimicked sexual excitation.

"He handed me his booty bag, put his gun to my head, and led me past the tellers. He told me not to resist, but that wasn't necessary because every move he made from that point on was under my influence."

Marie walked to each member of the group, held an imaginary bag in front of them and demanded all their money. The men shoveled invisible bills into her make-believe sack. The women cooperated less enthusiastically except for the psychiatric resident. Marie could spot a girl crush a mile away.

"When it was time to leave, we walked together like a pair of slow close dancers. No one waited for us outside the bank." She mimed opening the door, looking left and right.

"He told me to go back inside, if that's what I wanted. It would be my last chance because if I went with him, he'd never ask if I wanted to be free again." She paused and looked at the ceiling the way she'd seen telenovela actors do. "As if anyone wants to be free of love."

The ladies in group squirmed in their seats, so she'd gone a bit over the top, dramatically speaking. So, she shifted to a road chase that never actually happened, and when everyone was caught up in the escape, she dribbled in a few kisses that would have been right at home in PG-rated movies.

Marie borrowed freely from romance authors. Jodi Picoult and Nicholas Sparks were her favorites for flirtation, but Nora Roberts and Julia Quinn were good for betrayal and dramatic endings. She walked the group through the stages of romance, which were surprisingly similar to the stages of grief.

"We stayed together thirty days, stealing from the rich and living off the land." She let a single tear trickle from her left eye. A Pushmataha County Sheriff's deputy gunned down my first lover while he robbed a branch bank in a Homeland grocery store. Romance with a violent man is a temporary thing." She wiped moisture from her eye and scanned the group for effect.

Perfect execution.

"Tears are another weapon in a woman's arsenal." She locked eyes with the psychiatric resident. She waved her arm like a magician's assistant directing the doctor's attention to the men in her group. They were putty in her hands.

———————————

THERE WAS NO doubt Marie Ferarro was getting well. The staff attributed her improvement to group therapy and antipsychotic drugs, but Marie knew true love was the reason. Archie Chatto would come for her. Of that much she was certain. She didn't know how he'd manage her rescue, imprisoned as he was in El Reno Federal Penitentiary, but her Apache lover would find a way.

"It won't be long," she told Dr. Moon during their last private session. "You'll see."

Archie's plans arrived on the wind, while Marie sat on a concrete bench under a miniature forest of bald cypress by the koi pond. Archie didn't talk to her exactly, but that wasn't important. Men's plans could usually be summed up in three simple words. "Get it done."

Bless their single-minded hearts. Marie had learned long ago it's best to ignore a man's words if you want to understand his thoughts.

Doctor Moon believed she might do even better at another facility. One with a more relaxed environment where she might be allowed to communicate with Archie by telephone. Where Sarah could visit without restrictions. Such a thoughtful therapist. Such a radical departure from Marie's previous experiences. Small wonder he was famous.

Doctor Moon never failed to ask Marie about her daughter during their private sessions. At first she thought he might be interested in Sarah as a girlfriend, but the emotional balance of his words and body language was indecisive.

He was a hard man to read, but Marie would break his code eventually. She had never met a man she couldn't understand and then control once she set her mind to the task.

She wasn't surprised when he told her, "It's time to go, Marie."

Dr. Moon was an important man, no need to bother with paperwork or committee meetings. Just load a mental patient into his car and drive away. His attitude of entitlement and Marie's cooperation carried the day.

She knew she was being spirited away. The doctor's posture was too erect for this to be a hospital-approved endeavor. His voice had an artificially deliberate tone, and he stretched the spaces between his words to compensate for their clipped quality. He resisted the impulse to walk quickly by shortening his stride and tipping his head slightly backward to slow his forward momentum.

The man was stealing her. It wouldn't be the first time, but Dr. Moon would be her first psychiatrist-abductor.

"I hope it's a long ride," she said, "wherever we are going."

He acknowledged staff members and clients with nearly subliminal nods. He flashed a charming smile at the bored security personnel and walked Marie out of Flanders the way a champion ballroom dancer leads his partner onto the floor.

"Well done," she told him. "They have no idea what you are doing."

The doctor accepted her flattery in silence, but she could tell how pleased he was. Marie could feel the doctor's hand tremble when he placed it innocently on her lower back.

Gotcha.

"You are a remarkable woman, Marie." Dr. Moon opened the passenger door of his black SUV for her. He checked to see that her seat belt was positioned correctly and securely fastened.

A good start. Marie would have the psychiatrist in the palm of her hand by the time they reached their destination, wherever that might be.

"I'm taking you to Stringtown," he told her without being asked. "I think you'll like it there."

20

WHEN TI'MAMA COINPENNY answered the door of the Wise Owl Child Development center, she was confronted with a horrible sight. Two stern-faced white people, a man and a woman, stood before her holding clipboards.

The woman stepped forward and flashed a badge. *BOND AGENT* was printed across the gold shield in capital letters. Ti'Mama had seen badges like that but couldn't remember where. So many agencies and authorities. It was hard to keep track.

The white man stood back. That meant the woman was in charge. A sure sign these bond agents were social policemen. The man held his badge over the woman's shoulder. He made a zipper motion over his mouth.

To remind Ti'Mama of her right to silence? Usually they read from a laminated card like the ones deaf people trade for handouts. Maybe this white man didn't need a list. Maybe his crazy eyes and his zipper motion were good enough.

"I'm Agent Bible, and this is Agent Collins." The woman consulted the papers on her clipboard. Her lips moved slightly as she reviewed the case against the Wise Owl Center.

Nurse Coinpenny didn't try to read her lips. Words on official papers are written in a language only lawyers and politicians understand. Fine print. Much too fine for nurses of Haitian ancestry.

These agents didn't ask for identification. That was a good sign. Maybe they'd decided there were enough African faces looking through the bars of the county jail. Maybe these bond agents had come to check for safety violation, to count fire extinguishers and see if registrations were in order.

Ti'Mama gestured for the agents to come inside. Better to communicate with gestures since anything she said could be used against her. Policemen hit you, then arrest you for your bruises. They shoot you and then get a paid vacation. If there was one thing Ti'Mama Coinpenny understood completely, it was the futility of resisting white people with badges.

"We need to see the nursery right away," the woman told her. "Urgent police business."

Ti'Mama led the white bond agents to the babies. She walked at an agonizingly slow pace, like a rheumatic tourist on a hiking trail with a steep incline. That was another thing She'd learned over the years. When white people want to hurry, it is best to move slowly. So you have time to think. To change course before they stampede you into a trap.

The police never answered questions, but the time had come for Ti'Mama to ask one. "What are you looking for?" She affected a Creole accent that didn't really belong to her. It made her sound exotic and, perhaps, a little dangerous.

"A baby," the woman cop answered.

"We have five of those." Ti'Mama opened the door to the nursery enclosure. "Yesterday we had six, but baby boy MT186 was placed in a permanent home."

These officers weren't happy with the babies they found.

"Malnourished," the woman said. "Raw spots on their lips. Crusty secretions in the corners of their eyes."

Ti'Mama wanted to tell her that was not her fault. Babies didn't come to the Wise Owl Center from good homes. She would cure their infections, treat their rashes, feed them. Ti'Mama would give these ba-bies a glimpse of love so they'd be ready for the Land of Milk and Honey she imagined they'd be going to. Mr. Luna would see to that part.

The man held his note pad like a shield, looking over it in nervous fits and glances like the sight of these babies was more than he could stand. He fidgeted and shuffled around the woman cop, totally useless, the way men usually were in a nursery. Ti'Mama felt sorry for him, just a little, until he finally gained the power of speech.

"Records," he said. "Maybe we should look at the records."

After that she didn't feel sorry for him anymore. Mr. Luna was strict about her babies' records.

Nurse Coinpenny knew a lot about HIPAA regulations and patient confidentiality but not enough to wrestle policemen over the made-up rights of unwanted babies. Bad things happened to nurses who accepted such responsibilities. Mr. Luna was the one who should be deciding about the babies' records. He wasn't exactly white, but he was a political man. That was almost the same thing.

"Mister Luna might say you need a warrant." Ti'Mama looked at the floor as she spoke. She shifted her weight from her left foot to her right and back again. Her ankle bracelet of mercury dimes jingled like a pocket full of small change, reminding her of her heritage. Descended from African queens and kings. Stolen by Arabs, sold to Europeans, but the African gods still watched over her.

The woman bond agent showed her an Oklahoma drivers' license. "Is this the man you know as Mister Luna?"

Ti'Mama didn't want to look. Policemen had tricky things, like bond agent badges and false drivers' licenses. This one had a picture of Mr. Luna, but it said his name was Hashilli Maytubby.

"Indian Name," Ti'Mama said. She directed the statement to the male cop even though the woman was clearly the person in charge.

"Mister Luna is Hispanic. *Everyone* at the center knows that." Ti'Ma-ma hoped her statement might shift the agents' interest to the secretary or the other duty nurse, but that wasn't going to work. She heard doors opening and closing. She heard cars in the parking lot starting their engines. All the other members of the Wise Owl Center's staff were taking unauthorized personal time, leaving Ti'Mama alone with her babies and these agents. Why would the police allow the others to leave? She whispered a prayer asking the Loa for protection from these official intruders. She briefly considered running for the door, but she could not. She was the guardian of the unwanted babies. She changed their diapers and gave them formula and medication. She gave all the love she could spare to the little children with numbers instead of names. She wouldn't abandon them now, even if it meant going to jail.

But these two agents weren't arresting her. They weren't hauling out handcuffs and legal papers. They were arguing for her cooperation, trying to persuade her to show them the records. Ti'Mama was granted an epiphany, perhaps from Sobo, the Loa of strength, or Dumballah, the father Loa who protects women and children.

"Bond agent ain't police." She slipped deeper into the Caribbean dialect her grandparents spoke during religious ceremonies. It felt strange on her tongue, unnatural and holy. Ti'Mama had always held the African gods in deep respect. She'd given offerings and requested favors, but she never felt them as a tangible presence until this moment. "Bond agent is bounty hunter. Ain't given no authority." She could feel the strength of the Voodoo pantheon seeping into her body from the earth and the air around her. With the help of the Loa, Ti'Mama Coinpenny would delay the intruders until Mr. Luna arrived or until he sent the real police to cart them off to the white man's jail.

Ti'Mama would have held her ground if her concentration had not been broken by the slow steady drumbeat of heavy leather pads on the floor of the Wise Owl Center.

The thumping approached the place where Ti'Mama made her stand. Had it been a mistake to call on the African gods? Supplicants were known to die, even as their prayers were answered. Crossing the ocean on slave ships had left the African gods bad tempered. They were often unpredictable but always hungry for blood.

"Easy to anger and hard to satisfy." That's what Ti'Mama's grandparents said. Thoughts of destruction pushed resistance out of her mind.

Big Shorty lumbered into the enclosure where the babies were kept. He stopped in the center of the room, like a hologram, perfectly balanced on his stumps. Ti'Mama stood as still as a rabbit frozen under the shadow of an eagle.

Big Shorty didn't speak until a hummingbird darted into the room and hovered over his right shoulder.

"Give these people what they want," he said, as loud and clear as a used car commercial on AM radio. He repeated it three times, once for the Father, once for the Son, and once for the Holy Ghost.

He made a circuit around the room, keeping Ti'Mama in the center of his orbit. The hummingbird kept pace with him in fits and starts. By the time he lumbered out the door, Nurse Coinpenny was ready to co-operate. The order came from Baron Saturday himself, the Loa of the dead. Not the most powerful of the African gods but easily the most frightening.

It took her less than ten minutes to collect a stack of records representing every baby who had passed through the Wise Owl Child Development Center in the past year. She gave them to the woman without a word. She released the folders as soon as the female bond agent held them securely, mindful that magical power can be transmitted through ordinary objects. She crossed her arms over her queasy stomach and whispered the Lord's Prayer without a trace of Creole accent. Ti'Mama would wait with her babies until Mr. Luna returned. She hoped he wouldn't be too long.

———————————

IT WAS A short, quiet walk from the Wise Owl Center to Riverside Gardens Cemetery. An unasked question fluttered in the air between Robert and Sarah like an imaginary butterfly. Robert was the one who put it into words.

"The hummingbird. Was it Shorty's great-great-grandfather?"

Sarah didn't answer. She couldn't accept the idea, but she couldn't dismiss it out of hand. She clutched the eighty odd records against her chest and pretended she hadn't heard.

When Robert tried to ask the question again, she showed him her bond agent's badge and reminded him of his right to remain silent.

"We'll talk about it later," she promised. What was one more broken promise to a man like Robert? He must be used to it by now.

She opened the door to the caretaker's cottage.

Big Shorty had positioned his kitchen table in the middle of the room where the light was best for examining the Wise Owl records. It took Sarah very little time to locate infant MT186.

"It's Andrew Tiger. I can tell by the photograph." She sorted through the remaining records and set aside five other likely kidnapping victims.

"Healthy children within normal limits for weight and length. No chronic diseases or medications, no HIV or residual neurological damage from drug intoxication."

"Now what?" Robert asked.

"First we visit the public library," Sarah said. "Then we go to Kinko's Copies. We are going to fax these records, along with everything we know, to the police, the FBI, and to every Native American-owned business we can think of. Hashilli Maytubby's kidnapping enterprise is about to come to a screeching halt."

She drummed her fingers on the stack of kidnapped children. There was still a question that troubled her, and there was no diplomatic way to phrase it. "Who are you, Shorty? Who are you really?"

He showed her his friendliest smile highlighted by dental work from an era when gold was a sign of prosperity.

"Am I some kind of African God?"

This was the kind of question Sarah's mother might ask while she was deep into the manic phase of her bipolar disorder. She prepared herself to accept Big Shorty's answer as the truth—at least for the time being.

"I'm real enough," Big Shorty said. "Just a black man from the Cookson Hills hoping to win a wrestling match with death."

It was the answer Sarah expected but not the one she desired.

21

"*H*OW COME *BULLSHIT* is an acceptable public declaration but *shit* is not?" Albert Tiger tore his attention away from the afternoon news long enough to make sure Victoria was listening. "Is it because the extra syllable disguises the unpleasant truth."

The police spokesperson was a pretty girl, too young to appreciate the nature of her deception. Her hairstyle was post-coital. Her voice belonged on a phone sex hot line. Her bright red, collagen-injected lips were periodically moistened by a tongue with its own agenda. Albert tried to characterize her clothing, but he couldn't. It vanished before his eyes.

The hot, nameless news reader smiled like a thousand dollar call girl at a governors' convention as she read her statement from the teleprompter. A team of well-meaning but misguided citizens had interfered with the ongoing investigation of a serial kidnapping ring targeting Indian Casino management. The vigilantes had endangered the lives of the stolen children. Police wanted them for questioning.

"Three Native American men." The news reader's voice continued the narration, but police artist's renderings replaced her image on the screen. Albert guessed they were file drawings of previous Indian felons never apprehended. One looked a little like his father.

"Believed to be Creek or Chickasaw." The news reader pronounced each syllable of Chickasaw as if it were a separate word. "Anyone with information about these three vigilantes should contact police immediately."

"Not the kidnapper," Albert said. "Just the three unknown vigilantes." He was satisfied with that. He and Victoria knew what the police did not. Sarah Bible was the anonymous informant who had dumped information into the laps of the authorities in a manner they couldn't ignore. Sarah Bible, not three poorly-drawn Native American men, had brought Baby Andrew home. Just Sarah and her mysterious male companion. Albert appreciated the value of quiet heroism because he was a Native American man. Victoria accepted it because she was a mother. The couple expressed their gratitude to Sarah by telephone because visiting their own guesthouse would have meant acknowledging they knew about Sarah's live in friend. As a casino manager Albert knew all about plausible deniability.

"Stay as long as you want," he told Sarah. "Ask for anything we own, and it will be yours."

Victoria squeezed Baby Andrew hard enough to make him squirm. He had not been out of his parents' sight since social services brought him home. Two other kidnapped children had been recovered, and more would be found as the investigation proceeded. Hashilli Maytubby's elaborate scheme was coming unraveled. According to the police, it was only a matter of time until he was in custody. The Tiger family owed Sarah Bible and the mystery man a debt they never could repay, but that wouldn't stop them from trying.

"Don't tell anyone I'm here," she asked them. "And my friend...."

"What friend?" Albert almost said "Fugetaboutit," but that sounded too much like *The Sopranos*.

Victoria didn't say a word. She just kissed the phone. Albert wondered how long it would take her to remove the germs with a disinfectant wipe.

THE COPS WOULD take a dim view of liberating a client from a mental hospital even if Sarah had a very good reason. *But officer, he had to show me which grave to rob.*

She wasn't sure if impersonating a bond agent was a crime, but stealing records from the Wise Owl Center certainly was, even if she did it to disrupt a kidnapping enterprise.

There were lots of other embarrassing if not illegal details, like discussions with the wind, Native American witchcraft, Voodoo spirits, and a hummingbird that might be the ghost of a Cherokee freedman. By the time a clever interrogator finished with Sarah, she'd be keeping her mother company at Flanders.

The activity at the Tiger house was hectic. The police paid regular visits. Aunts, uncles, and cousins dropped by periodically. Even Professor Lindsay flew in for a short visit with his daughter and her only child.

Sarah and Robert watched the whole thing from the picture window of the guesthouse, ignored by family members and apparently unnoticed by authorities.

Their privacy was disturbed only one time, when Professor Lindsay knocked at their door. Sarah had anticipated her department chairman's visit. He was the one who'd made arrangements for her to stay there, after all. It was only natural he would drop by and check on her progress.

"Victoria didn't tell me you had a significant other." Professor Lindsay gave her a perfunctory embrace. Pro forma on the west coast but overly familiar in Oklahoma. He shook Robert's hand firmly and briefly, in the manner of a college dean passing out diplomas on graduation day.

Dr. Lindsay studied Robert's reactions, eager to place the young man within a social context, but Sarah didn't offer any helpful information and Robert's facial expressions and body language gave no clue to his cultural disposition. Variations in interpersonal space had no effect on him. He didn't back away when Dr. Lindsay became a space invader. He didn't close the distance when the professor moved away.

Sarah could have provided an explanation of sorts. Recovering schizophrenics—*if there was such a thing*—didn't respond to social stressors in expected ways. Hard and soft eye contact didn't trouble Robert. He didn't mind and probably didn't notice excessive scrutiny. Being ignored didn't bother him in the least. Dr. Lindsay wouldn't be able to find any stereotypical niche behaviors that would help him understand Robert.

The professor walked in a circle around Robert, the way a man might evaluate an automobile before tendering an offer. Rude behavior under almost any social circumstances, but his interest looked genuine to Sarah rather than intrusive, and Robert didn't even bother to follow Dr. Lindsey with his eyes.

"Very good." The anthropologist shook Robert's hand again, more vigorously the second time. "You're just the sort of young man I hoped Sarah would attract."

Robert reacted to this statement with a smile that stretched the corners of his mouth to their elastic limit. Sarah didn't smile at all, but she had taken enough social sciences to recognize the signs of denial, even when she saw it in herself.

Dr. Lindsay apparently recognized those signs as well. He winked at her. "Try not to overthink it, Sarah. Emotion wins over intellect every time."

She started to pose an argument but decided the best course was to wait for the conversation to drift to another subject.

"I understand someone sent the authorities a kidnapping conspiracy all wrapped up and tied with a bow," the professor said. "Someone who had the kidnapper's driver's license. Someone who knew the kind of car he drove. Someone who could identify Andrew Tiger's photograph in a record from the Wise Owl Child Development Center."

"That sounds like a fabulous senior project," Professor Lindsay said. "A student who could complete such a project would be certain of a place in graduate school." Over the years, Professor Carson Lindsay had accumulated a great amount of political capital at the University of New Mexico. Saving for a rainy day.

"Your forensic anthropology project is outstanding. First student ever to tackle an active crime." He winked at Sarah again and then at

Robert—more like a nervous tic than acknowledgement of a conspiracy. The department chairman had the reputation of never crowding the borders of academic ethics, but now it looked like he was ready to make a run for the wire.

Dr. Lindsay lowered his voice to a coarse whisper. He looked around the room as if he were checking for hidden microphones. "Archie Chatto called me from El Reno penitentiary. His trial date has been set for the end of next week. He wants to see you before then."

When Sarah was slow to respond the professor whispered a little louder. "Men like Archie are a dying breed. Like wolves, jaguars, Siberian tigers. Inconvenient but irreplaceable. We'll miss them when they're gone."

"And the man he killed?" Sarah moved beside Robert.

"Allegedly killed. There is often a presumption of guilt when Native Americans are accused of crimes, especially Apaches."

"Archie's appearance doesn't help his case," Sarah said. "It isn't hard to imagine him in the role of a murderer."

"Unfortunate, but true." Dr. Lindsay lifted a carefully folded piece of copy paper from his shirt pocket and handed it to her. It contained all of Archie's Department of Corrections particulars. "He thinks Marie is in some kind of serious trouble. He believes he might be able to help."

"From a cell in a federal prison?" Sarah made a show of studying the numbers, dates, and times on the sheet of paper. She refolded it and placed it in her purse.

"Never underestimate the abilities of an Apache warrior." Dr. Lindsay had no problem with stereotypes, especially if they were outrageously heroic. He turned his attention to Robert, who had yet to speak a single word.

"In spite of those blue eyes, I believe I detect some indigenous influence in your features. Tell me, young man, am I wrong?"

Robert invested several seconds studying Dr. Lindsay. He might be committing details of his face to memory, admiring the color of his eyes or reaching a conclusion about the professor's character. Sarah didn't have a clue.

She was reasonably certain Carson Lindsay was prepared to accept whatever Robert told him on face value, at least for the time being.

Sarah thought of the professor's worldview as Zen anthropology, but she kept that term to herself.

Robert remained silent, but he directed Dr. Lindsay into the kitchen with economical gestures that would inspire jealousy in a professional mime. When the professor and Sarah were seated and the quiet tension had built to the breaking point, Robert finally spoke.

"Let me tell you how the spirit of a Sinagua Singer came to live inside my body."

The professor reached for a ballpoint in his shirt pocket, but Sarah stopped him before his hand had moved more than a few inches.

She mouthed rather than spoke the admonishment, *This is not the time to take notes.* Fortunately he was good at lip reading.

"My parents were archaeologists," Robert said, "excavating a Pueblo ruin that had been abandoned for twelve centuries." His back-story, delivered with no emotional tone. A simple disclosure of facts.

"They celebrated an unexpected discovery in the way young lovers often do. How could they have known that a spirit had been waiting more than a thousand years for such an opportunity?" Robert had the pace of an accomplished storyteller.

Dr. Lindsay smiled as he settled into the most comfortable position the kitchen chair would allow. "Wherever did you find him, Sarah?"

"You wouldn't believe it if I told you."

22

"**I** LIKE TO have the corners of my graves as sharp as an axe blade. Backhoes can't do that." Big Shorty twirled his shovel like a baton. He tossed it into the air and caught it on the spin.

Robert wondered if all master gravediggers could do that. He watched the big man move around the bottom of the grave, cleaning up stray bits of caliche clay, patting the walls into a proper residence for the dead.

"Make it perfect, even though no living soul appreciates how fine it is." Big Shorty bounded up the stepladder he'd carefully positioned to avoid marking the walls. "No one but me and the dearly departed." He left the boundaries of the grave as smooth and slick as a chalkboard. "A man could list his secrets on those walls or draw a map to the next world if he knew the way."

The floor of the grave was level and perfectly aligned with the rectangle of space at the top. Big Shorty had created a rectangular polygon of air that would have passed muster with the most exacting mathematician.

"Four inches of tolerance on every side from the top to the bottom. Makes it easy to lower the vault into place." Shorty would be present for that phase of grave preparation, ready to correct accidental scrapes and scratches before the hourly-wage men filled his negative sculpture with loose dirt. "Four inches are as much as I can allow. Should be enough, but sometimes it isn't."

Robert knew all about the sacred number four. The wind had told him. God, how he missed hearing her voice.

"Four principal directions. Four seasons. Four days of fasting for a ceremony." Robert looked at the watch on Shorty's wrist. A timepiece had its uses, even for a recovering schizophrenic. Exactly forty minutes since Sarah went to Flanders. She'd promised her visit would be just long enough to be sure her mother was safe.

Safety is a relative thing inside a mental hospital, especially one that kept a Choctaw witch on staff. Hashilli remained at large. The police actively sought him and Mr. Luna, but they had no plans for the famous Dr. Moon. There was no way a famous psychiatrist could be involved in a kidnapping conspiracy. Not according to the experts.

Different fingerprints were on file for Hashilli, Mr. Luna, and Dr. Moon. The men had different ethnicities and demographics. The police were convinced they could not be the same person, in spite of media leaks to the contrary. Dr. Moon wasn't even a person of interest.

Robert let another four minutes pass. Wasn't that long enough for Sarah to check on Marie? He asked the wind, even though he knew she wouldn't answer.

SARAH BREEZED THROUGH Flanders's security without a hitch. She placed her name on the visitors list and proceeded to the commons.

No one stopped her. No one reacted to her name. No one asked her to explain her role in the escape of the schizophrenic client, Robert Collins.

Flanders was a special kind of a bureaucracy, part medical and part political, and the moieties were at odds. Paper rituals had been organized to reveal detailed personal information while simultaneously concealing identities. Some staff members knew who was who. Some knew what was what. Hardly anyone knew more than that.

The secretarial staff posed the greatest danger. They had computer consoles at their fingertips and special mental compartments devoted to bureaucratic speculation. They knew almost everything, and what they didn't know, they could deduce during their union-mandated fifteen-minute breaks.

Sarah walked the perimeter of the common area as though she were pacing off a temporary soccer field. She expected to find her mother in the center of a group of men actively competing for her attention. Marie Ferraro shared a fan base with professional wrestling matches, NASCAR races, and monster truck rallies. That is to say, males with testosterone-induced judgment deficits.

After three complete circuits of the commons, Sarah heard no male voices raised to the level of mating calls. She witnessed no strutting, muscle flexing, or mock combat. Either Marie was not on the floor, or she was off her game.

Sarah found a seat near a television set where a mixed-gender collection of clients discussed the dramatic nuances of *Days of Our Lives*.

Not many places to hide inside a mental hospital. Marie might be starring in one of her group sessions, or perhaps she'd had a setback and was confined to her room. If she didn't make an appearance soon, Sarah would be forced to expand her intelligence-gathering operation from simple observation to discrete interrogation. Asking questions would raise her threat assessment level on the color scale from yellow to orange if she chose her subjects carefully, all the way to red if she did not.

She wouldn't waste her time the psychiatric residents. Too little knowledge of the clients. Far too anxious to please. An enthusiastic resident might take Sarah's inquiries right to the administrative level. Damn the protests. Full speed ahead.

Nurses never answered questions. They were suspicious of interested relatives and nearly as dangerous as secretaries.

Clients were the safest resource. A man would be more helpful than a woman, not as observant, but less likely to harbor hostility for Marie. Sarah allowed herself ten minutes to select a candidate, but the problem resolved itself spontaneously, as problems often do.

A male client picked Sarah out from the opposite side of the commons and made his way across the floor with little regard for pedestrian traffic. The man was too thin to be considered healthy and too robust to be considered sick. He took long clumsy strides on legs as slender as pipe cleaners, and he made broad inappropriate gestures with arms too long for his body.

"My name is Ben," he told her. "No problem if you don't remember. People seldom do."

Sarah did remember Ben. He was the man who introduced her to "Dr. Collins" when Marie was having problems. Ben wanted to be helpful but was far too nervous to be discrete.

"Marie has gone away." He got right to the point, even before Sarah had time to ask her first question. "Doctor Moon pulled strings. Took her without the proper paperwork. Made the nurses angry. Even residents took notice." He rocked back and forth from heels to toes and back again.

He struck a series of poses that put Sarah in mind of a flamenco dancer. Ben got louder. His discourse grew in length and lost the thread of reason. Not only had Dr. Moon stolen Marie Ferraro, he had assassinated JFK, RFK, and MLK.

"Murdered all the K's," Ben shouted, cupping his hands around his mouth so he could broadcast the news to everyone inside the mental institution. It didn't take him long to catch the orderlies' attention. Two sturdy-looking African American men moved in to investigate the disturbance, but their eyes fixed on Sarah, not on Ben. Their expressions told her they were sorting through their memories. Incident reports, investigations, attempts to assign responsibility to someone who could be fired without creating a problem. Orderlies wouldn't forget things like that.

"Forgive me." She placed one of her feet on one of Ben's. The unbalanced client stood between her and the approaching orderlies. His body was too rail-thin to hide her, but the orderlies could not see the hand she placed on Ben's chest. A gentle shove and fate smiled on Sarah Bible.

When a client hits the floor, rules of triage set in quickly. All else is forgotten. By the time the orderlies had Ben back on his feet, Sarah had disappeared down a hallway.

She needed a disguise, something quick and simple.

Sarah pulled her hair into a severe ponytail and fastened it with a scrunchie retrieved from her shoulder bag. She lifted a soiled white coat from a laundry cart and carried it draped over her left arm. She held her back straight, kept her hips rigid, and walked to the cafeteria. No heterosexual male would give her a second glance.

The women could still see her. Nothing to be done about that. Women notice everything, even when they pretend to be oblivious. But women wouldn't interfere. Sarah was too determined, too busy, too much of a force to be reckoned with. The women would leave it to the men, and the men would do nothing—probably.

Sarah moved quickly through the cafeteria, sending employees scampering before her like a rag tag revolutionary army retreating before a superior force. Thirty steps and she was past the serving lines. Forty more and she was through the kitchen, opening the door onto the parking lot. Exactly the same route she had taken when she liberated Robert. The wind was brisk as Sarah moved beyond the grasp of Flanders security. It carried the scents and sounds of a road repair in progress somewhere to the west.

"Miss." The voice of authority called to her from the kitchen door. "Stop where you are, Miss. I need to speak with you."

Sarah turned to see a uniformed guard moving across the parking lot. He didn't wear a gun, but a spray can in a leather holster and a glittering pair of handcuffs dangled from his belt. Security guards usually traveled in pairs.

Because I am a woman, one is enough.

The guard was young and fit. No sign of paunch over his waistband. His shoulders were broad, and the contours of his shirt hinted at hours spent inside a gym. He'd catch her in a second if she ran. A bluff perhaps.

Flanders security guards weren't real cops. Undoubtedly, they could detain people within the confines of the institution, but did their authority extend as far as the parking lot? Sarah didn't know, and she'd bet the guard didn't either.

He looked decidedly uncertain as he drew closer. His eyes darted left and right, as if trying to decide between two images that both deserved his undivided attention.

The guard's approach slowed. He unsnapped a leather cover on a canister suspended from his belt.

Mace?

"Problem, officer?" Sarah put plenty of base into her voice and kept her consonants crisp, like the female lawyers on Court TV.

The guard didn't look at her. His eyes chose a target behind Sarah and to her right.

Robert Collins stepped from between two parked cars, his clenched right hand extended forward like a Roman soldier saluting the emperor.

"Something for you, officer." He rolled his hand over and opened it, revealing a neatly compressed pyramid of yellow dust on his palm. "Something you should see." His manner contained no residue of threat.

The guard did not withdraw his mace.

"Look closely." Robert spoke in a slow, regular monotone, like a stage hypnotist lulling an audience volunteer into complacent cooperation.

The yellow powder had the guard's full attention. He barely reacted when Robert blew the cloud of mushroom spores into his face.

The Flanders security guard blinked twice and collapsed to the ground as flamboyantly as a drama student committing insurance fraud. Robert carefully positioned the unconscious man, turned the guard's face away from the sun, kept his airway open.

"You followed me." Sarah wanted very much to disapprove, but she could not. "How did you know I'd need you?"

Robert pulled a red construction paper heart from his hip pocket. He pushed it forward, offering it for Sarah's inspection. The word love was written across the top with a black crayon in mixed upper and lower case letters. Two smiling stick figures were drawn at the point of the heart. They were holding hands.

"The wind carried it through the graveyard. Shorty said it was a sign."

Sarah took the construction paper heart and placed it in her shoulder bag, next to Archie Chatto's prison information.

She and Robert walked away from the sleeping security guard. They held hands as they walked, like the stick figures on the construction paper heart.

"Gotta love that wind." She wondered if the wind still thought she was pretty.

23

THE LITTLE CITY used to be called Springtown, but that wasn't odd enough, so locals changed the name to Stringtown. Clearly a higher note on the Okie scale of humor. Marie could name ten strangely-named Oklahoma towns right off the top of her head—Cement, Corn, Pink, Slapout, Gotebo, Bowlegs, Roman Nose, Beer City, Paw Paw, and Tin City. If pressed, she knew another baker's dozen. Most were hardly more than a gas station, a church or two, and a collection of name-related stories too weird for history books.

Stringtown had a minimum-security prison. That's what made it stand out in Marie's mind. Several of her moderately-notorious boyfriends had done time within its razor wire borders. It also had a mental hospital, but she had never heard of that until Dr. Moon brought her there. Marie had to admit the Stringtown Mental Health Facility was a pretty nice place for a crazy house.

According to Dr. Moon, the Choctaw Nation paid the bills. There must have been a lot of them. The place was far more modern than Flanders. Its rooms were nicer. Its common area was bigger. Its grounds had better landscaping. And its therapeutic style was nearly humanitarian—restraints tied with bows, stylish straitjackets, electro-convulsive units powered by dry cell batteries.

Marie felt like the queen of the asylum. It was the perfect place to wait for Archie. The staff was quiet and polite. Most were members of the Five Civilized Tribes, with the numbers slightly weighted in favor of Creek and Choctaw. The rooms were almost private—single occupancy but no locks on the doors. Medications were monitored carefully, and the more potent psychoactive agents were used only on the troublesome minority.

Dr. Moon was an important man at Stringtown, just as he had been at Flanders, but at Stringtown, no one except Marie called him Dr. Moon.

"Here I am known as Doctor Selene," he told Marie. But he wasn't cross when she slipped occasionally and called him by his old familiar name. Selene was one of the moon's many names, after all, and Marie was a client in a mental hospital. The staff would make allowances.

At Stringtown, Marie was Dr. Selene's special patient. He was her only therapist, and when Dr. Selene wasn't around, she had the run of the facility. The other doctors and the support staff allowed her to do as she pleased, as long as she didn't try to leave. They treated her like a royal concubine who was temporarily under house arrest but still a favorite of the king.

Their frequent private sessions were proof of that.

Marie and the doctor sitting in a tree, K-i-s-s-i-n-g. So far that was just a rumor, but things could easily go that way. They'd have passed the point of no return already if Marie hadn't known romantic terrain so well.

When it was time to apply the brakes she told the doctor, "Archie's presence is strong in this place." That always did the trick.

Psychiatrists usually keep a poker face in session. They sit outside the patient's range of vision. They speak in monotones, avoid emotionally charged language. Shrinks had many ways to avoid steering the discussion with inadvertent cues. Dr. Selene didn't use any of them. His face turned sour every time Marie mentioned Archie. Sometimes she'd put *Archie* in the middle of a sentence like punctuation, just to see what happened.

"When I was pregnant with Sarah—*Archie*—I never felt depressed." Worked every time. Like thumping an erection with a pencil. Marie learned that trick from an RN while visiting one of her boyfriends in a prison hospital. Hard to believe a man with a gunshot wound could be so easily aroused. Morphine, handcuffs, and critical injuries barely dull the urge. Marie knew a great deal about men, but she still hadn't figured out why they were so proud of having testicles.

"Archie." Marie said the name apropos of nothing. Dr. Selene's brow furrowed. He crossed his arms. Shouldn't a shrink know better than that? She suspected her sessions with Dr. Selene didn't fit into any accepted therapeutic protocol. She suspected her meetings with this doctor weren't sessions at all, at least in the psychiatric sense of the word.

Marie was pretty certain Dr. Selene was interested in more than her mind. Not too surprising. Men were naturally drawn to her the way male moths were drawn to pheromones secreted innocently by females of their species. Males were all alike. All horny bastards, regardless of genus, species, or even kingdom. When the necessary ingredients came together, things proceeded according to the laws of chemistry. As soon as a man breathed Marie Ferraro's pheromones, his passions ignited like a kitchen match raked across a rough surface.

Bless their hearts. A man's most complex patterns of behavior were at the mercy of that pesky Y chromosome. Once his buttons had been pushed, he reacted as predictably as a butterfly or a bull elk or a tomcat, and Marie had already embarked on the delicate process of finding Dr. Selene's buttons.

It wouldn't take long. she had manipulated romantically-inclined doctors before. Medical men were no more resistant to her charms than plumbers or politicians. With the right incentive, they would put aside moral codes and lifetime aspirations. They would give no thought to consequences until they had waded into the depths of scandal. They'd not panic until their reputations were caught in the undertow, far beyond the possibility of rescue.

But this time, Marie wouldn't slip into her old habits. She would handle Dr. Selene delicately. She wouldn't sleep with him unless it was absolutely necessary. She would remain true to Archie Chatto in her own fashion.

Nothing past second base, she told herself, unless it couldn't be avoided. Marie Ferraro was no callow heartbreaker. It had always been her policy to let a man down easy whenever it was possible.

"Archie is an Apache." Marie watched the doctor's reaction. Her lover's name made his complexion change. Sometimes he flushed. Sometimes he grew pale. It was a flight or fight reaction, she supposed. The psychiatrist didn't know whether to attack or retreat. That was good. Masculine indecision is a girl's best friend, much better than diamonds—except in a pawnshop.

"His great-great-grandfather knew Geronimo. Archie comes from a long line of warriors and medicine men." Marie recognized the signs of eminent collapse. The cracks in Dr. Selene's professional facade grew wider under the pressure of Archie Chatto. The man was a veritable Perma Jack commercial.

Marie fed the doctor tiny bites of boyfriend history, and it made him ravenous. Jealousy is a first-rate romantic appetizer. Her favorite author, Nicholas Sparks, had captured the concept perfectly in *The Guardian*.

Every favorable Archie Chatto statement would make Dr. Selene feel less adequate. He'd be forced to brag about his own accomplishments until she knocked the props completely out from under him with lavish praise for some insanely manly thing her jailbird Apache boyfriend had done.

A pissing contest. Wasn't that what men called it? Such simple creatures. The penis is the standard unit against which every aspect of their world is measured. Men know the exact length of their penises but have only a vague idea of their hat or shoe sizes. An astronomer had once told Marie that the earth and moon were separated by the length of 720,000,000 average length penises. Who could have imagined?

Time to let the doctor talk about himself. There wasn't a man alive who had trouble doing that. Before long he would talk himself into being in love with Marie Ferraro. His most cherished secrets would be hers for the asking. So would his points of vulnerability.

Then Marie would carry the psychiatrist in her hand, use him like a key to unlock the doors of the mental hospital where she was held against her will. Was she the first woman who had seduced the good doctor? Probably.

Once Dr. Selene was set in motion, Marie need only listen. She'd nudge and tease him in the appropriate direction with fine adjustments of tone and facial expression. Sessions were supposed to work this way. It was just a matter of determining who was in control.

———————

THE UNIVERSE RAN according to a rigid set of rules. Hashilli understood that, whether he was Dr. Selene or Mr. Luna or any of a dozen persona he had at his disposal. There were rules involving things like mass and velocity that couldn't be broken. But there were rules of social interaction that were more like cosmic suggestions. A shapeshifter had to have an intimate working knowledge of those social rules to make the world see him as he wanted to be seen.

For the first time in his life, his shapeshifting skills had failed him. Two of his personas were wanted by the police, and one of them was under suspicion. He wouldn't miss Mr. Luna all that much, and he could discard Dr. Moon if he came under too much scrutiny. But Hashilli—that's who he was originally. Everything started with Hashilli. Bits and pieces of him were integral in all the others.

He put those thoughts aside and concentrated on being the perfect Dr. Selene. It was hard to keep his mind on business in his private sessions with Marie. The woman had a way of disarming him.

"Can you heal a mind with words?" She smiled, eyes downcast, allowing him to assert dominance. It felt better than he expected.

"It requires a gentle touch." He understood what she was doing. Marie Ferraro was taking charge of the session, making it about him instead of her. "We listen to where the client wants to go and nudge her in that direction."

He laid one of his hands on one of hers. She didn't pull away. "Where is it you want to go, Marie? I'm listening."

"'I' want to go to Archie." She locked eyes with him, taking charge again. "He's so brave." She lifted her hand away from his and rubbed at the place he'd touched. "Not everyone can be a warrior, I suppose."

"The Apache are little more than savages." Hashilli was surprised at himself, talking to a client this way. He'd never felt it necessary engage in argument. But Marie Ferraro was different. For reasons he did not try to understand, he needed her exclusive approval.

"Apaches drink too much. They fight too much. They do everything too much." It was a sore point with Hashilli that the Five Civilized Tribes had never captured the imagination of the white man like the tribes from the old Wild West.

Euro-Americans heaped praise on the puffed-up philosophies of the Cheyenne and the Sioux. They found much to admire in the brutal warrior lifestyles of the Comanche and the Apache. But the Choctaw, Creek, Cherokee, Chickasaw, and Seminole were treated with contempt.

Hashilli supposed it was because the tribes of the American Southeast had met the white man first. They had seen their destiny written clearly in future history's ledgers and had struck the best deals they could. Because the civilized tribes had acknowledged their fate and made a relatively quick peace, the Europeans held them in low regard.

"Our history is as rich as the Apache," he told Marie. "Our warriors are as fierce, and our magic is as strong." Hashilli wanted to tell this woman everything. For reasons he could not understand, he wanted to fill her to the brim with respect and admiration for the Choctaw culture. Hashilli wanted Marie to recognize him for what he was, an exceptional member of an exceptional tribe. Before he quite knew what he was doing, he found himself telling Marie Ferraro how an attempted murder had established his credentials as a powerful Choctaw sorcerer.

"Catholic babies are adopted into the church with a sprinkling of holy water. Witches are baptized in blood." Hashilli had run his story through his mind so many times, practiced it for an imaginary audience so much, he had every nuance of tone and cadence worked to perfection. He paused and looked at Marie Ferarro the way a university lecturer solicits questions that he clearly hopes no one will dare to ask. She looked puzzled and interested but remained silent as he hoped.

"My grandfather was the most powerful Choctaw witch in centuries. He could poison an enemy's dreams with potions and smoke herbs that foretold the future. He could cure sickness or cast it like a spell. He could hear deception in a liar's voice and curse him with a stutter until he spoke the truth. You might imagine, a man like that made enemies— for things he'd done and things people only imagined."

Hashilli let his Dr. Selene persona go completely, showing Marie the identity he'd carried from the time he first became aware of his destiny. He spread his arms wide and turned in a circle, as if he were trying on a new suit and wanted her opinion.

"Grandfather consulted with his ancestors and selected me as his heir. I had no mother, which meant I had no clan." Choctaw family arrangements wouldn't mean anything to Marie, but having no mother invoked pity, so he moved forward with his story.

"Women of the Maytubby family took turns caring for me. Each morning the new nursemaid would paddle a jon boat across the Kiamichi River to Grandfather's cabin. She'd walk through the blood grass meadow that surrounded the house, whistling or singing so no one would take her for an intruder."

Marie perked up as he described the cabin. Hashilli hoped she was starting to realize how much better it was to be with a man of power than a brute Apache who was too incompetent to stay beyond the reach of the law.

"My favorite nursemaid—so they tell me—was an Italian girl who'd married into the family. Eleonora was her name. I'm told it means shining light. She was the only woman who ever touched me with love."

Hashilli told this story as if it was a memory rather than something Grandfather told him. He'd refined it, smoothed the rough edges and polished so thoroughly it seemed more real than any other thing in his past.

"She'd carry me through the four rooms of the shotgun shack—four rooms you could see through from one side to the other, you understand. She'd hold a bottle to my lips and sing as she danced me through the parlor and the kitchen."

In his mind he and Eleonora looked like the Madonna and Child sculpted by Michelangelo in the Church of Our Lady.

"She was dancing with me on the day an assassin came to take revenge on Grandfather." Hashilli stooped and pretended to be the killer making his way slowly through blood grass that left tiny scratches as it brushed against his skin.

"Murdering a witch is a dangerous business, but killing his heir was a much simpler matter—a clanless baby, carried by a nursemaid who wasn't even Choctaw. One clean shot and the line of magic men would be cut in the Maytubby family. The murderer moved close enough to be sure of his target. He aimed the gun as Eleonora danced from room to room."

Hashilli held an imaginary pistol in his hand, aimed down the invisible barrel. His hand jumped as he fired the fatal shot.

"Eleonora spun as he pulled the trigger. The bullet struck her in the neck above the collarbone. Severed arteries filled the room with a fine red mist that left its stain on everything. We fell to the floor, her body over mine, both of us silenced by her death. The gunman looked carefully through the kitchen window and then ran back to an anonymous life of nightly prayers and troubled dreams. Not once did he consider the gift of power he had given to the youngest sorcerer in the Maytubby family."

He gave Marie a moment to consider what that gift of power might be.

"The bullet might have killed me, but it took Eleonora instead. It collected a blood sacrifice on the way to its final resting place in the wall. The bullet is a talisman. The assassin turned Grandfather's shotgun shack into a shrine to the power of the newest Maytubby sorcerer."

Hashilli took a bow.

"You are the only one outside the family who knows the story of the magic bullet. In all these years, the only one I've trusted with this secret."

Marie clapped her hands the way she would at the end of a play. She smiled at Hashilli and held it longer than he expected. Her expression lost its sweetness as it faded. "I think I've been there." She looked as if she wanted to take that statement back. Hashilli was practically giddy with excitement.

"It must have been the same place," she said. "My first lover and I hid there, between bank robberies and shoot outs."

He lost a bit of his enthusiasm when she mentioned another lover. He had Archie to worry about, and that was quite enough.

"I saw the stains and the hole in the kitchen wall but never realized what they were." She shook her head as if she were trying to deny the miraculous fact of their intersecting histories.

"The blood grass was still there. No termites damage even though the place was very old. Insects didn't fly through the broken windows. The roof never leaked even in the hardest rain."

He took note of the rising pitch of her voice as she recited all the evidence of magic.

"No bird nests clogged the chimney," she said. "It still drew smoke from the wood fires we burned in the kitchen stove."

Hashilli recognized the signs. He had taken Marie Ferarro to the edge of surrender. It wouldn't require much to push her over. He played the philosophy card. "Fate has brought us together, Marie. When destiny decides, it's no use for mortals to resist." He grimaced as he quoted a line he once heard from a Lifetime TV movie, but it seemed like the sort of dialogue she would find appealing.

Marie was silent for a moment, thoughtful, perhaps a little vulnerable—all good signs. She took his hands, looked into his eyes, and said, "You paint a beautiful picture, Doctor."

He offered her his most charming smile. He would have kissed her, but she dropped his hands and leaned away from him.

"But I'm in love with Archie, and there is no such thing as witches, so I'm afraid destiny has got it wrong."

24

"HOW HARD COULD it be to track down a world-famous psychiatrist?" Sarah was a true believer in the gods of the Internet. With Google and a few well-chosen descriptors, she could find out anything about anybody.

"I'll start with an easy one." Her fingers clattered across the keyboard.

Famous Dr. Moon got her a Civil War physician—losing side—a Korean religious fanatic, and a cookie recipe.

"First try doesn't count." She added Oklahoma to the search line and clicked the mouse on *I'm feeling lucky.*

"How the hell does that lead to a real estate company in Claremore?"

"Can't find real indigenous people on computers." She could barely hear Robert's voice over the sound of Pella windows being pushed open and screens snapping into place. Soon, the wind was blowing through in every room of Victoria and Albert's guesthouse.

Robert told her, "They're hard to track. Especially if they don't want to be found."

"Damn!" Sarah liked dual-purpose expletives—half aimed at Google and half at the annoying man who still believed he could glean information from moving columns of air.

"It's not the heat. It's the humidity," Robert said, as if that explained everything.

Good heart. Bad brain. She had to admit he was better now that the voices were gone, but he hadn't given up being crazy.

"I suppose the wind told you all about tracking Native Americans?" Sarah immediately regretted the snide remark, but, as usual, Robert was oblivious.

He unpacked the three electric fans he'd persuaded her to buy and proceeded to create a mini-cyclone in the living room.

"Not natural but adequate," he said. She supposed his fixation on wind was better than the fascination most men had with breasts. They didn't mind if those were natural either.

"Hashilli's no ordinary man." Robert raised his voice loud enough to be heard above the breeze and the drone of Chinese-manufactured electric motors. "He's a witch, and witches are *way* hard to find."

"*Way* hard?" Crazy talk was bad enough without the pop culture adverbs. Sarah made several athletic sweeps of her mouse.

"Ah ha!" She couldn't resist gloating when she got a dozen hits with her new entry. "No one can hide from Sarah Bible, internationally renowned search-Injun scout."

But it didn't take her long to see that all her Google trails led nowhere. She found a number of newspaper articles in the *Tulsa World* and the *Oklahoman,* even a couple of human-interest stories in the *Norman Transcript,* but nothing in any other newspapers, not even in the six surrounding states.

The famous Dr. Moon had been a guest lecturer at the University of Oklahoma, Tulsa University, and the University of Central Oklahoma on topics ranging from criminal profiling to late onset autism.

Dr. Moon received a collection of honorary degrees from public and private colleges, featuring a variable first initial instead of a first name. H. Moon, Ph.D. (hon.), L. Moon, Ed.D. (hon.), and S. Moon, D.P.H. (hon.). All Internet dead ends.

He'd been given public accolades for organizing fundraisers and humanitarian enterprises by numerous state societies and religious organizations, but none of his endeavors withstood the scrutiny of the most cursory examination. He was on boards of charities that did not exist and attended meetings that never took place.

Feeding the imaginary poor with pretend food, like a little girl's tea party. Dr. Moon's fraudulent activities should have been transparent to anyone who cared to investigate, but apparently no one ever did. Newspapers printed stories based on information that must have been provided by Dr. Moon himself. Even that was inconsistent.

Journalists characterized his nationality as Asian, with oblique references to India, Sri Lanka, Pakistan, and Afghanistan, but no place of birth was ever specified.

His press-resume listed several foreign universities with exotic names, but when Sarah refined her search, she found that many of those institutions did not exist. Of those that did exist, most did not offer degrees in psychology or psychiatry, and those that trained mental health professionals did not list Doctor Moon as a degree recipient.

As I was going up the stair, I saw a man who wasn't there.

The good doctor was not a member of the American Medical Association or the Oklahoma Medical Association—which Sarah learned were merely political organizations—but he had a valid license issued by the Oklahoma Board of Medicine and a permit from the Drug Enforcement Agency allowing him to dispense and prescribe controlled substances. Neither of these organizations listed a first name for the famous Dr. Moon—that had to be illegal—and according to both, he lived and practiced at Flanders Mental Hospital.

By the end of her search, Sarah had not found so much as a telephone number, a street address, or an associate who might give her a viable lead.

"It seems that Doctor Moon is only world famous in Oklahoma."

Robert didn't say, "I told you so." He didn't punish her with a smug expression. Bad brain. Very good heart.

"Well, there are more ways to the woods than one." Years of doing stealth background checks on her mother's boyfriends had sharpened Sarah's skills as a social engineer. Her prepaid cell phone would give her all the anonymity she would need to tap the only resource she was certain would have information on the elusive Dr. Moon. She placed a call to Flanders Hospital pretending to be a reporter assigned to do a humanities piece on the good doctor.

After a few minutes schmoozing, she broached secretarial defenses and was connected with a mid-level administrator responsible for public relations. Sarah suggested that her call had been solicited by someone very high on the bureaucratic food chain.

"Wise men from the east, bearing gifts," she said. East coast or west, it didn't really matter. People with money always lived near the water. "I'm sure you know who I mean." Mid-level administrators often show their ignorance, but they never acknowledge it. Sarah knew the species well.

"Soft money is so hard to find these days." She tempted him with the attention of the National Institutes of Mental Health who seemed, of late, to have an open checkbook policy for institutions with a positive public image.

"Unsullied by scandal. Favored in the public eye. Blessed with a crisp exciting mission statement." Sentence fragments were good enough— large print sentiments suitable for a bumper sticker. Sarah sought coop- eration, not action. Verbs were superfluous.

She dropped names of grant application reviewers like a breadcrumb trail for her Flanders administrator to follow. Made up names, but who's to know?

Before long, the man was throwing information like confetti at a New Year's celebration. He opened the doctor's file and found answers to every question Sarah asked.

The problem was none of the information in Dr. Moon's personnel file was any use at all. The home address was fictitious, his telephone number was no longer in service, and the person to contact in case of emergency re- sided in Istanbul, Texas, a city that existed only in the doctor's imagination.

"Damn, that's what I get for talking to a public relations officer in a mental hospital." According to Sarah, anyone with that job description had to be a loser.

"Probably the first cousin of the governor's bastard son. Maybe just the second cousin." Someone in Flanders was bound to know where she could find Dr. Moon, but she'd have to climb a bit higher on the administrative ladder.

Doing voices was not one of Sarah's strengths, but with the aid of a generic European accent, she easily reached deep into the inner circle of personnel management. She presented herself as a full professor of humanities at the University of Oklahoma. When the personnel director picked up the phone, she added the ragged timber of a smoker to her voice. She spoke in smooth confluent tones that conveyed flawless skin, voluptuous curves, and the moral standards of a goat. She'd spent hours listening to her mother work a phone sex job during the *love recession* that followed 9/11.

"We are preparing a stipend check for your Doctor Moon, but we need some information for our records." Sarah kept a close eye on Robert and adjusted the strength of her improvisation based on his reaction. He was her sexual barometer, and a high-pressure zone was moving through the area.

Sorry, partner.

Robert's pupils expanded to the size of Arkansas blueberries. He leaned forward and fixed his attention on Sarah like a coyote appreciating a full moon.

"The doctor was a dear to speak to our little group. He had such an effect on me." Time to pause a moment. Exhale suggestively. Not a pant exactly but close.

Sarah snapped her fingers. She pointed at a chair across the room and motioned for Robert to take a seat. A third grader would have understood her perfectly, but he was thinking at a sixth grade level. A nasty little sixth grader with early onset puberty.

"I let him slip away without getting his address," she told the administrator. "Or even so much as his first name." The nervous laughter following Sarah's confession conveyed a sense of vulnerability men are seldom able to resist.

Kryptonite. Take that, Superman.

Sarah had learned this skill at her mother's knee, the way some girls learned to bake a pie or prepare chicken and dumplings. Marie enjoyed manipulating men, but Sarah never did. Sexual politics could have devastating results even on unintended targets. She could see the look on Robert's face—not love but infatuation.

Which is worse?

"I would be ever so grateful for anything you could tell me," she said. "The good Doctor Moon will never have to know what a naughty girl I've been."

Men loved naughty girls, even Robert. He'd resorted to mouth breathing. Not a pretty sight, but the only way to take in enough oxygen to fuel the metabolism of lust. Too late to make him leave the room. Sarah hoped her deception had a similar effect on the Flanders administrator.

The personnel manager clearly wanted to be helpful, especially after Sarah told him she would bring the check to him in person, "If only I can get some information for my records, you see."

She promised to be, "Ever so grateful," for the second time in less than a minute and would find a way to "Demonstrate my gratitude."

"We could go for coffee or for dinner or for something else. We can think of something else, I'm sure."

"Eager to please," was how the personnel manager described himself.

"Very, very eager to please," he said, loud enough to clear up any ambiguity about his willingness to accommodate the unknown temptress on the phone. But his information was in an unfortunate state of completion. He promised to update it and fill in the blanks as soon as Dr. Moon returned to Flanders.

The personnel manager couldn't say exactly when that would be. "He's on indefinite leave, you see, training psychiatric outreach workers somewhere in Africa."

Sarah decided then and there hospital administrators were idiot-school rejects in addition to being time-wasting SOBs. She was overwhelmed with the fierce urge to punish. Pinching was out of the question. Verbal abuse would have to do.

"Unusual project for a psychiatrist." Not all the sexual innuendo had disappeared from Sarah's voice, but her tone changed enough to put the administrator on the defensive.

"How so?"

"First of all," Sarah said. "Africa is a continent. If I wanted to tell someone where I would be working for the next several weeks, I wouldn't provide the North American Continent as my forwarding address."

"And there are only two countries on our continent," she continued, "While there are nearly sixty in Africa." Sarah knew how to suck all the warmth out of a telephone conversation.

She pictured the administrator on the other end. Midriff bulge pushing over his belt buckle. Clip-on necktie askew. His smile already turned into a grimace. His comb-over had come unstuck. His ego was shrinking so fast it might fall into the telephone receiver any second.

Sticks and stones can break your bones, but words can leave a nasty bruise on the self-esteem. Sarah knew this administrator would take out his frustrations on someone else once the quiver left his voice and he selected an adequately defenseless target. Secretaries were too dangerous. Maybe a custodian. A non-minority would be best.

"I'm certain Doctor Moon has gone to the country with the greatest need," he said. "Where he can help the most unfortunate people."

"Those pesky Africans. I suppose psychiatry is a pressing issue," Sarah said, "On a continent where twenty percent of the population is at war at any given time, a continent where AIDS is an epidemic, where obtaining therapeutic drugs is practically impossible, where children are unvaccinated, and starvation is a way of life."

She went on to tell the administrator that Africa was the spiritual home of the Horsemen of the Apocalypse, so "It's no wonder, people who live there are in such dire need of counseling."

The personnel manager assured her that psychiatry was much more than simple counseling.

"Ah, yes," Sarah said, "Doctor Moon must be kept quite busy teaching tribesmen with no training to administer drugs they can't obtain for illnesses they can't diagnose. If all else fails, he'll learn hundreds of tribal languages and teach talk therapy to his crew of barefoot analysts. The average bushman could pick up neurolinguistic skills in a matter of weeks since he isn't burdened with the unnecessary refinements of education."

"Madam, I hardly think—"

Sarah interrupted him with the three favorite words of nondirectional therapists. "Please go on." She drew an exasperated breath and exhaled loudly into the telephone.

"That's all they really need," she said. "Those three words are the heart and soul of talk therapy, just those words and a meaningful pause—that's a thirty second pause in layman's terms." She gave him one of those meaningful pauses so he could see just how effective it could be, but before it became truly meaningful, she heard a dial tone.

"Looks like our hour's up, you simpering bastard."

Robert's eyes lost their adoring look. He mumbled something that sounded to Sarah like an apology for the crime of being male.

She summoned up her most indulgent smile. It felt contrived. Probably looked that way too.

"I suppose I was a little hard on the poor guy, but once I got started, I couldn't seem to stop." Was that why parents beat their children?

Well, judge, when a little shake didn't shut him up, I shook him harder. Guess it worked. He's been quiet for a long time now. Sarah felt something nibbling at the edges of her conscience. It wasn't guilt. It was more like satisfaction.

25

"JUST LIKE ELECTROCONVULSIVE therapy." Robert had backed away from Sarah, far enough to give him a few precious moments in case she attacked.

"What?" Her voice still had an edge, not sharp enough for surgery but still dangerous.

He moved a tentative step closer. Women had so many ways to hurt a man. They could lay you low with a look. They could wound you with a word. They could strip you of your senses with an unspoken promise. Robert recognized the collection of conflicting emotions dominating his thought processes. Clarity—God, how he hated clarity.

"Watching you," he said. "Listening to your voice. It's like electroconvulsive therapy, only without the memory loss and the headache."

Sarah responded with a blank look and a shrug.

"Take it as a compliment," he told her. "Maybe I'm cured. Between you and Hashilli's mushroom dust." He took a moment to sort through his core values.

Less than ten seconds. A depressingly small inventory.

"Nope," he said. "Still crazy." He started to smile but thought better of it. Crazy people don't get to the dentist very often. He'd check on the status of his front teeth later. Concern about his appearance was a sure sign of returning sanity. Damn it. He was getting better.

"Don't you want to be… normal?"

"I can't be normal, but I can fake it," Robert said. "The wind taught me how normal people talk." He did a couple of one-sentence imitations—a cop dressing down a youthful offender, a restaurant manager who didn't allow crazy people in his establishment. Perfect execution. He knew it even before Sarah applauded.

"The wind is a good teacher," she said. "Think you can do a lawyer. A *quien es mas macho* kind of guy who drinks straight whiskey, files frivolous lawsuits, and talks dirty."

Robert stood silently in the breeze of his oscillating fans and considered the possibilities.

"Sure. The wind is full of lawyer talk, and I've watched hours of *Law and Order* and *Judge Judy.*"

He understood immediately. The mental health establishment was more afraid of lawyers than psychopaths. They couldn't drug attorneys into submission, and lobotomy was out of the question. A nasty lawyer with press connections might make the Flanders administrators give Dr. Moon up, even if it meant losing a sizable slice in the hospital's budget.

"Pigs crowded around a government trough," Sarah said. "They won't talk with their mouths full, until the slaughterhouse truck is in the parking lot."

"I can't drive a truck," Robert said. "But it always looked like fun, being a lawyer."

Sarah stood in front of him. She placed her right hand on his head and recited pseudo-Latin phrase she had read on the wall of the lady's room of the Student Union at the University of New Mexico.

"*Illegitimi non carborundum.* Don't let the bastards grind you down." She tapped Robert on the left shoulder, then the right, and then crossed herself. "By the power vested in me by the state of Pandemonium, I declare that Robert Collins is an attorney for the day."

She retrieved her cell phone and punched in the Flanders number.

"How many anthropologists have committed a mental hospital's number to memory?"

A rhetorical question. Robert was familiar with the concept, but this was the first one he'd ever recognized. Dear God, another sign of sanity.

Sarah's transformation to the personality-lite legal secretary of Robert's imaginary law firm was instantaneous and complete. Faint traces of a Hispanic accent colored her voice as she winnowed her way through the bureaucratic obstacle course and finally made it to an administrator allegedly responsible for admissions and discharge.

"Hold, please." Sarah muffled the phone under her arm. "Sounds like the personnel manager I just talked to. I don't think this is going to work."

Robert had only been a lawyer for a few minutes, and he wasn't going to miss his big opportunity. He extended his hand, made a grabbing motion with his fingers. Sarah handed him the telephone. She mouthed the words, "Be careful," as Robert embarked on his brilliant legal career.

At that moment Robert knew exactly *quien es mas macho*.

"This is attorney at law Robert Mariah speaking," he said, before the personnel manager could introduce himself. "My firm has been retained by Sarah Bible to secure the discharge of Ms. Bible's mother, Marie Ferraro, from Flanders Mental Hospital. This call will be recorded to assure no one's rights are violated. "Do you understand?"

The administrator didn't answer right away, but he breathed into his telephone like an obscene caller. "I guess so. Look, maybe you should be talking to the hospital's legal counsel."

Robert told him that was probably going to happen. "Unless we can straighten out our business here and now and save everyone a bushel basket full of trouble." He'd heard that colloquial metaphor on the one and only episode of *Matlock* he had ever seen. It had worked for Andy Griffith, and it seemed to break the ice with this mid-level bureaucrat.

"First of all," Robert said, "I need you to state your name for the record."

"Well, I don't know."

"If you make me come over there, mister, I will get your name all right. It will be printed in big bold letters on a subpoena. Then, unless I miss my guess, it will be printed on a pink slip that explains why you lost your job."

The administrator said his name too quickly for Robert to understand, then added, "You can call me Tim."

"Well, Tim, perhaps you can tell me why our court-appointed shrink is having such a tough time arranging an interview with Ms. Ferraro."

"I wasn't aware—"

"You fuck with me, Tim, and my head will be so far up your ass, you'll have Brylcreem on your breath."

"Really, I—"

"Think long and hard, Tim. A little dab'll do ya. Know what I mean?"

"I don't think—"

"You have three seconds to tell me where the lady is, Tim, and if you don't, it will be my pleasure to come over there and rub your nose in the biggest pile of legal shit you have ever seen. Am I making myself clear, or do I have to put that in layman's terms?"

"Marie Ferraro has been removed from the hospital by one of our contract psychiatrists. He did it without authorization, and we don't know where she was taken."

"That contract psychiatrist would be the famous Doctor Moon, wouldn't it, Tim?"

"Yes, sir."

"Anything else you would like to tell me? For the record, I mean."

"Well, sir." Tim sounded like his vocal chords might be having a second bout with puberty. Robert wondered if intense harassment might be the key to eternal youth.

"I'm waiting, Tim."

"Well, sir." Tim took the time to swallow a bolus of saliva that must have been the approximate size and texture of an egg yolk. "Just please don't come over here."

Robert ended the call with the push of a button. He didn't say goodbye.

Over the years, Robert had occasion to meet quite a few administrators of mental hospitals. Tim was the first one to call him sir.

"Being mean was sort of fun."

Sarah said, "You might have been a little over the top."

"Fuck yeah!"

"I can almost smell bourbon on your breath."

"Fuck yeah! Four fingers of Wild Turkey, neat."

"You can drop the tough guy routine now Robert." She turned a fan in his direction. It disturbed his hair but soothed his personality.

"Sorry. Any idea what our next step should be?"

"Archie Chatto," Sarah told him. "As much as I hate to admit it, Archie Chatto might be our only hope."

She was right. Robert could feel it in the depths of his borrowed soul.

26

A LOT OF important places were lined up along the remains of old Route 66. That was the only reason the Federal Department of Transportation hadn't put the mother road in a home. El Reno Federal Correctional Institution was on the road a little over thirty miles west of the Crazy Snake Gambling Casino. Not a long drive, unless your passenger was getting accustomed to his sanity and wanted to talk about it. Sarah tried her best to ignore Robert's discourse on the cosmic unity.

"Just imagine. People gambling in the Crazy Snake right now will eventually do hard federal time just down the road." It looked like he was prepared to say a lot more about the Alpha and Omega of criminal activity and the mystical connection between all things.

"Enough of that crap." Rolling down the windows of her Subaru changed things immediately. His monologue deteriorated into nonsense syllables as the wind blew across his face. Robert's canine-like reaction to the wind in his face was annoying, too, but it at least it wasn't New Age annoying.

"You've got the ID Professor Lindsay sent you?" Was the head nodding a response or part of some schizophrenic recovery ritual? She should have asked her questions before surrendering Robert to the influence of the wind.

"Can you hear me?"

He removed a laminated card from his shirt pocket and shoved it in front of her eyes, severely compromising her view of oncoming traffic.

"Good." She pushed his hand aside and used her peripheral vision to watch him return the card to his pocket. Passing Robert Collins off as Archie's spiritual adviser was a real Hail Mary, but Archie had insisted she bring her "male companion" when she came to visit him, and no one could visit a federal inmate without a photo ID.

"Do you know anything about the Native American Church?"

"Sure." Robert held his right hand out the window and made it perform a series of aerobatic maneuvers.

"Can you answer questions about the religion if the authorities quiz you?"

"I've heard ceremonies carried on the wind. I remember quite a lot."

"Why do you suppose Archie wants to see you?"

"Probably lonely," Robert told her. "And I don't think Archie wants you to travel alone."

Probably right on both counts. She doubted if Archie's friends and relatives would pass muster with the National Criminal Information Center, and his cultural background gave him no reason to be confident in the abilities of women.

Too late for second thoughts. But Sarah still had a few as she pulled into the prison parking lot. An armed guard stopped them at the gate. A plastic badge on his uniform shirt identified him as Sgt. Buford Troxel. He wore a matching name belt confirming his identity. As if anyone would pretend to be Sgt. Buford Troxel.

The guard was a suspicious man. He checked Sarah's name and Robert's against a visitors list. He took their photo IDs into a guard station and made a call. Sarah wondered if the guard's paranoia was a sign of thoroughness or a symptom of mental instability. Not that it mattered.

Sergeant Troxel returned their IDs. He produced a paper and read a list of rights visitors agreed to waive while they were on FCI property.

He made Sarah pop her trunk so that he could look inside. He put on a pair of rubber gloves and searched her shoulder bag. She watched his lips move as he read the label on a box of Tampons. Thank god she'd left Hashilli's pistol with Big Shorty.

"Can't take the bag inside," he told her. "Best to lock it in the trunk. The institution's not responsible for theft." The guard produced a saucer size, angled mirror on a stick—like a dental mirror for a giant. He inspected the undercarriage of her Subaru with the disinterested concentration of a gynecologist completing his final pelvic exam of the day.

"Don't usually take such precautions," he told her. "But the Vice President is here."

"In prison?" Sarah wondered how much time he'd have to serve.

"Just in the state. Can't have him killed here in Oklahoma."

Somehow looking at the reflection of a rusty drive shaft would keep the second most powerful man in the free world safe. Sarah wanted to ask Buford Troxel how, but she was afraid his answer might make sense.

The front entrance of the prison led into a large room that reminded Sarah of a hotel lobby. Her ID and Robert's were checked by a young African American woman in civilian clothes. She gave them visitor's passes attached to fiberglass loops they were to wear around their necks.

"Follow Officer Bryant." The receptionist pointed at a pot-bellied, uniformed man in his mid-fifties. He had a rim of bright red hair circling his sun-damaged scalp, like Bozo the Clown's evil twin.

They passed through so many sets of double-locked doors that Sarah lost count. They walked through a stationary metal detector. Something called an Ion Track Detection Unit found them to be free of narcotics, barbiturates, amphetamines, and explosives—everything you need for a Fourth of July celebration. They were just about to go into the visiting room when a young guard with crew cut, almost invisible, blond hair pulled them aside.

"Program lieutenant wants to see you," the guard said. He escorted them into an empty room and told them, "Make yourselves comfortable," indicating a circle of folding metal chairs that were totally inconsistent with the concept of comfort. "Won't be long."

Sarah checked the door to the room as soon as she was certain they were alone. Locked.

An hour later the door opened, and two men entered.

The taller of the two wore a blue blazer with insignia on his lapels that, Sarah presumed, indicated he held the rank of lieutenant. He introduced his companion but not himself. "This is the prison chaplain. He has some questions."

Why do bad things happen to good people? Sarah thought but did not say.

The chaplain seated himself in a chair on the opposite side of the circle from Robert and Sarah. The program lieutenant stood behind him, conveying the image of authority.

"The Native American Church," the chaplain said. For the first time, Sarah noticed the Bible in his right hand.

"The Native American Church." He pointed an index finger at Robert as if he were pretending to be a stick-up-man in a game of cops and robbers.

"I understand you are an ordained minister in that church. Tell me all about it."

If Robert was rattled by the chaplain's interrogation technique, Sarah could see no signs of it. Robert tipped his head from side to side, smiling intermittently as if considering the most appropriate way to answer.

"I'm not exactly a minister," he said finally. "My congregation thinks of me as a Roadman."

The chaplain moved his hands as if he were about to applaud Robert's answer. But doing so would have entailed thumping a hand against his Bible, an innocent action that God might easily misinterpret.

"On the peyote road." The chaplain forced a smile. Sarah couldn't tell if it signified happiness or an impending bowel movement. "By golly, I believe you're the first one I've ever met."

Apparently, Robert had persuaded the prison minister of his authenticity with a single word, roadman. She was pretty sure Robert had never been a member of the Native American Church. She was equally certain of his lack of any formal education in theology or anthropology. She doubted if he had graduated high school. Maybe he'd met an authentic roadman during his extensive walk with schizophrenia. She hoped the chaplain's interview/interrogation wouldn't explore his depth of knowledge too far, but the prison minister was clearly enjoying himself. The man's opportunities to discuss comparative religion were probably limited.

"Do you practice the half-moon ceremony?" The chaplain asked. He drew a deep breath as if preparing to add considerable detail to his question, but Robert didn't give him a chance.

"All roadmen participate in the occasional half-moon ceremony out of respect for the great Comanche founder of the faith, Quanah Parker."

The chaplain fidgeted in his chair like a four-year old. He squeezed his Bible, licked his lips, and waited impatiently for his turn to speak while Robert Collins, certified schizophrenic and ersatz roadman, told him things he already knew.

"Most favor the cross-fire ceremony. We find the trappings of Christianity comforting."

Sarah watched the prison minister digest Robert's "trappings of Christianity" statement. She could see an emotional outburst taking shape behind his eyes, pushing tears to the surface and then pulling them back again. She was in the process of formulating an apology and had almost found the right words when the chaplain surprised her with his unconditional approval.

"Outstanding!" The prison minister twisted his body in his chair so that he could make eye contact with the program lieutenant who stood quietly behind him. "Parker was wounded in a battle with U.S. troops. He would have died of infection if a group of Peyoteros hadn't treated him with decoctions of the sacred cactus." He turned back to Robert, bursting with pride in his knowledge.

"The Native American Church began with Parker's healing visions." The chaplain filled the room with wisdom so fast that Robert could not comment. He quoted Quanah Parker. "The white man goes into this church and talks about Jesus. The Indian goes into his Tipi and talks with Jesus."

The chaplain appeared willing and able to continue for the rest of the day, but when he began a monologue on the fabled white peyote of the Grand Canyon, the program lieutenant stopped him.

"So, it's all right for them to visit Archie Chatto?"

"Yes, of course." The chaplain apologized for his enthusiasm. "A spiritual advisor like Mister Collins is exactly what Archie needs." The prison minister rose from his chair and shook hands, first with Robert and then with Sarah.

"The Lord's work is a fascinating mystery," he said to no one in particular.

"So true," Sarah agreed. The only thing more fascinating was a recovering schizophrenic who could impersonate a lawyer one day and a roadman the next. Robert's skill as an impersonator was almost as good as Hashilli's. That observation made her a little uncomfortable. She brushed it quickly aside.

Archie walked across the visiting room with the deliberate dignity of a condemned man. He embraced Sarah briefly and shook hands with Robert as firmly and professionally as an insurance salesman.

"Thank you for coming." He led them to three chairs he had moved to the edge of the room and seated himself with his back against the wall. Sarah didn't sound convincing when she told Archie how happy she was to see him. She proceeded without noticeable interruption to tell him of Marie's involuntary stay at Flanders and how she had been spirited away by a contract psychologist who was also a kidnapper, a murderer, and, apparently, a Choctaw witch. "Professor Lindsay told me you might be able to help, but I don't see how that's possible."

Archie crossed his arms, stretching the fabric of his khaki prison shirt to its elastic limit. "I'm good at finding things," he said. "Lost possessions, animals, people who have been hidden away—I can find them. I can find your mother, once I am out of prison."

"My mother or my sister?" Sarah guessed it hadn't taken Archie long to penetrate Marie's deception.

Archie stage whispered, "Don't worry about it Jake. It's Chinatown."

Robert looked confused, but Sarah told him it was a line from her mother's favorite Roman Polanski movie.

"I knew everything important about your mom weeks before he met her," Archie said. "I followed Marie the way a timber wolf trails an antelope," he said. "I could pick out her tracks, identify her scent, predict the streams where she would take water and the meadows where she would graze."

The naturalist metaphor sounded perverse to Sarah. "You knew she was bipolar?"

"Incomprehensible, like all of Usen's best creations." Archie fixed his gaze on Robert. "The Apache have always appreciated such people."

Robert nodded. It would be inaccurate to say he wasn't a part of the conversation, even though he uttered not a single word.

"The silence of endless space and deep water," is how Archie put it. "The silence of dead ancestors and unborn children." Archie kept his eyes on Robert while Sarah absorbed his words. "This man will play a key role in my escape. I know it the way I know I am alive."

Archie's trial began in four days.

Sarah didn't attach much importance to the number four, but she knew Archie did. Four principal directions, four seasons, the four essential elements of the world—air, fire, water, and earth. Four was the most critical cipher in Native American numerology.

"Room three thirty-four in Judge Arthur Rakestraw's courtroom in the Oklahoma County Court House." The federal government had released Archie for trial by the state, even though it was a federal agent he was accused of murdering.

"No risk of double jeopardy," he explained. "If the state doesn't convict me, the feds can try me on a slightly different charge."

He told Sarah he'd been tried in Arthur Rakestraw's courtroom once before. "A three story drop to the pavement. No bars on the windows. They are practically inviting defendants to jump."

"Wouldn't you be killed by the fall?" Sarah asked.

"Your crazy boyfriend will figure out a way to catch me."

She considered denying Robert was her boyfriend but didn't. So many big mistakes. A little one like that wouldn't matter.

"Crazy games are won by crazy players," Archie said. "And Robert has the makings of a champ."

Two red splotches grew on Robert's cheeks. His eyes found a neutral spot half-way between Archie and Sarah. "In the land of the blind," he said, "the one-eyed man is considered delusional."

Sarah had no idea what he meant.

27

TWO TRIPS TO El Reno Federal Prison in three days. Sarah was practically on a first name basis with Sgt. Buford Troxel. She hurried Robert from the parking lot to the registration desk so they'd get through security before visitation started. She signed the proper forms and showed the proper identification, but the chaplain came to meet her before she walked through the metal detector.

"Archie wants to talk to the roadman alone." The prison minister was humble but firm. "Can't go against the inmate's wishes on this matter."

Sarah tried to object, but prison regulations were in place that would protect an inmate's religious freedom while the government locked him in a six by eight foot cell and took away everything else he held dear.

"Chatto's attitude made a substantial improvement." The chaplain escorted her to a conference room where she sat at table with three other rejected visitors. Apparently this sort of thing happened often enough to have a protocol.

"Sorry for your inconvenience," the chaplain told her.

She imagined he got a lot of practice saying that in an institution primarily devoted to punitive inconvenience.

A women with bad skin and numerous amateur tattoos on her arms asked Sarah, "What's your man in for?"

"Spiritual counseling." That seemed to satisfy everyone's curiosity. Sarah sat in silence for almost an hour while a psychotic fake roadman counseled a murderer on matters of faith and conscience. Was there any chance this nonsense would help her find her mom?

She had spent her childhood reacting to the whims of a mother who was certifiably unqualified to make important decisions. Now that she was all grown up, the actors were different, but the script was still the same.

MATTERS OF ARCHIE'S soul made for a tense ride back to Oklahoma City. Sarah used the master control of her Subaru to roll up all the windows so Robert would be forced to listen to her complaints.

"I thought it was especially touching that he sent word for me to deposit fifty dollars in his commissary account, but I suppose a man can't be expected to live on transcendental enlightenment."

"Think of it as cover," Robert said, fidgeting with the electrical control that up until now had allowed him access to the wind. "For the first time since he was incarcerated, Archie has money in his account, something to come back for."

"Fifty dollars-worth of canned soup, toothpaste, and chocolate bars." Sarah didn't think that was much incentive.

She lowered Robert's window half an inch, shaping his behavior the same way B.F. Skinner rewarded pigeons for pecking buttons in the proper order.

"I told Archie all of our adventures." The window lowered another quarter of an inch. "He was impressed with the way you broke me out of Flanders."

Another quarter inch of window sank into the door panel.

"And how you knocked Hashilli unconscious." Robert waited, but the window didn't move.

"Try harder." Sarah drummed her fingers beside the automatic window control.

"He was interested in the spirit powder, the way it knocks out most people but only made my voices go away. Something Hashilli and I have in common. For some reason, it doesn't anesthetize us." The window opened a full inch this time.

"Archie wanted to know all about Big Shorty. We're his troops. That's what he said." The window eased open to the halfway mark.

"He wants Big Shorty to be with us when he jumps to freedom. He says a man like that can be very useful."

What Archie's plan lacked in details it more than made up for with hubris. Sarah opened the window all the way. Let Robert enjoy the wind. She had a lot to think about on the ride back to OKC.

Prisoner jumps out of window. Co-conspirators catch him. What could be simpler than that?" Sarah turned on her car radio. She could barely hear the music over the wind.

No great loss. KROU, channel 105.7 played tunes from *Paint Your Wagon*. She listened to the last few refrains of "Hand Me Down that Can of Beans" and turned the radio off when a moderately talented baritone sang "They Call the Wind Mariah."

Damn. Maybe there was such a thing as magic?

SARAH SAID, "TOMORROW at three p.m., Archie Chatto is going to jump to his death, and there is no way on earth we'll be able to save him." Robert and Big Shorty were not ready to give up, but that was no surprise. Two thirds of Archie's rescue crew was *non compos mentis*.

And the third member is a quitter, that's what Sarah's mother would have told her. When Marie Ferraro was in her manic phase, it was her considered opinion that anything conceived could also be achieved.

But not this. Judge Rakestraw's courtroom overlooked a courtyard protected by two armed guards and a sturdy-looking security gate. There was no way to get in.

"If Archie is lucky," she said, "he'll be killed instantly." Sarah had to admit that scenario didn't sound lucky. Maybe Archie would reflect on that fifty-dollar commissary account and call the whole thing off at the last moment.

"Twenty years ago, it would have been easy," Big Shorty said. "Twenty years ago, there would have been no guard station and no metal gate blocking the only outside access."

"And movies cost a dollar and airport travel was trouble free and politicians were honest and colored people knew their place." *Whoops.* Sarah always went too far with hyperbole. "Okay. Maybe politicians weren't honest, but a lot of things have changed in twenty years."

It did no good to wax nostalgic about jailbreaks in simpler times. Oklahomans became security-conscious after the Murrah Federal Building Bombing in 1995 and even more so after 9/11. Gates and guards were everywhere. If Archie's escape team couldn't get into the courtyard, they couldn't catch the falling Apache.

Sarah suggested they consider a more traditional method of liberating prisoners of the justice system, something heroic, requiring exactly the correct proportions of gunpowder, bravery, and good fortune. Both Robert and Big Shorty agreed to give the matter careful consideration, even though it wasn't quite crazy enough to work.

A metal detector, a bag-check X-ray system, and two plus-size guards in khaki security uniforms protected the front entrance to the courthouse—a lot like airport security but without the motivation. The guards tried their best not to gawk at Big Shorty as he lumbered through the metal detector. Even when he triggered the alarms, not one of them suggested wanding him or looking inside his stump pads.

"We could smuggle in a gun." Sarah found it difficult to believe that she was the one suggesting an armed rescue from a secure building. So much for sanity.

"Look around," Big Shorty said. He didn't have to point out the armed guards and uniformed police who populated the first floor of the building. "They might be too polite to search me, but they would shoot us all without hesitation. It's more politically correct."

Big Shorty was right, of course. In addition to the surfeit of guards on the first floor, there would be bailiffs and maybe sheriff's deputies in the courtroom. Then there were the unbelievably slow elevators, which could probably be immobilized from a remote location. If everything went incredibly well, Robert, Sarah, and Archie might be able to fight their way down three double flights of stairs. It was impossible to imagine Big Shorty keeping up on such a literally unlevel playing field, and, aside from Archie, he was the only one among them who might willingly fire a weapon.

Courtroom 334 was a long rectangular enclosure with a podium at the north end, a jury box on the eastern wall, and a seating area for the public that might have been copied from a country church. Two ornate wooden doors were symmetrically placed behind the podium. Golden letters identified one as the entry to "Judge's Chambers." Sarah supposed the other doorway led to the jury deliberation room.

Robert pointed out the round institutional-style clock mounted opposite the podium so the judge could keep track of time.

"That's the clock Archie will use to time his jump." He made Sarah synchronize her watch with the courtroom timepiece as if the success of the plan depended on precision timing. There were seven windows overlooking the courtyard, and Archie had selected the central one as the site of his self-defenestration. Just as he had promised, none of the windows was equipped with bars.

"No need for bars." Robert leaned out a window and spat a tear-shaped blob of saliva into the courtyard airspace. The escape team watched it fall forty feet and splatter on the pavement. A jumper would suffer the same fate. He would break both legs at the very least, even if he should be lucky enough to miss the rectangular metal trash containers that lined the courtyard's interior walls.

Big Shorty pointed to the doors connecting the courtyard space to the interior of the building.

"Steel panels with bolts into steel frames," he said. "Take a bulldozer to knock them down."

Even if the doors were left unlocked, Sarah realized, opening them would trigger alarms. Things looked bad for Archie Chatto. If Marie's lover managed to jump through one of the unbarred windows of Courtroom 334, he would fall to his death expecting to be saved by a mysterious plan developed by his recently acquired spiritual adviser.

"I have an idea," Robert said.

Sarah should never have doubted the ability of an Apache to recruit allies capable of helping him perfect an impossible plan.

"A really good idea." Robert didn't take time to elaborate. He raced out of the courtroom, down the stairs, out the main entrance of the courthouse, and hurried across a busy street into an open green space landscaped with a red, white, and blue fiberglass buffalo and a number of uncomfortable benches. Sarah followed from a distance, maintaining a pace Big Shorty could match. She resisted the temptation to take his hand and lead him across the street. They waited for the light and crossed with a deliberate dignified pace that wasn't nearly fast enough to satisfy Robert.

"Quickly, quickly!" He waved them toward him like a traffic cop. "The wind is blowing stronger than it has all day."

"What's the wind got to do with your plan?" Sarah suspected she and Robert had significantly different planning styles.

"We stand together in this open space and sing," he told her, as if it were as logical as arithmetic. "The song is quite simple." He whistled a few bars and then sang with a voice as clear and sweet as an Irish tenor.

"Away out here they have a name for rain and wind and fire."

Big Shorty joined in after the second stanza and harmonized with a rich baritone that would have been equally at home in gospel music or classical opera. He took his work-worn gardener's hat off and laid it on the ground with its sweat-stained interior aimed at the sky.

"Call it camouflage," Shorty stage-whispered to Sarah between verses.

"This is a plan?" The song overwhelmed Sarah's question.

Robert pointed to tree limbs that gyrated in the wind like the batons of a team of conductors. He made a broad gesture indicating the litter that blew in a circle around the fiberglass buffalo. The wind modified the song, boosting the volume and the tone, making the high notes higher, and adding a timbre to the base notes that vibrated in the chests of passersby. People dropped loose change and dollar bills into Big Shorty's hat, and the wind did not disturb the proceeds.

"Really…?" Sarah raised her voice to a mild shout, but the wind pushed some of her words to the curb and carried others into the sky so that even to her own ears, she seemed to be speaking gibberish. She cupped her hands around her mouth and prepared to shout at her maximum volume. That would have been enough to override the effects of the wind if a nine by eleven pamphlet had not struck her in the face.

"What is it?" Robert stopped singing as soon as the paper found its mark. He lifted the pamphlet from her face with the care an archeologist might give the Dead Sea Scrolls. The wind stopped blowing while he read the page.

Sarah and Big Shorty asked, "What does it say?" simultaneously.

"I think this is the answer to our problems," Robert told them. "Tomorrow is big trash day in Mesta Park. That's not too far from here, I think."

"How does big trash day solve our problems?" Sarah asked, even though she was afraid to hear the answer.

"That depends," Robert said. "Can you drive a garbage truck?"

28

SARAH'S TEAM OF three stole a garbage truck in thirty minutes flat. A little less if you started timing after they cut the lock on the chain-link security fence. Did the *Guinness Book of World Records* have a section devoted to sanitation crimes? Surely that must be some kind of record.

"Keys are left in the ignitions," Big Shorty promised. "Tanks are full of gasoline. If somebody is supposed to be around to watch, he'll probably be sleeping." Apparently, he had known a garbage man or two in his time.

It took them longer to find coveralls, a necessity according to Big Shorty, even though sanitation workers mostly eschewed uniforms.

"No way for a pretty white girl to pass for an authentic garbage man unless she's wearing coveralls."

Sarah blushed at the compliment. Too pretty to be a garbage man. Shorty certainly had a way with words.

He rubbed dust on his hands and smeared it on Robert's face so he looked like a beggar in a Dickens novel.

"I learned deception from my grandpop." Shorty looked around as if he expected the old man to make an appearance. "Disguises never look exactly right, so we'll settle on a few strong details."

Sarah thought it just might work. She streaked her own face with a few lines of dirt in strategic places.

"No one ever looked too closely at a garbage man," Shorty said. "Like a duck decoys. Those things would never work if ducks paid close attention."

His explanation sounded logical to Sarah, and that worried her. "Our success depends on armed guards having powers of observation roughly equivalent to ducks." That sounded about right. "What do you think our chances are?"

"The plan is barely crazy enough to work," Big Shorty said. "A couple of distractions ought to do the trick. One to get you in, and one to get you out."

He wouldn't elaborate. According to Shorty, distractions worked best if they took almost everyone by surprise, and almost everyone included Sarah Bible.

The stolen garbage truck had an automatic transmission. That was a stroke of luck Sarah hadn't counted on, but the vehicle was big and cumbersome, with numerous controls mysterious to the uninitiated. Lucky for her it was big trash day in Mesta Park. While the morning was still young, Sarah navigated the tree-lined streets of the historic subdivision, mastering the finer points of turning corners without knocking over mailboxes. Only three minor casualties, and she was already getting the hang of it.

The truck was a marvel of automation. By 9:00 a.m., Sarah mastered the intricacies of the compactor. By 11:00, she could make the robotic arm snatch plastic mini-dumpsters from driveways and empty them into the trash collection chute. A few mishaps left the streets of the affluent subdivision littered with imported wine bottles and empty caviar containers.

"Serves them right," Sarah complained, already getting into the proper sanitation worker's frame of mind. "Those items belong in the recycling tubs."

By noon, she'd mastered the art of driving forward and understood most of the interior controls. She wanted to share her newfound knowledge with Robert, but his mind was opaque to all things mechanical.

"I never learned to ride a bicycle," he offered in his defense. "I never learned to drive a car, operate a computer, or set a digital alarm clock." Growing up in foster care and then going crazy in his teenage years had a definite downside.

"But I understand the wind. Not many people can do that."

"Thank God, the mental hospitals couldn't stand the strain." Sarah pulled the garbage truck into the entryway of Riverside Gardens Cemetery. She had at least two hours to practice backing up.

"The guards won't care if you scrape a few things," Big Shorty said. "Nobody expects a girl to be good at driving a Garbage truck." Sarah took a break while he glued inflated air mattresses to the top of the compactor.

"Sure Grip Lock Tight," Shorty told her. "Best adhesive ever made. Sets in seconds, holds like iron. I use it to repair broken angels."

Sarah's mouth dropped open.

"Cement angels. You know, cemetery sculpture." He layered the mattresses three deep, enough to cushion a full-grown Apache warrior falling at forty-five mph.

No one at Ace hardware had asked Shorty the purpose of his purchase, but then people hardly ever asked Big Shorty anything. Double amputees were always noticed, hardly ever acknowledged, and never confronted. Such was the power of a highly visible handicap.

Sarah remembered something from the 100-level philosophy course she took at the University of New Mexico. Friedrich Nietzsche said, "What doesn't kill me makes me stronger." No question about it. Big Shorty was as strong as Sure Grip Lock Tight adhesive.

Archie would come through the middle window of Courtroom 334 at exactly 3:00 p.m. as indicated on the clock behind the public seating area. He'd written the time on the back of Robert's hand with a ballpoint pen at their last visit. Under the number three, he added *MAYBE A MINUTE OR TWO LATE BUT NOT A SECOND EARLY* in neat capital letters that Robert refused to wash until the deed was done.

AT 2:50 P.M., SARAH drove the truck up to the security station that controlled entry to the courtyard. Robert slumped in the passenger seat beside her, pretending to sleep on company time. A woman would never be permitted to drive unless her male partner had more important things to do.

The gate opened, but one of the two guards had questions. "Log says you were here earlier today." The cop was African American. The name on his ID tag was Lemonjello Luper. Under other circumstances Sarah would have asked him how he got that name and how it was pronounced, but today she didn't have the time. Besides, it might be out of character for a sanitation worker to be openly curious.

"Last crew missed a dumpster." She tried her best to sound bored, as if she couldn't care less whether the guard let her in or not. "One of the judges complained, so here we are."

"Rakestraw," she added to give her story the ring of authenticity. "Placed the call himself." Would a sanitation worker say himself or hisself? Too late to worry about such details. "The human garbage these judges put on the street, you wouldn't think he'd notice one little dumpster."

Lemonjello Luper might have smiled a little as he copied the number of the sanitation company from the driver's side door.

"Have to call your supervisor." He shrugged apologetically. "We all got rules to follow." Officer Lemonjello would have followed those rules if Big Shorty had not appeared on the scene at that precise moment. Perfect timing for deception number one.

"Signs and wonders!" Shorty shouted as he waddled through the space between the garbage truck and the guard's station. "Where the hell is the goddamned popsicles?" He removed his broad brimmed gardener's hat, placed it over his heart, and sang a few words of the *Born in the USA*—just enough to demonstrate his amateur singing status and his professional commitment to America. Then he used his hat to fend off a swarm of insects invisible to everyone but him.

"I give my goddamn legs for this country and look what they give me in return. Goddamned Africanized bees." Shorty continued swatting foreign insects as he lurched past the open security gate and moved toward the courtyard much faster than Sarah would have thought possible. Officer Lemonjello was taken by surprise as well.

"Wait up, my man," the guard called out to the crazy double amputee who would have been maced and handcuffed by now if not for the sensitivity training mandated by the State of Oklahoma. He waved Sarah forward, warning her to check with him on the way out, then he and his fellow officer left the guard station to subdue the mentally challenged amputee who just committed public trespass. As Sarah drove past the scene of the disturbance, it was clear that Shorty wasn't going peacefully, regardless of the "compassionate" force employed by the two guards.

In answer to the reasonable demands of the officers, Big Shorty invoked the name of Martin Luther King Jr. and accused Lemonjello of being an unsatisfying dessert that wasn't even on the menus of the finest restaurants. He used the word "fuck" sixteen times in a single compound sentence and demanded the police summon an interpreter who was fluent in Ebonics.

Sarah forced her attention away from Shorty's distraction play and devoted her full powers of concentration to steering the cumbersome garbage truck into the correct position. The courtyard was considerably smaller than she expected, and she had only three minutes until Archie went airborne. She didn't have time to protest when Robert kissed her on the cheek. She was too preoccupied to interfere when he left the confines of the garbage truck and walked toward the ruckus at the guard station with both hands doubled into fists.

Was that part of deception number two? She looked up at the middle window of Judge Rakestraw's courtroom. *Closed!* Well, that was Archie's problem. She had less than two minutes to get the truck into position.

29

ARCHIE CHATTO SAT beside his court-appointed attorney, wishing he could steal a watch. Any watch would do, Timex, Bulova, Omega, something from a Walmart rack. A Rolex would be best. Its sweeping minute hand would time his jump with great precision, and he could sell it later—the essence of renegade punctuality.

Was that a Rolex on the prosecutor's wrist? Probably a cheap Chinese knock off. State lawyers were all about show. They only pretended to be thieves.

"What time is it?"

Archie's public defender flinched at the question. He crossed his lips with his pointing finger and made a shushing sound. A shameful show of disrespect. Archie thought he might take the lawyer's finger with him when he went through the window. Make a necklace of the bones. Sell it to a white woman in Santa Fe. Use the money to buy a watch, then throw the watch away. Indigenous symbolism, as meaningless as the American Flag, but the idea made him smile.

Under ordinary circumstances, a warrior did not clutter his mind with the arithmetic of minutes. Sudden changes in the temperament of horses, the unexpected appearance of a flock of crows, the scent of fear carried on the wind—these were the springs and gears of Indian time. But in Courtroom 334, there was only a round clock mounted on the wall, cleverly positioned so the judge and jury could see it easily, but the defendant could not. For the third time that day, Archie twisted in his well-worn wooden chair and checked the time.

His court appointed attorney nudged him and whispered, "Sit still, Archie. You're making the jury nervous."

Who could have imagined a jury of Archie's peers would be seated so quickly—seven men, five women, and an alternate of each gender? "Three Native Americans," his defense attorney had told him.

"That's a lucky break." The lawyer's name was Tim, or was it Tom? Archie'd had so many young white lawyers over the years, as interchangeable and inappropriate as clowns at a Shriner's circus. They saw no differences between the tribes.

White people thought of Indians as one large, dysfunctional family—a pod of red-skinned dolphins swimming in a sea of shared European oppression.

"Not an Apache among them," Archie whispered to his lawyer. There was a Creek and a Choctaw—that was to be expected in Oklahoma— but the third Indian juror was a Pima man. The Pima had been fighting the Apache for a thousand years, and from the look in this juror's eyes, they weren't done yet.

It was a good thing Archie had an escape plan. Medicine was strong in Robert Collins. The boy was no warrior, but luck and courage filled him to the brim.

Archie twisted in his chair once again. Two thirty, time to put his end of the plan into motion. He was no oral historian, but he would tell a story to this judge and this jury, and his story would end in splintered glass and freedom. Archie was prepared.

He'd braided his hair in the Lakota style, the way Sitting Bull posed for photographs. He wore prison khaki trousers held up by a buffalo hide belt beaded with colored porcupine quills. He wore a T-shirt with a picture of Geronimo, Cochise, and Victorio on the back and the words *Homeland Defense* written underneath. Pinned to the shirt was a button that advocated freedom for imprisoned Sioux activist and convicted murderer, Leonard Peltier. The myth of Indian solidarity.

Tim—or Tom—approved of the braids and the belt, but he didn't like the shirt or the button.

"Rule one is don't scare the jury."

Archie Chatto was the young lawyer's first Apache client. He didn't understand the function of intimidation in a culture built on heroic violence. He didn't understand that a warrior's most powerful weapon was the fear of his enemies. Storytellers used fear too. It put the audience in the proper frame of mind.

"Rule two is don't scare the judge."

Now it was time for Archie to scare his own attorney. "Tell Rakestraw I want to make a confession now." He crossed his arms over his chest and waited for the young lawyer's predictable response.

Tim—or Tom—reacted to his client's statement with a four-letter word. "What?"

American English is loaded with colorful expletives. Shit would fit the circumstances perfectly. Even a simple, "Damn!" would be okay. Archie was disappointed in the young man's limited vocabulary.

"Tell the judge I want to confess." Archie said it louder this time, loud enough to make the judge tap his gavel.

The public defender put his hand on his client's shoulder, then pulled it back when Archie glared at him. "The state's case is weak," the lawyer said. "The agent's body has never been found. We have three Indians on the jury. We just might win this thing."

The judge tapped his gavel again. Archie wondered how long the young man would have to practice law before he realized that a traditional Apache could never win in court. The Apache concept of crime was far too flexible to withstand the scrutiny of common law.

"The federal agent's blood is on my hands. I want to confess." He said those words loud enough for everyone to hear. Judge Rakestraw's gavel hammered like a nervous woodpecker.

Archie stood and addressed the judge. "I want to explain what happened here in this courtroom so the words can't be bent into new shapes by journalists and politicians." Pure Indian stereotype, like a line from *Black Elk Speaks*. Chief Dan George couldn't have said it better.

The judge told Tim—or Tom—to control his client, as if anyone in the courtroom thought that was possible. It wasn't proper for a defendant to confess without negotiation on his part by a competent attorney.

"You understand this is a death penalty case," Judge Rakestraw told Archie. "A confession in open court negates your opportunity for appeal. You don't get a second bite of the apple."

White men talked about apples when they were about to give in, something to do with the Bible and the treachery of women. Archie was making progress.

"One bite is enough," he said. "In the end, a warrior only has his story. I will tell mine now so people will know exactly how things were."

"Since Oklahoma became a state, no defendant had made an allocution in open court after a jury had been seated." Judge Arthur Rakestraw told Archie to watch his step. "Be careful, Mister Chatto. A great deal hangs in the balance." There was emphasis on the word hangs.

"Apaches are careful in a different way," said Archie. "I will confess carefully."

The judge made it clear there would be no chance for legal trickery. Archie had already made a public statement against interest declaring himself guilty of the crime. He could not retract it later. He would be allowed to describe the conditions and circumstances of the murder, but he could not attribute the act to accident or self-defense. "You are confessing to the crime of capital murder. Do you understand?"

"Is it all right if I pace while I confess, Your Honor? Apaches get nervous when they sit."

"You can skip around the courtroom if it makes you feel better," the judge told him. "So long as you don't run for the door." On Judge Rakestraw's cue, one of the two overweight bailiffs moved in front of the double doors.

Archie turned to face the public seating area. An old white man with suspenders and a tobacco-stained shirt sat in the front row. He flashed a broad toothless grin and nodded acknowledgement of Archie's attention.

Two journalists sat in the back. One jotted information onto a steno pad, and the other made entries on a PDA in violation of the judge's strict policy forbidding the use of electronic devices.

The minute hand on the clock behind the journalists jerked forward one notch in time. Two forty-one p.m.

Usen help me.

"I was warmed by the sun, rocked by the winds, and sheltered by the trees as other Indian babes," Archie said. "I was living peaceably when people began to speak bad of me. Now I can eat well, sleep well, and be glad. I can go everywhere with a good feeling." He repeated the same quotation from Geronimo every time he surrendered to authorities. He had said it so often, he no longer had to refer to notes. It was Archie's preferred way to end a struggle, unless there was a gunfight. The words didn't have the same impact if they were spoken from behind cover.

"I was not an easy man to follow." Archie paced back and forth in front of Judge Arthur Rakestraw and described how he jumped on a train passing through the Jicarillo Reservation in Arizona, then jumped off in New Mexico and stole a car.

"I drove the car until it was low on gasoline, then traded it for a mule. When the mule couldn't carry me any farther, I set out on foot. I have great respect for the federal man who followed me into the Oklahoma panhandle."

Archie raised and spread his arms to demonstrate just how much respect he had for the dead agent. In doing so, he demonstrated his impressive musculature and the large number of blue monochrome tattoos that started on his fingers and disappeared under his sleeves of his T-shirt. No one who saw those arms could have the slightest doubt that Archie Chatto was a dangerous man.

"Many tribes have passed through the narrow strip of Oklahoma where almost no one lives." Archie told the court about the blue-eyed explorers from the other side of the world who visited hundreds of years ago and recognized the special power of the place.

"They left ritual marks on rock walls shielded from the sun except for days of special significance, the summer and the winter solstices and the equinox."

Archie made a slow circuit around the rectangle of space defined by the lawyers' tables on the north, the judge's podium on the south, the jury box on the west, and the windows on the east. He paid homage to each of the principal directions with a pinch of imaginary corn pollen. The three Native jurors nodded their heads in solidarity, even the Pima man.

"Boundaries between the past and the present are thin at the high and low places of the desert plains. A quiet man can hear the echoes of ancient songs." Archie drew in his breath and held it to show how calm and quiet an Apache could be, even in a room filled with enemies. Judge Rakestraw held his breath as well. So did every person in the courtroom.

"I stooped and crawled among boulders that had rolled off the mesas when the earth was being made. I brushed against pictures scratched into slabs of rock by holy men who passed through that land before it had a name. Power marked my body where I touched the sacred stones." He told the jury how images of ancient petroglyphs glowed on his skin after sunset.

"It was a magic time. I heard the drums of ancient people. I smelled the smoke from their cooking fires, and in the silent moments between my heartbeats, I listened to stories the old ones told to pass the time."

Archie whispered a few words in the pure, untainted language of his people, incomprehensible to the judge and jury but as clear and powerful as thunder.

"Whether the federal agent heard the songs and stories, I cannot say. If he did, then he was a fool to pursue me any farther." Archie brushed his eyes across each person in the jury box, then turned to face the courtroom clock. The minute nudged the number twelve and the hour hand centered on the number three. Archie Chatto's story was nearly finished.

"We stepped into the distant past, the federal man and I, to a time and place where the authority of his government had not been born."

Archie smiled at his court appointed lawyer and watched the man shrink down in his councilor's seat.

"Warriors sat in a circle around a central fire. They passed a pipe and sent their prayers to the full moon on clouds of sacred smoke. Their medicine chief walked outside the circle, listening to the spirits of the night, waiting for a vision. On his fourth circuit, two strangers blocked his path. The medicine chief waived his staff at a stream bed that had been dry so long its muddy bottom had frozen into stone.

Archie stared at the worn oak floor of the courtroom so intently, the judge stood behind his podium to see if there was actually something there.

"I saw footprints pressed deep into the rock by a large animal who walked there while Usen made the world. Their meaning was clear to me."

Archie looked into the eyes of each juror, then back at the footprints he had summoned in their imaginations.

"The odor of fast food and automobile exhaust greeted me as I raced along the footprint trail. The doorway through time was only large enough for one. The federal agent might have reached it first, but he stopped to draw his weapon."

Archie paced in silence as if he was so lost in his story he didn't know what would come next. When he spoke again it was in a whisper that would make his audience strain to hear. "Bullets flew past me as I sprinted through the centuries, but nothing can stop an Apache warrior running in a sacred manner." He backed against the jury box faced the judge and shouted an Apache war cry as he sprinted toward the window.

He hardly felt the glass pane shatter into crystals as he flew through the central courtroom window. If he was lucky, everyone in the courtroom would be so stunned by the noise and the glittering display, they wouldn't notice Archie's Lakota braids came unfastened from his recently scissored hair and fell below their line of vision.

If anyone in the courtroom had rushed to the window quickly enough, they would have seen him bounce twice on the air mattresses glued to the top of the garbage truck, but he thought they would not. The people in Courtroom 334 had witnessed the miracle of human flight through time. They had seen an Apache warrior run in a sacred manner and knew it was pointless to investigate.

SARAH LOOKED AT her watch. It was 3:01, and the truck was parked beneath the central window of Courtroom 334. She'd wedged her front bumper against one of the metal doors that connected the courtyard with the interior of the building. If guards tried to open that door to apprehend a fleeing felon, they'd be sorely disappointed.

She gave her head and shoulders a violent shake, like a high jumper preparing to try for a new personal record. She was starting to believe this crazy plan might work. But there were so many reasons it couldn't.

If she managed to turn the garbage truck around, she'd never get it past the guard station. The security police would have subdued Big Shorty and Robert by then. Alarms would sound within the courthouse. Armed guards would swarm out the doors and descend on them. Without question, the plan was doomed to fail. Every one of them would be arrested. Sarah would be the only one who could not claim innocence by reason of insanity.

A perfectly parked garbage truck was still something to be proud of. It took another violent head and shoulders shake to eliminate those thoughts. By then she heard the sound of falling glass and the thump of something heavy on the Ace Hardware air mattresses.

Stage two.

Sarah had only a moment to consider how quickly the plan was falling into place—racing toward disaster at the most efficient speed.

Archie opened the garbage truck door and told her it was time to go.

"Leave the truck. We'll walk from here." He was putting on a corduroy sport coat rescued from the truck's trash chute. "It's amazing the things people throw away."

Sarah followed him without question, the way Apache women have been following men into desperate situations for centuries. She finally understood why Native women had such quiet ways. They were stunned by the calamity of the world they lived in. Nothing left to say.

Big Shorty and Robert waited for them at the guard station. Officer Lemonjello and his partner lay unconscious in a shady spot, their heads tipped back, their airways clear. Robert had put his first aid training to work once again.

"Spirit powder?" She realized that had been part of the plan all along, the second distraction Big Shorty had told her about without divulging details.

Archie took the officers' sidearms and stuck them in his belt. He rescued a handcuff key and put into his mouth.

"In case we are arrested," he said with no apparent speech deficit. He stepped into the guard station, opened a DVD recorder, and removed two discs. "My picture will be on the five o'clock news, but the rest of you will remain my anonymous accomplices."

"Shouldn't we hurry?" Sarah could hear police sirens, but she wondered why the courthouse guards weren't running into the street.

"When alarms go off, the elevators shut down, and the exterior doors automatically lock," Archie told her. "An emergency response team, most likely SWAT, will surround the building and then conduct a room-to-room search. Standard operating procedure."

"You got a haircut." Robert leaned forward and examined Archie's new look. The change in appearance hadn't registered with Sarah.

"I'm assimilating into the dominant white culture."

Sarah thought that would take more than a haircut, but the change was dramatic.

"Time for us to start searching for Marie," he told Sarah. "Did you remember to park a get-a-way car nearby, or will we be walking?"

30

MARIE LOOKED FORWARD to her first appearance in the Stringtown group session room. There were two one-way mirrors with high-end digital cameras mounted behind each one recording gigabytes of drama on DVDs. Psychiatrists and social workers would review them later for therapeutic insights and dinner table conversation. God, how Marie loved show business.

She fussed with her makeup—a little more concealer, a little more blush. Fluorescent lights washed out her eyes and made her skin look blotchy unless her liner, shadow, and foundation were in perfect balance. This was Marie's opportunity to establish her star credentials, and she didn't want to blow it. If things went as planned, her DVD would be in Dr. Moon's permanent collection, and the good doctor himself would be in hers.

The doctor would peer at her through the mirrors like a peeping tom. Men were suckers for that sort of shameful secrecy. She'd reveal some things he wanted to know and some things he didn't. Nudge him out of his comfort zone. It was a tricky process. Like tickling a tightrope walker, just enough to keep him off-balance but not enough to make him fall. The essence of the feminine mystique.

Dr. Moon liked to hear Marie talk dirty, but not too dirty. She knew that much from their private sessions. He was titillated by her extensive experience, but explicit description made him panic. Dr. Moon was a peculiar man. Weren't they all?

He had deeply hidden wants and needs. God only knew what they were. Foot fetish, bondage, golden showers, discipline—so many possibilities. Eventually, Marie would know exactly what turned the doctor on. Meanwhile she'd pretend.

The relationship had finally reached the touching stage. Nothing inappropriate. His hand would brush against her shoulder. He'd straighten a displaced lock of her hair with the backs of his fingers. He'd place a protective palm on the small of her back as they walked together through the halls. Almost sweet, but there was more to come. Marie knew where Dr. Moon hoped his innocent touching would eventually lead.

He moved in that direction incredibly slowly for a man of middle years. Dr. Moon wanted Marie but was clearly afraid of her. Not a bad combination from her perspective. The psychiatrist would not be her first spooky man, but he would be the first one she didn't plan to take all the way. A new frontier of seduction.

She offered her most dazzling smile to the members of her group. She gave each of the two-way mirrors a full-face view and a profile while resisting the temptation to scratch her nose. Movie stars never had an itch they could not ignore. That, plus stunning good looks, was the secret to success in the acting profession.

Crazy people seated themselves in an imperfect circle of chairs. A young male psychiatric resident sat among them. His nametag and his watch were the only things that set him apart from the clients. He looked nervous, but so did everyone else.

The resident had his agenda, but Marie had a plan. She didn't wait for him to coax the group into action. She stood and made a brief introduction loaded with enough barely suppressed emotion to pass for sincerity. When she stepped outside the circle of chairs, no one tried to stop her. Heads turned to follow her as she walked around the room. She changed direction a time or two, just to keep them guessing. After a couple of mood changes, she had their full attention.

Roll 'em.

"My boyfriend drove off and left me standing on a back road in Choctaw County. You could say that's where the most important part of my life began." Every true confession story Marie ever read opened with a line like that. It was the pulp fiction way of saying, "Here goes nothing."

She checked to make sure her face was visible in both one-way mirrors before she tracked her eyes upward and to the left. According to *Dr. Phil,* that was clear sign she was searching her memories and not telling lies.

"I was a pretty fourteen-year-old girl with flexible moral standards and had no trouble finding men who would take care of me... for a while, anyway."

She checked her audience reaction. Just as she'd planned. The women were busy judging her. The men judged her, too, but in a different way.

"Arthur Walkingstick." Marie accentuated the consonants in her old boyfriend's name. She ran the tip of her tongue over her lips relishing the taste of his memory without smudging her lipstick.

The resident's mouth dropped open as if he had something to say. But instead of interrupting, he squirmed in his seat, trying to manage physiologic responses that were firmly in Marie's control.

"Arthur didn't want to leave me, but we both knew from the beginning that a man with warrants never really has a choice." A single tear trickled from Marie's left eye and pooled in a dimple. That skill was the result of a lifetime of practice.

"Thank God the Carson and Barnes Circus had just settled into a field outside of Hugo." Mention of the Lord gave Marie an excuse to cross herself. She wasn't Catholic, but she'd seen actresses do it on the big screen and didn't want to miss her opportunity.

"You all know about the circus wintering in Hugo?" Marie took the time to remind those who didn't that the Big Top came to Choctaw County in November and stayed until the weather turned warm.

"Circus people loved Hugo. It was nine miles from the Texas border, so a quick trip was all they needed for a change in jurisdiction if the State Police were troublesome. Weyerhaeuser timber company left clear cuts that grew in with rich green grass, no good for planting crops but perfect grazing for camels and horses. And the people were friendly. If a couple of lions wandered onto private land, the locals didn't kick up a fuss. Everyone in Hugo loved it when the circus came to town."

Marie's group were all Oklahomans. The youngest members might not remember the celebrations when Carson and Barnes trucks drove through the city streets, but they'd all heard stories about lost elephants and clowns hiding out from the law.

"The winter was mild enough for the animals and local citizens were so polite they hardly looked twice at the human oddities. There was a fat man, a skinny man, a bearded lady, an illustrated man, and a pair of Siamese twins who didn't have to be a spectacle once they got to Hugo. Nobody stared at them—not after the first week or so—but the animals and trainers didn't mind a little curiosity."

The psychiatric resident scribbled a few notes on his clipboard. Marie didn't what he was writing about.

"I was on my way to watch the elephants bathe in Owl Creek, when Arthur Walkingstick drove past in his Oldsmobile Delta 88. He blew me a kiss and then vanished in a cloud of dust from the gravel road. Sheriff's deputies followed him about a hundred yards back, doing their duty without risking the paint on their new cruiser."

Marie mimed staring into the distance like an actress in a silent film, partly for the group but mostly for Dr. Moon. She checked her reflection in the mirror and figured the expression on her face was as close to perfect as she was going to get.

"I waited where he saw me last—for hours. When the sun went down, I began to cry." She made sobbing noises so she wouldn't have to explain why men are attracted to the sound of female tears. The psychiatric resident scribbled notes. Some of the men looked like they were ready to jump out of their seats and come to her aid. Even the women looked sympathetic.

"It wasn't long until Gideon came to my rescue. He was a tall, imposing man, with a back as straight as a German soldier's."

Marie lowered her voice a full octave when she repeated the first words Gideon Bible ever said to her. "Are you all right, Miss?"

"I threw my arms around him. Buried my face in his shirt. It was pitch black, and Gideon didn't look like anything more than a good-looking man who would make my troubles go away. It wasn't until I went inside his trailer that I realized my savior was the circus's illustrated man. By then it didn't matter. Love's dominoes had already begun to fall."

Marie smiled at that line. She'd read it in an old issue of *True Love* and had been waiting for the right moment to us it.

HASHILLI DIDN'T FEEL safe inside the observation room, even with the doors locked and the lights turned down. Bullets couldn't penetrate the one-way mirrors separating him from group session. The room was insulated against sound—good enough to pass muster on a television game show. The doors were metal, set in stainless steel frames with double bolts. The walls were steel-reinforced gunite, capable of withstanding a low yield thermonuclear blast. Nothing could get at Hashilli here, except perhaps Marie.

Her feminine mystique broached the room's defenses as if it were a house of straw.

Little pig, little pig, let me come in. Not by the hair of my chinny-chin-chin. She didn't have to blow Hashilli's house down. He would unlock the doors at her command. How the hell did she do it?

His heart raced like a drum roll at a colonial hanging as he waited for Marie to embellish her romantic story of statutory rape. What had she been like back then?

Pretty as she is now, for sure, Hashilli decided, but perhaps just a little bit more vulnerable.

He watched her pace around the group session room, looking past the women, locking eyes with the men, moving with the precision of a prima ballerina. She knew the effect of every line she struck, the impact of every change in position. None of her ammunition was wasted as she told the story of the illustrated man who won her heart in Hugo.

Hashilli listened while she described how Gideon Bible had transformed his body into a religious artifact with a tattoo artist's needle. "The *Old Testament* covered his lower body, beginning with the book of Genesis written on his feet. The Ten Commandments stood out in bold calligraphy below his navel. An appendicitis scar divided the book of Exodus, the way Moses parted the Red Sea."

There was music in Marie's voice as she described the holy pattern on the illustrated man—religious music. "The New Testament merged with the Old at Gideon's waistline, and the holy words moved up from there to the top of his bald head. Even his eyelids were covered by scripture."

She told the group that every human with a Y chromosome has desires as strong as a lion and resistance much weaker than a lamb. Hashilli watched the male clients accept this revelation with a stoic frown. The women agreed with a silent synchronized nod.

"But Gideon Bible was different," Marie said. "He found a way to absorb righteousness through his skin the way a salamander breathes under water."

Supernatural protection. Hashilli knew it was stronger than bullet-proof glass and steel doors. But a man's souls, his inner and outer shadows? How long could a tattoo artist's ink protect them? He felt sympathy for Gideon as he listened to Marie describe how the illustrated man's resistance crumbled.

"Gideon felt dressed in his illustrations." Marie looked as if she were staring right at Hashilli as she spoke. "He seldom wore clothing. Covering the living word with fabric implied a preference for some books over others."

She nudged a stray lock of hair back into place and winked at her reflection—and at Hashilli, hiding behind her reflection. He was sure of it.

"No part of Gideon's body was free of scripture. As you can well imagine, I had many opportunities to read passages that were normally abridged when he paraded across the carnival stage."

Hashilli imagined Marie reading his own fine print. The image was exquisitely detailed, down to a pair of gold rimmed reading glasses, a Victoria's Secret camisole, and a pair of black patent leather shoes with six-inch heels. His mind's eye could see from the reflection in fantasy-Marie's shoes that she wasn't wearing *panties*. The thought of that word made him shudder.

"Gideon never denied his interest," said Marie. "But he never once gave in, not completely. I asked God to tell me how to overwhelm the illustrated man with lust. It didn't work, of course. Jesus is not the man to go to for relationship advice."

She described her seduction repertoire in enough detail to embarrass everyone in her group. Hashilli considered turning off the sound, or distracting her by tapping on the mirror, but even though he thought listening might drive him mad, he didn't want her to stop.

"Out of desperation I went to the circus's Gypsy fortune teller," Marie said. "Love potions were Madam Dooriya's specialty."

The chemistry of love and obsession. Hashilli's knowledge of power plants was limited to poisons. And spirit powder, of course. Even Grandfather never mastered that aspect of magic.

Marie pantomimed stirring her potion into a pot of soup—the evening meal she would share with Gideon. "In an hour, the room started spinning. In two hours, the world vanished into a pool of black ink. In eight hours, we woke in each other's arms covered in the salty residue of dried perspiration. The ache between my legs told me Madam Dooriya's potion had done its work, but my memory was blank."

Marie managed a look that was simultaneously seductive and guilty as she told how their relationship had slipped back into old familiar territory.

"He said nothing about the lost evening, and as the winter weeks dragged on, I came to believe nothing had happened between us."

She placed her hands over her lower belly, where a baby bump would first be noticeable. "When my pregnancy became obvious, Gideon told me my child was the product of a righteous woman sleeping with the word of God. After a while, I believed it too."

Marie Ferraro closed her eyes and folded her arms. "The Lord's ways are mysterious."

She circled the group, forcing them to follow her as she moved around the room and came to a stop with her back turned to Hashilli.

Perhaps she doesn't know I'm here.

"Sheriff's deputies came looking for Gideon several months before my Sarah was born." Her tone was flat. She turned to face her reflection. Hashilli stood and moved away from the glass, away from her line of vision.

"Gideon had warrants from his sinful days. A man running from the law never really has a choice."

Hashilli watched as Marie turned her eyes exactly to the spot where he was standing. She gave him a moment to consider the implications of her power, enough time to draw a noisy breath and back up against the wall.

"Maybe God swore out that arrest warrant for Sarah's father," Marie said directly to him. "Maybe Sarah is the product of immaculate conception, just as Gideon believed."

"I'll let the experts decide." She placed her forehead against the glass, close enough to see into Hashilli's hiding place. He'd backed as far as he could go, but he pressed against the wall like a ledge-walker acknowledging his mortality.

A smile spread across her face as she analyzed his reaction. The smile of a cat who has pinned a mouse under her paw.

31

SARAH WATCHED A pair of plainclothes detectives going door to door at the posh condo complex near the County Courthouse. Downtown had become the place to be since the Oklahoma City bombing. If Timothy McVeigh had any idea how his act of terrorism would stimulate the city center, he'd have tossed his explosives into a landfill and spared 168 lives.

Sarah guessed the condo-dwellers were mostly retired lawyers. They'd been carried to the economic summit on the backs of accident victims and criminal defendants and wanted to stay close to the source of wealth and glory. She felt a flush of shame at that unworthy thought. Not nice to hate people you don't know, even if they're rich. But it's so easy. Class envy is the natural state of things when you're looking up from the bottom.

Was envy a cardinal sin or just one of the little venal ones? She'd Google it later. Right then Sarah had to concentrate on the assignment given to her by Archie Chatto, a person on an even lower rung of the social ladder than herself. Society's rules didn't apply to Archie. He was like ET with muscles and tattoos, a stranger in a strange land. He was an indigenous warrior let loose in twenty-first century

America. He routinely outwitted his enemies with a revamped eighteenth-century strategy.

Sarah finally understood Marie's fascination with Archie Chatto—not necessarily a good thing—but she was never going to understand the man. Her sketchy background in undergrad anthropology didn't help at all. Would Sarah Bible, BS, MS, PhD, understand Archie any better than Sarah Bible, BS-in-progress? Not a chance, but in the college of hard knocks, spending time with a renegade Apache might qualify her for advanced placement.

"We need a white cop on our side," Archie told Sarah when he laid out a complicated plan for the day. It involved photographs, a map of the botanical garden, and a kidnapped police officer. "Rank is good, someone with a detective's gold shield."

"Impossible." She knew that word didn't mean anything to him. It wasn't an argument, really. It was more of an expletive, like *awesome* or *super*.

"Don't worry. Apache warriors know how to catch a fish without losing the bait," he said.

Since Sarah was the bait, Archie's angling metaphor didn't put her at ease. "Traditional Apache's don't eat fish."

Maybe her anthropology studies would come in handy after all.

"Fish is good fertilizer," Archie told her. "It makes the corn grow tall."

Apache didn't plant corn either. They borrowed it by force from the Pueblos and never gave it back. But Sarah didn't waste time arguing with Archie. She listened carefully as he laid out a scheme so convoluted she had almost no idea what to do.

"Details make things complicated," he said. "Start by watching cops and improvise."

Policemen generally traveled in pairs, but the detectives Sarah watched were splitting up. They knew as well as she did an experienced criminal wouldn't stay within shooting distance of downtown OKC. But just in case he did, they were checking out the downtown area where politically connected people lived.

"Filling in the squares." That's what Archie called it. "They'll feel safe enough to split their teams. Pick a plainclothes cop with black hair and blue eyes and get him as far as the botanical garden." He looked at her until she nodded.

"Yeah, I know where that is." Sarah wasn't particularly inspired, but it didn't take her long to find a candidate.

The detective wore a checkered sport coat and green slacks that struck his ankles three inches above the soles of his wing-tip shoes.

White socks—how stylish.

He didn't look like Robert's twin, but he had the requisite black hair and blue eyes. He was in his mid to late twenties with no facial hair or distinguishing scars. Just what the doctor ordered, if the cop was open to the brand of persuasion Sarah had learned growing up. True confession stories and romance novels, instead of nursery rhymes and children's books. Thanks for the memories, Mom.

"Officer!" She carried one of the "Have you seen this man" leaflets the cops had posted all over this part of town. She approached the policeman with the same caution she would use with a stranger's pet rottweiler—bold but careful to make no sudden movements. She imagined an experienced lawman could detect the scent of fear at a distance of thirty yards. It probably reminded them of undercooked meat and sex.

"Excuse me." She consciously slowed her breathing and thought about the only useful things she had learned from her mother. Young men are full of pride and testosterone. They like their women nervous. He'd see her as a pleasant diversion. Maybe a potential conquest. Based on his wardrobe there was probably plenty of room on this young man's gun for notches.

"It's probably just my imagination." Sarah smiled, tipped her head down, and looked at the policemen through upturned eyes. She considered fluttering her lashes. But that might seem contrived, even to a man whose mind was stuck in the reproductive mode.

"Yes, miss?" He puffed up his chest a bit. He flexed his muscles and struck a pose Sarah had seen on the cover of *GQ* Magazine. He'd taken the bait. Now if she could set the hook.

"I think I saw this man." She pushed the paper toward his face too close for him to read but close enough for him to see the slight tremor of her hands and the droplets of nervous perspiration her fingers left on the margins of the page. When the detective took the pamphlet from her, Sarah retracted her hands and clasped them behind her back like a little girl who has been caught at something naughty.

Helpless. Completely at your mercy. It was so easy to manipulate young men. Like shooting fish in a barrel, and not a big barrel either. Sarah could tell from the policeman's crooked smile exactly what was on his mind.

"Sorry." She heaped self-deprecation into her voice. She ended every statement on a slightly elevated pitch, enhancing the verbal uncertainty men found so charming. "I'm sure it was nothing. I shouldn't have bothered you." She turned and walked away carefully striking her best lines as she retreated. She looked over one shoulder, imitating a pose she had seen her mother do, copied from a classic Grace Kelly pin up from an earlier more innocent time.

Maybe the policeman wouldn't notice Sarah wasn't actually Grace Kelly if she made her bottom sway just so.

It only took three steps. "Wait, miss."

Success.

"Where did you see this desperate character?" He flashed a patronizing smile and looked her over carefully.

Checking her out, she realized. Imagining what she looked like naked. That's all he'd remember when asked to describe her to his superiors later on. A naked girl with a smitten look who wanted to have his babies. Could have fooled anybody.

"By the botanical garden," Sarah told him, slowing her walk, moving him with the deliberate skill of a border collie rounding up a stray lamb.

"Silly me." She picked up the pace a little, as she retrieved her cell phone. "I took his picture." She fumbled with the instrument, running through a series of photographs Archie insisted she take—mostly unimaginative floral photos and poorly composed wide-angle shots of the cylindrical terrarium-like structure in the center of the Myriad Botanical Gardens.

"I believe he's just after the Crystal Bridge."

He wasn't just after the Crystal Bridge, of course. He was at least fifty pictures into her memory card.

"Ah, here. Not a very good photo I'm afraid. I didn't want him to notice me."

"It could be him." The man in the blurred picture was clearly either Native American or Hispanic, and his arms were covered with jailhouse tattoos.

They continued walking toward the botanical garden.

"Not much farther." Sarah had successfully separated the detective from his partner. Now if she could keep him busy, too busy to place a call.

"He wore a T-shirt," she said. "There were Indians on the back… Native Americans, I mean. There was something written under the Native Americans. I think it was 'Homeland Security.'" Sarah heard the leather soles of the detective's shoes skid to an abrupt halt. They had reached the edge of the Myriad Gardens Botanical Park.

"He wore a button on his shirt." Sarah's fish was on the line now. It was time to start reeling him in. "White with red letters. It said Free Leonard Peltier. Any idea what that means?"

The detective had reached the speechless phase of the operation. His game had changed from Vagina Quest to Cops and Robbers, but so far, it was still a game, and Sarah wasn't sure of the rules.

The policeman reached for his cell phone. Sarah's charms all but forgotten. Archie's plan hadn't included reinforcements, so this is where her improvisation came in.

"There he is." She grabbed the policeman's hand, the one that held his cell phone. "That's the man!" She gave his hand a shake violent enough to send his phone flying to the ground.

Archie Chatto stepped into the path leading to the Children's Garden trail. He saluted the cop with the middle finger of his right hand. Close enough to read the upside-down capital letter A. One fourth of the word, hate. A prison sentiment recorded so long ago the blue ink was already beginning to fade. Archie turned and disappeared down the paved trail before the detective could order him to stop.

Sarah raced ahead, crushing the policeman's cell phone under her shoe. She took another couple of steps forward before he sprinted past her, much faster than she expected.

Was Archie quick enough? She didn't doubt it for a second.

The detective was deceptively unfit. His wind failed after a few seconds. He kept pace with Archie through the short Homesteader's Garden trail but lost ground quickly when the chase led across a broad expanse of open ground toward the Crystal Bridge. The two men had run less than thirty yards when the policeman slowed his pace to a brisk walk.

Sarah followed the action from a safe distance and shouted words of encouragement as the detective's energy flagged. Her words kept him going, but she longed for pair of pom-poms and a cheerleader's pleated skirt. Archie slowed down when he pulled too far ahead of his pursuer. He turned around and walked backward for a dozen paces so the detective would be sure to make a positive identification.

Sarah could see how Archie struggled against the instinct to make a clean getaway. What would Geronimo think of him now? Two hundred years of Apache tradition cast aside for a white woman's love.

Instead of disappearing into the exotic foliage he dodged along a trail beside a one-acre water garden. He followed the winding pathway into a section of the park featuring water plants, ferns, and cypress trees.

The detective speed-walked forty feet behind his quarry under a footbridge and across a cement platform that served as a stage during festival days. He lost sight of Archie beside a faux waterfall that emptied into a pool filled with blooming water hyacinth and lotus.

But not for long. Archie emerged from a collection of rhododendrons that had peaked a few days earlier. He waved to the cop and disappeared behind a boxwood hedge being trimmed into a topiary display by a troop of Hispanic gardeners.

The detective shouted, "Stay where you are!" He waved his gold shield over his head as though a display of rank might persuade the fleeing fugitive to surrender. His command sent the hedge trimmers running in all directions, but Archie took the time to offer him another one-fingered salute before he vanished behind a stand of flowering azaleas.

The pursuit went on long enough to tire the detective but not quite long enough to make him give up. He chased the run-away Apache down trail after trail until he was totally turned around among a clever arrangement of fuchsia and lantana. Then when it seemed all was lost, there was Archie Chatto, sitting on a park bench in the exact center of a dead-end circle of terraced plants, holding a magazine.

Maybe it was Archie Chatto. The detective looked uncertain.

Black hair. Arms covered with blue ink.

He wore a T-shirt featuring renegade Apache, and a white button was pinned to his shirt, a white button with red letters.

Of course, it was Archie Chatto.

"Let me see your hands!" The policeman drew his side arm from a holster under his left arm. He held it in a double-handed grip and approached the suspect slowly while checking the surrounding area for pain-in-the-ass civilians who might be hit with a stray bullet.

He strutted toward his perpetrator, like a man on his way to a gunfight. Sarah let out a little yelp so he'd know there was an inconvenient witness if he decided to end his embarrassing chase with a shootout.

"Go ahead," the detective said in a clichéd Clint Eastwood impersonation. "Make my day."

The suspect didn't run. He offered no resistance, in fact. That was the only thing about this man that was not the least bit like the notorious Archie Chatto.

"Stand up! Place your hands on top of your head and lace your fingers!" It was the young detective's day for cool police quotations. He found his handcuffs after a brief clumsy search. Restraining criminals was usually the province of uniformed officers. He stepped behind his suspect and nudged the man's feet far enough apart to keep him off-balance. In seconds the man's hands were cuffed behind his back. That was the diciest part of arresting a dangerous criminal. It took two hands to secure a pair of handcuffs, and for a brief moment, the officer had to holster his pistol.

"Cuffs are for my safety and yours," the policeman said. "You're not under arrest at this time." He turned the suspect around.

"What's your name? Don't even try to lie to me!"

"My friends all call me Robert," the suspect said. "Is there a problem officer?"

At that moment the detective's eyes found the button on Robert's T-shirt. His face lost that edgy Dirty Harry look. The button didn't say *FREE LEONARD PELTIER*. It said *YES WE CAN!* His lips moved as he read the message.

"Dude! Were you a Barack Obama supporter?" Robert asked. "I knew there had to be another one somewhere in Oklahoma, but I never thought we'd meet like this."

"You're...." The detective touched Robert's Obama button as if he couldn't believe it was real. "You're not the man I chased through the park, are you?"

Robert smiled. Sarah thought it was a nice smile, but it didn't look like the detective agreed.

"You're not even Indian." The cop reached inside his jacket as if he was considering a gunfight in spite of everything. "Those aren't tats on your arms either."

"My little nephews did that with a Sharpie, man. That shit don't even wash off. You know?"

The detective choked a little. Sarah guessed it was an apology trying to break through like an uninvited gas bubble, but he stifled it.

"What were you doing here?" He resumed his authoritative tone of voice as he cast his eyes around the area where Robert had been sitting.

"What's that?" He pointed at a magazine Robert had been reading. It lay on the park bench, miraculously undisturbed by the summer breeze, and piled in the center of its cover was something that would arouse the curiosity of any cop—a suspicious substance in plain view, arranged in a neat little pyramid over the middle of a blond starlet in a bikini.

It was the wrong color for cocaine or heroin, but diabolical new forms of methamphetamine were always coming on the market.

"It's *People Magazine*," Robert told the cop. "Pictures of the fifty most beautiful people of the year. Angelina made it again."

"Is this Archie Chatto?" Sarah shuffled closer to the confrontation still holding her HAVE YOU SEEN THIS MAN leaflet. "It doesn't really look like him, does it?"

She approached Robert too quickly to be warned away by the arresting officer. She extended her right hand and ran over Robert's face in a perfect imitation of a blind patron of the arts examining a classical Greek sculpture.

"Not the man I saw."

The policeman was so intent on his serendipitous drug bust that he didn't ask how Sarah had kept up with him through the chase.

"Can I use your cell phone, miss?"

She seemed to be confused by the question.

"You stepped on mine." He ended the statement with a nervous laugh, as if he was embarrassed to mention the incident. "I have to call for transport. I didn't expect to make this kind of arrest. I don't even have an evidence bag for the suspect's drugs."

"Drugs!" Sarah managed to sound alarmed and thrilled at the same time.

The cop picked up Robert's magazine and carried it to her, like a garden party waiter offering a choice of canapés to an important guest.

He held his breath while she inspected the mound of yellow powder.

She waited until the moment the detective inhaled and then blew the mound of powder into his face.

It took three seconds for him to collapse. Sarah wondered if he had time to realize he had been duped by this young woman and the slacker he had just arrested—and probably by Archie Chatto too.

His eyes danced around under his eyelids. Sarah had seen dogs dream like that. The detective mumbled something that sounded like he might be Mirandizing a suspect. He coughed, opened his eyes for a moment said, "Krispy Kreme," and closed them again.

―――――――――

"I WONDER WHAT he meant by that?" Robert asked Archie Chatto as he joined them in the protective circle of decorative plantings.

"Maybe it's the password to cop heaven," Archie said. He conducted a thorough search of the unconscious man.

The first thing Archie took from the detective was a handcuff key. "Can't have too many of these." He uncuffed Robert.

Then, Archie relieved the policeman of his gold shield and his 9 mm Glock in its shoulder holster.

"Consider yourself deputized."

Before Robert accepted the fruits of their elaborate crime, he positioned the detective in the Red Cross approved manner. He held the pistol for a moment, then gave it back to Archie.

"I'll carry the weapon later," he said, "if you think I should." He opened the leather case that held the badge on one side and detective Jerald Daugherty's Oklahoma Bureau of Investigation ID on the other. Robert didn't think he looked much like the detective, but Archie said they could be brothers.

"Like you were fraternal twins who were separated at birth."

Robert looked at the picture again. Considering his childhood, anything was possible.

Sarah asked him why he didn't blow the spirit powder into the detective's face like they had planned.

He wanted to give her a flippant answer. He wanted to say, "Why should I have all the fun?" But he did not. He had become lost in the role he was playing. He had become the slacker doing drugs on a park bench so thoroughly that he hadn't been able to shake it off when it was time to become Robert Collins again.

"Don't play it so real next time," she said.

He wanted to give her reassurances, but he could not. That was the reason he did not want to carry Detective Jerald Daugherty's pistol.

32

"THE DICK ZOMBIE" was Dr. Selene's new name among the Stringtown janitorial staff. Orderlies called a "love sausage alert" when he walked onto the floor, and the nurses speculated on ways to muzzle his pet "trouser snake" before someone got a nasty bite.

Psychiatric residents were the bottom link of the gossip chain, so when Marie heard one junior shrink tell another about the doctor's "testosterone lobotomy," she knew the word was as out as it could get. Dr. Selene was in love with a client. It was only a matter of time until disaster struck.

No surprise there. Marie's love affairs always ended in disaster. But this time she laid out her plans like a demolition expert. She was lucid and alert and ready to resume her life with Archie Chatto. Maybe her fixation on Archie meant she was still crazy, but it didn't feel that way. She hadn't felt so clever and in control since she was fourteen years old—just after the police took Gideon away.

The doctor reacted to love like an inexperienced high school boy. His voice raised several decibels when he talked with Marie. He stumbled over words. He wrote her name in the margins of patient records. His respiration rate dramatically increased when Marie gave him the slightest amount of attention and sometimes when she didn't.

His confidence gradually grew stronger, as Marie knew it would. Slowly, tentatively, he nibbled at the edges of her affection, in much the same way he'd approach a tough cut of meat. Take small bites. Chew each one thoroughly. Hope you find the tender parts before you break a tooth. Everyone in the hospital could see Dr. Selene's behavior for what it was, with the possible exception of the psychiatrist, himself.

He took meals with her in the cafeteria. Not exactly an intimate setting, but they were together in a safe environment where he was still the doctor and she was still the patient.

Phase one. All systems go.

Then he took her away from the institution to eat in fancy restaurants in towns with state lodges on lakes built by the Army Corps of Engineers.

Phase two. Countdown in progress.

Then he brought her flowers.

Lift off.

There was no way the famous and influential Dr. Selene could pass off a dozen long-stemmed roses as cutting-edge floral therapy. Marie made preparations for the next step on the courtship agenda. She had studied the manuals and double-checked the figures. Who says romance isn't rocket science?

Dr. Selene shut the door to Marie's private room as soon as he crossed the threshold. He walked toward her slowly, stiff legged, stooped over in a sort of standing fetal position. He thrust his hands into his pockets and fumbled with something just beyond their reach. Unless the doctor had become a banana smuggler, love was on his mind.

His lips moved, but no words came out. Marie knew he had something important to say, something clever and romantic.

"Well...." He'd probably written a script and rehearsed it in front of a mirror, but now it was as irretrievable as the list of presidents he'd memorized in the eighth grade.

"It's like this, see...."

Marie took a seat on her twin bed and invited the doctor. "Come sit beside me." She coaxed him with soothing vocal inflections and hand gestures as if he were a nervous puppy.

Dr. Selene muttered something unintelligible. The poor man's saliva had thickened to the consistency of peanut butter.

Marie handed him a half-filled glass of water that was sitting on her bedside table. A prominent lipstick smudge decorated the rim, and she watched him turn the glass so that his lips were positioned exactly where hers had been.

"Something like a kiss," Marie told him.

Dr. Selene choked a bit, but he finished her water and released the breath he'd been holding since he first entered the room.

She could have put the doctor at ease if she had chosen. Marie was good at making men feel comfortable, but then he'd feel entitled to take their *relationship* to the next logical level, and Archie Chatto would not approve.

It always came to this when a man and a woman were together long enough. This was the point at which the character of the relationship would be determined. If things went according to Marie's plan, she'd have her way with Dr. Selene without giving him the medium of exchange every man desired. This was not the first time Marie Ferraro had practiced sexual brinkmanship, but it was her first time with a man Dr. Selene's age who was so obviously inexperienced.

He kissed her.

Archie wouldn't mind a kiss. Especially a kiss like that. Dr. Selene kept his mouth closed, his lips puckered tight, the way a boy kisses his sister. The back of his hand brushed across her breast, a contrived accident, totally expected.

The doctor followed a pattern genetically programmed into every teenage boy. When Marie didn't slap him, he grew bolder. He gave her another close-mouthed kiss and pressed the palm of his right hand over her left breast. He squeezed rhythmically as though he were strengthening his grip with an unaccustomed piece of exercise equipment.

Archie wouldn't mind that either. Men had been groping women in the same clumsy manner ever since God made Eve.

Dr. Selene eased Marie back onto the bed, never once considering a firm "throw down" would be far more consistent with his crude technique.

He lay on top of her, allowing her to appreciate the feel of his erection through the combined thickness of her dress and his pants.

Marie failed to suppress an involuntary shiver, but she knew Dr. Selene would interpret her tremor as poorly controlled ecstasy. Sometimes the most seductive thing a woman can do is to cleverly disguise her revulsion.

This adventure would not proceed as the psychiatrist hoped, but Marie wouldn't be the one to call it off, at least not directly. She analyzed the situation. What would serve her purposes more, a premature ejaculation or sudden erectile dysfunction? Not much time to decide. The doctor lifted her dress and was in the process of removing her panties. He employed the same economy of motion a mother might use to change a diaper on a toddler who has passed the optimal age of potty-training.

The doctor held Marie Ferraro's underwear in his hands much longer than was appropriate. He stretched them to their elastic limit and drenched them with palm sweat. When he tangled them in his zipper while dispatching his trousers, Marie knew it was time to act.

"I know what it is you really want," she whispered in a slow seductive hiss, barely audible over the central air conditioning.

"What?"

"I know exactly what you want," she whispered louder the second time. She had to because the psychiatrist pulled back several inches.

All men had their little sexual quirks. Scars left from careless parenting, she supposed. Marie had never met a man who didn't want something he was ashamed to admit. The psychiatrist was no different. He hadn't exorcised his own demons through years spent on an analyst's couch. Dr. Selene's secret desires were alive and well, and from the effect her obtuse statement had on his formerly vigorous erection, they must be particularly shameful.

"Before I give you what you want," Marie said. "There is something we should talk about."

Dr. Selene's romantic moment had passed, but discussion was going to be difficult with her panties embedded in his zipper.

"Archie has escaped from prison," Marie told him. She would have known this for a fact even if she had not seen it on the television in her private room. She would have been able to smell Archie Chatto's freedom in the wind.

"He'll come for me. You know he will."

The doctor managed to extract Marie's underpants from his fly. When she ignored his efforts to return them, he folded the panties into thirds and placed them on the bed beside her. His eyes lingered on them while she explained his current circumstances.

"He'll kill you." Her tone was as free of inflection as an automated answering machine. Press one if you are feeling faint. Press two if you would like to run out of the room. Press three to review the menu. Have a nice day.

Marie's indifference struck the psychiatrist with the impact of a hammer. Dr. Selene rose from the bed and backed away from her without breaking eye contact—all the way to the door of her private room. He found the doorknob through trial and error.

When he pulled it open, Marie heard the sound of clinic shoes retreating down the hall. Probably a nurse. By tomorrow the shameful story of Dr. Selene's romantic misadventure would be in its final form, complete with sound effects and erotic dialogue.

"Do you really know what I want?" The doctor brushed telltale strands of female hair from his shirt and checked one last time to be certain everything was properly tucked and fastened.

"I do."

"It doesn't trouble you."

"A bit, perhaps. Not much."

"I'll figure something out," the doctor said. "About Archie, I mean." Marie knew exactly what the doctor meant. He was about to be coaxed into a rash act by a woman he could not have. Like Julius Caesar. Like Sampson. Like Hercules. The good doctor didn't stand a chance.

33

"**H**IDE IN THE** tall grass," Archie said. "Pick a vulnerable animal from the herd."

Sarah and Robert weren't hunting buffalo. They were stealing an SUV. Archie said they'd need one to rescue Marie.

The tall grass was the golfers' parking lot at the OKC Golf and Country Club. Sarah's Subaru Outback was their hiding place. It was the least expensive automobile there, but it was clean and polished and only slightly out of place.

Robert sat behind the wheel, even though he couldn't drive. Sarah sat so close to him another person could have joined them on the narrow bench seat. They pretended to be lovers. It was not as difficult as Sarah had imagined.

All four windows were open. The breeze cooled Sarah and boosted Robert's confidence. His lack of driving skills was a serious handicap to car theft.

"You can do it," Archie promised. "A thoughtful hunter can overcome any weakness." His plan hinged on the fact that the Oklahoma City Golf and Country Club employed undocumented immigrants as valets to park guest cars. The Apache had always used the *medicine line* between the United States and its neighbor to the south. Some things never change.

"The Sooner Swing Dance Society will be at the country club this evening. Drinks and light hors d'oeuvres at seven. Dancing starts at eight." Archie had gleaned this bit of information from the social pages of *The Oklahoman*. "A hunter picks through the scat of his prey to learn their grazing patterns."

"Comparing the city newspaper with scat isn't much of a stretch," Sarah said. "But stealing cars isn't the same as hunting."

"A different way of living off the land," Archie told her. "Now that the buffalo are gone."

"Watch for a low-end, late model SUV." Archie had cut pictures from the used car section of the newspaper for quick reference. "More expensive vehicles will be equipped with GPS anti-theft devices."

Stealing cars was much more technical than Sarah had imagined. "Why not just break the ignition lock or cross some of the colored wires inside the steering column?" That's the way they did it on TV.

Archie knew how to do that, too, but stealing cars that way damaged the electrical system. "Turn indicators flicker. Headlights and taillights malfunction. Signs even the most disinterested policeman feels obligated to notice. Much better to steal a car along with the keys, one that couldn't be located electronically by orbital spies in the sky."

Archie told them they would be going to Choctaw country. He hadn't figured out exactly where, but that would come.

It made sense to Sarah. Hashilli's name, the Choctaw plates on his black SUV, and his connection with the Maytubby bone-house all pointed to a tribal affiliation. Even if they couldn't find him in the old Indian Territory tribal lands, they would certainly find clues that might eventually lead them to the place he'd taken Marie.

"But why has he taken my mother?" If Hashilli intended to harm Marie, he could have done so easily while she was still a patient at Flanders. If he wanted to keep her as a hostage to prevent Sarah's further interference in his activities, he would have contacted her by now with threats and demands.

"Don't think of Hashilli as an ordinary criminal," Archie told her. "He's a witch, and he has a witch's motives."

Sarah didn't believe in witches, but Hashilli's beliefs, not hers, were important here.

"Hashilli Maytubby is a shapeshifter," Archie said. "Did your anthropology professors ignore the subject?"

"Lycanthrope?" An outrageous idea with a Latin name. Or was this one Greek? It didn't matter. She couldn't speak either one. "I'm fresh out of silver bullets."

"Anthropologists take things so literally," Archie said. "Hashilli changes from an antiquities dealer to a psychiatrist to a social worker to God knows what. Think of a shape-shifter as a master impersonator—not a werewolf."

Could time spent with Archie Chatto could count as fieldwork? Sarah thought Professor Lindsay would be open to persuasion. "But why do we have to steal a car?" Her Subaru could manage the back roads of rural Oklahoma in a pinch.

"Rough terrain ahead," Archie told her. Four-wheel drive would be a plus, and size definitely mattered. "Your Subaru is too small. We need something large enough to carry all of us."

The "all of us" Archie spoke of included Robert, Sarah, Big Shorty, Marie, and himself. Five people would crowd the Subaru to its limit, but she didn't understand why Big Shorty was included.

"Hasn't Shorty done enough?"

"There's plenty left to do," Archie said. "And a man like Shorty is well worth the space he'll occupy."

So, Sarah and Robert sat in Sarah's Subaru, watching undocumented young men park cars. Archie Chatto was their invisible backup.

———

LOVERS MEETING SECRETLY in the parking lot. They did it all the time according to Archie. "No one cares. No one pays attention. No one will remember, as long as you make it real."

Robert sat behind the steering wheel because that was where men ordinarily sat. He placed his right arm around Sarah's willing shoulder. The summer breeze carried the odor of freshly cut grass through the open windows, but Robert didn't need the wind, for once in his life, to make his smile authentic.

"Don't get the wrong idea," Sarah told him, just before she kissed him softly on the cheek and lips.

"Kiss me back," she whispered. "With enthusiasm. You know, in case someone looks this way."

Robert slipped easily into his assigned role. Easier than a lawyer, easier than a slacker. He could hear and feel Sarah breathing in his ear. It was a warm and familiar feeling, like a whispered message delivered by the restless Oklahoma wind.

They didn't have to wait too long. Members of the swing dance club drove through the double lane entryway with alcohol-enhanced abandon. They passed their keys to Hispanic strangers and went inside to wax nostalgic to music that was new when Germany bombed England. During that short span of time, Sarah discovered a very interesting interface between psychology and physiology. A man and a woman need pretend sexual interest in each other for only a few minutes before hormones turn fiction into fact. This was something her mother had always known.

"Keep your mind on stealing cars," she told Robert. But she could see from the addled look on his face that stealing kisses was more central in his thoughts. Sarah adjusted the rearview mirror and evaluated her reflection. The vermillion border of her lips was deep red, filled with oxygen rich blood. Her pupils were dilated. Her eyes refused to focus properly. Addled, she decided, not as bad as Robert but addled all the same.

She made a show of straightening her blouse, even though Robert had been a perfect gentleman. Would she have let him go further? Sarah would figure that one out after they had stolen their late model, low-end SUV.

"There's one now," she told him. "An exact match to one of the pictures Archie showed us, and it's red, my favorite color."

At that moment red was Robert's favorite color too. He opened the passenger door and stepped onto the parking lot. The next empty valet parking spot was number 24. His double-digit destination.

Robert wore a light blue fall jacket purchased at Goodwill. It was a little too heavy for the summer evening, but it *almost* concealed the shoulder holster under his left arm.

"Let the valet see the weapon," Archie had counseled, "but don't draw it." No worries there. Even though Robert's pistol was unloaded, he would never point it at anyone.

IT WAS THE perfect interception. Robert appeared beside the SUV just as the young Hispanic valet turned the ignition off. He tapped Detective Jerald Daugherty's gold shield against the tinted window with one hand, while he opened the driver's side door with the other. Exactly as planned.

"Leave the keys in the ignition. Step out of the vehicle. Let me see your hands." Three short phrases verging on hostility.

"Is there a problem, officer?" The valet followed the script perfectly. His name was Alfonso according to the plastic tag he wore on his black OKC Golf and Country Club shirt. Men who parked cars didn't need last names.

"Some people back at the main office want to talk with you." Robert took an aggressive step toward Alfonso, and just as planned, Alfonso stepped back.

"Momentum," Archie had called it. "Once he starts moving, he won't be able to stop." Alfonso tried to run away, but he tripped over an untied shoelace. By the time he was back on his feet, his plans had changed.

Archie had warned Robert about things like that. "Luck can turn on a dime. When it does, you'll have to improvise." He wasn't specific about improvisation, so when Alfonso reached into the pocket of his uniform pants, Robert didn't know exactly what to do.

"I have a green card," Alfonso said, but what he withdrew from his pocket was a butterfly knife. He opened it with a stereotypical gangster flourish.

"Shit!" Was that what a cop would say? Close enough.

Alfonso swung the knife in an artistic arch that brought the tip of the blade within an inch of Robert's eyes.

He doesn't want to hurt me. He wants a chance to run.

Alfonso cut a figure eight in the air. He executed a spin that would have been the envy of the Sooner Swing Dancers, and he brought the knife around again. The boy had talent.

Robert drew Jerald Daugherty's unloaded Glock from its shoulder holster and moved it into the trajectory of Alfonso's blade.

The collision sent both weapons clattering onto the macadam surface of the parking lot. Alfonso locked eyes with Robert for a moment. He judged the distance between the policeman and the pistol and decided it was far enough.

The valet bolted for the golf course where he would find sanctuary among the cedar trees and sand traps long before this officer would be able to take aim and squeeze off a shot.

When Robert turned back to the red SUV, Archie Chatto was already behind the wheel.

"Go back to Shorty's place with Sarah." Archie told him. "I'll join you there after I swap tags."

The plan was back on track. Archie would trade license plates with another SUV of the same color and model at the parking lot of Will Rogers World Airport. If they were lucky, the owner of the SUV whose tag they stole would be on a long vacation. By the time anyone noticed the license plate exchange, the search for the stolen vehicle would be cold.

Sarah greeted Robert with a kiss as he slid into the passenger seat of her Subaru. He was pretty certain this one was not provided for the purpose of cover.

"Had a bit of a problem with Alfonso," he said.

"So I saw."

"I improvised."

"Well done."

Robert looked over at the valet station. The remaining attendants had disappeared. "I guess the swing dancers will have to handle parking by themselves."

"We've saved each of them at least a dollar," Sarah said. "They should be grateful."

She had a point, but Robert doubted the swing dancers would feel that way, especially the couple with the missing SUV.

He found the time to steal one last kiss before she drove away.

34

EVEN WITCHES NEED their sleep. Hashilli usually had no trouble collecting his eight empty hours at the end of the day. But lately his dreams were filled with the sounds of owls flying and images of Marie Ferarro wearing nothing but a pair of red high heel shoes designed by Salvatore Ferragamo. He knew this fashion detail because voices told him. Robert Collins's voice and Sarah Bible's and the voice of an estranged female cousin, Sissy McCurtain.

Hashilli hadn't heard Sissy's voice since she chased him off Maytubby land with a shotgun nearly thirty years ago.

Did Grandfather send those dreams? Or Marie? Or her meddling daughter? Or the crazy one, Robert Collins? Too many distractions. Not enough sleep. It was almost like having a conscience.

"You act like you have no family." Sissy McCurtain's voice again, not so loud while he was awake but insistent. All the living Maytubbys were against him—every aunt and uncle, all the cousins, even the family dogs.

But I still have the ancestors.

Mostly true. But Maytubby ghosts spoke in signs and visions that were easily misunderstood. They demanded much, criticized quickly, and were slow to offer praise. Had he read the cosmic Maytubby plan correctly or gotten it completely wrong?

The young bull vanquishes the old one and rules the herd. But when Hashilli vanquished Grandfather, the herd scattered to the winds. No blood tied him to the Maytubbys. No mother linked Hashilli with a clan. No wife. No sister. Hashilli had no women in his life until Marie.

The owl shadow had drawn circles around her and took a blood offering from her hand. He'd seen it. Marie's image condensed in his mind like beads of moisture on a cocktail glass. The Ferragamos were crocodile hide. The buckles were fourteen carat gold. Their color matched her toenails, her fingernails, and her lips. Marie's areola were perfectly round and pink. Her backside struck the perfect balance between esthetic and erotic. Her mouth invited his kiss. Her skin called for his touch. She was perfect except for her lack of Choctaw blood.

Grandfather had warned him about women like Marie. "Once they get inside your head, you can never make them leave."

Quiet, Grandfather. I don't need you anymore.

Hashilli stood before the Maytubby bone-house and spoke loud enough to catch the attention of the most distracted ancestors. "Do you finally understand? Have you finally forgiven me?" Hashilli hadn't sent Grandfather off with a knife between his ribs or a pillow over his face. The old man's inner shadow had been carried to the afterlife on the wings of power.

"Owl's wings, Grandfather!" His emotions added too much volume to his words. Would the ancestors consider it an act of bravery to raise his voice where the African god might hear, or would they think him foolish?

Were ghosts open to persuasion? For two decades they denied Hashilli an heir. He had offered them a hundred babies, and they rejected every one. Now he'd take matters into his own hands. His successor would be born in the traditional way.

Marie Ferraro had given birth to one child of power. Soon she'd bear another. Everything of value comes through the mother. Women are life givers, and men are life takers. That is a basic lesson of the ancestors. Every Choctaw knows it.

When the new boy-witch of the Maytubby family reached his

prime, he would send Hashilli's spirit flying just as Hashilli had done for Grandfather, with a tea made from moonflowers and spirit mushrooms. Perhaps the boy would find another way. Methodology was trivial as long as it was done with honor.

Hashilli closed his eyes. He stood quietly, waiting for a sign. Ghosts were not generous with accolades, so he was surprised to hear the dull rhythmic thud that grew louder with each passing second.

Spirit sounds? A mother's heart must sound like that just before the rhythm is lost in the trauma of birth. But this heart sound was not quite right.

"What the hell are you doing in that old boneyard?" Baron Saturday's booming voice startled the witch from his prayers. The large black god lurched toward the gate on his padded stumps.

Hashilli was only a little worried. The spirits of the ancestors could keep the Voodoo deity at bay. They wouldn't tolerate an African interloper on sacred ground.

But the black god didn't seem to understand. He lurched over the threshold of the Indian Baptist Cemetery. He paused only long enough to steady his broad brimmed gardener's hat. He crossed himself in the Catholic fashion and then closed the distance between them. Fearlessly.

Hashilli called out to the ancestors, but the only sign of ghostly activity was the raucous arrival of a flock of crows. They flew over the gravestones and around the bone-houses like an untidy formation of artillery spotter planes looking for an enemy target. He knew the birds were not coming to his aid. He had seen them mob hawks and even owls when the birds of prey ventured into the crows' territory. There was no stopping these black, winged creatures when they were on the move.

Baron Saturday took another step toward the Maytubby bone-house. He leveled an accusing finger at Hashilli. The digit was as thick and black as the barrel of a pistol.

Would the ancestors allow the Voodoo god to kill one of their own? How did this African spirit mean to dispatch a Choctaw witch? With a bolt of lightning? Would a crevice open in the fabric of the world and swallow Hashilli into an afterlife of zombies and winged serpents?

The Voodoo god shouted something, but his words were drowned out by the noise of the growing swarm of crows.

Baron Saturday lurched forward, following a broken path around the deadwood littering the little graveyard. The African carefully avoided brushing against the yellow mushrooms clustered on the rotting cotton-wood branches.

Spirit mushrooms. Could Indian magic turn aside a deity from the Dark Continent? The mushroom spores would send the inner shadows of ordinary humans into the half world between life and death. Only shape-shifters could touch the spirit powder and remain standing. An image of Robert Collins flashed in Hashilli's mind. The yellow dust had no effect on the wind talker. What would it do to the Guardian of the Dead?

Baron Saturday pointed his finger at Hashilli again. He raised his voice loud enough so the Choctaw witch could hear some of the words above the noise of the mobbing crows.

"Where have you taken Sarah's mother?"

Hashilli knew at that moment he had chosen the right woman to bear his child. Even Baron Saturday wanted her.

The African god lurched closer, almost close enough to touch Hashilli with that black accusing finger. The noise and activity of the crows increased with every clumsy step. The birds flew through the Indian Baptist Cemetery in tight circles, swooping past trees and headstones, missing Hashilli and the African by inches. Neither man flinched.

Hashilli did not raise his voice when he told Baron Saturday, "I will deal with you in the usual way." Perhaps the African would hear him over the sounds of wings and crow-calls, and perhaps he would not.

"The way I deal with all meddlers." In all his years as a sorcerer, Hashilli's spirit powder had failed him only once. That was something he would have to think about later, after his magic rendered the African harmless.

Hashilli reached into the secret pocket sewn into the tail of his shirt. Ordinarily, he would employ some simple but effective distraction. The powder would appear in the palm of his open hand as if by magic.

But the baron would not be impressed by sleight of hand, so Hashilli didn't bother.

The African stumbled back when he saw the mound of yellow powder.

So far, so good. Hashilli moved forward. On the offensive for the first time. The expression on the baron's face was proof his tried and true tactic would succeed.

Would the crows go away when the African fell to the ground? Time would tell.

Hashilli drew a deep breath and blew hard enough to cover Baron Saturday with the toxic mushroom spores. If the spirit powder didn't kill the African, he would be unconscious for hours, maybe days.

That is exactly how things would have gone if the crows had not spoiled the plan.

A mob of birds flew between the Choctaw witch and the Voodoo God. The flock absorbed the powder into their feathers like a great black sponge. The birds fell to the ground like feathered hailstones. Dead or sleeping, Hashilli couldn't tell. He didn't wait around to see what Baron Saturday made of this. He was off and running from the African God. He hurdled over the sandstone wall that no longer protected the Indian Baptist Cemetery.

When a Choctaw witch comes face to face with a Voodoo Loa, sometimes it is best to run away.

35

SARAH PULLED THE stolen red SUV up to the security camera at the mechanized gate at the Stringtown Mental Health Facility. She addressed the microphone much louder than necessary.

"I am Assistant State's Attorney Connie Rubirosa." She pointed a thumb at Robert, who sat quietly in the passenger seat enjoying the flow of air through his open window. "This is Detective Jerald Daugherty." After she got Robert's full attention with a quick kick to his shin, he produced his stolen badge and pushed it in front of Sarah's face toward the camera lens. He mugged the camera with an arrogant smile, tipped an imaginary hat, then resumed his ultra-relaxed, don't-make-me-come-over-there posture. The perfect civil servant.

Sarah marveled at the sincerity with which Robert played the part of a police detective. She had no doubt he could verbally bulldoze his way through the Mental Hospital's security zone if he were sitting in the driver's seat.

Members of the State's Attorney's office never chauffeured detectives around. That part of their ruse lacked authenticity, but there was no help for it. Even when he was well within his detective persona, Robert Collins couldn't drive.

Sarah spoke louder as she directed the hospital security team's attention to the passenger in the central row of seats behind her. She hoped the nervous tremor in her voice would be lost in the elevated decibels and low-quality sound equipment.

"We are accompanied by Doctor Baron Samady, who is authorized to interview a patient we believe you are holding in your facility illegally." She watched the camera move on its axis and focus on Big Shorty's grim face. He looked more like a death camp counselor than a psychiatrist.

"That's the beauty of it," Archie told Sarah when he laid out his plan for rescuing Marie. "The deception doesn't have to be convincing. It has to be confusing." Big Shorty's race, his handicap, and the vague familiarity of his foreign name would all be critical to breaking down the resistance of hospital security. Sarah would be the lawyer, Robert would be the policeman. Shorty would be their ace in the hole.

"The ace of spades," Shorty said, when Archie took away his gardener's hat and made him dress in burying clothes. "Death's business card."

Archie also chose Sarah's pseudonym. Connie Rubirosa was one of the beautiful and clever assistant district attorneys from the *Law and Order* series. No one remembered the names of supporting actors, especially the pretty ones.

"But it will ring a bell," Archie said. "Hard to think when bells are ringing in your head."

Maybe the security team would be too confused to notice Robert wasn't driving. Maybe they'd open the gate and send Marie walking out. Sarah looked at her watch. She turned the crystal toward the camera and tapped it several times. "We're waiting."

She fished a legal-looking piece of paper out of her shoulder bag and waved it in front of the camera. "This is a warrant, duly issued by the State's Attorney, permitting us to search the facility and to interview members of your staff. It also grants us access to such records as we deem necessary."

Sarah knew the guards couldn't read the warrant through an instrument as crude as a gate security camera. She counted on that. She'd produced the document using her laptop and a high-quality inkjet printer owned by Victoria and Albert Tiger. It looked convincing from a distance but wouldn't stand up to close scrutiny.

Back in Oklahoma City, Sarah had thought Archie's rescue plan was well developed, even unnecessarily thorough, but faced with a locked gate and a faceless team of security guards, she realized it was hardly any plan at all. She didn't even know for certain her mother was being held in Stringtown.

"Hashilli will take Marie where he feels comfortable and in control," Archie had explained. "Everything about the witch screams Civilized Tribes and whispers Choctaw." Hashilli had focused his kidnapping scheme on Indian casinos. Used a Choctaw-funded child development center to hide stolen children. Passed himself off as a dealer in Native American antiquities. Drove an SUV with Choctaw Nation tags. "Which everyone seemed to notice without writing down the numbers."

Sarah had been surprised and a little intimidated by the number of enterprises owned, controlled, or funded by the Choctaw Nation. Of all her Google-strikes, Stringtown Mental Health Facility stood out as most likely to serve as a hiding place for Marie. The hospital was built just after Sarah and Marie moved to New Mexico. Operational costs were covered by a combination of Choctaw tribal money and federal grants administered by a Choctaw committee. Most of the clients and a majority of the professional staff were Native American. No one named Hashilli, Luna, or Moon appeared on the public roster of employees, but a Dr. H. Selene was listed as a board member and a consulting psychiatrist.

Another moon name. Good enough for Sarah. Archie agreed after he "smoked it and dreamed it," whatever that meant. Robert went along because he liked the name, Stringtown, and because he would go along with anything that allowed him close proximity with Sarah.

The only dissenter was Big Shorty. "Can't change facts with a majority vote." He admitted Stringtown was as good a place to start looking for Marie as any other, even though he had a list of dont's. "Don't like the plan. Don't want to be a shrink. Don't want to wear a suit. Don't like the name Samaday. It's a French word. Don't like the French."

So easy to hate the French. Even a crazy cemetery caretaker can do it. Sarah wanted to ask Shorty about his Francophobia, but she was afraid he'd launch into a bigoted rant that would poison their relationship. Even worse, he might persuade her he was right.

The security gate didn't open when Sarah held her fake warrant in front of the camera. She had no idea what to do next, but Robert was already on the move. He opened the passenger side door, walked around the front of the SUV, kicked the chain link gate hard enough to make it rattle, and then took up a position in front of the camera too close for it to accommodate with a sharp focus.

"You will open this gate immediately." He spoke in a flat mono-tone as though he might be reading the words from a teleprompter. He moved even closer to the camera, opened his mouth wide enough to provide his audience a view of his uvula. He fogged the lens with his breath. He wiped a fingertip-size clear zone in the center of the glass and stepped back.

Sarah imagined a clear image of Robert's angry cop-face appearing on a television screen surrounded by a halo of blurry color. She hoped the effect would be as impressive in reality as it was in her mind.

Robert read names from the list of employees Sarah had taken from the hospital web site.

"These people will be arrested for obstruction of justice if we are not admitted immediately." He turned to Sarah. "Get ready to crash the gate." She pressed on the accelerator pedal and watched the tachometer needle move to three thousand. She placed her hand on the gearshift lever and prepared to commit criminal trespass at Robert's signal.

"On the count of four." Sacred number. That number would res-onate with Indian guards, even if they didn't understand why. Rob-ert might be crazy, but he was smart. Maybe he did have the soul of a Pueblo Shaman.

"One, two, three." No ambiguous pauses between the numbers. No doubt in Robert's voice. He flipped a finger up for each number. A clear sign of the digital age.

"Wait!" The degree of emotion conveyed through the tiny monotone speaker below the camera exceeded anything the designing engineers could have imagined.

Robert stood in front of the camera holding three fingers in the air like a demonic Boy Scout preparing to recite the Oath. There was a mentally awake clause, if Sarah remembered correctly.

"We will meet you at the gate!" The speaker wasn't engineered to deal with shouts. The anonymous guard's words lost their sharp borders and hissed into static. His exited exhalations over his microphone resembled wind sounds closely enough to give Robert an enigmatic smile the security team was sure to misinterpret.

"Our attorney wants to examine your warrant, then we will cooperate fully."

Their attorney. Sarah didn't like the sound of that. Why would a mental hospital have an attorney on the premises?

A green and white Land Rover equipped with a roof bar of rotating yellow lights parked ten yards from the security gate. Four uniformed guards and one man dressed in a charcoal grey power suit emerged just as the gate's electric motor hummed to life and swung the chain link barrier inward.

The five men moved toward Robert like a troop of soldiers with Power Suit in the lead. Sarah and Big Shorty remained in the car.

Power Suit introduced himself to Robert. "My name is Stephen Lonebear. I represent the hospital in the matter of our missing client."

Robert liked the name Lonebear. So many members of the civilized tribes had adopted the British, Scottish, and Irish names.

When the attorney with the Indian name asked for the warrant, Robert took it from Sarah. He held the piece of paper as if he were about to relinquish it, but he pulled the document back while Stephen Lonebear's hand was still reaching out.

"Missing client?" Robert held the fake warrant against his chest. He traded looks with Sarah and Big Shorty. Shorty rolled his window down and glared at the attorney but didn't say a word.

Attorney Lonebear asked for the warrant again, but Robert had some questions.

"Maybe the FBI should be involved," Robert suggested. "Maybe

Marie Ferraro wasn't illegally transported from one mental hospital to another. Maybe she's been kidnapped?"

Maybe I'll slap the cuffs on your delicate lawyer wrists and lead you off to prison where you will be a bad man's girlfriend. All implied with an intense stare.

The lawyer swallowed hard but said nothing.

Big Shorty spoke from his seat in the stolen SUV. "Where is Doctor Selene? He should be able to straighten this out."

The lawyer swallowed hard again. He told them Dr. Selene was missing too. "That's why I'm here, evaluating the hospital's liability in the matter."

"Stupid bastard." Shorty spit a wad of mucous-loaded saliva out the window. He didn't specify the target of his insult. He flashed the lawyer an alligator smile. "Hazardous waste crew can clean that up later on," he said. "Tell us what you know." Shorty drummed his fingers on the door panel. It made a sound like horses galloping over a wooden bridge.

"Now!" The force of Shorty's order knocked the lawyer and the security team back a step.

Robert told them, "The baron took his training at the University of Rwanda. They take a more direct approach over there. Best if you don't make him get out of the car."

"Well." Stephen Lonebear had the look of a man who just remembered an important appointment somewhere far away. "I'm not sure I should say."

The lawyer glanced at Dr. Samaday's hand moving toward the outside door handle of the SUV and got sure right away. "Doctor Selene's behavior has been somewhat erratic. Now may I see your warrant?"

The wind picked up as the hospital's attorney reached for the document. It rearranged his carefully combed hair, revealing the doll-head pattern indicative of hair plugs acquired at bargain basement prices. The lawyer pulled his hand back and brushed it over his hair, as if his secret could still be concealed from this unwelcome trio of intruders.

Sarah lifted her cell phone, punched a series of keys and held the instrument to her ear. "This is Assistant State's Attorney Connie Rubirosa. Yes, I'll hold for the Attorney General."

Stephen Lonebear made a time out signal with his hands. "I'll tell you what you want to know. Don't involve the Attorney General."

Sarah listened to the time and temperature and then ended her call. "Let's hear it."

The hospital attorney was a fount of information for about two straight minutes. Marie Ferraro had been brought to the hospital as Dr. Selene's special client. She had been admitted without the proper paperwork, and Dr. Selene had taken her away from the hospital without discharging or transferring her.

"Since the disappearance, it was brought to my attention that Doctor Selene has made some statements to staff and clients that cast doubt on his stability."

Robert pressed for details.

"He claimed he was being stalked by an African god." The wind continued to blow through Stephen Lonebear's hair making his plugs stand out like rows of corn. He needed a comb and styling moose to keep the hair in place, but his hands were totally insufficient. Finally he admitted defeat.

"A Voodoo god who walks on amputated stumps." The wind twisted the plugs into miniature vortices of hair. The lawyer seemed to be wearing a fright wig manufactured for Rastafarian consumers. When he made another reach for the warrant, Robert let him touch it, but the wind pulled the paper from his hand and carried it into the sky.

Robert asked, "Any idea where the doctor took Marie?"

"He said he was taking her home. That's all I know."

Big Shorty opened his car door. The wind stopped blowing when he stepped out of the SUV and lurched toward the lawyer and the guards. Chaos descended quickly after that.

One of the guards shouted, "Oh, my god it's all true!" Before he finished the sentence, the uniformed staff was off and running toward individual vanishing points on the horizon.

Attorney Stephen Lonebear put a dozen steps backward between himself and the African god, then turned and ran until Big Shorty, Robert, and Sarah couldn't see him anymore.

36

EVERY CUBIC CENTIMETER of Archie literally screamed, "I am an Apache warrior." From the maternal nucleic acids in his mitochondria to the stone-cold-killer look in his dark brown eyes, the man was quintessential renegade.

"Being civilized makes people afraid to die," he told Sarah.

"Afraid you're going to kill them." She adjusted his collar, brushed a few stray hairs off his shoulders. As if those things could make a difference. Sarah made a slow circuit around Archie, appraising him from every angle. "Still scary." No amount of fiddling was going to change that.

Archie Chatto's hair was trimmed and neatly parted. He wore a Tommy Bahama Hawaiian style shirt with its tail flowing casually over his Arizona Jeans. His hands were clean. His nails were more or less manicured. Archie was parole board pretty, but he would never pass for a peaceful, law-abiding member of society. He was a pit bull on the way to a dogfight, and dressing him in discount store fashions could not disguise that fact.

"You won't fool the Choctaw," Sarah told him. "They don't have two hundred years of white guilt dimming their vision."

"They'll talk to me." When Archie asked questions, people told him things. Maybe they didn't tell him everything. Maybe they told him little white lies. But they told him something, even if they had Indian ways.

Sarah handed him a picture of Marie. He kissed it gently and placed it in his shirt pocket. She gave him a Xerox copy of Hashilli Maytubby's driver's license. He glared at it and stuck it in the back pocket of his jeans.

"Next to my ass," he said. "Where he belongs."

"People call the police when they're afraid."

Archie smiled at Sarah's naiveté. Indians wouldn't call the cops because a dangerous-looking man was in the neighborhood. Indians were slow to bring the authorities into their lives, even the Civilized Tribes. "If they know anything about Marie, they'll tell me."

Hashilli was another matter. He might be a cousin or an uncle. They wouldn't talk about relatives to a stranger. Not the first time they were asked.

"If they hold back, I'll shake the truth out of them," Archie said. That wouldn't be too hard. Ordinary people start shaking the moment he walked into the room. Like Chihuahuas in the presence of a wolf.

ARCHIE MADE THE grand tour of Choctaw country without incident. No one took him to task when he checked out the tribal hospice program in Bryan County. Likewise, at the smoke shops in Pocola, Durant, Hugo, and Arrowhead. When he visited community centers in Bethel, Antlers, and Broken Bow, the administrative staffs were cordial and cooperative. Workers at the trailer manufacturing facility in Choctaw were equally obliging.

Archie got some funny looks when he brought urine samples to the tribe's corporate drug testing service. Security guards at Blue Ribbon Downs racetrack made him walk through a metal detector, but if anyone called the police, he never heard about it.

He visited patients at the Choctaw Nation Health Care Center at Talihina without triggering alarms. He made his way to eight different tribal clinics seeking information about HIV testing—anonymously, of course. He questioned strangers in the streets in Durant and Valiant. Conversations always ended the same way. "Never heard of a Choctaw named Hashilli. Good luck finding the woman." No hesitation. No signs of deception. No flashing lights or sirens.

It wasn't until Archie visited a dental office in Coalgate that he came to the attention of the police. Hashilli's Mr. Luna persona was a member of a community board that funded the dental practice through a National Health Service grant.

Archie knew Hashilli hadn't stashed Marie inside a dental office, but he followed the lead anyway. Maybe the hygienist had cleaned Mr. Luna's teeth. Maybe Marie came in with a lost filling. Anything was possible. His expectations were low, and so was his mood, when he walked up to the receptionist. He had a pained expression on his face, but he did not act like a man with a toothache.

The young woman behind the counter greeted Archie with an insincere smile. She spoke the crisp colorless accent of a television newsreader. No trace of Choctaw Country dialect. The streaks of gold highlighting the symmetrical curls of her honey-blonde hair suggested hours spent in a salon in Tulsa or Oklahoma City. Her nametag identified her as "Laurie." The name was underlined with a question written in all caps. *HOW MAY I HELP YOU?*

Archie pegged her as a grant item borrowed from an urban area to grease the wheels of a start-up dental practice that probably had to beat patients off with a stick. He showed her a Xerox copy of Hashilli's picture.

"This guy ever come around?"

It took the girl a few seconds to shift her eyes away from the jailhouse skin graffiti that decorated the backs of Archie's hands and traveled all the way up both arms until it disappeared underneath the sleeves of his aloha shirt. She had been in Coalgate long enough to know that Archie wasn't Choctaw. Not Creek or Cherokee or Chickasaw or Seminole either. None of the Civilized Tribes would claim him as a member.

Archie offered Laurie a convincing smile and redirected her attention to Hashilli's picture. "He might call himself Mister Luna or Doctor Moon. He might be traveling with a woman." Archie showed her Marie's photograph.

"Are you a policeman?"

Silly question. Archie intensified his smile. "You might say I'm involved with law enforcement." He shoved Marie's photograph at Laurie. "How about this woman?"

The receptionist took the photograph in both hands. She studied it carefully, the way a thief might evaluate the contents of a collection plate during Sunday services.

"Well, Laurie, have you seen her?"

The girl followed Archie's line of vision to her nametag. She covered it with her hand, a moment too late.

"Sorry, sir." Laurie placed the photo on the counter so her hands and Archie's would not be touching it at the same time.

A trouble-front moved through the waiting room. Archie recognized the signs. Mothers put down their *People Magazines*. Little girls hid Barbie dolls behind their backs. Little boys stopped making action figures talk. The world within the dental office went deadly quiet. Even the back-ground noise of dental drills and high-volume suction apparatus disappeared.

Archie's eyes drifted to the glass cover on a record cabinet behind Laurie. The reflection of flashing red and blue lights obscured a section labeled "Recall Patients."

Archie didn't think anyone in the office had called the police, but he'd been asking questions about Marie and Hashilli all over Choctaw country. People in small towns would notice him, and the police would eventually take interest.

Curious cops generally arrest someone, that was Archie's experience. They took suspicious people into custody and held them until their curiosity was satisfied. When they were wrong, the injured party got an apology, sometimes even a legal settlement. The problem was, the cops were seldom wrong. They were never wrong in Archie's case.

No point in speculation, no point in flashing a fake ID and pretending innocence. Men like Archie Chatto never invoked the traditional greeting offered by solid citizens to police officers everywhere. "Is there a problem, officer?" The cops knew there was a problem as soon as they got a look at him.

Archie placed the photograph of Marie in his shirt pocket and asked Laurie the one question he knew she dared not refuse. "Okay if I use the toilet?"

Laurie winced at the proper English word for the facility. "The patient restroom is occupied, but if it's urgent...."

"Ain't it always urgent?"

Laurie directed Archie to the restroom in the doctor's office. Every doctor's office Archie had ever seen had a back way out. If he could slip away before the police identified him, he could disappear. Apache warriors had been disappearing like that for a thousand years.

Local cops were territorial. They wouldn't call state troopers into the search, at least not right away. The Coal County deputies would find the pickup truck he'd borrowed in Atoka and would assume he was a hapless car thief with a dental problem. It probably happened all the time.

The dentist had an escape route all right. Archie eased the back door open an eighth of an inch and surveyed the rear parking lot.

Damn, even Coal County cops travel in pairs. In the old days, before the tribes grew fat from gambling money, rural counties had not been so affluent.

A sheriff's deputy had taken a position at the rear of the parking lot. His eyes scanned the back of the building while his hand unfastened the snap on his sidearm holster.

Plan B. Archie opened the door to the doctor's private restroom. It was tiny, not suitable for persons with disabilities. It probably violated code, but for Archie Chatto's purposes it was perfect. He climbed onto the cheap laminated vanity with no concern for the footprints he left behind. He lifted a large section of acoustic tile and looked into the space between the ceiling and the roof of the building. The metal framework suspending the tiles was sturdy. Archie thought it would hold a man's weight, but only if the man was very careful.

TOM LEFLORE HAD been a policeman for almost a decade now, and this was his first opportunity to chase down a real live felon. He'd studied tapes from the security cameras at the Choctaw clinic in Atoka, and he was certain the notorious cop killer and escaped prisoner, Archie Chatto, was in the area. Spotting his cousin's pickup truck in the dental office parking lot was a stroke of luck. A quick call to Cousin Billy confirmed the truck was missing. At the very least, Tom would make an auto theft arrest and firm up his value as an indispensable family resource. In the best of all possible worlds, Archie Chatto would be the car thief, and Tom would make a first-class felony bust that would cinch his bid for County Sheriff in the next election.

Tom introduced himself to the cute little office manager from Tulsa. He knew her name already. Getting acquainted with new people was an important part of the job, especially when new people were pretty as Laurie Tremble. She looked like a movie star, and she talked like one too. Exactly the kind of girl he wanted to protect and serve. He'd take her statement later, after the excitement was over. At the Brandin' Iron Café. No one would notice a couple of porterhouse steaks charged to the county.

"He's in the doctor's office," Laurie told him. "I knew there was something funny about that man as soon as he walked through the door."

Patients started leaving as soon as Tom Leflore asked his first question. He told Laurie she should leave as well. "We need to clear the building, in case there's trouble." He'd waited ten years to say those words.

The pretty receptionist smiled at him. She pulled shoulders back and made a point of straightening her name tag so Tom had a good excuse to look at her breasts. He tried not to move his lips as he read the all-caps question under her name, "HOW MAY I HELP YOU?" It was a fine day to be in law enforcement.

If the deputy lived in an urban center like Oklahoma City or Tulsa or even Muskogee, he'd call for back up, but all the backup he had was standing out in the rear parking lot hoping to get a chance to use the 9 mm Browning automatic the county had just bought him. The boy was trigger-happy, no doubt about it. Hopefully he wouldn't kill their suspect before they made a proper identification. It would be a shame to take a man's life over a fifteen-year-old pickup truck with a blue book value less than $1200. But if the suspect turned out to be the cop killer, then restraint could be applied in moderation. Tom hoped to squeeze off a shot or two himself, now that all the innocent bystanders had cleared out.

He opened the door to the doctor's office. Took stock of its contents. There was a built-in desk and a couple of office chairs like the ones on sale at Sam's Club. There was a laptop computer, a pile of insurance papers, a stack of throwaway journals, and the *Sports Illustrated* swimsuit edition. The girl on the cover looked interesting enough to be evidence. He'd confiscate the magazine later and look at it down at the station.

The bathroom door was shut, and Tom figured that was where he'd find his suspect, taking one last crap before being hauled off to the Coal County Jail.

It would have been nice to kick the door in, but fixing it would be an unnecessary cost to the department, and besides, it opened outward. A good solid kick would not only wreck the door, it would break or dislocate the frame. As difficult as it was to find a carpenter around Coalgate, it might take several weeks before doctor could take a leak in private.

He held his side arm in his right hand and tried the bathroom door with his left.

Unlocked.

It didn't take Columbo to figure out the suspect's plan of escape. Tom could see the set of footprints on the vanity, and one of the acoustic tiles was out of place. That's the way it was with lawbreakers. They weren't all that clever when it came to getting away.

Tom hefted himself onto the vanity, detached the flashlight from his utility belt, lifted the acoustic tile, and peered into the space between the ceiling and the roof. It was a perfect rectangle. Like most dental offices, this one was built to order like a cracker box without a single feature of architectural interest. Complete efficiency with no esthetic nooks and crannies. Heating and air-conditioning ducts offered some cover. Other than that, his fugitive had no place to hide.

Unless the perp found a way onto the roof, Tom had the bastard. He thought he saw a little movement behind the big duct that delivered regulated air to the waiting room. No trap doors that he could see leading to the exterior, no reason at all to alert his partner. This criminal was his.

For a moment he considered the words of his old football coach. "There is no *I* in Team." But Tom Leflore wasn't playing football now. He was laying the groundwork for a career in law enforcement. There was no "I" in that either, but what the hell.

———————————

AS SOON AS Archie heard the deputy crawl into the space above the drop ceiling, he shoved the doctor's office chair aside and crawled out from the little cavern in the built-in desk that was big enough to comfortably house a pair of casually crossed legs but barely large enough to hide a man.

He removed the casters from the doctor's chair. He eased the bathroom door closed and wedged the back of the chair under the doorknob. Cheap, low pile carpet covered the cement slab in the doctor's private office. That would stabilize the chair's rear legs for a while. Not as secure as Archie would like but enough to slow the cop down if he followed the natural inclination to leave the ceiling space the same way he had entered it.

How long would it take the deputy to figure out he'd been outsmarted? Archie hoped it would be long enough for him to disappear out the front door. He could be long gone by the time the cop got his feet back on the ground and explained his lapse in judgment to his partner.

One of the acoustic tiles bulged out and cracked, scattering chunks of sound-absorbing foam over the reception area. A khaki uniformed leg protruded through the ceiling and was quickly withdrawn. Curse words and the crackle of a two-way radio accompanied the thumps and bumps of the officer as he completed his futile search.

Archie left the building just as Deputy Leflore's partner kicked in the rear door. A series of gunshots followed. It wasn't really Archie's fault if the cop on the floor and the cop in the ceiling had a gunfight based on miscommunications, but he knew a grand jury wouldn't see it that way.

Felony murder. That would be one more charge added to his already massive legal record. He made his way to the police car and radioed for help.

"Officer down!" He recited the address of the dental clinic, even though it was the only dental clinic in town, and everyone knew exactly how to find it.

"Dispatch an ambulance, stat!"

The origin of Archie's distress call would remain a mystery in Coal County for years to come. Some of the locals would believe a neighbor made the call after investigating the source of gunshots. Others would claim it was the ghost of a long dead Federal Marshal who had been killed over a century ago while pursuing bandits in Indian Territory— still on duty after all these years.

No one would speculate the call had been made by career criminal and confessed cop killer, Archie Chatto. It would be inconceivable that a renegade Apache could show that depth of compassion.

37

S TEALING A CAR was hardly any crime at all in Archie Chatto's judgment. It was a complete mystery to him why the police should take such an intense interest in what really amounted to enhanced borrowing.

"Christians talk a lot about sharing." Archie shook his head in disgust. He seldom ranted about the disappointing moral standards of the dominant white culture in America, but that was mostly because he rarely had a captive audience.

Sarah, Robert, and Big Shorty nodded their heads in silent agreement while they watched him pour water out of his boots.

"There is precious little Christian charity when it comes to sharing automobiles." Archie's most recent experience at borrowing a vehicle from the parking lot of the United Pentecostal Church in Durant had reaffirmed his cynicism.

"Taking a car should have been safe during church service. They were shouting, 'amen,' and 'praise the Lord.' Somebody was speaking—no, they were shouting—in tongues."

Robert handed him a hotel towel while Sarah laid some dry clothes on the queen size bed.

"Talking with God is just about the best distraction you could ask for, but the car owner called the cops the very moment I drove that vehicle off the lot."

Archie had taken more than a dozen automobiles during the frustrating search for Marie. He had left almost every borrowed vehicle in a relatively convenient location. He left in as good a condition as he had found them, sometimes even a little better. He filled some with gasoline and never changed the radio stations or left cigarette burns in the upholstery. He ran one of them through a car wash after a particularly dusty ride.

The meticulous maintenance of stolen vehicles was a matter of pride for a modern renegade Apache. When Archie borrowed an automobile, he gave it the same degree of care his ancestors had provided for stolen horses. Living off the land was a tribal tradition that the civilized community, whether Caucasian or Native American, couldn't seem to grasp.

"It's the teenagers, the vandals, and the joy riders who've given car thieves a bad name. It's a doggone shame." Owners just naturally assumed the worst about the men who took their cars without permission. They never saw the bigger picture. The only automobile Archie seriously damaged in a four-county crime spree had been the one taken from the church parking lot.

"The owner was watching through an open window, keeping one eye on Jesus and the other on his late model Buick Regal. Called the cops in the middle of the sermon."

"Had to leap out of the car while I was crossing Lake Texoma on the Highway 70 bridge. It was a long drop into the water." He permitted himself a moment of pride.

"The cops were so impressed they never fired a shot." Archie figured them for Native American policemen. "Even the civilized tribes know acts of bravery when they see them."

He escaped without a scratch, borrowed another vehicle from an unlucky bass fisherman, and met up with Robert, Sarah, and Big Shorty at Bob's Lake Country Motel, just outside of Kingston.

"It's a damn shame about hypocrisy," Archie said. "Jesus would tell you that if he was here." He wrung a stream of water out of his Hawaiian shirt and watched it bead on the cheap motel carpet.

"Time for a good long shower." He carried his dry clothing into the bathroom and shut the door.

EVERYONE WAS FRUSTRATED that the search for Marie was taking so long. Sarah wondered if it might be time for an anonymous call to the authorities.

"Waste of time," Robert told her. "They don't do Be-On-the-Look-Outs for non-criminal crazies. It interferes with quality time at Daylight Donuts."

Sarah knew he was right. A missing mental patient was out of sight and out of mind as far as the police were concerned. Not a problem unless they were actually recovered. Marie went missing regularly during Sarah's childhood, and the police never found her unless her current boyfriend was a "person of interest."

Who could blame them? They had murderers to find and rapists and kidnappers. Not to mention speeders. Normal lawbreakers had understandable motives. They left clues. Locating Marie was like getting a fix on one of those small, almost imaginary subatomic particles that governments spend fortunes trying to find.

Sarah thought of it as the Marie Uncertainty Principal. You could sometimes find out where she was, and you could sometimes find out what she was doing, but you could almost never do both. The math and science were just too complicated. Conditions in Marie's sphere of influence were always in a state of flux. By this time, Hashilli might be her new love interest. He was a man, after all, and Marie was notoriously good at manipulating men.

"Even if she is no longer his prisoner, even if she's now calling all the shots, that doesn't mean she'll contact me." Sarah relied exclusively on prepaid cell phones. Her number changed with every new contract. Marie had never been sufficiently motivated to learn any of them.

"Even if she knows my number, she might not think to call, especially if she is in a new relationship."

Archie's frown deepened at the suggestion.

"Her history with men is pretty consistent," Sarah said. "Time and close proximity are the only two things she requires for a romantic adventure." Mom is a skank, Sarah thought but could not bring herself to say it, especially in Archie's presence. Marie had devoted her life to the search for the ideal man. She'd started at the bottom, gradually worked her way up but was still in the slime layer. At this point, Sarah's mother didn't have a high opinion of men, but that didn't mean she'd given up.

"Marie loves you, Archie. But you aren't with her now. There's no telling what she'll do."

He didn't speak for several seconds. Sarah searched his face for some insight into his thought process. Not a twitch. He didn't swallow. He didn't blink. Had she ever seen him blink?

"Things are different now." Archie's mouth moved, but the rest of his face remained solid as a bronze casting. "She's tasted a warrior's love. Marie will never settle for less again."

Sarah didn't bother to object. Her mother's lovers had the single-minded devotion of heroin addicts. They wouldn't mend their ways until they hit rock bottom. And rock bottom was Archie's home.

"Don't waste time considering the impossible," he told her. "We still need to visit the casinos."

"By we, you mean everyone but you." She knew Archie had been saving the gambling establishments for last. Casinos used sophisticated security. Federal and state bureaucrats were involved in every aspect of management. They communicated regularly with police departments and other casinos. High risk for a wanted felon under the best circumstances, and now local authorities knew Archie was in the area. But there was no help for it. They'd lost Marie's trail at Stringtown and couldn't pick it up again.

"When a team of hunters can't find fresh tracks, they spread out and search for droppings," he said.

Archie used way too many fecal metaphors, but Sarah agreed with his premise. She and Robert would cover Stringtown, Grant, Broken Bow, and Idabel. He could flash his badge and ask questions. Eventually, the casino management would tumble to the fact that he was a fake cop, but Indian gaming was on perpetually tenuous ground in the state of Oklahoma. They wouldn't be quick to call attention to themselves by verifying detective Jerald Daugherty's credentials.

Archie and Big Shorty would cover the casinos at McAlester, Pocola, and Durant. Shorty would ask the questions. The police were well aware that Archie was in the area, and they would have sent his photograph to every casino security team by now.

"I don't dare show my face again in Bryan County," he told Big Shorty. "I can't go near the casinos if you didn't need a driver." There was no getting around the fact that Big Shorty couldn't work the brakes or accelerator pedal of a stolen car.

Sarah thought there was little chance Archie would be spotted as long as he stayed in the vehicle. Every curious eye would be fixed on Big Shorty. No one would give a glance to his chauffer.

Not many double amputees walk into the casinos on stumps, so Shorty's enquiries wouldn't be exactly discrete, but people would tell him what they knew.

"You'll scare the hell out of them," Archie said. "No one will gamble while an African god is thumping across the floor. They'll answer your questions just so you'll leave."

Big Shorty looked like he might object to being called an African god but was distracted when a hummingbird flew through the open motel window and hovered over his shoulder.

"Grandpop. You're a long way from the cemetery."

38

A GOLD DETECTIVE'S badge was equivalent to a backstage pass at every Indian casino Robert and Sarah visited. Not one manager called an attorney or asked for a warrant. No laws were bruised, bent, or broken in Indian gaming establishments. All the really important ones had already been canceled in the interest of profitability.

Sarah watched customers feed coins into machines that paid back ninety-five cents out of every dollar invested by the gambling collective. All of this had been illegal in Oklahoma less than three decades ago, along with "liquor by the drink," full court women's basketball, and tattoos. It was incredible how fast the Baptist church had lost its hold on state politics. She heard her own voice mumble the words "slippery slope" a moment before she realized she was thinking out loud.

The daytime manager of the Broken Bow Choctaw Casino interrupted his guided tour long enough to ask Sarah to repeat herself.

"Nothing at all," she said. "Just commenting on driving conditions along Highway 259." Once again, she posed as Assistant State's Attorney Connie Rubirosa seeking a missing woman and the man who abducted her.

The manager hadn't seen either Hashilli or Marie but offered to provide copies of the casino's security tapes. "No need for us to break the law when hard working people are stuffing money into our pockets."

No business, past or present, compared with Indian gaming—at least in Choctaw country. Not bootlegging whisky, not cultivating marijuana, not even manufacturing methamphetamine. Nothing legal or illegal held a candle to casino gambling. When the economy was good, people gambled casually in local casinos and made trips to Las Vegas to find big time entertainment. When times were hard, they did all their gambling locally. The tribe made out like professional Caucasian bandits. They were in the process of buying back all the land stolen from them, an acre at a time. Mostly with white men's money.

"We haven't gone in much for entertainers here at Broken Bow," the manager said, "but Durant does pretty good." He recited the names of a dozen singers who had slid below the threshold of public adulation within the last ten or fifteen years. If Durant customers weren't interested in musical nostalgia, there was always something going on in the casino restaurant. "They offer a six-pound steak free to anyone who can eat it in an hour along with two sides and a large drink. Now that's what I call entertainment. Singers might come and go, but the appeal of red meat is eternal."

Every Choctaw casino Robert and Sarah visited was thriving. For the first time since statehood, people came from as far away as Dallas/Fort Worth and Tulsa to hemorrhage money into the local economy. No one tried to apply a tourniquet, and no one had seen Marie or Hashilli.

"Some folks say that God is dead, but the devil is alive and well right here in southeastern Oklahoma." The manager laughed at his own joke. Neither Robert nor Sarah cracked a smile.

"Nothing lasts forever," Sarah said, "except the basic flaws in human character." It was the kind of statement she thought an assistant state's attorney might make when confronted by the unbridled success of a business that sells no product.

The manager offered no defense of the gaming industry. He showed the photographs of Marie and Hashilli to every dealer, pit boss, and cashier in the establishment.

The tribe and state authorities were finally on the same side, Sarah realized. For the first time in history. Slot machines and blackjack tables worked where treaties failed.

The manager didn't object when Robert showed the pictures to the waitstaff and the bartenders. Three members of the custodial crew were actively involved in polishing brass, sweeping floors, and cleaning up occasional spills, but the manager authorized a fifteen-minute break so they, too, could look at the photographs. The greatest and the least among the casino employees were at the disposal of the authorities.

The chief custodian didn't recognize the people in the photos, but he recognized Hashilli's name. "Maytubby! There was Maytubbys down by Tuskahoma where I'm from. Some of them was troublemakers."

Sarah let him hold the Xerox of Hashilli's driver's license.

His lips moved as he ran through a mental list of the Tuskahoma Maytubbys. "Hashilli Maytubby!" The boss janitor smiled at the recollection of the worst troublemaker of them all. "Lived down by the Kiamichi River. Mean as a red-assed spider, if you'll excuse my French."

Maybe the janitor blushed. Sarah couldn't be sure. He gave her a careful look as he handed back the copy of Hashilli's license. He looked at Robert too.

Making a decision, Sarah saw the signs. The janitor's eyes moved back and forth between her and Robert, as if he were measuring the distance between them.

Too close. She took a baby step away from Robert. Government lawyers didn't stand so close to state cops. Was their cover broken?

The janitor smiled. "Billy, come on over here." He motioned to his assistant. "See if you can help this young couple out."

Sarah took another step away from Robert. "We're not...." What else should she say?

The janitor held up his right hand like a justice of the peace performing a marriage ceremony. "I won't say nothin' to nobody. Government rules can't keep young folks apart."

One cover was intact. But was another cover blown? What did the janitor see? Did Robert see it too? Sarah would have to think about that later on. She handed the Xerox of Hashilli's license to the assistant custodian.

He took the paper delicately. He gave the picture and the name a cursory glance, handed it to the chief custodian, and wiped his police-contaminated hand on the front of his shirt. "Mostly kept to myself when I was home." It was a policy he clearly didn't intend to change.

The boss janitor thumped the DMV photo of Hashilli Maytubby with his index finger. He made a clucking sound with his tongue.

"Longer I look at this one, the more familiar he gets. Family lived off an unmarked road between Clayton and Tuskahoma. This one was slick as buttered sin."

"I'm surprised he ain't in prison by now," the janitor said. "The law was after him years ago, after that business with his grandpa. Killed the old man, people say. Though it wasn't never proved."

The chief custodian looked directly at the gun-bulge beneath Robert's jacket. "Keep that thing clean and ready." He passed a glance from Robert to Sarah, nodded his head as if he'd come to some conclusion. "See this pretty little girl walks behind you if you go into them woods. Don't never drop your guard."

Pretty little girl? People thought of Sarah as serious, cynical, bitchy. Never a pretty little girl. Was that a smile she felt on her face?

Robert promised to guard Sarah with his life. The chief custodian wished them luck and went off to deal with a spewing beer keg in the bar area. Why couldn't Marie ever take up with a man like that, one who talked sweet and smelled like stale beer? Sarah didn't say a word to Robert until they reached the stolen red SUV that had been their transportation to the Choctaw Casinos.

"I lived in Tuskahoma." It had been more years back than she could remember, when Marie took a Choctaw lover.

"The town used to be the tribe's capital." There was a large brick council house that's still used for events. Lots of traditionals lived in the area. Maybe some Maytubbys were still around. Not much of a lead, but it was the only one since Stringtown.

Sarah tried to report their progress to Archie, but his pre-paid cell phone was turned off. A wanted man couldn't afford to have his stealth compromised by an inconvenient ring tone. Vigilant enemies could be alerted, even if the phone was set on vibrate.

Policemen and attorneys could use cell phones with impunity. Felons on the lam could not. Sarah and Robert would have to wait for Archie's call before deciding on their next move.

She drove toward their temporary headquarters at Bob's Lake Country Motel. Her phone played the ring tone version of *I can see clearly now* before she reached the invisible line that separated McCurtain and Choctaw counties.

39

S HORTY PAUSED AT the entryway of the Durant Casino Resort just before the point of no return. He checked at his watch. Eleven a.m., a slow hour for gamblers, the ideal time to intimidate the help. If he stood there much longer, he'd arouse suspicions. No doubt security cops were watching him already, sitting around their high-dollar CCTV screens wondering what in the hell had gone wrong with the picture.

The double doors were polished glass. If Shorty turned his head just right, he could see the reflection of a dark green, stolen vehicle with a killer behind the wheel. It was superimposed on rows of colorful video poker machines. Comfortably supernatural, like an image of Jesus burned into a piece of toast. When Shorty came out again, Archie would be waiting. That idea would scare the hell out of most people.

Time to go inside, where sin earns its wages.

The casino air was thick and cold. It carried hushed conversations, the sound of jackpot bells, and the scent of cheap whisky. Unsatisfying, not at all like the air of Riverside Gardens Cemetery. Big Shorty lurched across the floor. Blood pulsed in his wrists and fingertips. He swallowed imaginary saliva. If this was what fear was like, Shorty didn't care for the sensation. As he moved farther into the interior of the casino, the nature of the background noise changed. With every step, the conversational murmur diminished, and bells rang less frequently.

Security guards took positions between the rows of slot machines. Big Shorty counted four sturdy-looking Native Americans fresh from weight rooms and target ranges. Their fingers brushed across the holster flaps fastened over their pistol grips. They flinched with each thump of Shorty's stump pads on the casino floor.

The guards' malaise improved his mood. This was how it should be. People should fear the gigantic black man who walked without legs, not the other way around. Even death was afraid of Big Shorty. That's why grandpa hummingbird liked to hover over his shoulder.

The tiny spirit had been with him a few minutes earlier but flew away when Shorty passed through the glass doors of the Durant Casino. The interior was too cool and dark, while the interplay of chimes, whispers, and nearly subliminal music was hypnotic. A ghost bird would never willingly enter a place so similar to the Land of the Dead.

Big Shorty noticed with some satisfaction the patrons of the casino had all stepped back. The bravest were no closer than thirty feet. Seen from the cameras above, they would form a perfect circle with Shorty in the exact center. That was how fear translated into plane geometry.

Shorty moved his bubble of fear through the assortment of gambling machines to the poker and the blackjack tables. What would management make of his systematic erasure of their morning profits? He could bankrupt this casino if he became a regular. Eventually, that would occur to the management, too, and they would send someone to talk with him—a sacrificial lamb. Shorty rotated on his stumps like a ballroom dancer executing a pivot turn. It was smooth and graceful and totally horrifying to everyone who watched. The radius of the circle of fear expanded by another foot. The four guards were safe behind a wall of patrons now. They formed the vertices of a crude square. More emotional geometry—not the most ideal shape for a firing squad.

Big Shorty heard an unsteady voice demanding entry through the barrier of frightened gamblers. "Coming through. Coming through. Coming through."

The voice lost its tremor by the third repetition. Its owner was a twenty-something, Hollywood-handsome Choctaw man in a grey Armani suit with a red silk power tie. He made a series of arcane hand signs that were apparently clear to the security guards. One of them said, "Show's over folks," and the circle lost its integrity. In a few seconds the background noise resumed its previous tone, and the slot machine bells chimed again.

"Can I help you?" the low-level manager asked Shorty.

"Not exactly politically correct, are you?"

The manager shrugged and introduced himself. "My name is Thomas."

He started to extend his hand but interrupted the gesture of friendship in mid-motion. He brushed an imaginary piece of lint from his jacket.

Shorty waited several seconds for a last name that he knew would not be forthcoming. "Don't get many people like me in this place do you Mister Tom?" There were many ways to intimidate managers. A compound approach might be the best way to soften this one up for the kill.

"What... sir?"

Managers liked to keep customer interactions short, shorter still with racial minorities, shortest of all with handicapped racial minorities.

"It is difficult to hear in this place." Big Shorty raised his voice to a level suitable for announcing a fire. "Don't get many people like me here, do you?" On one wall of Shorty's caretaker's cottage was a print of Edvard Munch's *The Scream*. Mr. Tom's face became a reasonable facsimile of that painting.

"No! I mean it's not that at all!" The manager looked around to see if his indiscretion had been witnessed by anyone higher on the food chain than himself. "It's not that at all." His denial sounded slightly more reasonable the second time around.

Shorty lurched a half step forward. Then another half step. The manager struggled to hold his ground. He teetered like a man balanced on the ledge of a tall building.

"Well, what is it then?" Big Shorty knew that hidden cameras were recording his interaction with Mr. Tom. The scene would probably be incorporated into required casino sensitivity training. Shorty's face would be pixilated, and his voice would be distorted to protect his privacy. As if anyone watching would notice his face or remember his voice.

Big Shorty cupped his right hand over his ear, pretending Mr. Tom's labored breathing was a garbled message.

At last the manager summoned up an all-purpose pearl of wisdom. "I'm sorry."

A sincere apology fits *almost* every situation. But Shorty wasn't about to let Mr. Tom off the hook so easily. "What does that mean? Sorry for what?" Mr. Tom started to speak but choked on his words. He stumbled back a step. His eyes searched out the security guards, but they were busy looking at the floor.

"The guards won't help you, Mister Tom." Big Shorty smiled, showing the manager all the gold in the back of his mouth. Shorty thought of it as durable dentistry, but he knew what the manager would think.

Shorty lowered his voice so that only the manager could hear. "Give it up, Mister Tom. This crippled nigger ain't goin' nowhere till you give him what he wants."

"What is it you want? Whatever it is, you've got it."

Big Shorty unfolded Xerox copies of Marie Ferraro's photograph and Hashilli Maytubby's driver's license. "Tell me where I can find these people, and I promise you've seen the last of me."

It was an offer too good for the manager to resist. He studied the picture of Marie for a few seconds—no joy. He looked at Hashilli's driver's license photo.

"Aha!" Mr. Tom finally had a bone to throw to the big/short terrifying black man. "I can't be sure, but this photo looks a lot like a member of the Alcoholic Beverage Commission."

As Shorty expected, the commission member had a different name.

"Mister Allunare," said Mr. Tom. "Sicilian, I believe. Looked his name up—it means crescent moon."

Bingo!

As it happened, ABC member Mr. H. Allunare had paid a surprise visit to the Durant Casino Resort that very morning. "I'll take you to him." Mr. Tom started walking toward the back offices where the ABC representative was busy going over liquor inventory. He moved like a panicked Olympic speed walker. He came to an abrupt halt and was in the process of composing a politically correct apology for his burst of speed when Big Shorty slammed into him and knocked him to the floor. Mr. Tom sputtered the first half of a spontaneous statement of contrition when Mr. Allunare emerged from behind the bar.

The Sicilian ABC officer swirled a glass of whisky in his hand like a stage prop. ABC cops always researched the Scotch whisky thoroughly before signing off.

As soon as he saw Big Shorty, he tossed the fifteen-year-old single malt back like a tequila shooter. He moved in a wide arc around Shorty, putting as many patrons and gambling machines between them as he could.

"Mister Allunare," the manager called out from the floor. "Wait, this man needs to talk to you."

Mr. Allunare drew a snub-nose revolver from somewhere inside his standard ABC Board issue checkered sport coat.

Big Shorty moved toward the man in quick jerky movements. The casino seemed to shake in concert with the collisions of his stump pads against the carpeted cement floor. Shorty knew this was impossible, but Mr. Allunare must have felt it too. He stumbled as he brought his weapon into a double handed shooting position.

The three shots sounded like balloons popping inside the casino, but the slugs were real enough. The bits and pieces of plastic and metal cascading from the slot machines were proof of that.

Three more shots disappeared into the darkness of the casino, and then the hammer of the pistol fell onto a spent cartridge. Mr. Allunare threw his revolver at Big Shorty with the style and skill of a pre-teen who was not quite good enough to move beyond the peanut league. The gun bounced on the indoor-outdoor carpeting of the casino floor harmlessly. It didn't take one second off Big Shorty's time.

Mr. Allunare barely beat Shorty through the entryway, but his speed increased dramatically when he reached the parking lot.

40

"**A**LL THINGS COME to those who wait." Archie liked all the clever things white people said about patience.

"Little drops of water wear away big stones."

"All fruits do not ripen in a single season."

"An ounce of patience is worth a pound of brains." Slogans for children who wanted things they didn't have and adults who had things they didn't want.

"To lose patience is to lose the battle." This one worked for Archie.

Apache patience is an act of war, as different from its white-mainstream-cultural counterpart as a sword is different from a butter knife. Wait and watch, like a spider in its web. Wide open eyes. Blank mind. Pounce quickly before opportunity wriggles free. The trick is being ready when the moment comes—not a simple task when the wait runs long.

Vanity license plates were Archie's downfall. Trite, inscrutable, easy to remember, written under the bumper hitches of almost every car on the Durant casino parking lot. The row of tags in front of Archie formed a sentence. 2MNY SHY1S WNT2B MAMAS LUVR. It had the feel of a cosmic message. Something a warrior shouldn't ignore.

Archie was caught off guard when Hashilli Maytubby ran out of the

Durant Casino. Several seconds passed before he processed what was happening. An amazing stroke of luck, almost turned sour by the curse of literacy.

Hashilli jumped into to his black SUV and jolted its engine into action. There were many black SUVs on the parking lot, many of them with Choctaw tags. Archie had taken notice but had done no more than that. One flat tire on each of them would have done the trick.

Too late now. By the time Archie had his car in motion, Marie's abductor was on Highway 70.

Heading east. The direction of the rising sun. A slow speed chase was what Archie had in mind, like the LA police trailing O.J. Simpson to his Brentwood mansion but without the lights, sirens, and helicopters. Archie had been in prison when that happened. He watched the whole case unfold on Court TV along with dozens of other inmates doing time in Western New Mexico Correctional Facility.

An ounce of patience is worth a gallon of high-octane gasoline. Hashilli Maytubby would have a valid driver's license. If he were pulled over for speeding, the police would issue him a ticket and send him on his way. Not so for Archie Chatto, wanted felon driving a stolen automobile. It was almost enough to make a man rethink his life of crime.

The highways of southeastern Oklahoma were riddled with speed traps, every one a reliable source of police department income. Hashilli drove less than five miles an hour over the speed limit, but Archie wouldn't risk even that minimal violation of the law. He fell behind a half mile every thirty minutes. He hoped to catch up when they passed through Hugo, but Hashilli surprised him by taking the Indian Nation Turnpike.

Finally, a lucky break. Archie's stolen vehicle had a Pike Pass. It paid the toll electronically, shaving minutes off his time. Hashilli did not make use of this modern commuter's convenience. He pulled through the toll road's cash lanes and tossed quarters into an automated basket, sacrificing efficiency for the sake of anonymity. Archie appreciated the kidnapper's caution. A Pike Pass would document the route he traveled to anyone with the authority and the incentive to check the records.

When Hashilli exited onto Highway 2, Archie was a hundred yards behind him. No hesitation swerves or last minute turn indicators. This was a familiar route to a well-known destination, not a deceptive run for cover.

Beware the fury of a patient man.

By the time Archie reached Clayton, he knew he had a problem. A Pushmataha County police car pulled out from its hiding place behind a stand of red cedar and followed him at about the same distance he maintained between himself and Hashilli.

Archie didn't really believe the cop's presence was an inconvenient coincidence, but he had to act as if it were. If he lost Hashilli's trail at this point, he might never find it again.

Archie closed the distance between himself and the black SUV when Hashilli followed the 271 junction toward Tuskahoma. He considered sounding his horn, or even nudging the SUV with his bumper, something to scare Marie's kidnapper into a rash action, but the policeman behind him activated the bar of lights on top of his car and motioned for Archie to pull over.

Only one cop. Archie took a little longer than necessary to ease his vehicle onto the shoulder. The car was freshly stolen earlier that morning. It was just plain rotten luck the owner had noticed so quickly, and the cops processed the report and alerted the mobile units to be on the lookout. Police efficiency—go figure.

Hashilli's black SUV crested a hill as Archie pulled to a stop. In a matter of seconds it would be lost from sight. Escaping from a lone county cop shouldn't require much effort, but the cop held a microphone in his hand. Brother cops would be here soon. Time to act like a warrior.

It is a good day to die. Did the policeman think so too? Archie drew his pistol and fired three shots through his rear windshield into the radiator of the police cruiser, then sped after Hashilli. He watched the policeman in the rearview mirror.

Objects may be closer than they appear.

The deputy opened his car door and rolled out onto the highway.

He assumed a belly-to-the ground, double-handed firing position he learned in CLEET firearm training, but Archie's car was already too far for a pistol shot. A warrior-cop would have fired through the police car windshield, maintenance cost be damned.

Bravery and abandon only go so far. Disabling a police car was like the Lakota/Cheyenne victory at Little Big Horn. More troops would be on the way soon. They would overwhelm the Indians with sheer numbers. Hopefully the Choctaw witch would lead Archie to Marie's hiding place before the cops regrouped and pressed their pursuit in earnest. Next time, they wouldn't be so careful. Archie had fired his weapon at an officer of the law. That brought on a whole new set of police procedures. Taking him alive would be way down on the list.

He caught a glimpse of Hashilli's SUV as it turned into what appeared to be a dense growth of blackjack trees. Unfortunately a second Pushmataha County Cruiser made an appearance at the same time, dead ahead, just beyond the hidden turnoff.

The driver of the police car turned the cruiser into a hard skid completely blocking both lanes of traffic. Two county cops jumped out of the car and took up firing positions using their vehicle as cover.

Sometimes the most cautious thing a man can do is to take an outrageous risk. Archie slowed his stolen car just enough to let the policemen think their show of force might lead to his peaceful surrender. He sat up straight behind the wheel and made eye contact with each of the officers in turn. He read fear and ignorance in the faces of the two young men. They'd learned caution at the police academy instead of bravery, operational protocol instead of strategy. The rules they followed made them indecisive. The muzzles of their weapons dipped when they should be spitting fire. The men looking into Archie's eyes should have known he would not follow their rules, but training hijacked reason.

Without the slightest detectable change in posture or facial expression, Archie raised his pistol above the dashboard and fired three slugs through his windshield into a tight cluster over the police car's right front wheel well. Oil and antifreeze puddled onto the road.

Archie still had three unspent cartridges in his magazine. Cochise would have used his firepower to slay his enemies. So would Victorio, Nana, and Geronimo, but times had changed. These officers would live. They would receive commendations for bravery. Their lack of heroism would be used as an example for other policemen to follow, ensuring the success of Archie's tactics in the future.

He pulled his car into a hard right and slid down below the door panel as he accelerated into Hashilli's hidden turnoff. A volley of slugs crashed through Archie's side window and thumped against the body of the car. The electronic lock control popped off of the driver's door and landed on the seat beside him.

The cops used Glaser Safety Loads, bullets with civilized pre-fragmented slugs dressed in thin copper jackets with a soft polymer tips— maximum stopping power but minimum penetration. This kind of ammunition protected civilians from being killed in their homes by stray bullets and consequently confounded ballistics evaluations in cases of friendly fire casualties. These Pushmataha policemen had taken on the urban warfare constraints of their city cousins in Los Angeles and Chicago.

Thank God for civilized ammunition. A little glass and bodywork and Archie's stolen car would be as good as new. The owner wouldn't have to wash bloodstains from the upholstery. Composite slugs put golf ball size dents in the left rear fender and the trunk as Archie steered his car through a barely visible space between the trees and aligned his tires along two ruts of dirty crushed weeds. Would the cops follow him on foot or wait for back up? It depended on how pissed off they were at the wild Apache car thief who wrecked the county police car budget.

Tree limbs slapped against the sides of the car. Broken branches bounced off the hood. Some found their way onto the dashboard through gaps in the windshield left behind by gunfire. Broken limbs and a litter of green leaves marked Hashilli's path like the trail of a spring tornado that touched down in the forest. Easy to follow now, but in a few days evidence of the witch's passage would be swept clean by the wind and hidden in the camouflage pattern of shadows cast by the tangle of hardwoods and conifers that crowded over the country lane.

Archie saw a bright spot just ahead, a meadow cleared by wild-fire years ago, the fingerprint lightning leaves on the wilderness. He ducked under the dashboard once again. The clearing was a perfect ambush point.

He couldn't slow the car too much or it would bog down in the weeds. Next time, he resolved to borrow a vehicle with four-wheel drive. He noticed with some degree of guilt a bag of half-eaten M&Ms and a page of spelling homework had bounced out from under the front seat. The name, Melissa Haloka, was printed at the top of the page in the careful, quivering hand of a second grader. A smiley face was drawn in red ink at the bottom of the page with a word balloon containing the simple expression of praise, "Good Work!"

Daddy will be late picking you up from school today, Melissa. Archie Chatto is to blame.

The path of broken branches and fallen leaves spread out like a river delta as Archie reached the clearing. The forest did not filter the sunlight here. Archie's eyes needed time to adjust before they could find the trail again, but the way ahead looked smooth and free of obstructions, so he did not wait for his pupils to limit the glare.

The next thing Archie felt was the front of his stolen car plunging into a narrow watercourse that formed a botanically camouflaged border between the meadow and the forest. He slammed against his shoulder harness hard enough to crack a rib, just before the air bag punched its way through the steering column and bloodied his nose. His pistol rattled onto the floor of the vehicle and landed on Melissa's perfect spelling test. The seat belt did not release when Archie pressed the latch. He reached into his pocket and retrieved the Swiss Army Knife he'd pur-chased at an Ace Hardware store in Oklahoma City.

It took him several seconds to saw through the tough fibers of his seatbelt. By the time he retrieved his pistol, gasoline fumes and wisps of smoke found their way through the dash vents.

The doors were jammed, but lucky for Archie, the back windshield had been weakened with bullet holes and offered the perfect emergency escape route.

Flames poked their way through ventilation holes created by the wrinkled sheet metal of the hood while Archie climbed out over the trunk. He made a careless leap onto the trail he'd followed into the creek as the front of the car exploded into a fireball.

As Archie bolted for the forest, the two county cops pushed their way through the underbrush. They opened fire without ordering him to halt. Fortunately for Archie, these two young men were accustomed to firing at stationary silhouettes of men with white circles drawn on their chests. An Apache running through the woods was a much more difficult target.

Archie could have ambushed the officers easily. He had three shots remaining in his side arm, and that was one more than he needed to send their wives shopping for funeral dresses. But Archie ran from the police for the same reason grizzly bears run away from hikers in the wilderness. There were always more where these came from, and they would come in force to avenge a fallen brother.

So Archie Chatto did not fire a shot at the Pushmataha County policemen, and they did not chase him with any enthusiasm. Instead, they lagged back and jumped at shadows and sounds that always follow inexperienced men through the woods.

Within minutes Archie disappeared, leaving a trail they couldn't follow. He'd be out of the search area while they were still taking shots at noises, well before reinforcements arrived with dogs and helicopters.

41

MARIE KNEW HER kidnapper's name was really Hashilli, but she preferred to call him Dr. Moon. Titles keep a man off-balance, make him feel like he has something to prove. Doctors are intelligent. Doctors are patient. Doctors are restrained.

"How fascinating," she told the doctor. It didn't matter what he said. Marie would find everything about him fascinating, even the dirty little cabin in the woods he thought of as his shrine.

"This is the place where my life really started." Dr. Moon made grand gestures with his hands as if he were showing her a gothic cathedral instead of a rude little shotgun shack on the wrong side of the Kiamichi River. He'd promised to buy Marie a six pack of Sprite to settle her uneasy stomach, but so far all he'd done was walk her through four small rooms that really hadn't changed much since she hid out in them with her outlaw boyfriend before Sarah was born.

"How fascinating." The doctor wasn't so different from other men in Marie's life. More educated and more successful than most, but he still abducted her and took her to a little shanty in the woods. What was it about her that made the owners of that pesky Y chromosome behave so rashly?

Marie sent a thought to Archie. *Find me quickly.* She broadcast the message on the frequency of love. Robert Collins had told her all emotional messages would be carried on the wind, even those spoken in the mind. She'd believed it then, and she still believed it—sort of.

Archie would find her, given time. But she wasn't sure just how much time she had before Dr. Moon noticed something was amiss. He was a psychiatrist, after all, an MD with special training in the processes of the human mind. But the man was as irrational as a Czech art film. Nothing he did made any sense. She wondered if psychosis could be spread from person to person like the common cold. That would explain Dr. Moon's insanity. A hospital infection, a sort of MRSA of the mind, an occupational hazard for a psychiatrist.

Dr. Moon was proud of the pump in the kitchen sink. He showed her how it worked. There was a wood cook stove, probably picked up at an Amish yard sale, and an honest-to-god icebox.

"You have to go for ice soon," she demanded. "And I still need my Sprite. That drive through the woods made me nauseated." Marie felt that way a lot lately. Nausea was a common symptom in the early stages of her manic phase, but she didn't feel the least bit manic. She felt normal. She could not remember feeling quite so normal since giving birth to Sarah.

Dr. Moon laid a reassuring hand on Marie's shoulder and then pulled it away as if she were hot to the touch. Terrified of women. Not an uncommon type. Simple to manipulate such men, just alternate between bitchiness and flirtation, like a downhill slalom race. It could be complex and somewhat risky maneuver if carried on too long. At some point she'd have to cross the finish line. Then what?

"Ice!" She kissed him on the cheek and watched his face turn red. Sooner or later he would overcome his ambivalence, and then his thoughts would turn to sex or murder—or maybe both. One thing was about as likely as the other. Men were like pet tigers. They'd nuzzle you one minute and maul you the next.

"They'll have ice in Tuskahoma," said Marie. "And Sprite. You'd better get moving soon, before I have to throw up in that stinky outhouse."

She put her hands on her hips and tapped her foot. Surely a psychiatrist would recognize that as a sure sign of impatience.

Men never seemed to listen to Marie unless they believed they were on the verge of taking her to bed, and afterward, they hardly seemed to listen at all. Dr. Moon was in his bragging mode. He'd fixed the cabin up so that she would be comfortable. He wanted praise.

Sorry, doctor. Fresh out of kidnapper treats. She could see he'd cleaned the place up a bit, repaired the roof, mopped the floor, maybe even washed the walls, but that could hardly be characterized as comfort. No electricity, no plumbing, not even a real road. Motel Six would be a vast improvement.

"Most of the family lived in a big house just across the river," Dr. Moon said. "It burned years ago, just after Grandfather died. Maytubbys still own the land, but no one lives there anymore. This cabin is all that's left."

Dr. Moon thought of the place as a shrine, but as far as Marie was concerned, it was just a little shack so nasty even termites wouldn't touch it.

"We could go to a hotel," she suggested, "where they have restaurants and bathtubs and cable television." *You could pretend to be interested in sports. I could pretend to be interested in you.*

Dr. Moon shook his head. Archie had escaped from jail, and the renegade Apache would be looking for Marie. "He'll never find you here. People don't remember this place."

Marie looked out over the river through one of Dr. Moon's reglazed windows. He could be right. Archie might never find her here, no matter how many romantic vibrations she sent into the wind.

Dr. Moon told her there were four bridges. Only a vehicle with the proper wheelbase could cross them. "Just thick planks supported by railroad ties. Easy to dismantle. I'll take care of that today. Then the river will be the only way to reach the cabin."

He showed her his brand-new aluminum jon boat, complete with a battery-powered trolling motor.

He pointed to the old one covered by a protective layer of Virginia creeper on the other side of the river. "Old wooden boat is up on cinder-blocks, so it's probably still okay. Of course, it never had a motor. In the old days, the Maytubbys poled it up and down the Kiamichi."

Marie's eyes found the bullet hole in the kitchen wall. She started to explore it with her pinky finger, but Dr. Moon gently pulled her hand away.

"Not for you to touch," he said. "Not for anyone to touch." He repeated the story of his magic bullet word for word the way he'd told her before—as though it were recorded on a microchip. Even the spaces between the words were exactly the same.

Too perfect to be true. Marie wondered which parts were made up.

The bloodstains seemed authentic. She looked at her shadow super-imposed on the hole in the wall. The bullet would have passed through her neck right above the collar bone. Marie was exactly the same size as the woman whose life had been taken instead of the baby witch's. Could that have something to do with his attraction to her?

"I won't touch your magic bullet," Marie promised, "but we need ice and Sprite and other things as well."

Dr. Moon gave her a pen and paper and told her to make a list.

Marie was not good at grocery shopping, but her list was thorough. Supplies enough to last a month. That might convince this man she was resigned to stay with him, but if Archie didn't come for her soon, she'd find a way to escape all by herself.

Come quickly, Archie. Her lips moved as she broadcast that thought, but Dr. Moon didn't notice. She had a thought that might keep her ab-ductor off-balance a little while longer.

Marie added Trojan condoms, ribbed for her pleasure, to the list. She underlined it twice. She pointed the item out to Dr. Moon, in case he hadn't already noticed. "Be sure and get the lubricated kind."

He accepted the grocery list as if it were a death warrant.

"Don't forget the Sprite," she reminded him as he stumbled out the cabin door.

Marie turned her attention once again to the magic bullet hole. It didn't look quite right to her, but she couldn't say why.

WHEN DR. MOON returned with the groceries, he no longer want-ed to talk about the cabin. He loaded the icebox with provisions and bagged ice. He arranged canned goods and paper plates and plastic cut-lery in the pantry.

In addition to the party size bags of chips, soft drinks, and bottled water on Marie's list, he'd bought boxed cereal, fresh vegetables, Spam, Vienna sausages, and canned beans. He described each item as if it were a treasure rescued from the bottom of the Marianas Trench, but words failed him when he handed Marie the condoms still wrapped in their discrete Homeland pharmacy bag.

He stepped back when she exposed the box.

She said, "A gross of lubricated rubbers. Someone has big plans." She held the box of condoms in front of her, using them the way a vampire hunter might use a crucifix. Dr. Moon stumbled against the little cabin's front door, fumbled with the latch, then tripped down the single step, and fell into the yard.

"Perhaps you'd like to try one on for size." Marie perched like a bird of prey in the open doorway. "Maybe we'll have more luck this time." If a woman doesn't remind a man of his previous inadequacies, he starts rewriting history.

Dr. Moon wasn't ready to stand up quite yet. He crawled backward without bothering to roll over, moving away from the cabin toward his new jon boat like a four-legged, upside-down spider. He made sputter-ing noises but never managed to form words until he'd put twelve feet between himself and the cabin door. When he finally spoke, he used an emotionally uncharged voice, completely inconsistent with his means of locomotion.

"Not right now."

In a graceful, athletic twist that seemed to defy gravity, Dr. Moon moved his body into the standing posture of an alpha male. He tipped his chin toward the sky so that he seemed to be looking down at Marie, even though her position in the cabin doorway gave her a six-inch advantage in elevation. He dusted off his pants and smoothed the wrinkles from his shirt.

"I have business in the city." Dr. Moon didn't specify the name of the city or the nature of his business. He reached behind him and removed a black boxy-looking pistol from a holster he wore in the small of his back.

Marie's face betrayed no fear. She smiled and leaned against the doorframe, striking a line that best displayed the curves men found so irresistible. She tossed the box of condoms into the cabin with a skill of a stage magician. She moistened her lips with her tongue and composed a beguiling smile she'd practiced in bathroom mirrors since her teenage years. This was not her first armed and dangerous man.

But the others weren't so fearful. Marie would have to move carefully. If she pushed him too far, too fast, he might decide she simply wasn't worth the trouble.

But he hadn't made that decision yet. Dr. Moon blew gentle puffs of air over every dusty surface of his pistol. He removed the magazine and checked the breech for debris. He re-inserted the clip, touched the barrel of the gun to his lips, and then returned it to its holster. This would not be Marie's day to die.

Dr. Moon said, "We need to talk about something when I return."

A clear sign of trouble. In Marie's experience, men didn't want to talk with women unless they were laying the groundwork for antisocial behavior.

"About our relationship." Dr. Moon's voice still sounded calm, but he took two more steps away from Marie.

"About our future." He stumbled slightly as he took another backward step toward the jon boat. "About the restless spirit of a child waiting to be born."

Marie was certain all the color drained from her face, but by then, Dr. Moon was too far away to see. She watched him climb into his aluminum flat-bottomed boat and push it into the river. He kept his eyes fixed on her as the current carried him down stream.

Marie realized that Hashilli wasn't just a sexually frustrated man tempted by desires he pretended didn't exist. This man wanted something from her that he could not have, something she would not give him. She had no idea what he might do when he found out, but she could no longer wait around for Archie.

Sometimes a woman had to take care of business all by herself. It was not an idea that Marie Ferraro found all that palatable, but necessity was the mother of invention, and she was a mother too.

42

ROBERT RAN HIS hands over the SUV Archie had stolen from across the Texas border. It was red, like all the other vehicles they'd been using in their search for Marie. "Looks the same as the ones from Oklahoma."

He kicked the tires because he'd heard that's what people did before they took possession of a new car, although he wasn't sure if the ritual applied to stolen ones.

"It has a bigger engine and high suspension with four-wheel drive," Archie told him.

Robert nodded as if the concepts of suspension and engine size made sense to him.

"You'll need to go off road when you go looking for Hashilli," Archie explained. "Not that you'll be driving." He patted the lump on Robert's jacket where the pistol was concealed. "I'd feel better if you'd load that thing."

He looked like he might be thinking over the idea of Robert carrying a functional weapon. "Or maybe not."

Archie sorted through a collection of switched and stolen tags from similar vehicles in the long-term parking lot at the Tulsa Airport. "These probably haven't been reported. No one memorizes tag numbers since they put card readers in the gas stations."

He selected a license plate and cleaned it with a paper towel drenched in the Walmart version of Windex. "Wish I could go with you guys, but I can't go near that stretch of Highway 271 since I shot up those police cruisers."

He wiped his hands with window cleaner, dried them on his pants, and presented Sarah with the keys. "Drive her carefully. Should be safe enough if you keep under the speed limit."

Sarah took the keys. "Why do men refer to cars as she? Cars, ships, the ocean, hurricanes, weapons, mothers, and girlfriends. Things they like, things they want, things that cause them trouble?"

Robert ignored the question, studiously cleaning specks off the passenger side view mirror.

Archie finally answered her. "I knew a man in Gallup who called his pistol 'Little Charlie.'" He frowned. "Little Charlie killed his owner in the end. Barrel in the mouth. Bullet in the brain. Nasty way to die."

Robert understood tangible things like bullets, but intangible things like judgements left him confused. "Nasty?"

"Unnatural, I mean. Dying with the taste of sulfur in your mouth."

The mirror looked spotless, but Robert rubbed it for good measure with his jacket sleeve, climbed into the passenger seat, and rolled down the window. He'd open it all the way to begin with and negotiate the final position with Sarah as they set off on their mission. He took his empty pistol out of its holster and inspected it to remind her he had a part to play in the rescue of Marie, even if that part wasn't immediately clear to people without a diagnosis of mental illness.

Sarah complained from the moment she pulled out of the parking lot at Bob's Lake Country Motel, but she didn't make Robert close his window, so he didn't mind. Her anger was a kind of passion. It filled the SUV with emotional electricity that made his skin tingle. It gave him a feeling in his belly that was something very much like falling.

"If driving this car is so damn safe, why didn't Archie come along?"

Robert didn't bother with an answer. Sarah was talking to herself.

Talking to God. Talking to anyone but him. He paid close attention to her pitch and inflection. Her words were as energetic and free of meaning as a thunderclap. The combination of the wind and his girlfriend's voice gave him a thrill he was certain no one had ever experienced before. Sarah still didn't know she was his girlfriend, but she would eventually. Meanwhile, her perfect round tones reminded him of the voices he used to hear before his encounter with Hashilli's mushroom dust that sent everyone else it touched into an anesthetic coma.

Not everyone. Hashilli could handle the powder too. That was something Robert and the shapeshifter had in common. Both impervious to spirit powder. Both crazy. Robert wondered what other characteristics they might share. He checked his jacket pockets for the packets of mushroom dust Archie made him carry.

"CHECK THE MAP." Sarah jostled Robert to get his attention. He looked her way, but the blank expression told her he had no idea what she was talking about. She started to explain but had to hit the brakes as she came over a blind crest and nearly ran into the back of a *WIDE LOAD*—half of a prefabricated house—taking up most of Highway 271.

"Look in the glovebox." She eased beyond the center line and looked for oncoming traffic. Another hill, naturally, this part of Oklahoma was nothing but hills and curving roads. There had been almost no traffic, so she could probably make it, but that kind of logic bordered on something her mother might think was reasonable with during a manic phase.

"There's a road map in the glove compartment." She'd insisted Archie mark the approximate spot where they could find Hashilli's hidden road. She eased beyond the centerline again.

"Clear enough." She ignored the no passing zone and sped past the wide load, up a hill without incident, but when she reached the top, she saw the second half of the prefab house a hundred yards ahead. She pulled between the pair of wide loads as they approached a curve.

"One in front. One in back. It's a perfect hiding place." Robert stuck his head out the window and smiled into the full force of the wind. It wasn't very forceful because Sarah was forced to drive at thirty miles per hour.

"Look for the map." She leaned in front of him and popped the glovebox open. They wouldn't need a map if Archie had come along. She remembered the sour expression on his face when he marked an *X* on Highway 271 somewhere near the place they had to go off road.

"You'll know it when you see it," he'd told her. "The way I knew you'd be there to break my fall when I jumped out a third story window."

But Sarah wasn't an Apache warrior or a crazy person who was hooked into a cosmic GPS system.

Robert tried to hand her the owner's manual. When she refused it, he started poking through insurance and registration papers.

"It says Rand McNally in big yellow letters," she said, as if naming the map would help.

He found it just as she eased past the centerline again and saw a half mile long strip of straight flat road in front of her. Sarah pushed the accelerator to the floor and felt the power of the SUV's engine as she raced passed the second half of the prefabricated house. She silently cursed the family that would call it home.

"Got the map open?"

"Not exactly." He held his hands up, palms exposed, like a stage magician who had just made something disappear. "Wind blew it away when you went so fast back there."

She stifled a string of curses. "Well, maybe Archie was right. We'll know where to turn when we see it."

Robert shut the glovebox and went back to enjoying a private moment with the wind. Sarah kept her eyes on the road, but her mind was in Albuquerque, where she'd be studying anthropology with mostly sane people if she hadn't followed Marie to Oklahoma.

"I wonder if Margaret Mead started off this way." She considered for a moment that her career path was probably closer to Jane Goodall's—chimpanzees versus the certifiably insane. Had she inadvertently created a new sub-specialty of anthropology? Maybe there was an upside to the latest series of disasters in her life.

She felt the car run over the edge of the highway onto the shoulder and returned her full attention to the road ahead.

"Slow down," Robert told her. "The police are ahead, just over the next hill."

How did he know these things? She wanted to ask if the wind was talking to him again but was afraid of his answer.

"Nothing mystical," he said, as though he read her mind. "I saw the flashing lights when you were dodging in and out of traffic."

Sarah would have seen them, too, if she hadn't been thinking about the series of bad choices that led her to this part of Highway 271. A Pushmataha County deputy stood in her lane of traffic and motioned for her to pull over.

She applied the brake and drove onto the shoulder. The police car was parked just beyond the entry to the hidden road Archie had described. She knew it when she saw it, just like he promised.

"Let me handle this." She put the SUV in park. She turned the engine off and rolled her window down.

The policeman ignored her and walked to Robert's side of the vehicle. She considered accusing him of male chauvinism but decided this might not be the time.

The deputy was in his mid-thirties. His long dark hair would have hung to his shoulders if it hadn't been captured in a crisp ponytail. Archie had warned Sarah to watch out for tribal cops. This one was a rugged young man with a barrel chest and a grim expression. He had his hand on the butt of his pistol.

"Was I speeding, officer?"

Instead of answering her, he demanded Robert's ID. "Take it out slowly. Keep your hands where I can see them." The policeman's fingers closed around his pistol grip, and his eyes went flat and deadly.

Robert eased his hand into the inside pocket of his jacket and withdrew Detective Jerry Daugherty's badge and police identification.

That took the Native cop by surprise. He looked at the picture and back at Robert. He made the comparison several times struggling to decide if the face on the ID matched the man who was riding in the suspicious SUV.

Sarah had watched enough episodes of *Cops* to know what was coming next.

"License and registration."

"The car belongs to my mother's boyfriend, officer."

"Where is your mother's boyfriend now?"

"He couldn't come with us because he's with a friend who's in a coma." Surely Robert would understand what she was telling him. "Reaction to some mushroom spores. You know… those yellow puff ball things?"

The cop looked completely bewildered by Sarah's mushroom-spore-message. He rubbed his thumb over the color photograph on the ID as though his confusion were no more than a smudge.

"Want me to show you the secret handshake?" Robert asked. He extended his closed hand through the open window. The deputy stepped back as the hand opened and revealed a mound of yellow powder. He drew his weapon and shouted, "Hold it right there!" as Robert blew the powder into his face.

The policeman looked at the pistol in his hand as if he couldn't remember how it got there. He staggered onto the grass beside the highway and struggled to keep his balance.

Sarah left the safety of the SUV and rushed to his side. She steadied him while reality slipped out from under his feet. Robert grabbed him around the chest, lowered him to the ground and dragged him to a safe location in the shadow of his police car.

The deputy's eyes fixed on Sarah. He tried to speak, but the mushroom powder had already locked most of his vocabulary inside another world. The cop managed two last words before his identity crumbled. Something important, judging from the expression on his face, but garbled.

"What did he say? Did you hear?" Sarah asked as soon as Robert tipped the deputy's head so his airway was clear.

"Owl dreams," Robert told her. "Don't ask me what it means."

The wailing siren of a police car approaching from behind them left no time for speculation. Sarah started to move toward the SUV, but Robert held her back.

"That car won't take us any farther," he said. "Even in the woods, it'll be easier to follow than two people on foot."

The second police car skidded to a stop twenty yards back, and two policemen jumped out with their pistols drawn. Robert took Sarah's hand and pulled her into the trees just as the deputies opened fire.

She resolved to write a letter to the Pushmataha County Sheriff, complaining that these deputies had not ordered her to stop, and their warning shots were way too close for comfort.

"Keep as many trees between us and them as possible," Robert said. "One deputy will have to stay with the unconscious officer."

The shots continued to ring out, even when Robert and Sarah were deep in the cross timbers.

"If they can't see us anymore," Sarah said. "Why don't they stop shooting?"

"The county's paying for the bullets," Robert said. "They'll stop when they have to reload."

Archie had told Sarah that Pushmataha County had just equipped the county cops with sixteen round 9 mm Glocks—a bit of trivia gleaned from a front-page article in the *Clayton Today*.

By the time the cops emptied their weapons, reloaded, and chose which one of them would pursue the suspects on foot, Robert and Sarah were well out of range and completely turned around.

"You think they'll send out a search party?" Robert ducked behind a tree and looked behind them.

"Maybe." Sarah didn't hear any sounds of men crashing through the underbrush. No helicopters so far either. "We didn't shoot up one of their cruisers like Archie did, so maybe not."

Robert reached inside his jacket and checked to make sure Detective Dougherty's pistol was still there. "So, it came in handy, not having any bullets."

"Everyone should carry an empty weapon." Sarah pulled him deeper into the forest. With no idea which way they should go.

They waded a shallow stream and crashed through a thicket of thorn bushes. "Lost is lost," she said. "There's no such thing as more lost or most lost, is there?"

They stopped and listened for sounds of pursuit every few hundred yards, but there were always noises in the forest.

"If Archie was here, he'd know what to do," Robert said.

"So, what do you think he would say?"

"I think he would tell us to walk in the direction of the setting sun until we find Marie."

"And what if we don't find her?"

"We keep looking," Robert said. "Simple plans are always the best."

"Where does that leave us when the sun sets?"

"In the dark." Robert smiled. "I've been waiting to use that line ever since he first heard it in an Abbott and Costello movie."

"Your bucket list shows an alarming lack of ambition," Sarah said.

43

FROM THE FRONT door of Hashilli's cabin, Marie could see the ruins of the old house where the Maytubby family inner circle once lived. Foundation stones had collapsed in moss-covered heaps. A pool of stagnant water filled the old cellar. Cottonwood trees outlined the house's perimeter, strung together by inch-thick vines.

A four-foot-high mound of tangled greenery stood beside the ruined building. It looked like a mausoleum overgrown with vegetation, but according to Dr. Moon it was a boat.

"Resting upside down on cinder blocks," he'd told her, "dressed in a shroud of creeper." According to Dr. Moon, the boat was still sound, kept high and dry by the magic of his touch.

Dr. Moon was crazy as the rats that lived in the deepest recesses of the old Maytubby outhouse. Hard to believe she ever thought the man was sane. Hard to believe she ever thought his words could heal broken minds.

He'd fooled lots of people—staff members of two mental hospitals, educated people, sophisticated in the ways of mental process, who should have seen the signs but hadn't. The only person at Flanders who'd seen through the pretend-psychiatrist's disguise was Sarah's crazy boyfriend, Robert Collins. She wondered if her daughter had finally sorted that out.

Love is a lot like lightning. It strikes in inconvenient places and won't be ignored. Marie understood this perfectly because she was a lightning rod. She could feel the charge building up between herself and Dr. Moon, and she knew the discharge threshold would soon be reached. Condoms, fake menstruation cycles, and verbal assaults on tumescence wouldn't insulate her much longer. It was time to seek lower ground, time to take cover.

He wanted to talk about the restless spirit of a child waiting to be born.

Those had been his last words to her as he went off to take care of his business in the city. Calculating the motives of a crazy man required a special kind of arithmetic. Marie wasn't all that good with numbers, but she knew this would add up to something bad. In the end, it almost always did.

Almost. She clasped her hands over her lower belly, the place Sarah had lived for the only nine peaceful months of the girl's life. When a woman is pregnant, the truth is summarized in a single sentence that is crisp and clear and written at a third-grade reading level. "Keep the baby safe." It was a concept so fundamental even wild animals understood it.

How quickly Marie had forgotten that cosmic truth. She'd squandered the shiny coin of Sarah's childhood on penny candy, and there was no way to get it back.

But she could still be a better mother, if she survived.

Marie had the staples of life—lukewarm Sprite, bottled water, Spam, chips, and Oreos. She could live on the provisions Dr. Moon had brought to the cabin. Now she needed a weapon.

She found a butcher knife sturdy enough to push its way past muscle and ribs into the inner sanctum of the vital organs. Could she stab a man to death? It would be better to decide that now while she could still make other plans. Marie had never killed anything bigger than an insect, but under the right circumstances, she might be able to make the leap.

She looked at her reflection in the knife blade and did not like the doubt she saw in her eyes. A knife was no proper weapon against a magic man, especially one who carried a pistol. Then she remembered the bullet in the kitchen wall, the bullet that had started Hashilli along the sorcerer's road. Perhaps there was another way a knife could be used to fight a madman.

The plaster was old and brittle. The lath underneath was firm and free of dry rot. Oak, Marie realized. The cabin was built when hardwoods were plentiful enough to waste under plaster. It took a long time, but she finally chopped and pried a foot long piece of lath free of the two-by-six-inch studs that held it in place.

She tossed the broken lath onto the pile of rubble in the kitchen floor and prepared to dig the bullet out of deeper supporting structures of the wall.

Nothing. There was no bullet hole in the lath on the other side. Could the slug have made a series of turns that defied the laws of physics, like the bullet that killed John F. Kennedy? Marie chiseled away more plaster and chopped and pried more slats of hardwood. No bullet hole anywhere.

She retrieved the original section of lath and examined it more carefully. The hole did not go through. It took her a few minutes more to notch the wood so she could break the lath along the plane of the bullet hole. She was not surprised at what she found.

Nothing—no slug, no magic bullet, no human sacrifice, no baptism of blood for an Native American witch. The whole thing was a lie. But whose lie had it been?

Marie remembered the pride with which Dr. Moon told his story. Did he believe it? She thought he did.

Grandfather had been a clever old confidence man, as well-versed in matters of faith and conscience as the Pope. He'd planted the seed of Hashilli's legend in a child's mind and fed it with details until its roots were tangled in the boy's memory. A man doubts nothing learned before the age of reason. The imaginary bullet was the most important strand in the rope of lies used by the old man to bind Hashilli to the world of sorcery.

Perhaps the bullet could still be a weapon, even if it wasn't real.

———————————

THE COOL WATER of the Kiamichi River wasn't even up to Marie's waist, but the bottom was slippery, and every square inch of her was wet by the time she waded to the other side. Her butcher knife made short work of the creeper vines covering the old wooden jon boat. Before an hour passed, she pushed the boat into the river and pulled herself inside.

How far would the water carry her? Would she meet her nemesis along the way? Marie clutched the butcher knife in one hand and the broken piece of hardwood lath in the other. If one thing didn't work, she would use the other. She tossed the lath into the river and watched it float away.

What would Hashilli do when he discovered Marie had run off with his magic bullet? He would no longer want to talk with her about the restless spirit of a child waiting to be born. She was pretty sure of that.

Her quiet reverie was interrupted by gunshots. Lots of them. Marie had learned to recognize the sound by spending decades in the company of desperate men. These were far away. They sounded like knuckles popping. It was the rhythm that gave the nature of the sound away. A pistol was a musical instrument of sorts, and every man who played one followed his own score. Shave and a haircut, five cents! Gunshot tunes were simple and direct, like the act of murder. This was a duet, two gunmen taking turns, point and counterpoint. The two men weren't shooting at each other. That kind of tune would have a different meter. These gunmen worked together.

Marie grabbed onto an overhanging tree limb and pulled herself to the bank. A river offered no cover in a firefight. She dragged the boat onto the shore, pulled it into the underbrush too far for it to be seen by a casual observer. How casual would Doctor Moon be when he finally returned from wherever he had gone? Not too casual, once he discovered Marie was gone along with his magic bullet.

He might believe she had been abducted, the vestal "virgin" stolen from the temple along with the magic bullet that held a piece of his soul. He would see the jon boat had been taken, and he would search along the river.

It was a good time to be somewhere else. Marie nourished herself with a bottle of Aquafina and a bag of Doritos. She put the empty bottle and the empty bag onto the ground and turned the boat over on top of them. She used her butcher knife to cut seven saplings into stakes and positioned them in a rough circle around the boat.

Marie's stick symbols followed no magic pattern. She had no idea what she was doing, so she was fairly certain Dr. Moon would be confused when he finally found the boat, and she had no doubt he eventually would.

44

ROBERT TOLD SARAH, "There are more ways through the woods than one."

No point in trying to figure that one out. It took all her concentration to keep from tripping as they walked across the overgrown, uneven forest floor. Thank God she wasn't wearing her State's Attorney power pumps. Heels were good for treading on the rights of law-abiding citizens, but they were useless in the woods.

After a few hundred unsteady paces, the trees and dense underbrush gave way to a waist-high stand of grass. Sarah's tear ducts worked overtime washing away pollen. Her nose filled up with sneezes.

She looked and listened for sounds of pursuit every few seconds. That would have made her easier to catch if the policemen hadn't already given up the chase. They were probably afraid of poison ivy or chiggers. God knew there were plenty of both in this godforsaken wilderness.

"They've retrieved a stolen SUV," Robert said. "They've chased two desperate felons into the forest and emptied their pistols. All in all they've had a pretty busy day."

There was also the matter of the unconscious policeman lying in the shadow of his cruiser, posed like a model for a Red Cross CPR course. Who could blame his brother cops for remaining on the scene. It occurred to Sarah she'd seen four policemen rendered comatose with mushroom powder, but she'd seen none of them revive.

It was a little late to consider unpleasant possibilities, but that's just what she did.

"Do you think the powder is dangerous?" The yellow dust had put Victoria Tiger in the hospital and killed Jimmy Mankiller's wife. Grand theft auto was one thing—felony homicide was quite another. And then there was the moral issue. Considering that first would have been nice.

Robert told her, "It's safer than bullets." Years of psychotherapy had given him a facility for stating the obvious.

She'd checked the newspapers and the Internet for news of their exploits. No mention of comatose policemen anywhere. "It would have made the news if one of those cops died. Wouldn't it?"

"Not if the medical examiner thought he died from natural causes." Robert's comments weren't helping.

"It's not like we had any choice." She stared daggers at Robert Collins, daring him to contradict her.

"We always have a choice."

Damn you, Robert Collins!

Like Marie, like Archie Chatto, like Big Shorty, like the hundreds of crazy people Sarah had met in her short, eventful life, Robert didn't grasp the most fundamental rules of empathetic conversation. She sputtered at him for a few seconds trying to explain what he hadn't learned in two decades of human observation but gave it up as soon as she realized which choice he was referring to.

The nearly invisible set of ruts they'd been following through the weeds split into two equally undesirable trails.

"Left or right," Robert said. "One way looks as good as the other."

Sarah didn't think either trail held much promise. "No oil on the grass between the ruts, no bent or broken weeds, no tire impressions in the dry, dusty areas. Looks like no one has driven a vehicle this way in a very long time."

"Trails always lead somewhere," Robert said. "And we can't go back."

"What would Archie do?"

Even though Robert must have understood Sarah's question was rhetorical, he answered her anyway. "He'd sit quietly and watch the trails for animal activity."

That sounded right. Wildlife would be more cautious along the most frequently used trail. It was worth a try.

Neither Robert nor Sarah had the patience of a renegade Apache, but after a thirty-minute wait with a minimum of sighs and fidgeting, rabbits emerged from the underbrush and hopped along the right-hand trail. Birds and field mice also favored the pathway on the right. Only crows and other carrion eaters liked the left fork. The road most traveled by—take that, Robert Frost.

Robert and Sarah followed the *Archie trail*, keeping a careful watch for signs of human traffic. They saw scat from deer and coyote. They saw raccoon and javelina tracks. They saw a partially decomposed black Labrador retriever wearing a collar with one tag verifying his rabies vaccination and another that declared, "Hi, my name is Nig."

Sarah saw the racially offensive appellation as a bad omen, but they continued following the Archie trail because there was no reason to believe the other path would be better. The problem was there were hundreds of wild acres in this region of Oklahoma where no one ever went unless they were hunting out of season or cultivating marijuana. There would be a lot of trails through this empty land, but they would be confusing and infrequently used by design. Robert and Sarah traveled only a half-mile when they came to a second fork.

"We don't have time for another wildlife survey," Sarah said. In a few hours the sun would set, and all decision making would come to an abrupt halt as they fought off the mosquitoes and the evening chill. She tried to picture a map of the area in her mind.

"Lake Clayton is somewhere near," she recalled. "We might find camping sites there, maybe even cabins." Sarah hadn't quite decided to abandon the search for Hashilli's hideout, but with every setback, she moved more in that direction.

Robert was as optimistic as ever. "I know what Archie would do next." He grabbed up a handful of dried leaves and crumbled them into organic confetti.

"We'll let the wind lead us to Hashilli's place!" He spoke with the enthusiasm of a newly converted Christian. He tossed the leaf fragments into the air and watched the Oklahoma wind pick them up and carry them down the left fork, dropping bits and pieces along the way like Hansel and Gretel's trail of breadcrumbs.

"That's how Archie would do it!"

Sarah knew Robert was exactly right. If Archie didn't have time to rely on clues from the natural world, he'd let supernatural forces to make his decisions. As good a way as any. Whichever path they chose would take them somewhere, and somewhere was a better destination than nowhere.

They hadn't taken more than twenty steps when a rough voice that couldn't make its mind up whether to be male or female ordered them to stop. "Might oughta turn around real slow," the voice told them, "so my trigger finger don't get nervous."

Sarah and Robert automatically raised their hands and turned in response to the command. It was a woman who held the two at gunpoint, but Sarah didn't think her estrogen level played a very prominent role in her appearance. The woman's shape didn't look particularly masculine, but it didn't look feminine either. More like a fireplug, Sarah thought. A fireplug dressed in worn-out blue overalls with the words, "DeKalb Seed Corn" embroidered across her chest. The woman's hair was gray, and her face was the same color and texture as her brown work boots. There was a dense black mole on her upper lip covered with thick sprouts of hair.

Marilyn Monroe reincarnated. The thought took shape in Sarah's mind against her will. Marilyn, slapped ugly by Karma for the sin of vanity. No doubt about it. Sarah had spent too much time in the company of crazy people.

The most important thing about the woman was her double-barrel shotgun. It had two antique looking hammers, both pulled back. The stock was varnish free, and most of the bluing was worn off the barrels. The weapon might have been used to hunt squirrels sometime before statehood. The woman's dirty finger rested on one of the two triggers. She didn't look as though her conscience would be troubled by a couple of dead anonymous strangers.

"This is Maytubby land," she told them. "Trespassers wasn't never welcome here, especially them with a witch's name on their lips."

"You've got this all wrong," Robert told her. He stepped in front of Sarah, ready to shield her from the first load of buckshot that might fly out of the incredibly large shotgun barrels at any moment. Close enough to grab the muzzle, if he wanted to plunge headlong into the afterlife. Sarah realized he was ready to do that if it would prolong her life for even a few seconds.

Like a scene from one of Marie's romance novels. Suicide as statement of devotion. More personal than a card but way more expensive. Sarah hoped Robert would try negotiation first.

"I'm a cop," he told the woman with the shotgun. He placed a hand very slowly and carefully into his jacket pocket and withdrew Jerry Daugherty's badge wallet. He tossed it to the woman, hoping she would fumble the weapon. Instead, she poked him in the chest with the barrels.

She used her boot to flip the badge wallet open. She compared the face on the ID with smiling face of her captive.

"That ain't you!" She spat a murky wad of saliva onto the gold shield.

"Pick it up," Robert told her. "Look closer. You'll see."

She didn't pick the wallet up, but she did give it another glance. Sarah hoped it was enough distraction because Robert was reaching for one of the packets of mushroom dust he carried in his pocket. A little puff would send this woman off into the land of dreams, hopefully before she squeezed off a shot.

"Nothin' wrong with my eyes," she said and brought the butt of the shotgun around, clubbing Robert in the temple just as he withdrew his closed fist from his jacket pocket. "Nothin' wrong with my wits, neither."

Sarah sat down beside him. She cradled his bruised head in her lap. His pulse was strong and steady. His breathing was regular.

"Reckon he'll be all right," said the woman with the gun. "What mischief is he holding in his hand?"

Sarah pretended she did not understand.

"Open that hand," the woman said, "or I'll shoot you dead and open it myself."

Sarah held Robert's hand so that the woman could see it. She pried the fingers open one at a time until she revealed a small pyramid of powder in his palm.

"What is that?" The woman moved closer. The shotgun barrel wavered slightly.

Sarah drew a breath as deeply and silently as she could and blew into the pile of dust

Hard enough to take the icing off a birthday cake, she thought before a yellow cloud of puff ball spores covered the three of them. Hard enough to collapse a house of sticks. Hard enough....

Both barrels of the shotgun discharged, singeing Sarah's hair and spattering her face with hot sparks of nitrocellulose. Her ears rang with a cosmic test signal. In case of an actual emergency, tune to the following channel for instructions.

That was her last cogent thought for several minutes, and then the spirits of the forest danced into her dreams accompanied by the banjo soundtrack from *Deliverance*.

45

HASHILLI RAN OVER his list of clever statements, things that might impress Marie so much she'd let him fill her up with babies. The ones he'd tried so far had failed miserably. As far as Hashilli could tell, women's passions were mostly fueled with small talk. Things that made them cry also made them hot. But some sad topics gave them headaches. That explained why drug companies manufactured aspirin as well as birth control pills, but it wouldn't help a magic man get laid.

Tricky business, distracting women long enough to fertilize their eggs. Bring them flowers, give them chocolates, buy them jewelry, all while maintaining an erection. Act romantic—think nasty thoughts. It was a pornographic juggling act.

Women had it easy. They played hard to get, then when the time finally came, they just lay there pretending to enjoy themselves. A few grunts and moans and a little hyperventilation. That's all it took. Mother Nature is a bitch.

In the old days a witch would waste no time on courtship. He'd hold his woman at knifepoint while they both sipped an herbal aphrodisiac. Chemical motivators were quick, unlike romance, and highly predictable. Too bad Grandfather hadn't taught him herbal magic. Hashilli's next best hope was western science, and he had little confidence in that. American scientific wizards devoted their lives to perfecting bad ideas. Neurologists studied the chemistry of the brain in order to make tranquilizers. Physiologists analyzed the mechanics of menstruation so they could render healthy young girls sterile and make reproductively incompetent women give birth to litters. Physicists observed the nuances of subatomic particles and used their newfound knowledge for bombs and video games. Aerospace engineers launched satellites devoted exclusively to cell phone service and high-definition television. So little to admire in the accomplishments of western science.

Hashilli had been amused when the Nobel Prize in Medicine was shared by two pioneers in the chemistry of Viagra, but now he understood the importance of the work. He'd take two one hundred milligram tabs—twice the maximum recommended dose—then surprise Marie Ferraro at the cabin. His plan was elegant in its simplicity. The only critical issue was the timing. It would take an hour for the Viagra molecules to open up the vascular floodgates of his penis. Then he would charge through the front door and take her where he found her. He would seem like more of a gentleman if he escorted her to the bedroom and ravished her on the high-tech air mattress he'd purchased for that purpose, but the time for social niceties had passed. He had to complete the act before Marie could talk the tumescence out of him.

Was she doing it on purpose? It was hard for Hashilli to make a rational judgment about sexual motivations. He hadn't experienced any of those since his teenage years, and even then, his drive had been as pale and weak as green tea.

He didn't know how Marie was able to send him into a frenzy of lust. Part of it was the things she said, and part of it was the way she said them. Her scent played a significant role in Hashilli's level of desire, but surely the woman couldn't control that. Her facial expressions, the way she crossed her legs, the way she swayed as she moved across the room. Everything about her worked together.

Marie filled Hashilli's mind with images from X-rated movies and dialogues from steamy romance novels. He'd devoted time to both these forms of entertainment, not for titillation, but for enlightenment. He'd always wanted to understand the motivations of ordinary people so he could exploit their weaknesses. Hashilli watched human mating rituals the way a biologist observed the courtship behaviors of exotic birds. He'd seen what people do and what they say but had never understood why until he found himself caught in the sticky residue of sexual attraction. Like a mouse in a glue trap. Wriggling and struggling didn't lead to freedom. It just made him tired.

Within seconds after swallowing two one-hundred-milligram blue tablets, Hashilli felt a tingling sensation in his groin. It had to be a placebo effect, the expectation of success, but he was satisfied with that for now, anything that kept him rigid enough to complete the required task.

It was interesting—copulation didn't seem so undesirable while his penis was in its reproductive-ready-state. He imagined what Marie must look like naked. Best not to think of such things in too much flawless detail. An unanticipated birthmark, an unsightly scar, a collection of varicose veins on the real Marie might upset the applecart. Hashilli wondered how many times he would have to ravish her before a baby witch was conceived. No matter. He parked his SUV, crowded the pill bottle into his pocket beside his erection, and made his way to the aluminum jon boat hidden in the cattails. Maybe those old men with their chemistry sets deserved the Nobel Prize after all.

Walking with an erection was difficult. Hashilli had some dim memories of the experience during his post-pubescent years.

Homo erectus. Interesting name for primitive man. He wondered if he had inadvertently discovered the reason early humans walked in the Leaning Tower of Pisa posture that is so frequently represented in speculative anthropological illustrations.

By the time Hashilli navigated his boat halfway to the cabin, he'd already begun to wonder how long he could perform before the Viagra lost its punch.

At that moment his stamina showed no signs of having limits. *God bless those little blue erection pills.* He pictured himself taking her in all manner of positions, some only vaguely within the realm of possibility.

Just how flexible was a woman like Marie? Hashilli would discover that for himself. The owls in the forest would be awakened by her cries of ecstasy. They would flutter around the cabin and perch in the trees. They would carry news of his exploits to the spirit world.

He stopped for a moment to catch his breath. His chest felt tight. There was pressure behind his eyes almost as extreme as the pressure behind the fly of his pants. The dull harbinger of a headache found a home in the occipital region of his brain and worked its way forward. The light from the evening sun took on a blue tint that made Hashilli squint, even though his boat was in the shadows. Perhaps he should have started with a lower dosage.

The side effects didn't hamper his erection. It was larger than ever, if that were possible, and somewhat painful. There had been an obscure warning about erections lasting longer than four hours. Hashilli had brushed that off as false advertising. Now he wasn't sure.

Would sex metabolize the drug? He thought it might. He remembered reading something about stroke and heart attack and asking your doctor if you are healthy enough for sexual activity, but he couldn't believe that would be necessary. Not for a man of power.

What was the difference between an obsession and a hallucination? One was a thought process that was stuck in a single gear, and the other was a complex image in the portions of the brain devoted to the five senses. Every doctor of the mind understood the difference, and the famous Doctor Moon was no exception. But witches knew that elements of the mind had borders as fuzzy and transitional as the late, great state of Yugoslavia.

For a moment, as Hashilli's trolling motor pushed him up the Kiamichi River toward his cabin, he sensed Marie on the shore.

There was a flurry of movement among the reeds, probably a muskrat or a beaver. Then he saw flash of color. Was it the color of Marie's blouse? Hashilli couldn't remember what kind of clothing she was wearing when he saw her last.

There was only one consistent image of Marie he could hold in his mind, and that image was stark naked—with breasts that pointed at the sky and a butt that looked like a matched pair of soap bubbles.

He drew a deep breath. The Viagra had opened his nasal passages and activated sensory nerves that had been held in reserve for just such a moment. The scent of Marie Ferraro was in the wind. If Hashilli's headache and his erection didn't hurt so much, he could have pinpointed her location with the accuracy of a bloodhound. As it was he could not distinguish reality from fantasy.

"Marie!" he called out to the disturbance on the shore. No answer, and the pressure cooker of lust cranked itself up another few pounds per square inch. At that moment, he needed Marie Ferraro more than he had ever imagined possible. Was this what ordinary people described as love? If so, he couldn't wait to get the feeling out of his system. And there was only one way to do that.

He cranked the trolling motor up to as many R.P.M. as the battery would produce and set a direct course for relief.

HASHILLI WEAVED HIS way through the underbrush much the same way a male cougar might approach a large, dangerous female who has come into season. He had never felt so aggressive, not even when he committed murder. He'd always understood sex and violence were soul mates. Creating life and ending it were two sides of the same coin, and when a man like Hashilli tossed that coin into the air, it was anybody's guess which side would come up. He drew his pistol and approached the cabin, holding the weapon in two hands like a S.W.A.T. commander preparing to capture a dangerous criminal or a rapist about to have his way with an innocent woman.

Was any woman really innocent?

"Marie!" Hashilli's voice cracked when he called her name. His salivary glands alternately ran amok, then shut down completely.

He charged into the cabin, crashing through the flimsy paneled door instead of opening it. He called Marie's name again, sorted his genitalia into a more comfortable position. Most of the little cabin's interior was visible from his position, and the object of his desire was nowhere to be seen.

Hashilli saw the excavation in his kitchen wall. He walked over to the pile of lath and plaster on the floor and inspected the debris between hyperventilated gasps of country air.

"Marie!" Hashilli's voice squeaked like a rusty hinge that no amount of oil would fix. He charged through the cabin, inspecting and re-inspecting everything, opening cabinetry, searching behind canned goods in the pantry, looking behind every container in the ice box, as if Marie might have been reduced to the size of a Kosher dill pickle or transformed into an octagonal glass salt shaker.

Gone.

The woman had taken the magic bullet. She had in her possession the object that had transformed him from an ordinary human infant into a Choctaw sorcerer. He had to follow her. He had to get that bullet back before she worked some kind of female mischief with it.

Am I too late?

It didn't matter. Hashilli couldn't follow her right then, no matter the danger. The pressure of his lust had reached the boiling point. His groin throbbed even more than his head, and there was just one way to let the pressure off. He knew exactly what he had to do. Some skills are indelibly burned into the memory.

Hashilli went through the pantry desperately looking for some product that displayed a picture of a woman. There was a box of Wheaties, the alleged breakfast of champions. On the box was a female gymnast completing an uneven parallel bar routine. She wasn't Hashilli's type, exactly, but she was better than Aunt Jemima.

46

THE PULSATIONS AT the back of Sarah's head might be the prelude to a headache, but for the moment it was more like sound than pain. Raindrops falling on a canopy of leaves. Restrained applause after Tiger Woods sank a twenty-foot putt at Pebble Beach. Bird wings pushing through the dense black air of a summer night.

Yes, that was it, night fliers looking for an easy kill. She opened her eyes, thinking she would see the birds as they passed overhead, but the only thing she saw was the full moon floating much closer than it should have been. The dead world circling the earth was the home of Diana, Goddess of the Hunt. She presided over the fickle hearts of lovers, the level of the seas, female cycles of fertility, and the transformation of men into monsters.

"Even a man who is pure at heart...." Sarah could almost hear her mother reciting a poem from *The Werewolf*—the old black and white movie starring Lon Chaney Jr. According to Marie, it embodied everything a girl needed to know about men.

Members of the rugged sex were cunning and dangerous and eminently desirable. Fortunately for women, they were cursed with simple minds.

As Sarah's eyes adjusted to the moonlight, she noticed that the face on the moon wore lipstick. Galia 03 Rosy Nude. How had she missed seeing that before? The moon's mouth opened slightly, and the pink tip of a tongue traced the outline of those cosmetically enhanced lips.

The moon's eyes blinked. Could that be mascara?

"It's called the 'smoky eye,' dear." Sarah wasn't surprised to hear the moon speak with Marie's voice. "A girl has to look her best even when she's running for her life."

"Mother?"

"You know I hate that word, Sarah. It makes me feel old and… old."

"What are you doing here?"

"I might ask you the same question." The eyes blinked. The mountains and craters of the moon were highlighted with almost undetectable tints of Guerlain Terracotta Bronzing powder. Marie's face emerged on the surface of the barren world like a figure in a Gestalt illusion. It had been there all along but remained invisible until the pattern asserted itself on the mind's eye. Then it would never go away.

"I suppose everyone has to be somewhere," Sarah said.

"Exactly right. Now where is that young man of yours?"

A circle of birds flew around the moon, transforming Marie Ferraro's face into a surrealistic icon, the sort of image that might decorate the walls of a Christian Orthodox Church designed by Salvador Dali. It was then Sarah knew she was dreaming.

Owl dreams. Where had she heard those words before?

"Wake up, Sarah." Marie was no longer a disembodied head with a halo of night flyers. She had a body now. Marie had arms, and they were shaking Sarah, rousing her from her mushroom-dust-induced anesthesia.

"We have to get out of here before Doctor Moon finds us."

Sarah lay on a bed of leaves under a makeshift lean-to made of saplings and creeper. Her mouth tasted of stomach acid and nightmares. A thin film of oil coated her face.

"Is it morning?" The dregs of a night's metabolism had settled in Sarah's lungs and added a smoker's rasp to her voice.

Marie didn't have to answer her question. She could tell the time of day from the quality of the light that found its way through the wilting leaves of her shelter. Time had slipped past her without punching in or out on her biological time clock. Hours had gone missing, hiding in the past where they could never be recovered.

Marie gave Sarah a sip of water from a plastic bottle. "We don't have much time, Sarah. Everyone else is ready to go."

"Everyone else?"

The female thug who had held Sarah and Robert at gunpoint took her place beside Marie. She introduced herself as Thelma McCurtain but told Sarah that everyone just called her Sissy.

"Sorry for the misunderstandin'." Sissy McCurtain handed Sarah an opened tin of Spam and a bag of barbecue-flavored Fritos.

Sarah took the peace offering gladly. The salt and fat would add texture to her morning breath while the carbohydrates replaced those used up detoxifying the mushroom dust.

Sarah had never met a Native American with a name like Sissy. The woman looked like one of the deranged hillbillies who routinely represent Oklahoma and Arkansas on nationally syndicated daytime talk shows. But when Sissy McCurtain wasn't holding her shotgun in the murder-ready position, she displayed indigenous behavioral traits Sarah encountered all over Oklahoma, New Mexico, and Arizona. Sissy didn't make eye contact.

Unless she's taking aim.

She was soft spoken.

Unless she's making threats.

She didn't talk much.

Unless she's talking about her family.

Sissy gave Sarah a quick breakdown of her lineage—something Native Americans often did within minutes of an introduction.

"Momma was a Maytubby. Married a McCurtain back a while."

She apologized for Hashilli. "Momma's second cousin. We been trying to live him down for quite some time. Caused quite a strain when we heard the witch had brought a woman to the cabin."

She turned her eyes toward Marie as if she was looking for approval.

"Then other folks start comin' around. It was only natural we thought you was the enemy."

According to Sissy The Maytubbys took turns guarding the property, mostly without a plan. They wouldn't confront Hashilli. He was a relative and a man of power.

"Might shoot his friends though. We might put up with a dangerous cousin, but when strangers got into the act, it was time for the family to take action."

Sarah finished off her canned meat, chips, and bottled water. She was still thirsty, but the only liquid available was half a twelve-ounce bottle of Diet Sprite. She took a couple of short, gassy swallows and made a face.

Robert helped her to her feet. He had a bruise on his forehead the shape of a shotgun stock, but gusts of wind were blowing his hair into disarray, washing his mind clean of troubled thoughts. He smiled when Sarah explored his injury with tentative fingers. He didn't recoil when she kissed it, in spite of her bad breath.

"Sorry for the trouble," Sissy said. "Best to leave quick. My car ain't far, and there's no telling when *he* might come lookin'." She'd leaned her antique shotgun against a blackjack tree. She picked it up carefully and held it at arm's length.

"Somebody else can carry this if it makes you nervous." Sissy looked to Sarah's mother for an answer. Marie was the one who had found her lying unconscious in the woods.

"Anything you say," Sissy told Marie, "It's got my okay."

Sarah stepped between them. "You carry the shotgun, Sissy." That name made her cringe almost as much as *Big Shorty*, but no one seemed to notice. "Everyone else is afraid of it."

Marie nodded her approval. "We need to get moving before Hashilli shows up."

Sissy held her shotgun in the ready position when she heard her cousin's name. "Sometimes bad things come when you call them. Best not write the devil's name on the wall."

"Understood," Marie said. "Now we have to go find Archie, although I was pretty certain it would be the other way around."

Sissy set off through the forest as if she had a plan. The others, who clearly had none, followed close behind.

Sarah filled Marie in while they walked. "Archie's at Bob's Lake Country Motel. He and Big Shorty have attracted a lot of attention lately."

"Big Shorty. I had an old boyfriend who called his penis that," Marie said. "Love my oxymorons—*Now then*, I am *clearly confused.* Is this *Big Shorty* a real person? I find it *simply impossible* to believe."

"He's real enough," Sarah said. "Your wits have a particularly keen edge this morning." She'd seen Marie move through states of unbridled optimism and boundless energy before, but this was not simply the manic phase of her bipolar condition. She seemed genuinely happy, naturally alert, and mentally competent—under the worst possible circumstances. "Has the famous Doctor Moon found a cure for your bipolar disorder?"

"Archie is the one who cured me, at least for the time being. Sissy knows all about it. Knew it from the first second we met."

"It's nature's way is all." Sissy stopped the party's conversation as well as their march through the woods with an upraised hand. She pulled back the hammers on her shotgun and held it in position for a hip shot. She pushed through the branches of a red cedar and stood in front of a 1988 Plymouth Reliant was partially concealed by tall grass and saplings. Solar deterioration of the formally green paint and randomly spaced dents and rust spots made the car blend into the background like a soldier wearing camouflage.

She took up a guard position between the headlights of the rusting Chrysler K car and motioned for the rest of her party to follow. Marie sat in the front passenger seat, the place of honor. Robert sat behind her.

Sissy scooted in behind the steering wheel and handed the shotgun to Sarah, who was assigned the Sergeant at Arms position beside Robert and behind the driver.

Several gallon-milk-carton-size boxes were scattered over the back seat of the vehicle. Sarah pushed them aside, looking for a seat belt as Sissy drove the automobile along an escape route that only she could see. One of the boxes tipped over, spilling several dozen round lead pellets onto the seat and floorboard.

Sarah picked one up. Smaller than a marble but not by much. "Damn, what are these things?"

"Double ought buckshot," Sissy told her. "I reload my own shotgun shells." There was also a box of brass-tipped red plastic tubes, a can of smokeless powder, and a container of primer caps.

"I don't bother with store bought wadding," she said. "Strips of my Old Papa's underpants is good for that. Old Mama give them to me when he passed."

With one final tooth-rattling jolt, they were on the road, headed for Bob's Lake Country Motel.

"It's a Maytubby business, sort of," Sissy said. "Bob's my mother's second cousin twice removed."

Sarah didn't understand the intricacies of extended family relationships.

Sissy explained, "Not exactly a Maytubby. Not a McCurtain neither. Old Papa would have called him an asshole cousin." She made a point of concentrating on the complexities of forest navigation. Sarah could see in the rearview mirror that Sissy McCurtain's face was turning red.

"Sorry for the dirty talk," Sissy said. "Hope you'll pardon my French."

"*Ça n'est pas grave!*" Sarah said. Everyone inside the Plymouth Reliant waited quietly for her translation.

"It means, I pardon your French." One of the few phrases she retained from the University of New Mexico's foreign language requirement. Very useful, along with, *bonne chance, je ne comprends pas*, and *où sont les toilettes?* Before that moment, she had never fully appreciated the value of a liberal-arts education.

HASHILLI WOKE TO the screech of a mockingbird asserting its territorial imperative. He reflected on Harper Lee's astounding misjudgment of the character of those winged bullies.

He held his wristwatch at a close approximation of the optimal focal distance for his morning vision. Cracked crystal. God only knew how that had happened, but the timepiece still worked. Already six a.m.

Witches made a point of rising earlier than their enemies, but it had been a rough night.

Memories of his dreams haunted him, pubescent girls dressed in patriotic bathing suits doing erotic floor exercises while Marie applied a vice to his groin and Robert Collins squeezed his head to the point of exploding. Hashilli would never feel the same way about female gymnastic competitions or Wheaties again. All things considered peyote is a better pathway to a vision than Viagra.

But a vision is a vision, no matter what the source. Wisdom filled the vacuum left in Hashilli as soon as lust receded. The scales were lifted from his eyes. He saw the truth about Marie Ferraro and Robert Collins—as clear as the crack in the crystal of his Rolex watch.

Collins had been unaffected by the mushroom powder, just like Grandfather and Hashilli. The boy impersonated a police officer at the White Owl Center, at Stringtown, and at casinos all over Choctaw country. Robert Collins was a shapeshifter. His skills were rudimentary, but there was no sense denying their existence.

Hashilli had made a dreadful mistake when he locked Collins in the Maytubby bone-house. The ancestors weighed the hapless schizophrenic, they measured him, and they did not find him wanting. The Maytubby ghosts chose Robert Collins as Hashilli's successor.

Grandfather was involved in this. The old man's bones still had power, like a saint's relics. They made things happen, even from their resting place at the bottom of Lake Texoma.

A witch could take precautions against magic, but Hashilli had done nothing. He hadn't even looked to see whether the boy's shadow took the shape of an owl. He had always assumed the ancestors would select a child to replace him. He thought he would have twenty, perhaps thirty years to ease through the transition.

But spirits are impatient.

The ghosts recruited an outside agent, a woman to seduce him. They tricked him into bringing her to the cabin. He'd shown her the wall where the magic bullet was buried. Now she owned a piece of Hashilli's spirit, the tiny seed from which all his power grew. She would give it to Robert Collins, and he would find a way to use it. Grandfather would help him. The old ghost still resented his murder, and for the first time in his life, Hashilli sympathized with his predecessor's attitude. But things didn't have to go as the ancestors planned. The shadows weren't infallible. Hashilli would track Marie down. He had a pretty good idea where to start looking.

On his Viagra-fueled trip back to the cabin, Hashilli had sensed Marie Ferraro's presence along the river's southern edge among a collection of cattails and reeds. If he had taken the time to investigate, he might have ended the woman's treachery then and there, but his thought processes were dimmed by pharmacologically induced lust. That was finished now. He knew exactly what to do.

After he killed Marie, Hashilli would grind her bones to dust and scatter them in the river so her outer shadow would not find a resting place. Perhaps he'd keep part of her as a souvenir, not enough to give her ghost a purchase point but enough to bind her to him. Perhaps a finger-bone necklace or a breastbone whittled into a crucifix pendant.

Yes, a crucifix. A marriage of indigenous and Christian symbols, like the Voodoo gods who masquerade as Catholic saints.

Now that the ancestors had abandoned him, perhaps Hashilli could learn a thing or two from the Africans. He'd not worked out Baron Saturday's part in Robert Collins's game, but there would be time for that once his other enemies were vanquished.

REEDS LAY BENT and broken in a path exactly the same width as the stolen jon boat. Hashilli jacked a bullet into the chamber of his semi-automatic pistol and reassured himself the safety was in the off position before he steered his boat along the all-too-clear trail the seductress left for him. It didn't take long to find the drag marks on the shore where Marie pulled her boat away from the water's edge.

Stronger than she looks. He still admired the woman who betrayed him. Thoughts of Marie fanned the coals of lust into a smoldering fire, but the emotions were manageable. Nothing more than a Viagra hangover.

In spite of his best efforts to steer his thoughts away from weaknesses of the flesh, Hashilli found himself wondering what Marie would look like dressed in a U.S. Olympic uniform, competing in a balance beam routine before an audience of millions. How long would it take to wash his mind clear of the woman's influence?

The wooden jon boat wasn't well concealed. She'd known he would follow her. She'd known he would find the boat. What measures had she taken?

Hashilli saw seven sticks driven into the ground in a rough circle, like funeral stakes in a traditional Choctaw burial. No one did that anymore. All of the old rituals had been abandoned. Most of them forgotten.

He removed the stakes one at a time, saving the shortest one for last. It wasn't placed on the western side, as it should have been. Was this some kind of magic he did not recognize, Voodoo perhaps? Something she had learned from Baron Saturday?

No trip wires attached to the boat. Hashilli didn't think it would be booby-trapped, but he couldn't be sure. Marie Ferraro was a white woman. Her kind was far more comfortable with explosives than magic.

He slipped his fingers under one side of the jon boat, flipped it over and dove for cover in one easy, uncoordinated motion. After a slow count to thirty, he raised his head—no Claymore mine, no poison gas, no nest of rattlesnakes. There was an empty plastic water bottle and an empty individual-serving bag that once contained Doritos. The blue plastic lid was screwed onto the bottle, and the bag was crawling with ants. What did it all mean?

While Hashilli pondered the mysteries of symbolic magic, his cell phone rang. Bob's Lakeside Motel, according to caller ID. Hashilli owned a majority interest in the resort. He was so broadly diversified it took him five rings to remember which persona to assume.

"Mister Neumond speaking." Hashilli tweaked the words with a hint of German precision. He'd circulated rumors of Nazis in the Neumond line. No one in Choctaw country would ask Mr. Neumond any embarrassing questions. Everyone in this part of Oklahoma was far too polite for open curiosity.

"This is Bob, sir."

The motel had been popular with German visitors over the past few years, and Bob must have wondered why none of them looked like Mr. Neumond.

Hashilli had let some family secrets slip to satisfy his manager's curiosity—Grandfather Neumond's service in the SS, the old man's villa in Argentina. Wasn't that where all the runaway Nazis went after their misadventures in the Great War? Maybe all descendants of Nazi war criminals had bronze skin and black hair—Fascist evolution. He doubted Bob would even consider the possibility that Mr. Neumond was a disgraced Maytubby cousin.

"That colored man you told us to watch out for is staying at the motel," Bob said. "The one without no legs."

"Ah, yes."

"He's staying with another man," Bob said. "Looks to be an Indian, but he ain't from no local tribe."

"Thank you, Robert. Your report is most useful." Mr. Neumond told Bob to keep the information between the two of them. "There won't be any trouble, Robert, if you can be discrete." Hashilli ended the call without saying goodbye. His distant cousin would be grateful for Mr. Neumond's economy of words.

Archie Chatto and Baron Saturday had gone to ground at Bob's Lakeside Motel. Undoubtedly, Marie would go there too. With just a bit of luck, Hashilli could clear the entire nest of vipers in one fell swoop.

Mr. Neumond could take the blame. These interlopers had already cost him four personas. Dr. Moon, Mr. Luna, Dr. Selene, and Mr. Allunare, all carefully developed and documented—years of work erased by acts of treachery.

He headed back to the reeds where his boat was tied. There were places around the motel where a man could hide, places with some elevation where an assassin with a high-powered rifle could do a lot of damage.

47

THE AIR INSIDE Sissy's Plymouth smelled like burned oil and half-burned gasoline. The translucent cloud of smog spewing from the tailpipe looked like a primitive mosquito-abatement program. The automobile's engine made mysterious bubbling noises, and something rubbed intermittently under the right rear tire well. The car was a testimony to the engineering genius of Detroit and Oklahoma's lack of a vehicle safety inspection program.

Sarah didn't miss her shoulder bag until they passed by Durant, eighty miles from their point of origin by the Kiamichi River.

"Raccoons won't take it," Sissy reassured her. "Nor possums nor coyotes."

Sarah wasn't worried about the forest creatures making unauthorized calls on her cell phone or stealing her identity. "There was a pistol in the bag. Archie insisted I bring it along." She could see Sissy's eyes conducting a search of the back seat in the rearview mirror.

"We're still well armed," Sissy said. "There's my shotgun, and it looks like your fella's got a pistol."

Robert pulled the semi-automatic pistol out of his shoulder holster. He jacked the chamber open and closed, removed the magazine, and shook it beside his ear. "No bullets. The gun is just for show."

"Robert pretends to be a policeman, so he has to carry a weapon," Sara explained.

"Not much use in a gunfight," Sissy said. "But we still got my shotgun if it comes to that."

Sarah searched the back seat for more shotgun shells, but Sissy told her not to bother. "The two inside the breech is all we got. Maybe two is all we're meant to have." She patted Marie's shoulder and threw what must have been a smile in her direction.

"When I opened my eyes and seen Marie, my first thought was 'Momma's here. Now everything's gonna be all right.'"

The Plymouth vibrated violently and backfired several times as its worn out engine pulled them over a gentle hill. "Shakes like a hound dog shittin' peach seeds," Sissy said. "Nothin' works right about this old car, but she'll get us all to Bob's."

Sissy smiled at Marie again and coaxed the ancient Chrysler product over the next rise. As the land gradually leveled out, the old automobile got its second wind and picked up speed. By the time they reached the bridge over Lake Texoma, they were traveling fifty miles per hour, close to the vehicle's upper limit.

"Car runs on regular gasoline and miracles." Sissy licked her right index finger and drew a cross on the windshield.

Just when Sarah was beginning to relax and turn her problems over to a Choctaw country version of a higher power, Sissy underwent a change in attitude. "Holy shit!" Her attention locked onto an image in the rearview mirror to such an extent that she nearly scraped against the concrete border of the bridge.

"Holy shit!" Sissy was a woman of few words, and none of them very descriptive. "Get that shotgun ready. Hashilli Maytubby is comin' up behind us. I'd know that black SUV anywhere."

Robert helped Sarah crank her rear window down. She held the shotgun in her lap and waited for Hashilli to catch up.

"Scootch down in your seats," Sissy said. "The witch has seen this car before, but he don't necessarily know you're in it."

Marie laid her head in Sissy's lap, and Robert and Sarah scooted their heads down well below the back of the seat. Sarah pulled the hammers of the double barrel shotgun into the firing position. The act gave her a momentary sense of power, but the feeling passed quickly. She had never fired a weapon like this. Not even once in her life.

She placed her fingers on both triggers and waited for Sissy to talk her through her first shotgun assault. Things would happen quickly if Hashilli knew they were in this vehicle.

"Fate is what it is." Sissy licked her pointing finger and drew a second cross on the windshield. "He's pulling up close behind us now." She waved to his reflection in her mirror. "No point pretendin' we ain't family."

Sarah watched Robert reposition himself so the wind would have more access to his face. If he was worried about their impending doom, there was nothing in his demeanor that showed it.

"Guess I shouldn't be surprised," Marie said. "All my relationships turn into attempted murder in the end.

"Do they always end that way?" Robert asked.

"Not always," Marie admitted. "Sometimes my boyfriends get arrested first. Warrants, you know. There are always warrants."

Sissy said, "I'd take that as a sign."

Sarah thought that Sissy took almost everything as a sign.

"You think he'll really try to kill us?" Robert asked.

"Y'all get my shotgun ready." Sissy said. "We only get one chance."

When Hashilli crashed his SUV into the back of Sissy's Plymouth, Sarah doubted they would have even that. She rose up in her seat—no point in hiding any longer.

Robert held Sarah's legs as she cantilevered her body out the rear passenger window. She pushed the shotgun stock tight against her shoulder and positioned its business end so that Hashilli's head was centered between the barrels. She thought he would pull back when he was confronted with the blank dead stare of the double barrel weapon, and she was prepared to squeeze off two shots before he retreated beyond the gun's killing range.

Instead of retreating, Hashilli veered into the lane beside them. He raked the bumper of his SUV down the left rear fender of the Chrysler K car. Sarah's aim was thrown wide by the collision, and the two barrels of double ought buckshot shattered the black SUV's passenger side window and most of the windshield. She saw Hashilli wipe blood off his right ear and brush safety glass shards out of his hair as he dropped back. The noises from the Plymouth's engine had diminished to a barely audible level, and the rubbing sounds under the right rear tire well vanished completely.

"Wonders and miracles. He's fixed my car." One more thing Sissy was sure to take as a sign.

Marie resumed her upright position in the passenger seat. "I know how to stop him," she said. "I know exactly what to do once he realizes we're out of bullets."

Hashilli rammed the back of their car with his SUV and quickly pulled back again.

Marie leaned over the back of the front seat and poked around in Sissy's reload boxes. She was jarred substantially by a couple more rear end collisions delivered by Hashilli's SUV, but she found what she was looking for. She held a ball of double ought buckshot up for everyone to see.

She said, "A man can be undone by a lie even more easily than the truth. Roll down your window, Sissy."

HASHILLI IMAGINED THE grill of his SUV must look like a set of broken dentures. A thin strand of steam trailed over the hood and drifted through the shattered windshield, covering his face with droplets of coolant and filling the interior of his vehicle with the scent of hot rubber tubing. It was clear the SUV could not withstand many more collisions with the apparently indestructible relic Sissy McCurtain drove.

He pulled close to the rear bumper of the Plymouth and then dropped back. He repeated this action several times, and when no one fired a shot at him, he surmised they had no ammunition. He would take them while they were still on the bridge, where they would have no opportunity for escape.

Hashilli pulled into the overtaking lane and eased his SUV beside the Sissy's Plymouth until their front side windows were aligned. He raised his 9 mm semiautomatic pistol and prepared to send a shower of lethal projectiles flying at his enemies. He had plans for each and every slug.

Marie would be the first to die and then Robert Collins and Sarah Bible. After everyone else was dead, he would put a bullet into Sissy Mc-Curtain's head. When the Plymouth finally skidded to a stop against the concrete perimeter of the bridge, he would sort through the wreckage and find his magic bullet.

Like picking thornless blackberries. Like taking candy from a baby.

Hashilli saw that Marie understood his intentions completely, but the woman showed no fear. She held a small round object between the thumb and fingers of her right hand.

My prize!

She raised the object to her lips and kissed it tenderly.

My magic bullet!

Then she flicked the sphere of lead in front of Sissy's face across the intervening space between the vehicles, through the shattered front passenger side window into Hashilli's SUV.

Hashilli released his steering wheel, dropped his pistol, and scrambled to catch the flying ball of lead, but its trajectory had been complicated by the differing speeds of the two vehicles and the forces exerted by the wind between them.

Sissy dropped back. She positioned herself behind Hashilli's SUV and drove the Chrysler K car into the truck's right rear corner.

All of Hashilli's attention was focused on recovering the power object Marie had thrown his way, and finally he did recover it. He held the lead sphere delicately in his left hand and marveled at the pristine regularity of its surface.

How could something so soft and delicate have passed through a woman's neck and lodged itself in a cabin wall?

He had just about decided that it couldn't when Sissy pushed his SUV through the concrete guardrail and into Lake Texoma. It was a very long fall.

48

THE AFTERNOON SUN cast long shadows behind the slender headstones inside the Indian Baptist Cemetery. Big Shorty stood on the path leading to the Maytubby bone-house and pointed out the yellow puffballs Robert missed the first time through.

"Can't clean the place up until every last one of those mushrooms is gone." He directed Robert to a rotten cottonwood branch that was partially obscured by moonflowers. Shorty hadn't decided whether to remove the Datura plants or the sandstone wall that separated the Native American graveyard from the rest of Riverside Gardens Cemetery, but he had already painted over the white owl on the Maytubby bone-house door.

Sarah felt the spiritual boundaries of the little cemetery dissolve as Robert used one of Shorty's kitchen knives to scrape the mushrooms off the deadwood. He and Shorty searched out the remaining puffballs with the enthusiasm of children on an Easter egg hunt. Archie, Marie, and Sissy stood around the perimeter of the little graveyard like fans at a sports event, cheering the home team on to victory.

Sissy McCurtain was clearly impressed with Big Shorty. "Don't see a man like that too often."

How could Sarah disagree?

"You think he's got a woman?"

Sarah didn't answer. She wouldn't discourage romantic interest, no matter how unlikely it was to work out. She had learned that at her mother's knee.

When Robert bagged the last of the puffballs, Big Shorty motioned for everyone to come inside the sandstone wall.

"I'll care for this place now that the witch is gone." He didn't seem to notice Sissy standing by his side.

"I can help," she offered. "I don't know much about these bone-houses, but I've got relatives who'll tell me."

Shorty nodded his head in the affirmative. Sarah wondered if he had any idea what he was getting into.

Sissy walked over to Sarah's mother. She took Marie's left hand in both of hers and kissed it gently.

Like the final scene from *The Godfather.* There was something going on between Sissy and Marie that Sarah didn't understand. It started when Marie found them unconscious in the forest.

"The Maytubbys is all done with magic men," Sissy said. "That finished when Hashilli drowned." She placed a loving hand on Marie's belly, then she moved her fingers firmly but gently, the way a doctor might check for enlarged lymph nodes.

"The next one won't be a Maytubby—won't even be a Choctaw." Sissy walked back to stand beside Big Shorty, but she kept her eyes on Marie. "The ancestors have made their choice, but they won't help you none."

Marie smiled. She and Archie exchanged a look.

"Archie will take care of us." Marie's voice was steady, unmodified by manic energy or depression. Sarah looked into her mother's eyes and saw something she had seen only rarely in all the years they had been together. The look of sanity.

"What's going on?" Sarah had been Marie's confidant since she was five years old, but now her mother seemed to be sharing secrets with Sissy McCurtain, a stranger she had known for only a few days.

Sissy took up a new position putting Big Shorty between Sarah and herself.

She peered over Shorty's shoulders and held her hands up as if she were surrendering to an armed posse. "Didn't mean to give away no secrets." She took a half-dozen unsatisfying breaths, then lowered her arms.

"The cat is definitely out of the bag," said Marie. "I'm pregnant, Sarah. Sissy thinks there's more to it than that. I'm not so sure." She looked to Archie for support. He placed an arm around her shoulders but did not speak. He retreated to the safety of his Indian ways.

Sissy stepped out from behind Big Shorty. "Owl dreams came with the mushroom powder sleep. I figured you had them too," she told Sarah. "The ancestors had given up on Hashilli. They wouldn't let him find an heir."

Marie said, "That's why he stole the babies, Sarah. With Native Americans, nothing is ever about money."

Robert fastened a twister seal around the last trash bag of mushrooms, dusted his hands off on his pants, and came to stand by Sarah. He didn't look surprised to hear what Sissy was telling her, but then Robert was a man who was accustomed to hearing voices in the wind. It would be hard to shock him. Sarah saw with some satisfaction that he did look surprised when she reached out and took his hand.

"Your mother's baby is next in the power line," Sissy said. "It don't matter who the father is. Everything really important comes through the mother's blood."

Archie pulled Marie closer to him. He kissed her cheek and favored Sarah with one of his hundred-watt smiles. She wondered what Geronimo could have accomplished with a smile like that.

Sissy appraised the afternoon sun. "Showin' beats tellin' every time." She walked to the newly painted door of the Maytubby bone-house and motioned for Sarah's mom to join her.

Marie stood at the threshold and allowed Sissy to adjust her position as though she were a supernatural television antenna.

"Here we go." Sissy stood back, evaluating Marie's shadow. She pointed to a spot in front of the shadow's belly that would be occupied by Sarah's new sibling in another six months. "Look careful, now." Sissy used her own shadow's finger to trace the faint outline of an abstract owl shadow on the door. It was barely visible but was definitely there.

"It'll get clearer as birth time draws closer."

Sarah saw the silhouette of the owl, but she also saw how it blended with the shadows of cottonwood leaves and branches moving in the wind.

There is always a rational explanation.

Marie took no position on the matter. Neither did Big Shorty or Archie, and Robert never took a position on anything. With or without magic, this part of the adventure was finished. The next part was about to begin.

Archie told the group that he and Marie would move to the north-eastern quadrant of Oklahoma. "The Cookson Hills. It's always been outlaw country. A good place for a renegade Apache to hide out."

Big Shorty would remain in Riverside Gardens Cemetery, waiting for his opportunity to wrestle death. He hadn't offered Sissy McCurtain an invitation, but it was clear that she intended to stay with him, and Shorty did not object.

"I guess I'll go back to Albuquerque," Sarah told the group. "It looks like I'll need a new roommate now that mother is moving out."

Robert accepted her offer with a smile. The voices in the wind were gone, but Sarah's voice was loud and clear.

www.ingramcontent.com/pod-product-compliance
Lightning Source LLC
Chambersburg PA
CBHW051214130726
47988CB00001B/88